MURDEROUS MUTTERINGS

SARA GODDEN

APS BOOKS
YORKSHIRE

APS Books
The Stables,
Field Lane,
Aberford
West Yorkshire,
LE25 3AE
www.andrewsparke.com

APS Books is a subsidiary of the APS Publications imprint

©2024 Sara Godden

Sara Godden has asserted the right to be identified as the author of this work in accordance with the Copyright Designs and Patents Act 1988

All rights reserved.

First published worldwide by APS Books in 2024

No part of this publication may be reproduced, stored in or introduced into a retrieval system, or transmitted, in any form, or by any means (electronic, mechanical, photocopying, recording or otherwise) without the written permission of the publisher except that brief selections may be quoted or copied without permission, provided that full credit is given.

A catalogue record for this book is available from the British Library

MURDEROUS MUTTERINGS

For Richard

Thank you for all your love and support

Detective Inspector Jake Jones took a deep breath. Then he announced, "Mrs Darnley was found dead in her garden this afternoon by her neighbour. We have a witness who places Miss Firth at the scene. We're led to believe you were the last one to see her alive!."

"I only moved here a few weeks ago; no one knows me. I don't understand" Dee stammered as she rushed to the office toilet, tears falling.

"Can Miss Firth escape out of there?" the Inspector asked.

"No" came the reply. "She's going nowhere."

Chapter One

This particular morning Dee had taken the shortcut through what was known locally as a snicket - she would call it a ginnel - which led to Gamblewood High Street in order to give herself plenty of time. As was usual for her, things hadn't quite gone to plan.

Dee had visited the street only twice before today, since moving to Gamblewood. It had brought back fond memories of a coach trip she had taken with her gran to the Shambles in York. Like the Shambles it too was a selection of quirky old buildings lining both sides of the high street, each building hosting a little shop below. Every now and again there were breaks in the buildings and narrow alleyways led off to other little buildings or cottages nestled in behind.

Dee's first visit had been to go to the bank to set up a new account, and her second was to the post office. As a result of her move Dee was on the lookout for a new job. She had decided to put an advert in the window of the post office listing the reception and secretarial services she could offer if anyone was interested. No one had been more surprised than Dee when within the week she had received a phone call from a Mr Gill.

This morning was turning into a disaster as far as Dee was concerned. After all, how hard could it be to find an address in a place the size of a postage stamp. But she couldn't find it. On the verge of giving up and about to go home, an elderly gentleman had pointed her in what he thought might be the right direction. Although the gentleman had not been totally right, Dee had somehow, probably by some form of divine intervention, found her way to 110 Lay Street. The piece of paper bearing the address was now screwed up and shoved in her pocket out of sheer frustration. Dee was annoyed at her own tardiness. She hated being late and she hated it when other people were late. If only she had asked for directions earlier. She chastised herself for wasting so much time. Being late was unacceptable and embarrassing in her book, especially on the first day of a new job.

Thrusting her arms into the sleeves of her navy-blue jacket, Dee tugged at it in an attempt to straighten out its crumpled edges. She pulled at her curly red ponytail in the hope of taming it and pushed her shoulders back. After all, first impressions do count.

Dee now found herself stood staring at the old tatty brown door in front of her. Realising that she was starting to feel incredibly nervous, Dee took a deep breath and knocked on the door. There was no reply. The horrible door with its out-of-date frosted glass, tucked away off the high street, hidden from passers-by, etched with the name P.D Gill, remained closed.

Dee knocked again, her impatience growing and feeling hot and bothered, she tried the door handle. The door opened easily. She peered round it to see it led into a corridor with three steps up to another brown dull door with the same frosted glass once more etched with the same name - P.D Gill.

"Well here goes nothing," she thought out loud.

On entering the corridor Dee shivered, feeling as if she was being watched. She knocked and entered the second shabby door.

"Hi I'm Dee" she said with her best smile but Mr Gill didn't answer. Dee knew he was Mr Gill as he had a name plate on his desk which she thought very old fashioned. She started to apologise for her lateness but he just gestured to her to come in and pointed at the only spare desk in the office, continuing to tap away on his mobile.

Taking in Mr Gill's attire, something Dee always noticed about people, she saw he was wearing a T-shirt and jeans. Both had seen better days.

Dee felt overdressed. She realised if she was going to continue to work there, she would hopefully never have to wear a suit again. This pleased her enormously as she was wearing the only business suit she owned.

She hung her crumpled jacket on an antique coat stand and sat down. 'He can't be married either,' she thought. She could see in the reflection from the window behind Mr Gill that he was playing Candy Crush on his phone. Taking a moment to look around at her surroundings, she was considering if she should just make an excuse and leave. 'Edward wouldn't be happy working here,' she thought.

Dee had moved to Gamblewood to be with Edward. They had met purely by chance in Dee's old local coffee shop. He was up North for a meeting that had been cancelled and she had been getting a skinny latte as usual for her boss. She had forgotten her purse that morning. It was at home on the bedside table. With no means to pay, Edward had come to her rescue and spared her further embarrassment as she was trying to explain her predicament; he had offered to pay for both hers and her boss's coffees. The rest was history and six months later Dee had packed a suitcase, upped sticks and moved to the pretty little village of Gamblewood, into a converted stable block with the man she already had plans to marry.

Edward had encouraged her to sign on with an agency; the very thought of anyone putting an advert in the local post office was a weird and antiquated notion to him. "You might get some nutter phoning you, Dee, you never know," he had said.

"I'll give it a try and if I don't hear anything I'll sign up with an agency, I promise," Dee had replied.

'Maybe I should have listened to Edward.,' she now thought while glancing around the office. It had three old desks; his and hers, and one with a mass of papers on it. The old hat stand stood next to a set of drawers that looked like they might collapse at any moment. A kettle, four mugs - but no tea or coffee - sat upon it with a tin box. In the corner stood a grey, metal filing cabinet. There was a door to the left of the filing cabinet and another to the right of Mr Gill's desk, 'God only knows what's behind them,' she thought.

The whole place needed a damn good clean and brightening up. Everything was so brown. Edward's office was a glamourous affair, all white plastic and not a thing out of place, just like their home.

Her thoughts were interrupted. "Miss Firth? Hello; sorry about that. Toilets in there," he pointed to the door to the left of the filing cabinet, "and you can see where the kettle is. You can bring your own coffee or tea bags if you want."

Dee smiled realising she didn't have a choice unless she wanted to go all day without a drink.

Mr Gill continued pacing up and down within the confines of the office "Find it alright?"

"No not really. Sorry I'm late," Dee tried to explain. "You see, I wasn't too sure what I was looking for and the P.D - I now realise it stands for Private Detective - isn't that obvious really. I must have walked past your door twice, if not three times, I'm not sure how your customers find you; it's not easy at all," Dee stammered a little at the end, realising by his raised eyebrows she was saying way too much. She attempted her best smile. "Sorry, it's just an observation, I shouldn't…"

Mr Gill interrupted her before she could say any more. "Well, Miss Firth, first they're not customers but clients. Secondly, clients prefer discretion; they don't want the whole village gossiping about them being seen coming in or out of here and finally P.D does not stand for Private Detective, although that's quite astute of you to think that. It stands for Peter David; which is my name," and with that he returned to his desk.

Dee sat for a moment thinking of how to break the ice and nothing was coming to mind other than to run.

Mr Gill spoke first "Miss Firth…"

"Please call me Dee," she was trying to be as friendly as possible.

"Dee; I do like that. If you look in the top drawer there's some unopened mail. Mary used to deal with all that and I understand you have some book-keeping skills too from what you said on the phone."

"Yes, just the basics."

"Well, there's a computer in the cabinet, over there," he pointed at the grey metal cabinet. "The key to it is in your top drawer too. We keep everything locked away; confidential reasons."

Dee nodded partly in agreement and partly in bewilderment.

Peter continued. "Mary had everything up to date and in files. She said you'd find it all easily enough and she's taped the password to the computer under your desk. Are you ok just to get familiar with where things are, open the mail and sort it?"

Dee just nodded. "Can I use the bathroom first, please Mr Gill?" Dee said as she stood up.

"Yeah sure, but no more Mr Gill, Dee; Pete or Peter please," he said with a soft smile, making Dee feel a little less uncomfortable.

Escaping to the bathroom, Dee took a minute. 'Not off to the best start, I'll sign up with a job agency tomorrow. I'll just stay here until I find something else'. She was not too surprised to find the bathroom was as brown and dull as the office. She was certainly not going to sit on that toilet seat until she had cleaned it herself, although the knitted pink dolly covering the loo roll made her smile. That must have been Mary's contribution to brighten up the place.

On returning to her desk a bottle of water had been placed upon it.

"Bit stuffy in here today; thought you might like a bottle, "Peter said.

"Thank you, that's lovely, and yes I'll remember to bring in some coffee and milk tomorrow."

"We don't have a fridge; Mary and I just used the powdered stuff."

"Oh, it's fine. I'll sort it," she hated powdered milk and now knew her new best friend was going to be the little coffee shop she'd walked past several times that morning. She bent down and removed the taped piece of paper from under the desk. It had the word *Jasper* written on it. "Jasper? Is that Mary's dog?"

"Yes, it is. Look at you playing detective. After my job?" Peter winked.

Dee chuckled; the ice was broken.

Peter could sense another question coming and before Dee could ask, he went on to explain that Mary had moved to the coast to help look after her grandchildren. Mary had felt the sea air would be good for her and Jasper.

Dee opened the top drawer of her desk to find it full to the brim with mail. She pulled a face. Using two hands she scooped the unopened letters onto her desk. She was horrified by the growing mound in front of her. As she emptied the drawer of its contents, she touched something sticky. With the final envelopes out of the way, she found the grey filing cabinet key neatly taped to the bottom of the inside of the drawer.

Pete looked up from his mobile.

Dee could feel him looking over and asked pensively "When did Mary leave?"

"Five months ago."

After a morning of opening one envelope after another, while Peter seemed to spend the morning playing games on his mobile, Dee had three neat piles upon her desk. One pile was bills and one was mail outs and rubbish. The last pile comprised letters from clients; some even had cheques attached. She decided this was an appropriate time to frequent the local coffee shop. It had taken her all morning to sort that mail and she was craving a latte and something to eat. "Is it ok if I nip out to get some lunch, please?"

"Of course, are you ok to get me something?"

"Sure, what would you like? I was thinking of trying the coffee shop."

"Good choice; just one of their iced buns please," Peter replied, "Money's in the tin next to the kettle, I don't expect you to pay for it; take enough to get your own." Just pop it on the petty cash sheet that Mary kept."

Dee did as she was instructed and left the office.

The little walk to *Coffee Creams* - 'such an appropriate name,' she thought - had brightened Dee's spirits. The brown tones of the office and the monotony of opening all that post had left her feeling a bit down in the dumps. However, on the upside, she didn't need to pay for her lunch. Maybe things were looking up.

Dee walked into the shop. The little bell over the door tinkled. Dee was greeted by a pretty, dark-haired girl probably not much older than herself in a pink spotty apron asking if she could help her from behind a glass counter filled with the prettiest cakes Dee had ever seen.

"Definitely a skinny latte please, but these all look amazing," Dee said, pointing at the delicacies on show. "Gosh I'm so tempted to have one, which is silly since I've just ordered a skinny latte but I don't know which to choose."

"Then I'll make the choice for you. I'm Alison and you are..?"

"Dee, I've just moved here and I'm working at the Private De…" She stopped short.

"Pete's new secretary. I take it he wants you to take him back an iced bun?" Alison rolled her eyes.

"Yes, he does. Take it he eats a lot of iced buns?" Dee said laughing.

"Him and Mary both." Alison continued. "We do miss Mary. She used to come in here with Jasper - that's her dog - every weekend, told us titbits from cases. I loved her stories."

"Oh, I thought Peter insisted on discretion."

"Mary never mentioned any names, no names at all. She'd always keep us guessing, just giving us enough of the details to get you hooked. You always wanted to know more. She probably made most of it up to be honest, you know, to make them sound more interesting, but I liked hearing them anyway. Well, I'd best get you this latte and a surprise treat, plus one iced bun to go. Take a seat."

Dee decided to sit at the table in the window, with its pink dotty cloth that matched Alison's apron. She looked out at the comings and goings of the high street, lost in thoughts of how much and how quickly her life had changed since meeting Ed. She recalled the day after moving in with him, how he had taken her to see his office. He was showing off a little she had felt at the time, or showing her off; Dee wasn't sure which. Either way she had called him Ed and he had insisted that in future she call him Edward in front of his colleagues. Dee had found this a little pretentious and it had annoyed her.

"Here we are," Alison said placing down a huge slice of Victoria sponge and a large skinny latte. "Hope you like it. Let me know?"

"That's just what I need. Perfect choice," Dee said looking hungrily at the slice of cake.

"Enjoy, and just to let you know, on a Thursday night about seven we hold a book club, in case you're interested."

"Ooh, yes, I'd like that. Thanks Alison."

Dee loaded up her cake fork and plunged a huge piece of the cake into her mouth. It was every bit as delicious as it looked. Dee felt so much happier after eating the cake. Who wouldn't she asked herself. Full and content with the world, she went to find Alison to pay.

"That was gorgeous, thank you so much. How much do I owe you?"

"On me, as a welcome to Gamblewood," said Alison handing over Peter's bun.

"That's really kind, thanks." With a little wave Dee closed the brightly painted pink door of *Coffee Creams* behind her.

Walking back to the dreary office, iced bun in hand, Dee felt she might have found a friend. As much as she loved Edward every girl needs a good friend. There are just some things you can't discuss with your boyfriend and with all her old friends back up north Dee had started to feel a little lonely. She really was missing female company to chat nonsense and share a bottle of wine with.

Arriving back in the office Peter had not moved and neither had any of the piles of opened mail on her desk. Dee handed Peter his iced bun, returned the money to petty cash and pleasantries about *Coffee Creams* were exchanged.

Dee asked Peter to remind her where the computer was kept and he pointed at the grey filing cabinet. She unstuck the key in the drawer. All very *Hart To Hart,*' she thought; another one of her gran's favourites.

She retrieved the computer from the filing cabinet. She was shocked to find the contents of the filing cabinet so neat and all in alphabetical order. Mary had obviously been very tidy and well organised. She now pictured Mary as a Miss Moneypenny character in tweeds. She was going to be a hard act to follow.

Mary's organisation of all the files on the computer did not disappoint either. For an older lady, this grandma sure knew her way round a computer and Dee was quickly able to work out where everything was or went. Within no time the three mountains of mail were reduced to half their size, much of it having to be thrown away, which was fortunate as Peter couldn't be bothered reading it.

Just as Dee was finalising cheques to go to the bank, marking them as paid on one of Mary's many perfect spreadsheets, the dull brown door opened. Standing in the doorway was a tall man with greying hair, very neatly dressed and highly polished shoes.

Dee felt embarrassed by the drabness of the office and wished it looked more like Edward's. "Hello, please come in. Can I help you?" she piped up, not sure if that was the right thing to say. Out of the corner of her eye she saw Peter put his mobile down and sit up straight in his chair.

The man, probably in his late fifties, looked sombre and upset. "It's my wife. It's been a living hell," he shook a little as he spoke. "I took our Susie to the park the other day, she was playing happily, running around and then she was gone! I've no idea where or what happened." The man took a deep breath "My wife can't sleep with worry and keeps bursting into tears. It's all my fault for not keeping an eye on her apparently. The police aren't interested either, I just don't understand how she could vanish like that, in broad daylight too!"

Dee felt she wanted to hug him, the poor man.

Peter spoke calmly "Now then Mr?"

"Whitman," he replied.

Peter made a sign for Dee to take notes as he offered Mr Whitman a seat on the old wooden chair next to his desk.

Looking for something to write on Dee opened the second desk drawer to find two notepads, a pack of pencils, pens and highlighters. There was also a camera and a recording device. She grabbed a notepad opened it up and tried her best to look professional. She wrote *Mr Whitman* and underlined it. Not sure what else to write, her thoughts wandered back to the camera and voice recorder sitting in the drawer.

"Dee, did you get that?" Peter said a little too loudly.

"No, sorry. You were saying?"

"Two days ago, Susie went missing."

"Where did this happen?" Peter asked.

"In the park over there." Mr Whitman pointed out of the window behind Dee. "I can't believe it. Where could she go?"

Dee turned to look out of the window. Sure enough in the distance was a park. 'I must pay that a visit,' she thought, picturing her and Edward sharing a romantic picnic. Her thoughts were interrupted.

"Two days ago - Dee, write the date down."

Dee said sympathetically, "I'm so sorry, Mr Whitman. You and your wife must be so upset about your daughter."

The office fell silent.

"Daughter!" Mr Whitman shouted before bursting into a roar of laughter.

Peter looked across at Dee. His face had a very odd expression, one Dee could not comprehend.

Mr Whitman finally said, "Susie is not our daughter, nor even our grand-daughter. She's the bloody dog!"

Peter sat back in his chair, folding his arms and all Dee could focus on was her new employer's raised eyebrows.

Dee remained silent after apologising for the confusion and at length Peter returned to questioning Mr Whitman about Susie. Dee carefully wrote down all the answers until Peter discussed the matter of fees and asked Mr Whitman to leave his address, phone number and a photo of Susie with Dee.

Once Mr Whitman had left, Peter picked up his car keys and said he was going to the police station to see if they had picked up any dogs matching Susie's description. "Odd, you know," he said on his way out. "That's the third dog in two weeks; looks like we have a dog-napper in Gamblewood."

"Or a dodgy takeaway," Dee chimed in.

"Might have where you've come from, but Mr Wang is a pillar of society, does a lot for the community and if you haven't been to his restaurant yet, I suggest you do. Best Chinese you'll ever eat!" With that he left shouting back that he wouldn't be long.

Dee sat back to reflect on the situation she had got herself into. Peter seemed to blow hot and cold. She wasn't sure if he liked her or not, or if she liked him. Maybe she was just saying all the wrong things and speaking her mind too much without thinking first. The pay was alright though. Maybe it would be ok to stay a few more days.

'I'll try and impress him and have Susie's file typed up before he gets back.'

Dee found a whole file on missing dogs, filed perfectly under D for dogs. She copied how Mary had typed up a previous file on a dog called Ollie which had gone missing back in May. Not difficult as Mary had left a template on the computer to use. Mary had thought of everything and Mr Whitman had forwarded the photo from his mobile to Dee's so all Dee needed to do was print the photo and attach it to the physical file.

The printer refused to play ball. It had printed the file out from Mary's computer but Dee couldn't pick up the printer on her mobile and link to it. Turning the printer on and off had no affect.

Mary didn't seem to have left an office e-mail address that she could forward the photo to and then print it off from the computer. Dee found this odd and decided to give up. She could print the photo once she got home on the home printer and bring it back in tomorrow. She could just ask Peter for help when he returned but felt it was better to leave that for another day. She felt she had irritated him enough already.

When Peter returned from the police station, Dee couldn't tell if he was happy or not. "Any luck?" she asked.

"No," he went to sit down behind his desk before adding, "Interesting though – they've had an increase in missing dogs around here, and from the park too. Mr Whitman had reported Susie's disappearance, but as usual the police have better things to do than look for dogs," he sighed. "Odd, isn't it?"

Dee wasn't sure if he was asking her a question or making a statement. So she kept quiet.

Peter put his hands behind his head. "How are you doing with everything?"

"I managed to find Mary's file on missing dogs, so I've typed up the file on Susie. I just need to attach the photo. Most of this post is sorted -

just a few more letters I need you to read and any cheques that were attached are ready to go to the bank," she felt quite pleased with herself.

"Well, I think that's us done for today." It was only three thirty.

"Do you want me to call in the bank on my way past and put these in for you?" Dee asked, picking up the paying-in book she had found under *B* for bank account in the grey cabinet.

"Oh, yes, if that's ok? Mary did all that. Well, it's been a busy first day for you. It's not always like that, a client coming in. To be honest we can go weeks with no one at all," Peter checked his watch "I'll see you tomorrow. Is ten o'clock alright? Gives you time to get here. I notice you don't have a car."

"No, I used to borrow my gran's car, where I lived before."

"I must remember to give you a set of office keys too, you know, just in case I'm out, or you need to lock up; that sort of thing. Mary did give them to me. Just can't quite put my finger on where I put them."

"Shall I set up a file on the case of the missing keys?"

Peter laughed. "Sense of humour. I like it."

Dee reached the bank just in time, the bank was in the last building at the far end of the high street. There wasn't a cash machine outside which Dee hadn't noticed on her first visit.' Must be a listed building. There'll be one inside,' she thought, making a mental note for future reference. She joined the queue. She could not see a cash machine inside either, but her attention turned to the two ladies in front of her gassing about someone with the unfortunate name of *Muttering Margo.*

"What's she up to?" the one in the summer dress said.

"Who knows; bonkers that one; mad as a box of frogs!" the other lady in white trousers and a blue top crowed back.

"All that barking, it's driving Vicky mad. She says she never walks them."

"Someone should report her. Could you imagine, as nice as those cottages are, living next door to that old bat? poor Vicky." The lady in the blue top reached the counter, withdrew some cash and left gesturing to her friend to give her a call.

Dee deposited the cheques and asked the bank clerk about withdrawing cash to be told that it was withdrawals over the counter or there's a cash machine at the garage on the outskirts of the village if that's handier.

The walk home was pleasant; the day had cooled a little. It felt like it was going to be one of those Indian summer evenings that she and her gran so loved. She reflected on her first day working for Peter. She had lots to tell Edward over dinner tonight.

"Dinner! Shit!"

She had said over breakfast that she would cook. As yet she hadn't confessed to Edward that her cooking skills didn't stretch beyond shepherd's pie, and she hadn't got round to buying any food either. Time was ticking and most of the shops and the little deli she was passing were putting up their closed signs. 'Take out, that's what we'll do.,' she remembered Peter mentioning Mr Wang's. 'A pleasing solution to their meal problem and a perfect way to end a strangely perfect day.'

Or so she thought.

Chapter 2

Dee woke up the next morning with a self-inflicted hangover. Her eyes were puffy from crying and she was furious with herself. If only she had made an effort to cook. All of the horrible words from the previous evening came flooding back to her. She and Ed had had their first proper argument. He'd come home and threw a strop on finding her dressed up to go out to Mr Wang's for Chinese.

"I'm not going out; I've got that meeting tomorrow. I've got to work tonight, that's why you said you'd cook - so I can work. You know this is big for me. I've got so much to do," he had yelled at her.

"I'll get take out."

In a sarcastic tone he'd said, "Do you know how many calories are in a Chinese? Do you? And how cold will that be by the time you get back."

"I'll take your car. I can drive you know."

"Not my car you're not; you're not insured for it."

"You said you'd put me on the insurance. You said you would."

"As if I had time to do that. This advertising campaign is more important than anything else right now!" Ed had shouted and stormed off towards the little room that he called his office. He may not have slammed the door but he had definitely closed it.

Dee had never felt so unloved. She didn't know what to do. She made sandwiches and left Ed a plate in the kitchen with a note saying *Sorry, Love Dee xx*. She had grabbed a bottle of wine from the fridge and gone upstairs to watch television in bed. She'd kept hoping that Edward would come in and they would hug, kiss and makeup, but he never did and she had cried herself to sleep.

Dee checked the time. It was only 6.30 am. Realizing that Edward had not come up to bed at all, she brushed her teeth, brushed her hair and went downstairs to find him. The sandwiches still sat on the kitchen counter where she had left them, untouched. Edward's coat was gone and so was he.

Dee had gone from upset to fuming. "What an arse," she said aloud to the empty kitchen. "You could at least have said goodbye."

She had a hot shower, a hot coffee, two paracetamols and trowelled on as much makeup as she dared to hide her reddened eyes. Once again, the weather looked promising and it was going to be a lovely rain free day so she decided to wear cream trousers and a coral blouse with coral shoes. No suit required.

Then, walking into Gamblewood, she decided to treat herself to a morning latte at *Coffee Creams* 'I'll give him calories in a Chinese 'she thought.' I'm not over weight and I'll eat what I like. I'll have two cakes and up yours, Edward Holloway; up yours.'

Dee tried the door of *Coffee Creams* but it wouldn't budge.

Alison turned round to find Dee's nose pressed against her window, like a cartoon character. She unlocked the café door to greet her new acquaintance. "You're up early. It's only just gone eight. We aren't open yet," she said. Then noticing Dee's eyes and all the make-up she changed tack. "Look I'm all sorted really. Fancy a quick coffee and a chat before I open up?"

"Sorry, I didn't look at the time. Are you sure it's, ok?"

"Of course." Alison practically dragged Dee into the shop by the arm. "Now sit down. I'm going to have a large coffee with a croissant, fancy one with me?"

"That would be great, thanks."

While Alison prepared the promised coffees and croissants, Dee sat quietly, looking out along the high street. An old man was unlocking the bookshop, a van bearing the name *Flowering Fancies* had pulled up outside the florists and the lady in the summer dress from the bank yesterday was walking down the path chatting away on her mobile. She checked her mobile several times but Ed had not called or sent any texts.

"Now what's going on. Tell me all about it. I can see you've been upset." Alison's tone was carefully soothing as she placed the plates and cups on the table.

Dee blurted everything out that had happened the previous evening. "He didn't once ask how my day had been. It was just I've got to do this, I've got to do that," Dee paused to get her breath then continued. "He even shouted at me, asking if I knew how many calories are in a Chinese. Who gives a Figgie Pudding!"

Alison couldn't control it any longer and burst out laughing. Dee looked up at her from her coffee and started to laugh too.

"That's better, it sounds to me like he's under some pressure at work and you've just got the brunt of it. Maybe he did just want a night in and I'm sure once this meeting is over and done with today, you'll be back to your loved-up selves in no time, God only knows how many spats Jim and I had when we first moved in together."

"Jim?" Dee enquired.

"Jim owns the local garage. We were childhood sweethearts as my mother used to say. Jim took over his father's garage and I took over here. It was my mother's coffee shop before she went to live in Spain."

"My mum lives in Spain too – Murcia," Dee jumped in, not quite believing the coincidence.

They chatted happily about how Alison's mother had nursed her father when he was ill until he passed away two years ago and had then gone to visit a friend who ran art classes in northern Spain, decided to fall in love with the scenery and stayed. Dee in turn talked about how her mother had gone on holiday with her boyfriend and had met another man. They'd decided to set up a bar together and despite her mother's pleas for Dee to join her, she had moved into her Gran's house aged fourteen.

There was a knock on the door.

"Oh my! look at the time, Dee." Alison jumped up and unlocked the door. It was ten past nine.

Alison apologised to the old gentleman. "So sorry Albert. Usual, is it?"

Albert shuffled his way to a table at the back. He waved at Dee from across the table. "New to Gamblewood?" he asked.

"Yes; Alison's making me feel very welcome."

Dee cleared the table for Alison feeling it was the least she could do. "I'll leave you to it," she said. "Ta Alison, for everything."

"See you soon. Do you want a coffee to take with you?" Alison shouted from behind the counter.

"I'm fine, thanks. You'll be sick of seeing me in here" Dee said as she headed for the door.

"Don't forget about Thursday – book club."

"No definitely not."

Dee realised that she had not thought about Ed at all for the last forty-five minutes. Alison was one clever cookie.

She still had time to walk to the book shop before work. The old man she had seen earlier was tidying books in a crate outside the shop into neat lines.

"Hi, going to be a lovely day," Dee said

"Yes, we do get good Septembers here in Gamblewood. Are you new to these parts?"

Dee explained that she had only lived in Gamblewood a few weeks and that she'd just started working for Peter.

"I do miss Mary and her stories," the man continued. "Wonder how she's getting on?"

Dee saw the sign on the door for the book club at Alison's, advertising the recent book they were reading. Without answering the old gentleman's previous question she said "Oh I'd better get that book please; do you have a copy in?"

"That I do; last one."

Dee paid and tucked the book into her bag. It was a romance. She laughed to herself at the irony; she would start it tonight.

The outside office door was already open as Dee approached. Peter was bent down behind it picking up the post.

"Morning, are you okay?" he asked, noticing she was wearing too much make-up. It looked like she'd been crying or got one hell of a hangover - maybe both.

"Yeah, good," Dee lied.

They walked into the office in silence, and Dee remembered she'd brought no tea or coffee with her. "Shoot, I forgot about drinks," she was looking at the hat stand as if it was suddenly going to produce Yorkshire tea or Nescafe.

"Got water, if that's any good?" Peter said and disappeared behind the door at the side of his desk.

"Is that another office in there?" Dee asked trying to peer round him as he closed the door.

"No, it's my living quarters. A little flat or I think you'd call it an apartment nowadays. Anyway there's only me, so it suits. Easy for commuting."

Dee giggled. However, Peter, realising Dee was going to ask more questions, stopped her in her tracks just as she opened her mouth to speak. "No. there's no Mrs Gill. Never found anyone to put up with the unsocial hours and impracticalities of being a detective," he sighed a little as he sat down.

Thinking back to last night Dee couldn't help but think that Peter was better off not being in a relationship. "Has there ever been anyone special?" she asked.

"Now then, Dee. I could lie and say plenty but no - married to the job as they say."

Dee retrieved the computer from the filing cabinet and grabbed the file on missing dogs to attach Susie's photo. She had printed it off using Edward's printer in his home office before he had got back. While attaching the photo Dee found herself going back over the argument. She slammed the stapler hard, forcing Peter to look up from his phone. Dee could feel the anger in her rising at the thought of how it was all so unnecessary and how quickly everything had been blown out of proportion. Then she remembered the cutting comments and Edward leaving without so much as a goodbye. She could feel herself starting to well up and headed for the bathroom. Safely inside, the tears began to fall.

After a few minutes from the other side of the bathroom door Dee could hear the chatter of a female voice, very friendly and engaged in what sounded like quite an animated conversation with Peter. Dee wasn't sure she wanted to interrupt but knew she'd been in the toilet far too long already. Wiping her tears away and trying to look like she hadn't been crying, she put on her best smile and opened the bathroom door.

"Hi. Are you Dee Firth?" the woman asked.

"Yes," Dee was trembling a little. For there in the woman's hands was the biggest bouquet of flowers Dee had ever seen.

"Then these are for you."

Dee was speechless, something that didn't happen to her very often.

"Well, either he likes spoiling you or he's done something really bad," Peter said, unaware how near the truth he was.

Dee managed to get out, "They're amazing," while fighting back the tears.

"Well Pete, I'll get off. Lots to do and all that."

"See you around, Paula."

The flowers had blocked Dee's view of the two of them. If they hadn't, she would have seen Paula mouth to Peter that Dee was obviously upset and to tread carefully. The flowers were from Flowering Fancies, so Paula must have been the girl she saw earlier in the florist's van.

Dee opened the envelope to read the card that was poking out of the array of flowers. It read *Chinese tonight? Ed x*. Trust him to try and make a joke out of the situation.

While she was examining the card, Peter had retreated to his flat. He was not good at dealing with emotional women - or any type of emotion. He felt it was safer to be out of the way than in the office until a reasonable amount of time had passed for him to risk peeking his head out from behind the flat door.

He watched as Dee blew her nose into a tissue then tried to wipe away the large droplets that were falling from her face onto her desk. Unsure of what to do, Peter adopted a soothing tone. "Look, I don't know what's happened, but they're beautiful flowers. It's really thoughtful of him."

Dee's eyes had become puffier and redder than ever. She had re-read the card over and over again, noticing that there was no *Sorry* or *Love* written on it. She blew her nose again.

"I know!" Peter shouted out, taking Dee by complete surprise. "The park," he pointed out over her shoulder at the view behind her. "A good breath of fresh air will do you good. Go take a walk around the park. Take as long as you need."

"Hmm, I'm so sorry. This is so embarrassing but do you mind?" Dee struggled to speak between sobs and her running nose.

"Get yourself off. See you when you get back," Peter made it sound like an order and Dee did as she was told. It was such a relief to be outside in the fresh air. The dull office and the scent from the flowers had been suffocating her.

Peter relaxed back in his office chair and texted Paula, thanking her for the heads up. 'That's what young love must be like,' he thought to himself while smiling about the drama that Dee had brought to his little office. 'This would never of have happened to Mary.'

The sun was now shining through and the day was warm with a soft breeze wrapping itself around Dee's shoulders like a cosy blanket. She could see the park entrance in the distance and headed towards it. 'Peter must think he's hired an absolute nightmare. He's been so kind to me. Wonder if two iced buns in two days might give him a heart attack.' Her mind was restless, away from home and the wisdom of her Gran. Everything was weighing heavily on her. Inside the gates she sat down on the nearest bench overlooking a little duck pond, convinced that Peter was going to sack her and Edward was going to ask her to leave, saying it was all a huge mistake.

"Things happen for a reason," her Gran would say. Dee closed her eyes, the warmth of the sun on her neck helping her to relax and she began to picture her Gran telling her to stay positive. "Good things happen to good people."

Back at the office Peter was flicking through the' missing dogs' file. He'd made numerous calls since Dee left to go to the park but all to no avail. 'Alison might have heard something or Paula. Should have asked Paula this morning,' he thought. Annoyed at himself for not thinking about it earlier he decided he'd get some fresh air too and pay the girls a visit.

Peter was surprised at the warmth of the day and quickened his step a little. He was not a sunshine person; he much preferred the winter. 'Won't be long before it all changes and the cold dark nights draw in,' he thought. He went to Alison's first.

"Hi, Peter. Doing okay?" Alison asked.

"All good," he replied, raising his eyebrows.

"Coffee, is it?" Alison was already holding the coffee pot over the cup. She already knew the answer. She also knew the raised eyebrow look.

Peter nodded and sat down. "Hi, Albert, how're you doing?" he asked the old man sitting at his usual table.

"Good, good. Missing Mary, Peter."

"Me too," said Peter. "However I've a new girl Albert. Her name's Dee; interesting."

Albert returned to his paper and as it was quiet Alison sat down opposite Peter. Handing him his coffee she couldn't help herself. "Interesting. What do you mean?"

Peter explained what had happened with Dee at the office.

"I know. She was here this morning. We talked about it. You know it can't be easy; new job, new boyfriend, new village, no family here. Can't put my finger on it but there's something about her. I like her, Peter. She's going to be good for you, you'll see."

Peter nodded. The pair fell silent.

"Are we having an iced bun with another coffee?" Alison said.

"No, I'm good ta. Think I need to lose a few pounds. And talking of losing things, have you heard anything about dogs going missing?"

"No, not me."

Alison went back behind the counter with Peter's now empty coffee cup in hand and Peter turned to call across the tables. "What about you, Albert? Heard anything about dogs going missing in the village?"

"No, can't stand dogs or cats. Like fish though," Albert answered without even looking up.

Peter realised he had drawn a blank and rose to pay Alison for his drink. "I best be going."

Just as Peter was nearly out the door Alison remembered something. "There was a man here yesterday looking for your place. Mentioned he'd lost his dog. Smart man, nicely dressed."

"Alison, you know I don't talk about cases. Nice try." Peter was laughing as he left.

Albert put his newspaper down to tell Alison, "I do miss Mary. I really do."

Dee had made a decision. She was not going to feel sorry for herself and if it all went wrong; she would just go home to her gran's and start again. Sitting in the warm sunshine, listening to the ducks quacking and watching the world go by had helped to heal her woes. Feeling much better and more back to her usual self, Dee thought she'd take a quick walk and see what was at the other side of the park.

The grounds were beautiful at this time of year and, as she made her way, she passed young children giggling as they played on the swings, a couple stealing a moment and a gardener enjoying the day's toil.

In the distance was a pretty row of cottages. 'I'd like to live there,' Dee thought. She let her imagination run away with her and she imagined herself inside one of the pretty little cottages. There was a Christmas tree in the corner with twinkling soft lights and she was wrapped in a cosy blanket by an open fire with a good book, sipping wine while carols played in the background. By the time Dee had come back to reality, she'd unknowingly left the park and was looking over a white picket fence into the garden of one of the cottages.

"Hello. I don't get many visitors or are you selling something? No money me, you know." The voice came from a tiny lady, probably in her eighties, dressed in a nice dress for someone her age with a green pinny over the top that didn't match at all. "I say, no money here if you're selling things."

"No, no, I'm not selling things," Dee said bewildered at how she had come to be standing there at a garden gate facing an elderly woman who had appeared as if from nowhere.

Thinking fast Dee explained she was new to the village and was just walking past and that her garden reminded her of her gran's back home.

"Come in, come in," the old lady beckoned. "Don't just stand there, I'll show you my back garden. It's my pride and joy."

Knowing how her gran had talked of the loneliness some of her friends had experienced, Dee gave in and followed the lady into the house. "I'm Dee."

"Yes, yes. I'm Margaret. Now then come along. come along."

Margaret's cottage was homely. She had logs on the fireside and flower print cushions scattered on the furniture. Dee was so thankful that there was none of that old lady's smell that infested some of her gran's friends' houses. The inside of the cottage was as well-kept as her picture-perfect garden. The walls were adorned with paintings and framed photographs perched on the mantlepiece surrounded by vases of flowers. Dee loved it immediately.

"Lemonade, girl? Do you want lemonade? Hot day, hot day you know," Margaret shouted from the kitchen.

"Yes, that would be lovely," Dee replied nearly tripping over the dog now seated at her feet as she tried to make her way towards the kitchen. "Oh, you have a dog. What's his name?"

"That one is Ginger," Margaret replied, and headed out towards the garden through some patio doors carrying the two filled glasses.

For an old woman Margaret could move and Dee noticed how steady Margaret was on her feet compared to her own gran.

"Come out and sit down. Sit down."

Dee petted Ginger and made her way through the lounge to the garden, passing a side table holding three framed photographs and an ornament of a lady riding a horse. To make conversation, Dee mentioned the ornament.

"Yes, had that a long time. Been in the family for years. Daisy's weeds you know," Margaret said, adding something under her breath which Dee couldn't hear her for sudden barking.

"They want to come out," Margaret exclaimed as she leapt to her feet.

Dee watched her move around the garden. The old lady was so agile and nimble, Dee wondered if she'd ever been a dancer.

The garden was spectacular. Margaret must have help. It was like something out of one of those design programmes she'd heard her gran talk about. 'Alan somebody on the telly…' Dee knew nothing about gardening. 'One day, one day I will,' she thought, taking a sip of lemonade.

Next moment Margaret returned surrounded by a pack of dogs.

"Oh my. You have a lot of them," Dee said bending down to try to give each one of them her attention.

"Company, company," Margaret said giving one of the dogs a tickle.

"What are their names?" Dee asked, putting her lemonade down before it could be knocked out of her hand.

Margaret pointed at a yellow-looking dog. "This is Custard. That one's Bourbon. Here's Shortbread. Don't know where Cookie is. You've met Ginger and here's my little cutie, Florentine."

Dee was impressed with how good Margaret's memory was. "I don't know how you remember them all?" she said but Margaret wasn't listening. She was talking to herself. Something about birds.

Dee spoke louder, thinking the old lady might be a little deaf. "Nice photos. Family?" She pointed towards the three framed photos just inside the door.

"Aye, aye. Heiress there. You're an heiress?"

"Yes, my Gran said she's going to leave me her house when she passes. I don't like it when she talks like that."

Margaret didn't acknowledge what Dee had said and began talking about dog food, once again mainly to herself. Then she said, "Finally, Cookie where have you been?" bending to stroke the latecomer's ears.

Dee giggled at the thought of the dog answering her. 'How funny would that be.' She was ready to leave. She'd finished her lemonade and had had enough of petting the dogs and trying to make conversation with someone who would seemingly rather speak to herself. "Thank you for the lemonade, I must get back to work."

"Yes, yes" said Margaret getting up and they both headed back into the house.

"I can call again, if you'd like me to?" Dee offered.

"That would be nice, but I know you young ones are so busy."

Then, as Dee stepped back to turn round and leave, she felt herself falling. She grabbed out for the arm of the sofa to soften her landing and missed, hitting the floor with such a bump she really wasn't sure if she could get back up. She was somehow entangled with Cookie.

"Are you alright, dear. That dog gets under my feet all the time. Can you get up?"

"Yes, I think so. That's embarrassing." She patted herself, checking to make sure nothing was broken. Now she was just desperate to leave.

"Cookie, your collar," Margaret shrieked. "Can you pass me it, dear. It's half under the sofa."

Dee reached down to retrieve the little blue collar with its name tag in the form of a little silver bone. Engraved on it was the name *Ollie* with a mobile number written underneath. Dee remembered that Ollie was the name of the dog she had so recently copied into a file. She handed over the dog-collar and Margaret retreated to the kitchen throwing the dog collar on top of the kitchen worktop and turning on the taps.

"Do you know, I think I've left my mobile phone on the table outside, Is it okay if I just go out and check?"

"Sure, dear," Margaret said without turning round from the kitchen sink.

Thinking quickly and hoping that Margaret wouldn't come out, she checked two of the other dog's name tags. The one she'd called Ginger had the correct name on his collar but the one Margaret had called Custard was tagged Benji. She panicked, needing to tell Peter straight away. "Thank you for the lemonade, got my phone," she shouted to Margaret who was now drying the glasses with a checked tea towel.

"Not deaf. No need to shout," Margaret tutted under her breath then started talking about grass seed. Dee headed for the door and Margaret was suddenly right behind her.

"See you again." Margaret said with one hand on the door handle, but somehow her tone left Dee feeling it wasn't much like an invitation to return. She walked as quickly as she could back to the office, convinced she'd heard Margaret say, "Good riddance," as she'd closed the door behind her.

"Peter?" Dee said as soon as she got her breath back.

"You've been gone a while. Feeling any better?"

"Much better, thanks." Dee removed the large bouquet of flowers from her desk to the floor.

Peter watched her carefully. She seemed in a flap with excitement. "Dee, has something happened?"

She turned to face him holding the lost dog file she had retrieved and opened out on her desk. "I knew it!" She could hardly contain herself. "Ollie, I've found him. He's at this old woman's house and there's other dogs too!!"

"Ok, sit down and start at the beginning."

Dee explained how she'd ended up looking into one of the cottage gardens and being invited in to see the back garden by Margaret. Peter had to interrupt a couple of times to keep her on track. Dee had a tendency to waffle and Peter wasn't interested in hearing about photographs in pretty picture frames and horsey ornaments.

"Ginger, Cookie, Bourbon…are you kidding me? Do you think Susie could have been one of those dogs, Dee?"

"Could be. Thinking about it, there was one she called Florentine that seemed shy. I couldn't check them all without her noticing. What do we do now?"

"We need to go back. Are you sure these names are correct?"

"Yeah, she definitely said her name was Margaret."

"No, not hers. The dogs' names. Dee think about it; what do they all have in common?" Peter was now out of his seat, pacing the floor behind his desk.

"Common? No idea."

"Biscuits, bloody biscuits. Custard as in cream, Ginger…" Peter gestured with his hands.

"Oh God, yeah, Bourbon. You must think I'm a right idiot, why didn't I put two and two together."

"You're not an idiot. You went back out into the garden to check as many dogs as you could without getting caught. Good use of your gut instinct I'd say."

"What now?" Dee asked, finally sitting down in her chair.

"Like I said we – and by we, I mean you, have to go back, to take some photos of the dogs and their name tags. Then I can call Jake and let him know what we've found."

"Jake?"

"New chap at the police station; sharp mind; like him a lot."

Dee said that Margaret had seemed quite annoyed when she was leaving. Even though Margaret had said "See you again soon," deep down she didn't think for one moment that she'd meant it. "Shame, Peter. She was so lovely till Cookie's collar fell off."

"Exactly. I suspect she knew you might be on to her."

"Really? Well, what reason or excuse do I have to call round there again?"

Peter looked as if he was hoping thin air would give him the answer and then announced, "I'm peckish. Let's head to Coffee Creams and get a bite to eat and see if we can come up with something."

Alison couldn't help but notice how well Peter and Dee seemed to be getting on. Whilst eating their sandwiches and drinking their tea, they chatted and laughed. Dee looked so much happier than the woman who had been sitting opposite her that morning. Alison noticed that the two of them kept lowering their voices when anybody else walked past their table so she went over to see if they wanted anything else. "Case work?" she enquired.

Peter replied with a smile. "Bit of brainstorming, that's all, but yes it's about a case, so don't ask. You know not to ask."

Alison pulled a face and said, "Are we having cake?"

It didn't go unnoticed by Alison that Dee convinced Peter to try the Victoria sponge rather than his usual iced bun and when they got up to leave, Alison shouted after Peter's back. "Told you she'd be good for you!"

"What's that all about?" Dee asked once they were outside.

"Alison being Alison," was the droll reply.

On their way back to the office they called in at Paula's shop. Paula was surprised to see them and said as much when they said they needed horticultural advice. They needed to tell someone that Dee's gran had sent her some bulbs to plant, but as Dee's Garden was all concrete with no grass or soil in sight, Dee would say that she thought that the someone could make good use of them.

"Daffodils," Paula suggested.

"Love them," Dee said. "They're one of Gran's favourite flowers."

"Always smell of pee to me," Peter said under his breath.

The plan was in place. They had agreed not to go the next day as it seemed too soon, but the day after. Peter felt that would be more appropriate.

They re-entered the office, which as dull as it was, had been lifted by the scent of the bouquet Edward had sent her, but Dee realised she hadn't checked her phone or thought of Edward once since meeting Margaret.

"Type up everything for the file. Include every detail even if it doesn't seem significant now. It might be later," was the instruction issued as Peter disappeared into his flat. Dee was hammering away on the keys on her keyboard when her phone flashed. *Booked Chinese for seven. Edward x* the text read. Dee replied with nothing more than a kiss. 'Not giving in that easy,' she thought returning to her typing.

When Peter came out of his flat he was holding a piece of rolled-up paper. Laying it flat on his desk he said, "Come over and have a look."

"It's a map of the village."

"It certainly is. Can you point out which house it was. I want to do some background digging."

"Where are we?"

"Right there," Peter pointed.

They traced her walk as best they could. There were only two exits at the other end of the park. It was obvious which one Dee had taken, as she would have naturally come across the exit on the left before the other one which came out opposite Gamblewood Primary School and Dee was clear that she had definitely not seen a school.

"Did you go down any lanes, cross any roads?"

"No, I just crossed the road from the park to those three cottages." Dee's finger was poised over them on the map.

"Well, I never. Are you sure you went into the cottage on the right?"

"Yes. Why? The old lady was nice. Well to start with she seemed nice enough." Dee folded her arms.

Peter was checking his phone. He'd missed a call. "Jake's called, probably wanting a catch up over a drink. If we go to Muttering Margo's day after tomorrow, I can tell him all about you and finding the dogs over a pint."

"Muttering Margo? I heard some ladies talking about her in the bank when I went to pay the cheques in." Dee looked shocked. "They said she was totally barking. Pardon the pun."

"Yes, she walks around the village muttering and talking under her breath. Didn't realise you were talking about her with you saying she was called Margaret."

"Wonder where Margo came from?"

"Probably a nick name. You had a lucky escape. Surprised she let you out once she'd got you in there," Peter declared.

"So Muttering Margo is our dog napper, and bonkers by all accounts. Do you seriously want me to go back there on Friday?" Dee's voice was getting higher and higher. "How do you know that's her house, Peter? Could you be wrong?"

"Definitely her house. Albert lives in the first cottage on the left. He's been there years. A young family live in the middle and then Muttering Margo's cottage is the one on the right. She spends all her time talking to her plants and flowers. They're probably the only ones who'll listen to her."

"Vicky.." Dee blurted out. "The ladies in the bank said that Vicky was sick of all the barking coming from the dogs next door. Vicky must live in the middle cottage. They said her neighbour was batty; mad as a box of frogs! That's what they said."

"Well maybe like you said, she's just a lonely old woman who needs some company. I'll just go and return Jake's call." Peter was waving his mobile in the air as he disappeared into his flat.

Dee sat back down behind her desk. She was trying to figure out when her role - secretarial duties with a bit of book-keeping thrown in - had developed into her turning amateur sleuth and going undercover in an old lady's house to take photos of dogs. Shrugging her shoulders, she reminded herself how boring her last job had become as she had constantly moaned to her gran. Boring this wasn't. But on the other hand, going into a mad woman's house seemed stupid even to her. 'Think positive,' she told herself. 'Think of the people like Mr Whitman's wife or Ollie's owners who will be so pleased to have their dogs safely returned. It's got to be a good thing I'm doing. Just hope Margo...Margaret doesn't get into too much trouble.'

Peter returned and reclaimed his seat behind his desk to read through Dee's typed report of the day's events.

"Very good. You've got quite the eye for detail," he praised her, making her feel quite good about how her day had turned around. She had solved the case of the Gamblewood dog-napper and Peter seemed proud of her. She did feel a little smug if she was being honest. Her phone flashed. Another text from Edward. She turned her phone over without reading it.

"Hi," said a voice from the doorway. She hadn't even heard the door open while she was busy congratulating herself.

"Umm, hi." was all that Dee could manage.

"Jake, hello," Peter said. "I just tried calling you. Could do with a little catch-up about a dog or two over a pint, if you're free Friday evening, although I know how it is. Sorry Dee, this is Jake, the DI I was mentioning earlier."

"Yes," Dee answered, not really able to speak. Jake was a good-looking, well-built chap with dark curly hair and a thin, clever, smiling face and he'd caught her totally caught off guard.

Jake nodded. "It would be nice to catch up but I'm here on official business."

"How can we help?" Peter said.

Jake's attention turned to Dee. "Sorry about this Peter," he carried on, Now he was looking directly into Dee's eyes. "Are you Deandra Firth?"

All Dee could manage by way of reply was a nod.

Someone else standing in the corridor behind the inspector moved alongside him. Peter recognised him as a Detective Sergeant; Tom something or other.

"Hang on, Jake. What's going on here?"

Jake ignored Peter and continued "I'm Detective Inspector Jones. Miss Firth we would like to ask you some questions down at the station regarding Mrs Darnley. Would you mind coming with us please?"

Dee just sat there, shocked.

"Mrs Darnley?" Peter interrupted.

"Yes, you might know her in the village as Muttering Margo."

Now Peter was on his feet and at Dee's side.

"What's this got to do with Dee. Why do you need to question her?" His detective brain was kicking in, knowing how the police worked.

Dee could not move a muscle. She felt she had lost all mode of speech and just sat there staring at Jake.

"I'm sorry but we need to speak to Miss Firth. Mrs Darnley was found in her garden this afternoon by her neighbour and we have a witness who places you at the scene. We're led to believe you were the last one to see her alive!."

"I only moved here a few weeks ago. No one knows me. I don't understand," Dee stammered, tears falling. Pushing past Peter, before anyone could stop her, she took refuge in the office toilet.

"Can Miss Firth escape out of there?" Jake asked.

"No," said Peter.

"Then we'll wait."

Chapter 3

Peter paced up and down outside Gamblewood Police Station. He knew how awful questioning could be. After all he had been on both sides of the table. When Dee finally stumbled down the steps in tears, she threw herself at him nearly knocking him over.

"Are you okay? Let's get back to the office. It's getting late and you can tell me all about it." Peter dragged an exhausted Dee into the passenger seat of his car.

"Your car's nice." The inconsequential remark was a sure indicator of extreme stress.

"It's nothing special, but reliable and cost-effective to run."

Dee was staring back at the police station as Peter pulled out of the car park. She had no idea where to begin in telling Peter what had happened to her.

"You went easy in there, Jake?" Tom said.

The two of them were looking out of Jake's office window watching Peter and Dee leave the station car-park.

"Yes, she was in a bit of a state of shock I think. I'll bring her in again, soon."

Jake turned away from the window, went over to his office chair to retrieve his mobile phone from the inside of his jacket pocket. He waited till Tom left his office to go back to his. He then texted Peter. *Need to meet for that drink – tonight.*

Safely back in the office, each with a takeaway coffee from the petrol station, Peter urged Dee to start at the beginning and to try and remember word for word as best she could what they had said to her. She told Peter as much as she could between renewed bursts of tears.

"They obviously don't suspect foul play. They're quite routine questions to be honest, Dee. You've got nothing to worry about. You were probably genuinely the last person to see her alive, that's all."

"Do you think so? God, why did I go into her flipping house, and now she's dead. What are the chances of that?"

Peter's phone vibrated. He checked it to discover the message from Jake.

"Dee, Jake wants to meet for a drink tonight. So, see nothing to worry about. I'll sort it all out tonight. Do you want me to take you home? It's getting late and those flowers will be awkward to carry."

Dee accepted and Peter drove her home. She had forgotten all about the flowers and going out to Mr Wang's. She had just over an hour to spare before they would have to leave to go to the Chinese.

"Shall I come in and explain what's happened to Edward. It is Edward, isn't it?"

"No, I'll be fine, but it's really nice of you to offer."

Peter watched Dee get out of his car and walk up the drive. She looked so down and brow-beaten, he was more than a little surprised at his own protective feelings towards her. Picking up his mobile he texted Jake that he would be at the Star and Crown in thirty minutes.

"Hi, you got the flowers then? Thought you might have sent me a thank you text" Edward said with a bitter note to his tone and Dee burst into tears. He turned to face her. "Look it all got a bit out of hand yesterday. Think I was just worried about today; you remember the meeting in London?"

"Yeah." Dee was trying to smile as the tears ran down her face. "I've had a really bad day…."

About to tell him the events culminating in her police interview, Edward interrupted her. "You don't have long to change for Mr Wang's. I'm really looking forward to it. Heard great things about the food."

Before Dee knew it, she was upstairs, showered and tying her curls into a high ponytail. She didn't normally wear dresses - she thought she looked awful in them - but she was determined to make the effort to wear one now after the row the night before. Edward seemed full of vigour and excitement despite his early start to London. Dee looked in the mirror and felt flat. The day had taken its toll, the tears had made her face look tired and puffy. The blue dress didn't look bad, probably because she had not eaten most of the day. She grabbed a tissue from the box and stuffed it in her bag, thinking she might need it.

"Come on Dee, we don't want to be late. Are you nearly ready?" Edward shouted up the stairs.

"Yeah, coming," she shouted back while slipping her left foot into the silver strappy sandal. She looked back into the mirror for a final check before going downstairs. Not too shabby for someone who's been interrogated for hours she thought. Then she felt suddenly sick.

The Star and Crown was in Amberleigh, a market town much bigger than Gamblewood where people were much less likely to know Peter or Jake. It was easy to talk openly over a pint without stares and others trying to eavesdrop. The only person who appeared to know them was now sitting down with a pint in hand, chatting merrily away with the landlord. The latter could recognise a cop a mile off but they didn't seem to be watching him or anyone else in the pub. The landlord relaxed. After all they had been nothing but pleasant and they'd been in a couple of times before without incident.

"Hope you went easy on Dee?" Peter was finally asking Jake once the niceties were out of the way.

"How could I not. She looked terrified and constantly kept bursting into tears."

"I asked Dee to write her account of meeting Margaret who we believe has been taking dogs from the park. Here, have a read. That copy's for you. You'll see she's quite good at the little details; does go off at a tangent though; but read it through and see if that ties up with what she said to you today. I'll go get us one more."

"Just a shandy for me." Jake picked up Dee's typed account from earlier and settled himself back to read as Peter headed to the bar.

At Mr Wang's, Ed had been nothing but complimentary about her dress and hair. He explained how he hadn't wanted to wake her when he'd left early to get the 5 o'clock train. Dee just nodded and smiled.

The waiter brought over their order. Dee had gone from feeling sick to ravenous. The wine she had just downed had calmed her nerves and she started to pour herself another glass.

"Gosh, you're putting it away. I'll have to order you another bottle at this rate." Ed laughed and started to eat.

Between mouthfuls, Ed continuously talked about his visit to London, how amazing the office was that he had visited and how professional and sophisticated the staff were. At some point Dee tuned him out. She found herself going back over the interview, playing the question-and-answer session over and over in her head. She ceased to hear a word that Ed was saying and realised, if she was being honest with herself, she really didn't want to.

Suddenly snapping back to reality Dee spoke, just a little too loudly, announcing to Ed, "I was taken in for questioning by the police about a woman I thought might have been pinching people's dogs who's now dead."

The whole restaurant went deathly quiet and all eyes were on them.

Ed looked around, completely baffled. "Everyone's staring. What? What's happened? Forget it, let's go home; you can tell me there." Without waiting for her to react, he stood, pulling his jacket on, and then grabbed Dee by the elbow as she was pouring the last bit of wine in her glass down her throat.

He flung some banknotes onto the table. "That should be enough," he whispered into her ear. Let's get out of here. This is so embarrassing."

"What do you think, Jake. Does it all tie up?

"Exactly what she said, with less tears. It's just unfortunate that she seems to be the last person to see her alive; usual thing, wrong place, wrong time. You're right about detail; she's very good. You've taught her well." Jake nodded, raising his pint to his lips.

"It's all her, trust me, I've not taught her anything. She only started with me this week. Poor thing - what a week she's had." Peter went on to explain about Mary leaving and hiring Dee and that he'd checked Dee out before he hired her. She came with no baggage and he'd liked her initiative in putting her advert in the Post office. "So, are we thinking a fall, over one of the dogs maybe?"

"That or she tripped up in the garden and banged her head. Sad isn't it to die like that." Jake replied.

Peter looked across at Jake, his cogs turning. He knew Jake well. "The dogs. What's happened to them?"

"They're in the pound at the moment behind the station. Don't suppose you have time to find their rightful owners do you?"

"Well, we were going to go back on Friday to get more evidence before I called you. It's lucky Dee noticed the dog's name on the collar was different to the one Margaret used. Anyway we've already been approached by some owners who've lost dogs in the park, so I'm sure we can tie it up pretty quickly."

"And get paid!" Jake interrupted him with a smirk.

"Of course," said Peter with a wink. "I taught you well."

Dee sat on the sofa and blurted out the whole sorry tale from start to finish. Ed didn't say a word. He just kept pouring wine and thinking how this would affect him.

"It was so awful, Jake - that's the detective - was trying to be as nice as he could but it was still awful; truly awful." Dee's exhaustion was plain. Going through it all again and reliving it had done that. The wine was now mixing with the Chow Mein and Dee suddenly had to flee to the bathroom where Ed could hear her being sick.

He just sat bewildered in the chair opposite the sofa, sipping his wine.

'Why Dee?' he thought. He could feel the anger rising in him at her stupidity, going into someone's house who she didn't know, trying to be so nice as usual and look at the mess she'd got herself into. Ed rubbed his forehead, it hurt. 'That Peter must have connections. Peter must be able to help, if only she hadn't gone to work there, if she'd just listened and got herself a decent job through an agency none of this would have happened. What a mess.' He turned to see a green-looking Dee come out of the downstairs bathroom.

"Hope you've cleaned that up?" he shouted across at her.

"Course I have. Thanks for asking how I am?"

"How you are? What about me?" Ed was now storming towards the fridge, wine bottle in hand. "How do you think I feel? We'll be the talk of the village; village gossip, that's what we'll be."

"I doubt it. No one here knows who we are. It's not like we're heavily involved in village life and I've only just moved here!"

They both stood glaring at each other.

"Look I'm not feeling great." Dee deliberately softened her tone. "It's really upset me all this. I'm so annoyed at myself. I can't see why this has had to happen to me."

"No," Ed said. Coming over to her side, he popped an arm around her shoulder and Dee could feel her body relaxing into him.

"Let's go to bed. Peter's told you, you've nothing to worry about. We both need to get a good night's sleep and stop all this arguing." He bent to kiss her on the top of her head. "I'll just lock up. Go on you, get yourself tucked in"

Dee absent-mindedly thanked Ed for the flowers and headed upstairs as she'd been told.

When Ed could hear Dee in the bathroom, he poured himself another glass of wine from the bottle in the fridge, put his feet up on the sofa, laid back into its soft cushions and raised the glass into the air as he congratulated himself on his successful day in London. Somehow Dee's problems had ceased to matter. At least for now.

Chapter Four

Dee woke up happy that things were much better between her and Ed. Once he had eventually come to bed they had kissed and made up. Now he was up and gone - an early start at work he claimed. Dee sat up and swung her legs over the side of the bed, suddenly the anxious sickly feeling of yesterday rushed over her.

"Poor Margaret," she said out loud to the empty bedroom without realising what she'd done.

She eventually decided to wear black, even though the sun was shining once again. She felt black was appropriate. Her Gran always wore black when someone she knew had died.

Peter looked Dee up and down as she entered the office, trying to be funny and to avoid the onslaught of Dee's likely questions. "Anyone would think someone had died!"

Dee did laugh and sat down at her desk. More post was on it and a bottle of water Peter had placed next to it.

"Thought you might need that. Glass of wine too many?"

"No, I threw the wine and my chicken Chow Mein up in the downstairs bathroom. Not pretty." Dee started to giggle and Peter let out a belly laugh.

"Seriously, what did Jake say last night?" Dee's head was down. She was too afraid to look at him.

"It's all good. Looks like she took a fall in the garden, fell over one of the dogs maybe. Jake will have it all sorted. The dogs are in the pound. Fancy coming with me? See if any of them match up to the missing animals on our file."

"Gosh, I forgot about the dogs. How does that work? Do we just take them from the pound, return them to their owners and get paid?"

"Well, if I get paid you get paid so that's got to be a good thing plus… you get the credit of finding the dogs at Muttering Margo's house and returning them to their rightful owners."

Dee pointed at the post. "Shall I just do this first?"

"No. It'll still be there when we get back. Come on. We can grab a coffee from Alison's on the way."

"Hi Peter," beamed Alison "Usual?"

"Yes, please and whatever Dee normally has to go. She's in the car."

"Okay." Alison carried on as she made Dee a skinny latte "Heard about Muttering Margo. Must have upset one of her plants." She chuckled a little. "No I don't mean that. It's truly awful, isn't it. People are saying she fell."

Albert, at his regular table, piped up. "Nasty one that. Always muttering about someone or something - never made sense - always going around saying things, telling stories. Hope someone takes those dogs away - so sick of their yapping."

Peter turned. "Albert, I'm heading over to the dog pound now to get them. Did Margo always have a dog or dogs?",

"No idea," Albert said from behind the newspaper he had picked up. "Didn't bother with her. I know Vicky went round to complain about all the barking keeping her youngsters up at night. Can't say I noticed barking before. Probably over the summer it started. What do I know? Mad that one."

Peter took the take away cups from Alison and thanked her but Albert interrupted. "Saw your new girl at Margo's house yesterday - went inside she did. I told the police when they asked if anyone had been hanging about."

Peter stopped dead in his tracks. "Thanks Albert, you've cleared one thing up."

"One thing?" Albert's head popped up over the top of his newspaper.

Peter didn't answer. He was half way out the door, his detective brain in overdrive.

Albert looked over at Alison. "Have I said something wrong?"

Alison shrugged her shoulders and carried on drying the cup in her hands.

"Need that," Dee said to Peter as he handed her the coffee.

"Well, I've cleared one thing up. I didn't want to push Jake too much last night, but didn't you wonder how someone recognised you outside Muttering Margo's house."

"I did to be honest, and how would someone know I was the last one there? Someone else could have gone to see her after me."

"Albert's just told me he recognised you, probably from going into the café. You don't know Albert at all do you?"

Dee looked shocked at the question and answered angrily. "Of course I don't. I've only ever seen him in the coffee shop. I didn't know he lived in the same place as Muttering Margo until you told me…showed me on that map. God, you've got me calling her Muttering Margo now!"

"Wonder if he's a curtain twitcher?" Peter said aloud breaking the silence which had fallen as they drove off.

"Curtain twitcher? We call them nosy parkers where I come from, thinking about it - that old man has really landed me in it. The whole thing makes me feel sick, poor woman, nice or not. Peter, who do you think found her?"

"Interesting that. I've been thinking the same. It's got to be Vicky. Jake said a neighbour found her and Albert didn't mention anything just then. Got to tread carefully though; Jake can only say so much. Intriguing though, the case of Muttering Margo ends with death by falling over a dog."

"That's not funny. I hurt myself tripping over one of her flipping dogs. I've still got the bruises," Dee said, grinning.

"Here we are," Peter announced.

Dee felt lightheaded as they entered the police station car-park. The memories of the interrogation came flooding back, filling her with dread. "Don't you think they'll find it strange, that Jake I mean. I was interviewed about Margaret dying and now I'm here again?"

"Not unless you know something I don't. Look it's Jake that's asked us to come and sort the dogs out. You're worrying over nothing, Dee. It was just an accident. You've got to stop feeling sorry for yourself, like I've already told you, you were just in the wrong place at the wrong time and that's all. Come on." Peter jumped out of the car.

Dee could sense his annoyance at her. She followed him into the station, her heart skipping a beat as the officer behind the desk stared at her. Peter could sense a couple of looks from other officers milling around behind the front desk coming Dee's way. They would all have had a rollicking if he was in charge. Peter asked to see Jake, his voice one of authority and it took Dee by surprise. The officer responded and said that he would be back in a minute.

A couple of the officers had obviously recognised Peter. He couldn't hear what they were saying, but he knew it was about him just by the glances. Dee kept her head down; she felt so embarrassed by the staring policemen and was convinced they were all talking about her having been questioned yesterday.

Tom came out from behind a door that led into the reception area. He kept one hand on the door, keeping it open. "Peter. Hi. Come through. Jake's just tied up on the phone at the moment."

Recognising Tom, Dee looked away, pretending to read a poster on a pin board.

"You remember Dee? she's with me," Peter spoke calmly but loud enough to let everyone know.

"Yes, come through."

As they passed the front desk, Dee heard one of the officers say, "Looker that one. He's done alright."

"Gorgeous," said another.

Jake sat in his office, rubbing his hands together, something he only did when he felt anxious. There was a knock at his door. "Enter," he commanded. It reminded Dee of her school days.

Tom opened the door but stood back to let them enter first. Jake pointed at two seats and Tom came in and sat behind them in a chair in the corner of the office. Peter shook Jake's hand and they swapped greetings. Dee kept quiet, looking down at the floor. Not for the first time she'd noticed how good-looking Jake was and wished she'd made more of an effort. Her black outfit felt very dull compared to his lilac shirt.

"Are you okay, Dee? do you need some water?" Jake asked and nodded at Tom who knew that meant he should go and fetch some.

Dee looked up. "Yes, yeah I'm fine. It's being here, just really don't know what to say after all that's happened."

Peter interposed himself into the conversation. "So the dogs, Jake? Do you want to take us through to the pound and we'll crack on." He wanted to save Dee from talking too much and from further embarrassment. Her cheeks were already flushed.

To Jake Dee looked tired and strained. Whisps of curly red hair had escaped from the high ponytail and framed her pretty face in falling spirals. He turned his attention to Peter and looked him straight in the eyes. "The PM has come back."

Dee could feel Peter stiffen in his chair. "And?"

Mrs Darnley didn't fall, or rather she did but only after she'd been hit over the head with a blunt instrument."

Dee sat bolt upright; her eyes wider than ever as the realisation of the situation hit her. "She was murdered? Is that what you're saying!"

Neither Peter or Jake responded at first. Then as Peter nodded, Jake said, "Afraid so, Miss Firth. We need to establish where you were between noon and 1.30 on Wednesday, twenty-third of September."

Dee couldn't think straight or get a single word out of her mouth. She had begun to shake from head to toe.

"You can't think for one minute this has anything to do with Dee." Peter was almost pleading.

Jake's gut feeling was usually right and in his heart of hearts he couldn't see Dee as a killer but someone was and Dee had to be eliminated from his enquiry. After all, apart from the killer she was the last known person to see Margaret Darnley alive. "Of course, I don't," he said. "You know I have to ask these questions though."

Tom returned with the water and placed them down on the desk. Dee reached to pick up one of the glasses but her hand was trembling. She went to put it back down and a little water popped over the top of the glass and splashed onto the hardwood of the desk.

Dee was close to sobs. "I thought you said we were coming here to sort out the dogs not to charge me with murder!"

Peter put an arm around her. "We can get this sorted. Think it through. What happened when you left Margo's house?"

"Nothing, nothing at all. She was alive when I left, I swear but she wasn't that nice to me. Like you said, probably because she realised I'd picked up on the dogs. Then I walked as quick as I could back to the office to tell you what had happened. We went to Alison's to make a plan. Then we went to the flower shop." She was out of breath, gulping loudly, her mouth so dry.

"Have a drink," Peter said passing her the same glass she'd spilt a moment ago. "Jake, I'm sure you can check these timings out. This has nothing to do with Dee - or me for this matter."

"Definitely," Jake said, "Tom, can you get on to this please."

The sergeant left the three of them alone and once the door had closed behind him, Jake said, "Peter and I are good friends, Miss Firth…Dee. Peter taught me everything I know. We go back a long way. Now, in my position I don't want to come across as unprofessional in front of Tom. I've met killers before and trust me I know you're not one of them. I just have to go through the process - Peter knows that. We need to eliminate you, that's all."

"He's right, Dee, we'll have this cleared up in a jiffy," Peter said trying to comfort her.

It felt an age before Tom returned. "It all checks out. There's CCTV of Miss Firth leaving the park and the owner of *Coffee Creams* confirms that you were there eating cake - apparently she remembers as you…" Tom stopped to point at Peter. "You don't normally have cake, which is why she remembers it. Flowering Fancies has CCTV so we can check that out now, but the proprietor says you both bought bulbs which she thought was odd as you…" Tom pointed at Peter again, "…live in a flat and she reckons that was just after one thirty; maybe two o'clock. I've sent someone to look at it now," he closed his notebook and took a step back as if waiting for applause.

"Very good, Tom. Can you chase them up at the flower shop?"

"Sure," said Tom leaving again.

"I feel sick," Dee announced.

Jake explained where the ladies was and Dee practically ran down the corridor.

"Now we're on our own, down to business," Peter declared. He took out his own notebook. "Tell me all you have so far."

Dee looked in her bag for a hairbrush. Her curls had come loose and mascara had run down her face in thick dark lines. Just as she was taming the last strands into her ponytail a female officer came into the toilets.

"Are you alright? I've been sent to check on you."

"I'm fine, ta," Dee replied.

"Fancy a cup of tea; maybe a sugar in it or two?"

Dee just nodded. Her whole body ached from vomiting and she noticed her hands were still trembling. Trying to pull herself together she followed the officer into a side room opposite Jake's office. She gestured for Dee to take a seat and asked "Sugar?"

"Please, just one. Wouldn't normally but you're right I need it." Dee spoke so quietly the officer was struggling to hear her.

"I'm Claire - Detective Constable. I'm new here, just started."

Dee tried to relax and took some deep breaths; she was worried that this was going to be another form of questioning. "Me too, moved here to be with my boyfriend. Do you have a boyfriend?" The DC looked too young to be married and there was no ring on her finger either.

"No, but I think the Inspector's a bit hot. Don't you?"

"I like his shirt."

"You like his shirt? What's wrong with you?" Claire blurted out between fits of laughter and a moment later Dee began to laugh too. Just then the door opened and Jake, Peter and Tom entered the room. Claire jumped to her feet. "Sir," she said.

"You're okay to go, Miss Firth" Jake declared.

"Didn't know I wasn't," Dee chirped back, giving him the worst glower, she could manage.

"Let's go," Peter said. He was already halfway out the door. Dee followed him and they didn't speak again until they were outside on the steps of the police station.

"What about the dogs?" asked Dee.

"We can sort that tomorrow. We need to get out of here. Quick get in the car!" Peter spoke rapidly and was pushing her into the passenger seat. He'd recognised a car that had just pulled in. It was Ruth a local journalist and he knew it wouldn't be long before the press got hold of the murder and he didn't want to see himself or Dee in the paper or on the regional news. "I'm taking you home; you look terrible. Stay home and don't go out today, Dee. Promise me." Peter looked agitated.

"Alright, but why? What's this all about?"

He explained about the press as he drove her home. Then Dee checked her phone and found she had four missed calls from Ed. Apparently, he wasn't coming home tonight. They had an early start with the campaign and he thought it better to stay overnight than get up early and drive to London again in the morning. Dee felt an odd sense of relief.

On arriving at Edward's house, Peter was also relieved to find no one hanging around. He was convinced someone at the station would tip someone off about Dee's involvement in Gamblewood's first murder of modern times. He waited in the car as he watched Dee go in. He heaved a heavy sigh as she waved and closed the door behind her. He texted her to close the curtains and that he would pick her up at ten the next morning so she didn't have to walk to work. It was all he could do for her.

Dee did as he suggested. She closed the curtains and headed upstairs for a bath. As she looked out of the bedroom window, she saw Peter's car pulling away.

What Dee did not see was the green car that pulled in moments later.

'I'm not going anywhere; I think I'll have a glass of wine,' she told herself. She nipped down with just a towel wrapped around her body, grabbed what was left in the wine bottle from the previous night and headed back upstairs. In the bedroom she spotted the romance novel for the book club. She hadn't read a single page.

"Might as well start now," she said speaking aloud although she was alone. 'I'm turning into Muttering Margo,' she thought.

After her bath she laid on the bed with the novel by her side. She managed one chapter before her eyes felt too heavy to continue. It was still early in the afternoon and she was fast asleep, completely oblivious of the man who'd been trying to peer through any chink he could find in her downstairs curtains.

Chapter Five

Dee woke to find the day as sunny and bright as she felt. She nipped downstairs to grab a cup of herbal tea and immediately headed back to the bedroom, pausing briefly to open the curtains and let the sunlight in. She had slept so well and was shocked to find it was only minutes after six in the morning. She had only woken up once during the evening when Ed had called to say goodnight. Now she was in no hurry; she had till ten o'clock before Peter was coming to pick her up. Plenty of time for a leisurely morning. Snuggled back in bed, cup of tea in hand, she picked up the book that had laid beside her whilst she slept, and she started the second chapter.

Elsewhere, Peter had had the worst night's sleep he had experienced in a long time. He was worried about Dee. He'd even thought about going back and sleeping there. He had tossed and turned most of the night, worried about the press but something else at the back of his mind was troubling him more.

Dee wasn't sure about the book. It was a love story set sometime in the eighteen hundreds; two families feuding. It wasn't exactly her normal read but 'Maybe that's the point of a book club, getting you to read a book you wouldn't normally opt for.' It suddenly struck her that she had missed last night's book club meeting. She made a mental note to apologise to Alison as soon as she saw her.

Peter was restless. It had just gone seven and he was already showered and ready for the day. Not being one to eat breakfast he realised by eight o'clock he was getting nothing done. He thought he'd grab a coffee from somewhere on the way to Dee's to delay him a little. He knew he would be there early but he felt sure she wouldn't mind.

Knocking on the door of Dee's house, he was thinking, 'This Ed must have some money,' as Dee opened the door. He noticed she was looking better, closer to being her own bright self as she floated around the centre block of the magazine-worthy kitchen, offering him toast as that was all they had in. He noticed her puffy eyes had gone down and she had much less make-up on which suited her and the green blouse she had on really made her green eyes and red hair pop.

"All okay?" she asked, thinking Peter was looking at her really strangely.

"Yeah. Just thinking how much better you look this morning. Sleep has done you good."

"More knowing I'm not wanted for murder helps," she said in a sarcastic tone and continued, "Did that Jake really think I could have done that to someone? Really it's beyond belief."

"Just doing his job; been there and done that."

They had agreed that toast wasn't going to cut it and with Peter turning up much earlier than expected if they set off to the office now with a bit of luck Alison might already be in Coffee Creams prepping. Peter had thrown the excuse of a coffee he had bought from the local garage out of the car window on the way to Dee's.

Alison was busy cleaning tables and placing salt and pepper pots on them. Dee hadn't turned up last night to the book club which was probably for the best as she had been the main topic of conversation. Some were saying someone new to the village had been arrested for killing Muttering Margo. Others were quick to correct them saying they'd heard a girl was been interviewed and was helping the police. Alison liked Dee, she'd warmed to her as soon as she'd met her and she was not about to let this bunch of ladies tell tales and spread gossip about someone they hadn't even met. Alison was deep in thought about the book club meeting when she suddenly jumped back bumping into and causing the table behind her to wobble. There at the window stood Peter and Dee staring in with their noses pressed against the glass, so Alison went to unlock the door.

"What are you two trying to do, freak me out! You could just have knocked on the door." Alison spoke with annoyance.

"Sorry," Peter jumped in. "We know we're early. Any chance of some breakfast?"

"Oh you're fine. Get yourselves sat down. I'll grab you some menus. Like your blouse, Dee. Really suits you."

Dee waited for Alison to return and immediately apologised for missing the book club. "From what the ladies were saying, I think you've been a bit busy." Alison spoke soothingly but stood waiting for Dee to explain. Her curiosity wasn't immediately satisfied because Peter stepped in with their order while Dee just smiled and turned away to look out of the window. Alison got the hint and went to cook two full English breakfasts for them.

"People are talking about me already?" Dee whispered across the table to Peter.

"Small place Gamblewood; everyone knows everyone. Don't worry about it; they'll soon find something or someone else to gossip about."

Peter was trying to be reassuring but Dee wasn't buying it at all. She would have to leave. Ed was right; they were the talk of the village.

Reading her thoughts, Peter said, "No need to leave. Things have a way of sorting themselves out, and everything happens for a reason" He added a "Thank you" to Alison as she brought their teas over.

"Leave? Who's leaving? Not you Dee?" Alison asked.

"No, she's not. It's just been a very difficult couple of days, hasn't it, Dee?" She nodded. "Need's a friend to talk to, Alison. Couple of glasses of wine and a takeout; maybe you and Jim would be free at the weekend?"

"Peter please, that's so embarrassing," Dee hissed. Then turning to Alison she said, "Sorry, you don't have to do anything of the…"

Alison interrupted her. "I think that would be nice. Good idea, Peter. We don't get to do the couple thing very often. It will be a nice change. What's your number?" Alison pulled her mobile out of the pocket on the front of her spotty apron and popped Dee's number into her contacts. Then she screeched, "Oh bacon!" and turned and ran to the kitchen.

"Peter, she really doesn't want to. Jim might be funny too. He's never met us."

"Give over," Peter replied. "Jim's a lovely guy and they're a nice couple. Do you good to go out and let your hair down."

Peter couldn't help thinking of the spotless, neat, never-a-cup-out-of-place interior of Edward's house. If that was anything to go by, it was

Jim he felt sorry for, having to spend a night with the perfectly boring Edward.

"All sorted, I've just spoken to Jim. I'll cook. Come here for seven tomorrow night then you can walk and don't need to worry about driving." Alison beamed as she placed two large plates of food on the table.

"Are you sure, I don't want to…"

"Looking forward to it already" Alison smiled and said she'd better open up otherwise Albert would have her guts for garters and indeed, just as they were finishing their breakfasts, Albert arrived.

"Morning, Alison," Albert shouted, as he did every morning and she waved to him. She was already preparing his morning tea.

"Now look at that." Albert stopped beside Dee and Peter's Table. "Quite a to-do outside your office this morning. Are you hiding in here?"

"No, Albert, but thanks for the heads up. Thought that might happen."

"What might happen?" Dee was totally confused.

"Press," Peter said looking fed-up. "A murder in a little village like this will definitely cause a stir."

"Not wrong, Peter," Albert quipped as he went to sit down. As he unfolded his newspaper he turned to look at the pair of them. "A murder in Gamblewood. Who'd have thought?"

"He thinks I did it." Dee was once again hissing over the table.

"Well he's wrong, isn't he? Come on, let's go."

"Well, that's one way to drive my customers away!" Alison shouted at Albert.

"What did I say?" he said, looking sheepish.

"You know exactly what you implied. Don't you think you've landed that girl in enough trouble telling the police she was at Margo's house."

Albert put the paper down and looked at Alison. "But she was. She might have killed her."

"You might have killed her; you were always moaning about Margo." Alison was on a roll.

Albert picked up his newspaper. "I, I wouldn't do that," he stammered.

"No, neither would Dee. Do you really think a murderer would work for a private detective agency for goodness sake. Just give her a break, Albert."

Alison was heading back behind the counter carrying Peter and Dee's empty plates when Albert retorted. "No, I don't, but it would be a good cover-up."

Alison put the plates down, threw her hands in the air and stormed into the back kitchen afraid if she listened to Albert any longer, she might throw him out.

In the car, Dee asked, "Are we not going to the office?" Peter had turned left and it had thrown her.

"No, we're heading straight to the police station. Let's get these dogs back to their rightful owners and see if Jake's in. Maybe he might have more information by now."

"Why would he tell us?"

Peter pulled the car over coming to an abrupt stop. "Something's bothering me, Dee. It has been ever since all this started. There's more to this than meets the eye."

Dee felt if her eyes got any wider her eyeballs would pop out.

Peter continued, "You see, this might be someone with a grudge against me or the agency, trying to frame you."

"Frame me, why?" Dee was aware her voice had gone up an octave.

"Someone might have watched you go into Margo's house, using you so to speak. Could also be a coincidence of course that you left and then the killer went in after you, which in that case you were lucky because if you were still there they might have killed you too, or is it someone who knows you work for me, I've put a lot of people behind bars, Dee."

"I don't understand. I only started working for you this week. No one knows me here. I'm only your secretary. I don't want to be involved in any of this, I really don't!"

After a momentary silence, Peter announced, "Think logically. What motive would anyone have to want to kill an old woman? Muttering Margo was annoying, yes; but to warrant murdering her? It just doesn't make sense."

"What about if someone saw her stealing their dog and they went to get it back and it just got out of hand or Vicky next door lost it and came round to ask her about all the barking then bonked her on the head…and then there's Albert."

"Albert?"

"Yes, Albert. It annoys me how it's okay for him to imply that he saw me at Margo's house and that I might have killed her, yet why was he watching me or was he watching Margo's house and as you say he's using me or made me into a what do you call them?" Dee paused searching for the word. "A scapegoat!"

"You've put a lot of thought into this."

Dee was about to tell him that she had literally just come up with those scenarios but he continued, "One thing's for certain, Dee; something's not right and we're going to get to the bottom of it."

"We? I'm just here to do secretarial duties. You're the detective not me."

"Don't you want to know who did this and why?"

"Well yes, but…"

"Thought you might. Also I'm not having all those good-for-nothing gossips think that an employee of mine's involved in a murder. We're going to help Jake solve this, if not solve it ourselves. Then all those busy bodies can eat their words when they find out we've helped to solve the Murder of Muttering Margo not flipping committed it."

Dee sat quietly, mulling over what Peter had just said. He was right of course, the whole village did probably by now think she'd done it. She had to clear her name. Then she would persuade Ed to leave Gamblewood for good.

Jake was gathering his things to get ready to go back over to the crime scene. Muttering Margo's house had been gone over by forensics and he just wanted another look. Something was playing on his mind. Something felt wrong. He hated that nagging feeling. He'd only had it on one other case and he hadn't been wrong. Fortunately, the missing child was found just in the nick of time as they were dying his hair to change his appearance. If it hadn't been for that nagging doubt Jake had felt the little boy would probably have been gone forever.

"Ready boss?" Tom shouted through the door he was holding half open.

"Yeah, just about. Can you ask Claire to come with us. She might just notice something us chaps might not."

Tom nodded and went to get Claire thinking it was a bit of a sexist comment on Jake's part.

Claire was thrilled. She'd not been to a murder scene before. She was bubbly for a Detective Constable and that made a change. Most female constables Tom had met had ideas above their station and thought they had to prove themselves when they came out of training but not Claire. She seemed to keep it real, and fitted in well with the rest of the troops.

The three of them were just coming down the steps when Jake spotted Peter's car coming into the car park. He told the others to go ahead and he would catch them up.

Peter was already winding down the window as Jake approached. "All okay, Jake? We've come about the dogs."

"No issue, Peter. Just heading over to Margaret Darnley's house. Dee; Miss Firth; would you like to come with us?"

Dee didn't even look at Jake. "No, I'm not getting in a police car, people here are already saying I did it and if I was seen in that-" Dee pointed at the police car "-that would add more fuel to the fire as my Gran would say."

Peter said, "Tell you what, Jake. If it's okay with you, we'll be as quick as we can here and then I'll drive Dee over. Wouldn't mind a look for myself if that's permitted?"

Jake nodded and asked Peter to text him when they were on their way.

Once the Inspector was out of earshot, Peter turned to Dee. "Rude that. Your Gran would be ashamed."

"Shut up. Me in a police car? Not happening. There's enough talk already."

Peter smiled to himself. 'A little fiery that one. Maybe more like Mary than I thought.'

Jake took a good wander around the garden. To say Margaret had so many dogs the garden was immaculately kept. Jake looked back at the house from the bottom of the garden. It was a beautiful-looking cottage. How could something so horrible happen in such a lovely place. He was suddenly startled by a voice behind him. "Need a cup of tea?" It was the neighbour Vicky leaning over the wall that separated their gardens.

Jake declined but did make a mental note to go round to Vicky's himself. He wondered how easy it would be for her or anyone else to enter from Albert's garden and climb over the garden walls without being seen.

"Sir," Claire shouted from the patio doors.

Jake left his thoughts in the garden and went to see what Claire and Tom had discovered. Tom was in the kitchen, looking through a drawer but Claire was at the fireplace looking at the painting above it of a winter's scene.

"What do you make of that, sir?"

"Lovely. I like that sort of art."

"Sir, I'm no expert, but that's not just a print. I think it's an original. Might need to get someone to check it out. Could be worth a bit that, sir," Claire continued. "Look at the little ones of the horses hung over there. I wonder if they're by the same artist?"

Jake was starting to see the inside of the cottage in a whole new light as his phone started to vibrate in his pocket. Making his excuses he headed back into the garden to answer it, and to find that Peter and Miss Firth were on their way.

Peter and Dee had not spent too long sorting out the dogs. It had however been frustratingly difficult to get in touch with some of the owners. Still, all of the animals had been claimed or would be over the next few days except for Ginger. He actually matched the name on his tag and, unfortunately, wasn't chipped like the others. Dee had felt bad about leaving him knowing once the others had been collected Ginger would be on his own and likely to end up at the nearest Dog's Trust for re-homing.

"I'm a bit nervous, Peter," she said quietly as they pulled away from the police station car park. "What if her ghost is there or you can see blood where she was killed?"

"I don't think her ghost will be there. If it is, maybe it can tell us who the murderer is," he replied.

"I'm being serious; don't you think it's scary going into a house where someone's been killed?" Dee asked biting her bottom lip.

It dawned on Peter that in his line of work he had been fully trained to handle the many crime scenes he'd attended whereas for Dee this was her first time and might indeed prove upsetting. He conveyed as much and promised he would look after her and that she should stay by his side the entire time they were there.

"Are you driving past the office?" Dee asked.

"Yeah, just to see if they've all gone. The press I mean. Hopefully, they all got bored of waiting for us to turn up."

The little alleyway leading to the agency's scruffy brown door was clear. "Well, that's one less thing to worry about."

Dee's mobile was telling her she had a text. The sender was a real surprise. "My Gran has just sent me a text. She's never done that before. Wants me to phone her."

"Phone her if you want; we're only a couple of minutes from Margo's though."

"No, it's fine. We could be on the phone for hours. I'll send her a quick text back to tell her I'll phone tonight."

As she was texting her reply, her phone went again. She took the call but made it brief.

"You're Gran already?" Peter asked.

"No, it's Ed. Says he's on his way back from London and he's tired and fancies an early night."

"Too much information for me!" Peter laughed as he pulled over opposite Margo's cottage.

"That means he's genuinely tired."

'How boring,' Peter thought but didn't say it.

From the gate of Muttering Margo's cottage there was a clear contrast to be had. Margo's cottage and front garden were pretty and well kept while Vicky's looked as if it could do with a little bit of TLC and Albert's, although tidy, wasn't a patch on Margo's.

"Gloves!" Tom shouted.

Dee was about to touch the handle of the garden gate. Peter grabbed her making her lose her balance a little. He held on to her as she wobbled.

"What is it with me falling over and this house?" Dee exclaimed.

Peter handed her some nitrile gloves from his pocket. Dee started to ask why he was carrying gloves about his person but thought better of it as Tom beckoned them in.

Apart from patches of white powder in various places and tape around the outside, the cottage looked just the same as it had when Dee last saw it, minus the dogs and Muttering Margo of course. Dee felt sad.

She thought of her Gran. Would she have to do this one day: go into her Gran's empty house? She felt overwhelmed with grief just for a moment.

Peter took hold of her elbow, "You, okay?" he asked.

Dee nodded. Claire saw Dee and waved, mouthing that she liked her blouse. Dee waved back and Jake came in through the patio doors smiling.

"Hi, this might be a bit strange, Miss Firth."

"Please call me Dee. Are you allowed to do that?"

"If it's okay by you then it's fine by me. Like I was saying, this might be a little odd, but can you have a good look round and see if you notice anything; anything at all?"

"Like what?" Dee questioned

"I don't want to put ideas in your head, Miss…Dee. Is it the same as when you were here for example?"

"Yes, I think so."

"Have a mooch, Dee. Take it in. Take your time. You never know, something might come to mind." Jake spoke gently to her before motioning for Peter to join him in the garden.

"Will you be alright? I'm just going out for a word with Jake?" It wasn't really a question, more a statement.

Dee nodded and went over to join Claire. "Hi, weird this," she said.

"It's my first murder scene too." Claire whispered.

"Hope it's my first and last."

In the garden Jake was filling Peter in on some more of the details. "And that's about it? Not much at all, apart from Albert seeing Dee. No one heard or saw anything; nothing's been stolen as far as we're aware and there wasn't a break in." Jake shrugged his shoulders.

"So, she knew her killer?"

"We presume so." Jake was wringing his hands in frustration. "There just doesn't seem to be a motive; no motive at all."

"It's only been a few days, Jake. There'll be a lead soon, I'm sure." Peter was expressing a confidence he didn't really feel Some crimes you never solve.

"Hope so, Peter. I don't like this; don't like it at all."

Peter didn't answer. The thought of Gamblewood having a murderer on the loose was almost unbelievable, but that was the situation and it made both men feel very uneasy.

Dee had not noticed anything useful at all. She showed Jake where she had fallen and he showed her where Margo had died. Dee had gone through all her movements, over and over again, but nothing jumped out. The cottage was as she had left it. Claire had mentioned the paintings but none of them could make out the signature, only their quality.

Time had gone on and Peter wanted to get back. So making their excuses they left. Nestled in the safety of the office, with no press hanging around outside, Dee resumed her daily task of opening the mail and Peter checked a couple of e-mails on his phone.

"Peter, you've been invited to a garden party at The Manor," Dee said excitedly.

"God, I hate going to that. They have it every year. Henry's knocking on a bit now. I don't think he's been well."

"Henry?"

Peter explained that Henry was the so-called Lord of the Manor. Gaitley Manor to be exact. "When is it?"

"Next Sunday," said Dee.

"Hope you aren't busy next Sunday and own a nice dress. You're coming with me."

"Me!" Dee looked surprised.

"You'll like old Henry. He likes to know what's going on in the village and who's new. You'll be fine. You'll enjoy it. I suppose we have to formally reply?"

"Yes, we do," Dee said, still staring at the invitation in her hand, it was rather posh.

"Then crack on with the post and I think we'll call it a day Dee."

"We've not had anything to eat; do you want me to go and get you a sandwich or anything and what about sending the invoices out for the missing dogs?"

"We can send them out next week. Let folks enjoy having their pooches back before we send bills out for finding them. Forgot about lunch to be honest Alison's breakfast kept me nicely full."

Dee agreed and they chatted briefly about the virtues of a good breakfast. While Dee was packing her things away she put the invite into the top drawer of her desk.

"Need a lift home?"

"Do you think it'll be okay for me to walk, press and all?" Dee had her fingers crossed.

"There's been no one hanging around since this morning. I think you'll be fine."

Dee left the office feeling upbeat. The afternoon was warm. The sun caught her blouse as she walked and the man behind the camera lens sitting in the green car was astonished at how it complimented her green eyes and red hair as he snapped away.

Saturday night arrived. Sipping the cold white wine that Alison had poured, Dee followed her into the *Coffee Creams'* kitchen to ask if she needed any help. Alison had told her it was all under control. "It's only lasagne and salad followed by chocolate mousse."

Dee looked out of the kitchen to find Jim and Ed in an animated discussion about cars. "Thanks, so much for this," she told Alison. "It's been the oddest week ever."

Alison didn't comment. She was hoping Dee would go on so she carried on chopping the tomatoes. The tactic worked and Dee started to tell Alison all about going back to visit the murder scene. When she'd told Ed the night before he hadn't seemed at all pleased to hear about it but Alison was all ears, topping up their glasses and urging her new friend to supply more details.

When Dee finally stopped, Alison said, "Never dull when Peter's around. So pleased you're alright about it all. What's that Jake like? I've heard a few rumours but never met him myself."

"He's alright. Peter keeps telling me he's just doing his job, but I think he's standoffish. There's a new DC called Claire though. She's nice."

Alison had in fact briefly met Claire when they came to question her about Dee and Peter's movements and to confirm that they had indeed been in Coffee Creams at the time of the murder. Rather than reminding Dee that she was her alibi, Alison just said, "I met her locking up one night and she seemed lovely."

The lasagne was ready to serve, and Alison got the clearest possible impression from Dee that Muttering Margo's death was not to be mentioned at the table tonight in front of Edward. She had noticed that Dee had been constantly checking that Edward couldn't hear what they were talking about. Alison had taken an instant dislike to Ed. She didn't know why; she just didn't like him but the meal passed with humour and fun and Jim, who was now trying to sell Edward a car, received a boot from Alison under the table.

"These are our friends!" Alison laughed. "Not a customer, Jim. Give the car talk a rest. You spend a lot of time in London don't you, Edward? No need for a car there."

Unfortunately, that put Edward centre-stage to talk about the advertising campaign and himself. Time had gone on and Dee had tried to change to subject but Edward was having none of it. He just kept bringing the conversation back to himself and that's when Alison, who was a good judge of character, realised why she'd taken such an instant dislike to him. "Coffee anyone?" she said gathering the empty dishes together.

"Yes please" Dee piped up. "I'll help you." She was already on her feet wanting to escape and feeling nothing short of embarrassed. She followed Alison into the kitchen of *Coffee Creams*. "You know, I meant to mention it earlier but I never realised it was so big back here. Sorry about Edward. He can go on a bit."

Alison had no intention of upsetting Dee by agreeing with her so she did the right thing and smiled in a don't-worry-about-it way whilst grabbing some little biscuits from the cupboard she'd made earlier to accompany the coffee. Sitting back down Jim had brought up the garden party to be held next week.

"I'm going to that," Dee announced.

Edward looked surprised. Dee hadn't mentioned a garden party last night, but before he could say anything, Alison jumped in. "That's great. We go every year. Henry invites most of the business owners to the party. Are you both going?"

"Yes…I mean no. I'm going with Peter. It's him who's invited really. Well, he invited me to go with him. Actually thinking about it, I think he just told me I was going with him; says I need a posh frock. What are you going to wear?"

"Same old, same old. Haven't bought anything new for ages," Alison replied.

Jim joked that he would be wearing exactly what he had worn for the last three years and Edward sat quietly looking completely put-out. They talked a little more about Henry and the party and Jim told a story of how he had once accompanied his mother to the famous garden party as a child and knocked over his mother's wine. Jim was hilarious at mimicking his mother's reaction and the scolding he had received. They all laughed except for Ed who managed a smile whilst sulking like a two-year-old.

"It's been a lovely evening," Dee said grabbing her coat from the back of her chair. The night was starting to turn a little chilly and so had Edward's demeanour.

"It's been great; really enjoyed it, haven't we, Jim?"

"Absolutely; good cook my Alison," He put a loving arm around her.

Alison unlocked the door and they all said their goodbyes but as the door was opened a gust of wind flew in whipping it out of Alison's hand. The bell tinkled as the door banged back hard and a picture fell from the wall.

"My god, what happened there? The wind's really picked up," Dee said, bending down to retrieve the photograph from the floor.

"Is it broken? Oh no; is it? Alison asked, not daring to look.

Dee checked but the picture seemed to be intact. "That's a really nice photo. Is it you and your mum?" She handed the picture back to Alison who checked it carefully, tracing her finger around the older lady's face.

"No, it's my mum when she was little and my grandmother. I can't believe it didn't break. How lucky was that? I love this photo of them cooking together; just love it." She had gone off into a sort of trance.

Until Dee shouted out one word. "Shit!"

The others stood there looking at her and it was Ed who piped up first "There's no need to swear."

Alison asked, "Did you cut yourself on the glass?"

Dee stood stock-still as if in shock, her eyes wide. "I can't believe I missed it. I must tell Peter. You know I said I went back with the police to Margo's house…"

Alison nodded. Ed was rolling his eyes.

"It's the photo, Alison. There was a photo of a lady holding a baby on the side table in the lounge. You walked past it to go out into the garden. It's not there. It's gone!"

Chapter Six

Dee had tried phoning Peter much to Edward's annoyance. "It's Saturday night. Leave the bloke alone. He could be out with his missus," he'd said with a sarcastic edge.

As they passed the alleyway leading to the detective agency on their way home, Dee checked but Peter's car wasn't parked up in its usual spot and no lights seemed to be on in his flat. After one more try at calling him, she gave up. After all, Ed might be right; Peter might be out with someone or asleep already.

In fact Peter was out. He was sitting opposite Ruth eating pasta in the little Italian in Amberleigh. He was trying to convince Ruth not to put a photograph of Dee in the next edition of the local newspaper. "Come on, Ruth, I've given you some insider knowledge, and you know the police won't tell you anything. It all helps your story. Just say Dee's helping with enquiries, nothing more."

Ruth shrugged her shoulders. "Pretty little thing; photographs well. Soft spot there, Pete?" Ruth asked, holding the photo up to show Peter.

"She does actually photograph well," Peter said, grabbing the photo out of her hand. "But you know me Ruth, married to the job. No one sane would have me."

Ruth picked up her wine glass. She had fancied Peter for ages. Their paths had crossed many times over the years on cases Peter had been involved in and that she had reported on. Unfortunately, she knew he saw her as no more than a journalist looking for the next scoop. She had already started to regret the amount of time she had spent getting ready, hoping finally he had genuinely asked her out for a meal, only to be disappointed once again when she realised it was to talk shop.

"I'll make sure we don't print the picture and I'll keep Dee out of the article as much as I can, as long as you promise that I'm the first to hear of anything new on the case," Ruth reassured him.

Peter nodded, took her hand and kissed it. "You are one special lady, Ruth."

Ruth wished he had really meant those words. However, she knew better, and pulling her hand back, told him, "Sod off!"

Edward had risen early on Monday morning for work; he'd been kind enough to bring Dee a coffee in bed and kissed her as he left.

Dee too was desperate to get to work. She wanted to tell Peter about the photograph since he'd not returned any of her calls.

October was upon them and Dee felt the summer was officially over for there in the sky were dark clouds full of rain. She had finally caught up with her gran over the weekend to tell her all about the murder of Margaret Darnley and unlike Edward, her gran could not stop asking questions and wanting to know more. Dee finally mentioned the invite to the garden party and how posh it all sounded, and they ended up agreeing that she should wear the pale blue jumpsuit and not a dress as Dee always felt uncomfortable in them. "Be a little different, Dee. You don't have to be like all the others" her gran had said. "Plus you can put that nice cardigan with the beading over it if it's cold."

Dee once again checked the weather out of her bedroom window and put on a heavier jumper for warmth and tried to find the raincoat that she knew she had brought with her. She still had unpacked clothes in a suitcase under the bed in the spare room. Unfortunately, Edward didn't have as much wardrobe space set aside for her as she had hoped for when she moved in. She retrieved the raincoat from the suitcase and her brolly. It wasn't raining yet, but at any moment she knew it was about to pour.

Peter had finished his morning exercise routine, and gone to see if any post had been delivered. The rain was heavy and the postman had an annoying habit of not putting the post all the way through the letter box.

"Morning," Dee said, in the doorway.

Peter laughed for there in front of him was a wet-through, soaked--to the-skin secretary. "Umbrella not working?" he asked mockingly

"No. I forgot I broke it on its last outing."

"I'll get you a towel," Peter said disappearing into his flat.

Dee hung up her coat on the antique coat stand. The rain-coat was dripping onto the carpet leaving a wet mark but Peter didn't seem to notice when he returned with a couple of towels. "I'll leave you to sort yourself out," he said and vanished into his flat once again. Dee retreated to the horrible office toilet to towel her hair and hoped the bottom of her trousers would dry of their own accord as there was no hand dryer. About fifteen minutes later, she was emerging from the bathroom as Peter returned.

"Better?" he asked.

"Yes, ta. Just need my trousers to dry. Over the weekend…I tried phoning you."

"Did you? Sorry about that. Bit of an issue charging my phone."

"Is it broken?"

"No, I lost the charger. Found it down the side of my car seat last night, on my way back from fishing."

"Fishing!" Dee was smirking.

"Nothing wrong with fishing. I like it. I went with Jake. It's good to take your mind off the job. Fishing gives you space and time to think."

Dee shook her head. "I was phoning you to tell you I'd remembered something about Margaret's house."

Peter went to sit down knowing he was in for the long haul. Dee started telling him about the meal at Alison's, then all about the wind and the picture falling off the wall. Finally, Dee got to the point about the missing photo of Margaret with a baby.

"Type it all up as quick as you can. Then you can print a copy off for Jake." Peter seemed excited at her news.

"He doesn't need to know all the details, does he? Like what we ate, the wind…"

"No, you're right. Just type a quick version. We can tell him the rest in person." Peter wasn't looking at her. He was already swiping his phone, sending Jake a text to say they were on their way shortly to see him if convenient.

Jake's reply was instant. He was already on his way to re-interview the next-door neighbour so if they could give him an hour, he would meet them at Margo's house. *Great* Peter texted back.

Tom was driving Jake to meet Vicky so he heard the latest news from his boss as soon as Jake put his phone back in his jacket pocket. "Peter and Dee are meeting us at the house. Turns out Dee's remembered something."

"That's good. Let's hope it's a lead."

"I do hope so. We need a break on this case," Jake said looking out of the window at the depressing rain.

Peter and Dee had decided to grab takeout coffees from *Coffee Creams* en-route to Margo's house. They could be sat outside waiting for Jake for some time. You could never put a time limit on how long any interview was going to take and Dee said she wanted to call in at Paula's to grab a bunch of flowers for Alison as a thank you for Saturday night.

Peter's arrival at *Coffee Creams* was marked by the tinkling of the little bell above the door.

"You can't stay away at the moment," Alison said with a twinkle in her eye.

"Two coffees to go please." Peter was smiling.

Albert was already there, hiding behind his newspaper. Alison wasn't best pleased with him because of how he'd spoken to Peter the last time, so he sat quietly hoping Peter wouldn't notice him. His hopes were dashed.

"Is that you Albert?" Peter asked.

Albert lowered the paper and looked across at Alison standing at the coffee machine making Dee's latte.

"All good Peter. You?" Albert managed to spit out.

"Albert, how well did you know Margaret?"

"Didn't know her at all." He stammered, remembering Alison saying he could have killed her just as easily as Dee.

"Do you know if she had any children?"

"Not that I know of, but then why would I?" Albert raised his newspaper again as if to shield him from any further questions.

The bell tinkled again and it was Dee with the flowers for a delighted Alison who headed into the kitchen to find a vase to put them in. Returning as Peter and Dee were leaving she called after them. "Mary once told me Margo's husband didn't live very long after they were married. Maybe that's why she didn't have any children. Just a thought."

Peter nodded and thanked her.

"Children?" Dee asked as they walked to the car.

Jake and Tom were on the sofa inside Vicky's house. Jake really wanted to have a good look around the garden, but felt it would be rude not to drink the tea she had made first. Vicky's little ones were running around the coffee table in circles. It wasn't an ideal situation for any interview.

Vicky's house was nice enough but not charming like Margaret's. The interior gave the impression it was pretending to be one of the new modern four beds that had been built on the outskirts of Gamblewood. Quite unlike the cosy cottage it actually was. Jake didn't like it at all.

Vicky finally settled down in the chair opposite the police officers. She was excited and it showed. Usually, the only highlight of her day was opening a bottle of wine once the kids were tucked up in bed.

Tom asked some basic questions to settle Vicky's nerves. Not that she was showing any. She was fully made up to the nines and if she continued fluttering her eyelashes at Jake one of them might fall off. She had seen the drop-dead gorgeous Detective Inspector a couple of times and "Who wouldn't fancy that," she'd told her friends. Jake was paying no attention to her flirtation though. He was almost dismissive as he stood up, popped his tea cup down on the coffee table and headed towards the patio doors that led out into a much smaller garden than Margaret's. It was filled with little plastic slides, swings, a trampoline, lots of toys, a wooden hut that had seen better days and a table with benches for seats. "Not into gardening?" he asked Vicky.

The sarcasm passed Vicky by. She replied in what she felt was a sexy tone. "I only drink wine in it!"

Jake looked across at Tom who knew that look and started to question Vicky about the day she found Margaret. Vicky explained the dogs were constantly barking - much more than usual - and she'd climbed on one of the benches to have a look at what was happening.

"She was just lying there, I shouted to her, but she didn't answer. Thought I'd go round, but the kids, you know - so I called for an ambulance." Vicky may have been responding to Tom but she wasn't taking her eyes off Jake.

"Is it okay for me to have a look outside?" Jake interrupted.

"Yes, of course you can," Vicky beamed and as she moved past him to unlock the patio door, she made sure to brush against his side.

"Mrs Wright," Tom said loudly.

"Vicky, please." She turned to look at the sergeant.

"What happened after you called the ambulance?"

With Tom continuing the questioning, Jake took his opportunity to check out the garden. He went around the perimeter of the garden wall that separated the three cottage gardens. Without a bench or something to climb on, it wouldn't be easy to climb over. They were head height, which explained why Vicky had needed to stand on a bench to look over into Margo's garden. He went across to the wall that separated Vicky's garden from Albert's. There were no plants and no soil for footprints because the garden had a concrete path around the perimeter with a square of grass in the middle. It looked like the children's playground it obviously was. 'Time to pay Albert a visit,' Jake thought.

Finishing the interview, Tom joined Jake in the garden. "Anything out here, sir?"

"Unfortunately, not."

They re-entered Vicky's lounge through the patio doors from the garden and thanked her for her time. She gushed that if she could be of any further help they shouldn't hesitate to get in touch. " Just need an hours' notice to sort the kids."

"More like an hour to tart herself up," Tom suspected

At the gate, Jake stopped and asked Tom, "Where's Mr Wright?"

"Works in London all week, travels a lot too," Tom replied checking his notebook.

"Interesting," was Jake's reply.

Dee's hair was a frizzy mess. As much as she tried to do something with it, the rain had done it's worst. Peter watched her struggle to tie it up in a ponytail and was amazed at how long her hair was when it was down. Then he spotted Jake and Tom chatting at Vicky's gate and got out of the car to go and meet them. Dee, still struggling to tie her hair up, followed a moment or two later and Jake noticed as she walked across to join them how fresh-faced she seemed compared to the overly made-up Vicky and how her hair was swishing behind her as she walked. Then he turned away sharply as if he knew he had been caught out staring. Peter saw and smiled.

"Let's get inside. Looks like it might rain again any minute."

They all followed Jake through the garden gate to Margo's cottage door where he asked them all to put gloves and over-shoes on.

"Everyone sorted?"

They all nodded and Dee had the urge to hold her hands up for inspection. As they entered Jake spoke to her. "Have a really good look around. Take your time but what have you remembered?"

Dee went straight over to the little table near the patio door. "Here," she pointed. "There was a photo of Margo holding a baby. It's not here now." On the table were two other photographs and the little statue of a lady riding a horse. "This has been moved to cover the gap."

"Please check every room, Dee. See if you spot it. Tom you go with her. Margo might have moved the photo, swapped it around, put it upstairs for a change."

Dee went over to the fire place to look at the painting that hung above it. It was mesmerising.

Jake was more interested in the statuette. He picked it up. "Heavy!" He looked over at Peter.

"Murder weapon?"

"Could be."

"So, you don't have the murder weapon then?" Peter asked.

"No, not as yet. I've just had a look round the garden next door. Thought maybe someone could have thrown whatever they used to hit Margaret with over the wall or if she's our murderer she might have hidden it in the garden or the shed but it's just a playground next door and the only thing in the shed were outside Christmas decorations and a lawnmower."

Peter nodded and went to look at the statuette himself. "Nice piece this. Wonder who it's by?"

Jake opened the patio doors. Dee and Tom had gone into the kitchen and could be heard opening drawers.

"Think you should take this into forensics. You never know," Peter said.

"Definitely. Weird things going on here, Peter. Margaret came from a large family but had no family of her own. So, who's the baby in the picture? Why would anyone steal a photo? Why not take cash, jewellery, even a painting? Claire thinks that'll be worth a bob or two."

"There's a specialist in Amberleigh, Jake. Why don't you see if they'll come here to have a look: see what they say."

"Yeah. I'll do that."

Jake wandered out into the garden. He was renting a flat on the far side of Amberleigh and would love to have a garden like this.

Peter said, "How did it go at Vicky's?"

"Nothing major. I'll go through Tom's notes when we get back to the station, but she said the same thing as before. The dogs were barking so much it was getting on her nerves. She looked over the wall to see what was going on and saw Margo lying on the path. She'd shouted, got no response and ran inside to call an ambulance."

"Did she come round to check on her?"

"No. Said she couldn't leave the kids. She said she just kept looking at her from her garden till the ambulance arrived in case she moved."

"The ambulance crew had no issues getting in?"

"No, the door was unlocked so there were no access issues. Most people leave their doors unlocked during the day when they're in, don't they? Nothing unusual in that."

Peter nodded in agreement.

Dee felt like an intruder in Margaret's home. Tom was opening drawers in Margaret's bedroom, but she couldn't bring herself to search through or touch Margaret's things. It was intrusive and disrespectful and she told Tom as much.

"You can't think like that. If you find just one clue as to what happened, who could have done this, think of the peace and justice that would give Margo."

Dee nodded; she hadn't thought of it like that.

"Spot anything?"

"No, the photograph isn't in here and I don't know if anything has been moved as I didn't come upstairs. It's a nice room though isn't it?"

For Dee the neat and cosy cottage was reinforcing her determination when this was all over and her name was cleared, that she and Edward would leave Gamblewood for good. She didn't want to live in a square new-build like the converted stable block they shared now. Their next house would be a cottage like this with its little nooks and crannies and beams on the ceiling. Tom brought her back to reality, banging into her as they crossed the landing. He kept apologising profusely.

The rest of the upstairs was a bathroom and a spare bedroom. Dee didn't go into the bathroom but merely bobbed her head round the door. It was decorated in small white tiles, had pale grey lino on the floor and a shower fitment over the bath. All the towels were neatly hung up.

Dee heard Tom shouting for her to come into the spare bedroom. On the window sill were two photographs and a lovely ceramic bowl holding potpourri. Dee picked up one of the photographs. The first was of a young girl on a horse. The other was a wedding photo of Margaret and her husband. Dee spent some time looking at it. Margo had been good-looking in her younger days; she had a fabulous figure and the wedding dress, although dated, was beautiful. Dee popped it back on the window sill.

Tom had looked through the drawers to no avail and was heading out to the landing when Jake shouted to see if they were finished. "If so, come downstairs." When they were back in the lounge, he asked, "Anything?"

"No, the photograph isn't here," Dee said looking despondent.

"So Muttering Margo's dead and a photo of her holding a baby is missing. Anything else, Dee?" Jake asked hoping there was.

"No." Dee shook her head. "What's happening with that?" Jake was holding a bag containing the statue of the lady riding a horse.

"Taking it to forensics. Margaret was hit with a blunt instrument that we haven't found yet."

"You think someone might have hit her with that?" Dee was shocked and Peter stepped in. "They have to check every possibility."

They headed towards the door but Dee stopped suddenly in her tracks "I need to go back upstairs."

"Really, why?" Peter asked.

"I need to check something. Can I go, please?" Dee was asking Jake who passed the statuette to Tom and said, "Come on. I'll go with you."

In the spare room Dee went straight to the window sill. She picked up the photo of the young girl riding a horse. "Here, look." She passed the photo to Jake. "You see the girl riding the horse; that's the same girl who was holding the baby in the missing photograph."

"Are you sure?"

"Yes, definitely."

"I don't think that's Margaret riding the horse," Jake declared.

"It is. She's just young that's all."

"It isn't, Dee. I swear it isn't."

"Then who can it be?"

They stood there staring at the photo, hoping the answer would miraculously occur to them.

Peter bobbed his head around the bedroom door to find them huddled over the photograph that Jake was holding. They looked totally baffled.

Chapter Seven

On the way back to the office Dee went on and on about the photograph. Peter zoned out; he was thinking of what steps to take next. Dee only finally stopped talking about it once she realised Peter wasn't listening to her at all and changed the topic to the garden party, asking if it was okay if Edward could join them too. Since Saturday night Edward had not stopped nagging Dee to get him an invite.

"Yeah, whatever," Peter replied, not sure what he had just agreed but too caught up in his own thoughts to care.

"Thanks, that makes my life a lot easier" Dee said.

Dee couldn't get the photograph out of her mind and was having a hard time concentrating on typing up the latest case developments. She had taken a picture on her phone when Jake wasn't looking before he could take it away and hand it to Tom to go into one of those plastic bags to be taken to the police station.

Watching Dee staring into space was annoying Peter, and he knew he had to ask "What is it? Out with it."

Dee looked across at him. 'How does he know what I'm thinking?' She said, "I can't stop mulling over those photographs. It really did look like Margo on that horse. If it wasn't her, do you think it could be one of her sisters? Alison said she was from a large family."

"Hmm…it's got me thinking too. Shame we couldn't see the back of the photograph. There might have been a date on it when it was taken."

"Do you think Albert would know about Margo's family?" Dee asked, waggling a pencil about

"He could, but he didn't seem very helpful the other day. Think the library is our best bet. We need hard facts; birth, death, marriage certificates. that sort of thing,"

"Good idea. Where is the library? I don't think I've seen one in Gamblewood." Dee was now tapping the pencil against her forehead.

"No, it's in Amberleigh. We just have a mobile van that comes here once a week; parks up near the school."

"Shall we go then?" Dee asked impatiently.

"Not today. We need to get those invoices out to the dog owners and I want to see if Jake finds out anything first; give him a little time; you never know what he might dig up."

"I wonder if the little statue was used to kill Margaret, it's too lovely a thing to be used as a murder weapon." Dee spoke quietly thinking of Margo and a feeling of sadness swept over her.

"I'm sure Jake will let us know, but I imagine if it was it would have been wiped clean."

"Hm, yes. So, I'll carry on with this then," Dee said, pointing her pencil at the computer.

Tom and Jake had two objects in front of them.

"The frame's nice Jake. Could be worth something."

Jake nodded. "Think we need to get these off to forensics. Is Claire around?"

"I'll go and find her," Tom said.

Jake opened the top drawer of his desk and found a pair of gloves. He then proceeded to take the photograph out of the bag. The girl in the picture - she was only a girl, maybe fourteen or fifteen - looked like Margaret but it wasn't her. 'It has to be her sister or a cousin maybe.' The frame was pretty. Jake could see a stamp on it, so, he knew it was silver, not cheap. Tom was right about that. Jake went to take the photo out of the frame. The fastenings weren't budging and he didn't want to break it. 'I'll ask forensics to do it.' His last thought before Tom returned bringing Claire with him.

Dee had finished typing up her account of her findings at Margo's house, and her stomach made an unusual growling sound causing Peter to look up from what he was reading. She definitely needed a sandwich and a latte and asked Peter if he was getting hungry too.

"I'm fine but if you're going to Coffee Creams can you bring me back an iced bun? And take money out of the tin to pay for lunch."

"Look, I can't keep taking money out of here. I'm starting to feel guilty now. I can get my own."

"Wouldn't hear of it" was Peter's answer as he returned to his reading.

Dee nestled herself into a comfortable seat by the window inside Coffee Creams holding a warming latte between both her hands and looking out of the window dreamily down the high street. Alison was making her a tuna salad sandwich. A couple of other tables were occupied and Albert sat in his usual spot reading his paper. She could hear him swapping pleasantries with an elderly couple on the adjacent table.

"Dee!" Alison made Dee jump as she placed the food down in front of her.

"Gosh I was away with the fairies, then."

"Fancy coming shopping with me Wednesday afternoon? I close early on a Wednesday. Wouldn't mind something new for the garden party."

"I'd love to, but I'm not sure what Peter would say. I'll ask him. Can I text you to confirm? Where will we go. There's not much here in the way of shops."

"Amberleigh's got one or two nice boutiques. I'd appreciate the company. I'm rubbish at clothes shopping."

"Let's hope Peter's okay with it." Dee held up crossed fingers.

"If he isn't, tell him there's no more iced buns from me!" Alison was laughing as she turned to welcome a new customer.

Jake was not happy. His worst nightmare had arrived at the front desk in the shape of Ruth from the local newspaper. She wanted an update. He hated the press and being interviewed. He hadn't met Ruth before.

He'd managed to avoid her the week before and was trying to come up with some excuse now, but he knew he'd have to face her sooner or later. "Better to get it over with," Jake said to Tom, sighing.

"She's in two. Want me to sit in?"

"No, it's okay, dealt with many journalists in my time," Jake said gloomily.

Dee finished her sandwich and paid Alison. Albert was leaving at the same time and he opened the door for her.

"Walking my way?" Albert asked Dee.

"Heading back to the office; invoices to send out."

"Then I will walk with you. I go home through the park." Albert declared.

"Albert, did you or your wife know Margaret, I mean Margo at all?" Dee asked, trying not to appear too nosey

The answer was simple enough. "No, not really" but Albert felt compelled to enlarge upon it. "My Annie would chat to her and I know Mary would go round for a cuppa sometimes. Margo spent all day talking to the flowers or herself. That one was mad she was; mad."

Dee took a deep breath she was frustrated at Margo being written off as simply mad. "Did you know her husband?"

Albert stopped walking, "So tragic. Died young he did. They hadn't been married long. She never married again. Mind you who'd marry that."

The remark almost seemed calculated to anger Dee but she managed to keep her composure as they started walking again. "You said Mary visited her? Peter's Mary, I mean."

"Yes, couple of gossips they were, Mary was a sucker for a tale or two, and Muttering Margo had plenty and what she didn't know she'd make up!"

Albert seemed annoyed so Dee put a hand on his arm.. "Are you okay?"

"Yes love" Albert answered solemnly. "Well, you're here" He nodded down the alleyway that led to the detective agency. "See you again."

Dee found herself shouting her goodbyes and waving to the back of Albert's head as he ambled up the street towards the park. He didn't look back.

Jake had finished his interview with Ruth. He had been hoping to gain as much information from her as she was from him but he'd not given her much to go on and so in return, when he started firing questions at her, she didn't feel obliged to give any information back. The meeting was brief and Jake was soon back in his office in need of an expresso.

Ruth sat in her car outside the police station tapping her long fake fingernails on the steering wheel and checking her face in the rear-view mirror. Not bad girl; you've still got it she told herself. The rumours of a new handsome DI in the village were not incorrect and there was the added bonus that he was single. Ruth told herself that even though she was a little older than he was, age was just a number these days. Her tapping continued while she thought of a way to lure Jake out for a meal at the little Italian in Amberleigh. Jake, looking out from his office window, saw Ruth still sitting there in her car. He watched and waited for her to leave unaware that he had become her new love interest.

Dee gave Peter his iced bun and agreed with him that Albert wasn't very forthcoming, maybe even a little frosty when asked about Margaret. "He did mention that Mary used to go and see her, they'd have a cuppa together."

"Really," Peter looked surprised. "Mary never mentioned Muttering Margo; not to me anyway."

Dee wanted to ask him more about Mary, but Peter's mobile rang. He rolled his eyes, and said, "Hi Ruth," almost too nicely so it almost sounded sarcastic. Taking the phone with him, he disappeared into his flat.

Dee had finished the invoices and was putting her coat on to go home by the time Peter finally re-emerged from the flat to sit back down behind his desk. The banter he usually deployed with Ruth had all but disappeared. He felt she'd been very formal with him - not her flirty self at all. It had unnerved him a little. Dee could see he looked troubled and asked him if he was okay. "Yeah, I am," he said but Dee didn't think he sounded convincing at all. She still took advantage of the moment to ask if she could go shopping with Alison and had her fingers and toes crossed that he would agree.

"Course you can," he said still thinking about Ruth. Then an idea came to him. "How about we go earlier and do some research on Margo's family at the library?"

Dee had a feeling of excitement whelming up inside her. She was desperate to do some digging and was pleased that Peter had asked her along. "Definitely; brilliant idea. I'll let Alison know I can make it and I'll find out what time she wants to meet."

"She closes at two on a Wednesday, so I bet it will be nearer to three. Gives us plenty of time."

"It's getting dark earlier," Peter said looking out of the window. "Sure you're okay to walk home? I can run you if you like?"

"Thanks, but I'm fine. I like the walk," Dee said. She wanted to phone her gran on the walk home anyway.

The telephone conversation went as Dee might have predicted. It pleased her gran immensely that Dee was making new friends and she wanted to know all about progress on the case. She was insistent on Dee calling her again on Wednesday evening to update her on their library visit and told her not to spend money on more clothes because the pale blue jumpsuit that Dee already owned would be perfect for the garden party.

Amberleigh didn't have a large library and the records it held could not be described as extensive. The librarian told them that if they didn't find what they were looking for the church might still hold records too. They thanked her and were now trying to find copies of Margaret's marriage certificate. "Wouldn't it be quicker to do that ancestry thing? My gran has a friend that uses that - found she was connected to royalty," Dee suggested.

"You could use the computer over there if you want," Peter replied, hoping that Dee would save him the task. She would probably be quicker at it than he would.

"Okay." Dee went over to the computer and typed in *Darnley*. A lot of Darnleys flashed up on the screen before her and she started to scroll through. Finally, she came upon a George Darnley. Not from Amberleigh but the address looked familiar. Dee clicked on the name and shouted across to Peter triggering a mum who was choosing books with her toddler to shush her. Dee mouthed an apology but the women then ignored her.

"What you got?" Peter whispered,

"Is that Margo's address?" Dee asked quietly.

Peter nodded. They both stared at the screen. In front of them was Margo and George's wedding certificate. He was down as being an insurance salesman and Margo as a landscape gardener.

"That explains why her gardens are so beautiful and why she loved her plants," Dee whispered

"Can you find anything on George's death?" He stood up straight, placing his hand in the small of his back to relieve the ache from being hunched over while Dee tapped away.

"That's sad." Dee pointed at the computer screen. "Car accident."

"Can we find her mother and fathers name, siblings etcetera? Get as much info as possible, and take photos on your phone."

"I'm sure we can print them off, if we ask."

"Up to you. Keep digging." Peter was pleased with her; she was turning out to be very useful.

Dee met Alison outside the library bang on three o'clock. Peter had already left armed with all the information they could find on George and Margaret Darnley.

"How did it go? Get much?" Alison asked.

"Did you know she was a professional gardener and she had three brothers and a sister?"

"No, I didn't know. Fancy that. Had her down as more of a matron, battle-axe type," Alison said before she was distracted by a dress in the shop window on the opposite side of the road. It was a dark maroon colour, and the sleeves were three-quarter and edged in black, while the hem of the dress flared out and was edged in the same black trimming as the sleeves. It was simple but elegant. "Come on!" Alison was already heading across the road and Dee had to run to catch her up. "What do you think?" Alison asked her.

"It's gorgeous, might be pricey."

"Let's go in and find out."

"Welcome ladies. We love customers, new and old" said the slender woman in the size zero dress, sporting a high bun so tight she didn't need a facelift.

Dee didn't speak for draped over a mannequin in the corner was a beautiful sea-blue scarf that had caught her eye.

The shop owner knew only too well when someone fell immediately in love with one her garments. "Beautiful isn't it; sparkles like the sea," she said, unwrapping the scarf from around the mannequin and handing it to Dee.

"I like the dress in the window" Alison said.

"Yes lovely isn't it. Unfortunately I've just sold it to Petra Gaitley. Not your size anyway." Turning back to Dee the woman said, "The colour is amazing on you."

"Thank you." Dee stammered trying to find a price tag.

The woman turned her attention to Alison. "Now then, I think I have the perfect dress for you; let me see."

Alison looked across at Dee for help.

Dee asked, "Do you have this dress in any other colours?" She meant the dress in the window.

"No, I don't. What about this?" The shop owner was holding a wrap dress as high as her bun in a shimmering lilac colour with silver embroidery on the cuffs. Alison finally plucked up the courage to ask if she could try it on and if there were any other dresses that the owner thought might be suitable.

After trying on four different suggestions, Alison came back to the lilac wrap dress. "I'll try it on again, is that okay?" Alison said returning to the little changing room as the woman said, "Take your time, no rush here."

Alison reappeared from behind the curtain and Dee had to agree that Alison looked amazing in it. The dress hugged her in all the right places and brought out the colour of her eyes.

Alison hissed, "Dee, come here."

"What?"

"There's no price on it. What should we do?" Alison looked in a flap.

Dee smiled and holding the curtain up a little called to ask how much the dress was.

"It's on the sale rail, so I'll knock you twenty percent off." The woman shouted as if she was doing them a favour, before answering the actual question Dee had asked her. "It's one hundred and twenty pounds and the scarf is sixty-five."

"Did you hear that Alison - one hundred and twenty," Dee said in a hushed tone.

"Yes, I think I can afford that. It is for a special occasion and I haven't had anything new for ages." She continued to look at herself in the mirror.

"Take it then. Jim will love it. I'll just go and pay for this scarf. It's so beautiful!"

Dee left Alison in the changing room admiring herself in the mirror.

"I'm going to take this please." Dee was plainly excited at her purchase.

"Do you know, I've had a good day today sales wise." The lady grinned, nodding towards the dress in the window. "So, for a new customer I'll take ten percent off the scarf."

"Really? That's so kind of you" Dee stuttered as the woman reached into a drawer and pulled out some black tissue paper.

"I'm only being nosey and I know it's already sold but how much is that dress? The one in the window." Dee felt like she was about to be chastised for asking.

The lady bent forward and whispered over the counter, "Well I suppose you'll never meet her." Then after a stagnant pause, "Three hundred and forty-five pounds."

Dee was speechless.

Alison came out beaming, carrying the lilac dress. They both watched as it was wrapped in black tissue paper and put into a black and white bag, tied with a black ribbon just as Dee's scarf had been. They both left pleased with their purchases and as they turned to wave goodbye to the shop owner, she turned the sign to *Closed* as she shut the door behind them.

"I love that dress." Alison was so happy. "Are you going wear that scarf on Sunday?"

"Yeah, I think it will go perfectly with what I'm going to wear, Alison. Hey, take a guess how much that dress was in the window."

"I'm rubbish at stuff like that." Alison looked skywards for inspiration. "Two hundred pounds? Could be more if Petra Gaitley bought it." Alison had a sarcastic note to her voice.

"Three hundred and forty-five!" Dee revealed, pleased at herself for asking.

"That's Petra Gaitley for you," Alison said smirking.

"Who's Petra Gaitley? That lady in the shop said she'd only tell me the price because I was never going to meet her."

Alison laughed out loud. "Just shows you how wrong you can be. You will definitely meet her." Alison put on a posh accent. "She's Lord Henry's wife!."

Chapter Eight

Dee couldn't believe what she was seeing. There was a big white board resting on an old easel between her desk and Peter's. It was so big it swamped the entire side of the office and made it feel tinier and more cramped than ever. To make matters worse, to allow space for it her desk had been pushed nearly up against the filing cabinet leaving her minimal room to get in or out. She stood speechlessly in the middle of the office taking it all in.

"Morning. Haven't used this in years!" Peter declared as he came into the office.

"Okay, why do we have a great big white board in the office?" Dee was both baffled and annoyed that her desk had been moved to make way for it.

"This is going to be our sounding wall - ideas, theories - it's all going up here," he said excitedly,

"Hmm, okay, like what?" Dee placed her hands on her hips.

"All the info from yesterday. I thought you might like to start?"

"Peter, I don't understand."

"Look." Peter picked up a blurred image of Muttering Margo and stuck it to the white board. He wrote *victim* above the picture and her name underneath.

The penny dropped with Dee. "It's like what you see on telly. Let me have a go." Peter stepped back handing her the pen he was holding, She didn't have a printed photo of herself so she drew a picture of a stick person wrote her name beneath it and the date she had visited Margo. Above the stick person she wrote *Last person to see Margo alive?*

"You've got it," Peter said placing a hand on her shoulder and then removing it quickly as it felt too personal. "Why the question mark?"

"Well, I wasn't the last one to see her alive, was I? The murderer was." She handed the pen back to Peter. "I'm going to grab us some coffees. We might be at this all day. I'll get you something to eat. Iced bun?"

"No ta, Dee. Think I need to rein in the iced buns. A sandwich for lunch might be nice though. Surprise me. You know where the money is."

Dee armed with cash from the little tin box headed off to *Coffee Creams*. Just as she was closing the door behind her, she took a quick peep back into the office and saw Peter staring at the white board. The saying that her gran used 'Happy as a pig in muck' came to mind.

Jake was unhappy and Tom knew it. Jake was quiet in sound but loud in his gestures of annoyance. "Do I really have to go to this?" he asked, pointing at an invite to a Garden Party at the Manor. "Who has a garden party in October?"

Tom knew better than to answer and made his exit from Jake's office as fast as he could saying something about coffee. "He's not happy about having to go to Henry's," Tom told Claire as they passed in the corridor.

"I'd love to go to that. Tell him I'll go instead."

Tom thought that might not be the worst idea she'd had and ran along to the kitchen to fetch two coffees.

Jake sat back in his chair. He hated things like garden parties. He was flapping the invite around like a fan. People were always awkward at these sorts of things, they never knew what to say to him, always too polite, never a real conversation. 'How do I get out of this one?' he thought to himself? His phone beeped to let him know he'd received a text, it was from Ruth inviting him out to dinner on Friday evening, supposedly to discuss the recent death in the village. He threw the phone down in frustration. He hadn't taken to Ruth, not just because she was a journalist but she was too flirty and he felt she was as fake as fake could be. Her nails had grated on him during their meeting the other day as she had continuously tapped them on her note pad. He swore blind he could hear that tapping noise long after she'd left.

Tom entered and placed a hot coffee down in front of him. "What if me and Claire go on Sunday rather than you?" he offered.

Jake took the idea seriously but knew he couldn't duck out of it really. "I've had a better idea," he said. "We'll all go."

"I'll let Claire know," Tom said. "Are we in uniform?"

"No, you can wear what you like." Jake replied feeling much better. Now he just had to deal with Ruth.

Back in the office; Peter took their sandwiches from Dee and put them in the fridge in his apartment. Dee had tried to look to see what the apartment was like on the inside, but as he went through the door Peter thwarted her by quickly closing it behind him. By late afternoon with the sandwiches eaten the white board was filing up. There was a family tree of Margo's family, dates and time of her death, the weapon clearly stated as *blunt instrument* and a question mark underneath a drawing of a horse that they had used from the internet as they didn't have a photo of the real figurine from Margo's house. A picture of her cottage and the address. "So, what links them all together?" Peter asked.

"The missing photo of the same girl in that photo I found upstairs?"

"Wish we had a picture of that photo."

"We do. Here on my phone."

"You are very shrewd, Miss Firth. When did you take that?"

"When Jake wasn't looking, just before he bagged it up."

"Very good, Dee." Peter was grinning like a Cheshire cat. "Let's print it off and get her up on the board."

Dee had finally sussed the printer although she did mention to Peter that a new one might not be such a bad idea. As with Margo, a blurred image of the girl in the missing photo was shortly in place on the board.

"I think she's the sister, Elizabeth," Dee interrupted Peter as he was thumbing through more papers on his desk.

"Yes, she probably is. Did we find a marriage certificate for the sister? Just wondering."

"I didn't look," Dee said apologetically.

"They're all named after royalty, Margo's brothers and sister."

Dee thought for a moment. "Yeah, I noticed that; original isn't it."

Ruth was not happy; in fact, she was positively fuming. She had received a reply from Jake saying he had plans at the weekend including the garden party at Gaitley Manor and was unable to make it. She was put out. It was rare that she was turned down. Tapping her nails hard on the desk she questioned what he could be doing that was better than going out to dinner with her.

One of the press photographers, walked past her desk, "Hope the wind doesn't change; your face might stay like that" he said, sarcastically.

"Naff off!" Ruth replied and then thought better of it. "Going to that garden party at Gaitley Manor, Shane?"

"Yep, unfortunately. Got to get some pics for Laura's gossip column."

"Mind if I tag along?" she asked.

"Not your scene, Ruth. Why would you want to go?"

Ruth thought fast. "The murder of Muttering Margo - you know Margaret Darnley. Might be some local gossip I can pick up on."

Shane shrugged his shoulders and told her it was no skin off his nose if she went with him or not. "Meet me outside the grounds early as I want to snap people arriving."

Ruth was pleased with herself, her mind full of scenarios of what could happen. She would make sure that she casually bumped into Jake. She suddenly came back to reality and grabbed her bag from under her desk.

"Where you going?" shouted a dark-haired girl from the corner desk in the open plan office.

"Retail therapy," Ruth replied. As she left the building, she recalled seeing a beautiful maroon dress in one of the shop windows.

The remainder of the week had been quiet for Dee. She and Peter had returned to the library but no marriage certificate for Margo's sister Elizabeth could be found. They had visited the church to see if any further records of Margo's family were held there, but to no avail. The vicar told them a sad tale over a cup of tea and chocolate cake: any records which had been stored there were ruined when a storm blew the church roof off and to the vicar's horror at the time anything that was stored in the top of the church went with it.

Peter realised they needed a jump start, just that one bit of information that would put them on the right track. "Think I'll phone Jake. See if he's had any breakthrough," he told Dee. "We don't seem to be getting anywhere fast, do we? I just don't understand why. I'll drop you home and see if he fancies a pint."

Dee was happy to accept the lift home. The dark nights were definitely drawing in.

Jake's week had to come to a close but he was never one to stop working. Tom had asked if he fancied joining him and some of the others for a drink at the local, but Jake had refused. He was too engrossed in the murder of Margaret Darnley to make polite conversation. He just couldn't find a motive or worse still the murder weapon. Even forensics weren't helping; Kathy had come back to him about the photograph which they'd removed it from its frame but there was no name or date on the back. Another dead end.

"On my way-out, sir" Claire said knocking as she entered his office. "These have just come back. What shall I do with them?" Claire was holding the photo back in its frame and the horse figurine.

"Pop them on here please." Jake patted the edge of his desk.

His phone rang as Claire placed the items down carefully and left. Jake waited until she'd gone. "Hi Peter, all well?"

"Fancy a drink tonight, usual place?"

"That's just what I need. I also need to pick your brains, Peter."

"And I yours," Peter replied and they hung up.

Jake picked up the photograph and lightly brushed his fingers over the girl's face. Talking aloud to the image in the photo he asked, "Just who are you and what have you got to do with the murder of Muttering Margo?"

Chapter Nine

It was the day of the garden party. Jake had risen early with a nagging feeling at the back of his mind. He and Peter had gone over and over the case on Friday evening but drawn a blank. He sat at his dining table with a large mug of steaming coffee and went through once again in his own mind what they had discussed.

All Margo's brothers and sister were dead. All of her brothers had died quite young, the youngest brother of cancer a good fifteen years ago. None had ever married. The sister died young too - in a riding accident. They had discussed the parents and how horrific it would have been to have four of your children die before themselves and the pressure on Margaret as the only surviving child. No link had been found to a baby or young child in the family and the only conclusion they could come to was that he or she belonged to someone outside the family.

In essence, Margo's family had not had a nice life – too full of illness and tragedy, finally ending in Margo's own death. They agreed it was a sorry tale. "Dee thinks the girl in the missing photo is Elizabeth," said Peter. Jake agreed that was probable but wanted actual proof and where was he going to get that? Claire and Tom had found no further photographs at the cottage during their search apart from Margo's wedding album and no children were pictured in the album which depicted what looked like a registry office wedding. There was another couple in the photos, presumably the witnesses but, in Claire's opinion, as they weren't wearing wedding outfits, they could have been just a couple walking past the registry office at the time. Jake hadn't wanted to waste any time on them so they were crossed off the list and the photos included neither bridesmaids nor other family members. A low-key affair indeed.

So, Margo had been the last in her family and Jake was waiting on details of the will hoping that might shed some light on the matter.

They had discussed the weapon used but Peter could tell Jake was starting to get frustrated as a thorough search of all three gardens had not thrown up anything like a viable blunt instrument and he was a little narked at forensics for not being able to be more precise and to tie it down to a particular object such as a hammer. All they could say for sure was that Margo had received a blow to the back of her head with a blunt instrument that had a sharp edge and that she had been killed instantly. The rest of the trauma to Margo's head had occurred from banging her head with force on the plant pot as she fell to the ground.

At that point in their discussion the landlord had noticed that the two of them looked a little forlorn and sent over two pints on the house. Jake smiled to himself. The landlord obviously recognised that it didn't do any harm to keep the police onside.

Jake's letterbox rattled making him jump but it was just the local rag. He retrieved it from the hallway and took it through to read over his coffee.

Peter topped up his coffee and grabbed the local newspaper. He had plenty of time to get ready for the afternoon event and settled himself on one of the kitchen stools. Opening the newspaper he slammed his cup down hard. There on the second page was a picture of Dee next to an unsettling image of Margo. "Shit!" He jumped as the coffee spilled onto the worktop and he cursed under his breath. "That bloody Ruth. Wait till I see her. I'll have her guts for garters!"

Dee, was showered and downstairs in her bathrobe. She was deciding whether to tie her locks up or leave them down. Edward was still upstairs pampering himself. It took him way longer to get ready than her and it was becoming annoying. He seemed to have more lotions and potions than she had ever owned, even his night-time routine seemed to take forever. 'What happened to men using soap and water?' she thought to herself. On the other hand it was probably a good thing that he took care of himself. She remembered one of her friends from home whose boyfriend seemed to avoid any form of personal hygiene at all.

"Made you a coffee," Dee shouted up the stairs knowing full well he wouldn't hear her. He would be fixated on the day's highlight. If he'd mentioned the garden party once he'd mentioned it a thousand times. The way he'd carried on anyone would think he had received a personal invite to mix with royalty. She plonked herself down on the sofa and turned on the telly. She found she had become engrossed in some Sunday cooking program when sometime later Edward appeared.

"I think I've got it just right," he announced. Standing on the stairs he was looking like something out of a country style magazine.

Dee raised her coffee cup up to her face to hide her smile. She was finding it hard not to burst out laughing. "Think you'll fit right in," she managed.

Edward was preening himself. "Picked this up in London," he said fingering the tweed waistcoat and matching jacket. "Looking good." He disappeared back upstairs to the bedroom.

Dee shook her head. He really was all or nothing. She turned the telly off and went to join him upstairs. "Time to sort this mop out," she declared, running her hand through her curly red hair. That was if Edward could stop hogging the mirror.

Ruth had checked herself a hundred times if not more in the mirror. 'Jake stands no chance today. One look at me and he's all mine.' She had gone all out. Although the maroon dress she had seen in the boutique window had been sold the lady who owned the shop had a very good eye and had slid her into a navy and white summer dress that grazed her ankles and skimmed her slender figure. She had also invested in new lingerie leaving her feeling sexy and ready for what was inevitable as she saw it between her and Jake. She picked up her navy clutch bag and headed out. Such a shame she had to go so early to meet Shane. She checked her watch one more time and hoped she still looked like she did now in two hour's time when her prey arrived.

Like Peter, Jake was fuming. The local newspaper had been thrown on the table in disgust. 'What does that stupid woman think she's playing at?' The article implied that the police were getting nowhere and stated that if anyone knew anything, anything at all, to contact him at the local police station. They had even printed the telephone number.

He paced up and down the little rented flat. 'Why mention Dee in her report? Doesn't she realise that Dee's a target for gossip and lord only knows what else if the murderer thinks she saw him or her.' His thoughts were of anger towards Ruth, his mind whizzing as he realised the station would be bombarded with crank calls resulting in extra work as any information received, no matter how useless, would have to be followed up.

He went back to the newspaper article, looking at the picture of Dee. The camera had caught her at just the right moment. The same couldn't be said about the picture of Margaret. It was blurred and she looked as if she was giving someone the evil eye.

"You're getting a visit tomorrow" he said aloud surprising himself while tapping his finger hard on Ruth's byline at the bottom of the article.

He picked up his mobile to call the station and, when one of the young PC' s picked up the phone,. he explained the situation but he was too late. The calls had already started to come in.

Peter set off to collect Dee and Edward. He wasn't looking forward to Dee's reaction to the newspaper article, but with a bit of luck she wouldn't have read it and hopefully he could break it to her gently.

"He's here," Dee shouted to Edward who came running down the stairs. As he passed her to open the door while Dee grabbed her bag from the sofa the smell of aftershave was over whelming. "Have you used the whole bottle?" she asked between coughs.

"Better too much than too little," he retorted.

Peter couldn't get over the sight of Edward's attire. He really had decided to play the role of country gentleman. Dee, however, looked serene in a sea of blue; a scarf shimmered around her shoulders and gently moved as she walked towards the car, her red curly hair was down at the back and he noticed the sides had been twisted and pinned up when she ran back to check that she had locked the door. Edward was by then already in the back of the car and Dee apologised as she climbed in. "Can't help it. I get it from my Gran. Always best to check. You never know."

"No, you don't," Peter agreed and as he pulled out of the drive, he opened his window. "Do you mind?" he asked Dee in the front passenger seat.

"No, not at all." They exchanged a look of agreement. Edward reeked to high heaven.

Jake met up with Tom and Claire so they could all go in together.

Claire had on a summer dress with little red flowers on it and a red shawl wrapped around her shoulders. "The weather's amazing," she said. "Who'd of thought for October would be like this?"

Neither of the men answered. Tom was staring at Claire thinking how pretty she was while Jake was looking in the other direction at a man standing outside the gates that led to the Manor holding a camera.

"Who's that?" Jake asked Tom.

"I think it's the photographer from the local rag. Do you want me to go ask him?"

"No not right now. Remember we're just hear to listen to any gossip, ask a few indirect questions. Got it?"

Both Claire and Tom nodded.

"You two look very dapper. You both clean up very nicely" Claire said pulling a face.

"Ta" said Tom feeling proud that Claire had noticed the effort he'd made but Jake was already walking away. He couldn't care what he looked like. He was on the hunt for a killer.

Ruth was on her second glass of champagne. This really wasn't her sort of thing. She'd been monopolising one of the local shopkeepers for so long they had both started to look around in boredom for someone else to talk to. The garden party was filling up though. Guests were still arriving but the hosts were nowhere to be seen.

"Where's Henry?" Shane made her jump, sneaking up behind her.

"No idea. Why?" Ruth asked.

"Need a good shot of the Gaitleys as they make their grand entrance down the steps. They probably know that people are still arriving, I'll hang around with you till they come out and grace us with their presence." He grabbed a drink off a tray as a waiter went by.

Dee was blown away by the Manor House exterior and its gardens. The marquee was filled with white tables surrounded by gold and white chairs to sit down if you felt the need, although most guests were still standing around chatting and drinking. She didn't recognise anyone she was looking for. 'Alison and Jim must be running late,' she thought.

"Lots of people here," Peter observed.

"Yeah. I was just seeing if I could spot Alison and Jim. I'm sure they'll arrive any minute."

Peter nodded.

Edward said, "I'll go fetch us another drink."

"I'm fine for now." Dee's champagne glass was almost untouched.

Edward went off anyway. The truth was that he didn't like Peter and wanted to mingle. He wanted to get his name out there and to let people know that his attire was from London, whether they asked him or not.

Dee turned to Peter. "Thank heavens. Thought he was never going to go. So, what's the plan today then?"

Peter put an arm around her shoulder. "No plan; just listen, keep our eyes and ears open; that's all we can do." He was almost whispering and Dee had to strain to hear him.

"What's going on here you two? Something to share!" It was Alison, obviously in jovial mood.

Peter let his arm fall from round Dee's shoulder and she said, "I've been looking for you. You look gorgeous; absolutely stunning. Doesn't she Peter?"

"Yes, you're husband is one lucky guy."

"That I am," Jim said leaning in to give Alison a peck on the cheek.

"Talk about looking gorgeous, that's a simply stunning photo of you in the gazette. We both said so didn't we, Jim?"

Dee looked flummoxed. "Gazette, photo, what…?"

Peter interrupted. "Nothing! I'll show you tomorrow. It's nothing, honestly. Just says you're helping the police with their enquires, and it is a lovely photo."

"There's nothing bad in there and you should see the horrible picture of Margo, looking like she's about to kill someone!" Alison said, placing her hand on Dee's arm for extra reassurance.

Jim took this as his cue to leave in search of drinks for them.

Peter said, "Alison I'm enlisting your help today."

"You are? How exciting. To do what?"

"Just the same as Dee. I need your eyes and ears. Push people a bit about Margo; see what people say, but try not to be obvious."

"I can do that, no problem." Alison was smiling from ear to ear.

"Thanks. Right now we need all the help we can get. Let me know tomorrow if you hear anything, no matter how small or even if you don't think anyone's said anything at all, they might react. Good to notice people reactions too. That goes for you too, Dee."

"Sure" Dee replied.

"Hi all." The voice had to be Jake's baritone and they turned to see Claire and Tom following behind. Dee thought Claire looked lovely, all dressed up and not in trousers and trainers. She told her as much once they'd joined the group.

"Peter, can I have a word?" Jake asked, pulling him aside so Tom announced he was going to find a drink and the three girls began chatting about their outfits and the weather.

Ruth had already seen Peter from the corner of her eye but then Jake appeared beside him. "I'm going over there," she told Shane, pointing with her glass. He wasn't bothered whatever she did. He was fiddling with his camera getting ready for the big shot he craved of the hosts. 'What on earth was taking them so long to put in an appearance.'

Jake and Peter had only just started exchanging thoughts when they were rudely interrupted by Ruth. "Gentlemen! What can I say? You both scrub up so nicely, I wouldn't know which one of you to choose." Peter glared at her and Jake looked almost as angry but Ruth merely carried on. "Jake, I could do with a drink. Fancy coming with me and helping me find one?"

Peter cringed. This was Ruth at her flirtatious worst and he grabbed her by the elbow before Jake could respond. "You're coming with me. I'll get you a drink," and he pulled her away from Jake's side before she could attach herself. Once out of earshot of the rest of the group he spat out, "How dare you? We had an agreement about Dee and don't for one minute think he's impressed either. And in case you didn't get it, I mean Jake."

"What the hell are you playing at?" Ruth looked like she was going to burst into a fit of rage "Don't you ever speak to me like that. There's no agreement. You've given me nothing. Nor has Jake so I presume it's exactly as I've written and you're both getting nowhere" She took a deep breath. "I've got an editor on at me. We can't all be our own boss. I had to write something and don't for one minute have a go at me about your assistant. I was nothing but nice and we even printed a decent photo of her!"

"Ruth, you're putting her at risk. Maybe even yourself. There's a killer out there!"

"So what? She's a big girl and so am I, Peter. Just for the record…"

Suddenly all attention turned towards the Manor House steps for making their grand entrance were Lord and Lady Gaitley.

"I haven't finished with you," Peter said.

"Is that a promise?" Ruth flicked her hair at him and walked away.

"Keep smiling, dearest. You can go back in soon." Lady Petra Gaitley managed between fixed smiles.

Henry didn't even acknowledge her. He was scanning the crowd, looking for people he knew. Petra seemed to have invited more than usual this year, but that was Petra; never one to listen. He thought the gardens looked beautiful and was pleased to be outside, it had been a while. Petra pulled him forward towards the edge of the steps, Henry hesitated and wobbled as he found his feet, and eventually they managed to make the journey, arm in arm, from the top to the bottom in one piece.

Peter had re-joined the group in which Jake was now chatting happily to Jim, while Claire and Tom were deep in conversation. "Thought the old boy was about to take a tumble."

"Yes, not like he used to be, our Henry," Peter joined in. "Usually fit as a butcher's dog that one. I've heard he's not been well."

"Me too." said Alison. "Such a shame. I don't think he's that old, you know."

"He's coming over!" Dee said excitedly, and indeed Henry was so Peter moved to offer himself as a walking aid.

"I'm not that old yet!" Henry smiled brushing Peter's arm away.

"You've not changed, Henry; stubborn as ever." The pair were laughing as they traversed the short distance to join the group of friends and police colleagues.

"Hello Henry," said Alison planting a kiss on his cheek.

"You do know how to make my day, dear." He patted Alison's arm and then turned to Peter. "Now then, introduce me to Gamblewood's newest detective. I've been reading about you this morning."

"I'm not really a detective, Sir," Dee said.

"No need for the Sir. I'm Henry to my friends. Now would you like a look around the Manor? Can't do with all this palaver and small talk anymore."

"Really, are you sure? Yes please." Dee spun round all excited and noticed that Alison looked a little put out. "Would it be possible for Claire and Alison to come too?"

"Absolutely, of course; and you must be Claire." Henry held his hand out,

Claire attempted a curtsey while shaking his hand. "PC Claire Brown Sir Henry," she blurted out.

"Henry, please. Always Henry to my friends," he repeated. "Now then, which of you lovely fillies are going to walk me to the Manor?" It was less a question than an order but Dee had already stepped up, used to the unsteadiness of her gran at times. Henry smiled. "Come on then ladies let's get ready for the tour!"

Jake rejoined Peter in time to watch the foursome walk away. There was no sign of Jim - who'd been accosted by another business owner in the village - nor of Edward come to that.

"Refills?" Tom asked.

"Just one more please, Same for Peter. Then I need you mingling. Ask about a bit; take your time."

"Will do, sir."

"Well, he's a card," Jake said. "Henry, I mean"

"Sure is. I've only been invited inside Gaitley Manor once, and that was years ago when I first came to live here. Quite the honour. He'll be asking Dee and Claire for information about the murder you'll see."

"Really; think so?" Jake said looking around.

"Henry always knows what's going on in Gamblewood, although we don't see him out and about like we used to. Getting older and I guess, illness can be cruel."

"What's wrong with him? "Jake asked.

"Not sure to be honest. Don't think it's cancer or anything. Could have a word with Dr Glen. Not that he'd tell me."

"Probably not, but if you're worried about him, it's only polite to ask. I think that was Margaret's GP too."

"Get where you're going with this, Jake, no need to ask twice. Time to circulate methinks," Peter said as Tom returned with the drinks and the three of them agreed to meet back in an hour to see if they had learnt anything new.

Petra was trying to look interested in the young man talking to her about his suit. She smiled and laughed but in truth he was boring the pants off her, or would have if she'd bothered to wear any. At last over Edward's shoulder she spied someone she was much more interested in talking to, the new DI she'd heard about from her housekeeper and as she hadn't met him yet, this was her perfect opportunity. "Excuse me," she said to Edward and sashayed her way towards Jake.

Edward was annoyed. He had been trying to impress her, not least because she was more than pleasant to look at - stunning in fact. He had come to the garden party to make connections and standing with Petra at one moment during their conversation he was imagining himself at her side as Lord of the Manor. Then she had practically stopped him mid-sentence and dismissed him like a child.

"Fancy that do you?" Jim said.

"Fancies herself that one; all fur coat and no knickers," Edward said, sarcastically.

"Probably. Another drink?."

Petra smoothed down the tight black dress as she walked in Jake's direction. Her red shoes and ruby jewellery added a brilliant hint of colour to her outfit. Her black hair was elegantly tied up in a French plait, and she smiled politely, knowing everyone was watching her, giving them all some form of performance. A lady tried to accost her as she passed but Petra was having none of it. She wafted her hand in front and carried on walking. If she had hung around, she would have heard herself called a *stuck-up tart*.

Jake was talking to the owner of the old book shop. He didn't seem to know anything about Muttering Margo or if he did, he wasn't telling. Their conversation was coming to an end as Petra joined them. The old gentleman greeted Petra, but as she only had eyes for Jake, he left them to it.

Petra outstretched a perfectly manicured hand, "Hi, I'm Lady Gaitley - Petra to my close friends. I don't think we've met before?"

"No" Jake said, taken aback a little by her beauty. "D.I. Jones - Jake to my close friends.

Petra let out a shrill laugh which caused a few people to turn around. She linked arms with him and asked if he fancied a walk round the walled garden. Jake didn't particularly but was unsure how he could decline.

Salvation came in the unwelcome form of Ruth. She had spied Petra making her move and wasn't going down without a fight. Jake felt like a piggy in the middle or perhaps a rose between two thorns. Ruth smiled insincerely. "Lady Gaitley, I saw Henry heading into the house. Maybe he's not feeling well. Do you think you should check on him?"

Petra didn't release her grip on Jake and smiled sweetly back. Through gritted teeth she managed to get out, "Henry's fine. Tummy trouble that's all. The housekeeper will look after him." She then turned all her attention back to Jake, her dark eyes gazing up at him. "Now where were we, before we were so rudely interrupted?" Jake couldn't fail to notice the dirty look Petra shot Ruth as she said it.

"Pardon me but I need to talk to Tom, so I'll catch up with you two lovely ladies later." Somehow he managed to loosen Petra's grip and make his escape leaving the two rivals for his affections stranded and glaring at each other.

Dee was gobsmacked by the opulence of Gaitley Manor. "My gran's house would fit in your hallway."

Henry smiled, liking both her youth and her openness. "Come through here; I just need this." Henry grabbed a walking stick that was leaning against the wall. "Petra didn't want me to use it when we made our grand entrance," he said.

Dee and Alison felt sorry for him while Claire didn't notice. She was a little behind looking at something on the wall. "Sir Henry," she called.

"Henry, dear Claire, just Henry." Dee noted that although Henry was wobbly on his feet there didn't seem to be anything wrong with his hearing.

"Who's this? She's lovely." Claire was standing in front of an oil painting of a lady dressed in blue with a diamond and blue tiara on her head.

"My mother, beautiful inside and out. Now come on through – in here." He led them into the next room, gesturing them towards two cream, high-back sofas separated by a gold and marble coffee table.

Dee looked around the room trying to take in the grandeur of it all - duck egg blue paintwork, the ceiling so very high, the fireplace large and ornate and the grand piano adorning the corner of the room. There were also ornaments and pictures galore.

"Stunning Henry, simply stunning. Do you live in the whole house or just part of it? Dee asked.

"The whole house, dear. Lived here all my life."

"Did you decorate it yourself?" Claire asked.

"It's evolved over the generations, but Lady Caroline had a huge input."

"I never met Lady Caroline," Alison said. "Albert always speaks so fondly of her."

"Is that Albert who lives in the cottages near the park?" Henry asked.

"Yes," Alison replied. "Comes in every day for his morning cuppa and teacake."

"Haven't seen Albert since Annie left. I miss our chats.".

"Did Annie work here?" Dee asked.

"Yes, she was our housekeeper for many years; lovely woman. Now then, talking of Albert, he lives or should I say lived near Margaret Darnley; so, Dee, is that your actual name? Apart from what I read in the paper, what is really going on?"

Dee laughed as the door opened and a neatly turned-out lady in her sixties walked in carrying a tray. "Thought you might like these," she announced placing glasses of juice and an assortment of canapés down on the coffee table.

"Thank you, Ms Bay. That's very good of you." Henry was smiling.

"I saw you all come in. They're now serving food outside, Sir, so, if there's nothing else Lady Gaitley said I might join in the festivities for the afternoon."

"Of course, Ms Bay. Of course, enjoy yourself," was Henry's reply.

The door closed and Henry relaxed back into the sofa. "Now where were we?" He looked straight at Dee.

Tom, Peter and Jake had finally re grouped.

"Anything," Jake asked.

"No, Margo wasn't popular. Seems like she was a bit of a gossip," Tom answered.

"Peter, you got anything?"

"Same here. Not getting anywhere." Peter changed the subject. "The girls have been awhile; Henry will be enjoying their company that's for certain. But Jake, talking of company what happened with the ravishing Ruth and the perfect Petra?"

"What is it with these women? I'm here to catch a killer not a wife!"

Jim was starting to look around for Alison. They'd been gone much longer than he thought they would have been and Edward was as dull as dishwater. He constantly talked about himself and his plans as to where he was going to be in five year's time. Jim didn't care where

Edward was going to be in five year's time and he was so grateful when one of his customers came over to talk about cars because Edward clearly didn't know the first thing about them and was only too pleased to make his excuses and leave them to it having spotted Petra was standing alone.

Ruth was fed up. Little rounds of bread with things on top was not food. 'It's no wonder Petra's so thin.' She looked over to see Petra enjoying the company of some overzealous young man dressed in a tweed suit. She would bet that Petra was keeping an eye on Jake to see if he noticed the young man paying her so much attention but noted that Jake didn't look Petra's way once. She decided to call it a day. Her feet were hurting her and she was hungry. She looked around for Shane to let him know she was leaving, but, unbeknown to her, Shane had left over an hour ago and was already in the pub enjoying a pint with his mates.

Sir Henry had enjoyed the company of the three ladies. Their interest in him and in the history of the house had been deeply gratifying. Unfortunately, Dee hadn't been forthcoming with much information about Margo's murder; either Peter had trained her well or the newspaper article had been correct and they didn't have much to go on. He had always prided himself on knowing the comings and goings on in the village before this stomach bug had stopped him in his tracks. He hated getting old.

"Now then, Dee. You never answered the question about your name."

Alison turned at that. "Yes. What is your real name. I don't know either."

Dee felt like a big spotlight was on her. "It's erm…"

"It can't be that bad," Sir Henry assured her.

"It's Deandra," Dee said looking down at the empty glass in her hand.

"That's beautiful; such a lovely name. Very exotic."

Dee smiled at him.

"Oh and talking of things exotic…" Henry slowly raised himself from the sofa. "Follow me ladies. I would like to show you all my pride and joy; my orangery."

They all followed back into the Hallway and then through a much smaller lounge - Sir Henry referred to it as a *snug* - and through the patio doors into the orangery.

"Looks like a huge greenhouse to me," whispered Claire to Alison.

Alison nodded in agreement. It was full to the brim with flowers, plants, fruit trees in pots and placed in the centre was a pretty table with two matching chairs and a gold plant pot.

"Oh my, this is amazing. Henry, do you look after all this?" Dee asked him.

"Yes, I do, and I want you to meet my Caroline."

"What do you mean?" Dee asked anxiously.

"Here!" Henry was pointing at the roses in the gold plant pot. "These were cultivated here; one of a kind. They named it Lady Caroline; perfect and beautiful, just like her."

All three of them had to agree. The roses were wonderful indeed.

On a window sill, hidden by spider plants, Claire spotted a few old photos. "Henry, is that a picture of Lady Caroline?"

"Yes." Henry reached over to pick out a photo in a pretty frame. "Petra doesn't like me having pictures of Caroline around. She won't come into the orangery, so I hide my Caroline in here along with a few other old photos I like to keep."

"Can we see?" Dee asked.

"Certainly." The photograph of Lady Caroline was handed to Claire, another to Alison and a third to Dee.

"How old was she when she…passed?" asked Claire passing the photo on to Dee.

"She was forty-seven. We had been married twenty-nine years. I miss her." A flash of sadness came over his face.

Alison and Dee looked at each other. Alison said, "You've been married to Petra for some time now, Henry."

"Yes. Fifteen years; if my health carries on worsening, she won't have to put up with me much longer."

Dee said strongly, "Now Henry, I'm sure you don't mean that. Don't talk like that. Tell me, who are all these people in this photo?."

Henry brightened and came over to look at the picture Dee was holding. "Those were the days, Dee. That's myself and Lady Caroline; a proper Lady she was. We'd not been married long, only a few years, when that was taken." He paused as if he'd had a fright.

"What's wrong?" Dee took Henry by the arm afraid he might fall over.

"That's my mother and father in the background and the rest are staff," he said, looking away.

"You all look so happy." Then, asked pointing to a figure at the back of the photo, she asked, "Who's that?"

"As I said, that's us and my parents. Then that's old Barry the Head Gardener next to Margaret. She was his assistant. Eventually old Barry's back was so bad he retired and then Margaret took over till…"

"Until what?" interjected Claire.

"Till she got married."

"Can I have a look at the picture please?" Claire said, dropping into police mode. Dee passed her the picture, mouthing something that Claire couldn't make out. "Henry, could any of these people from Margaret's past have something to do with her murder?"

"Of course, not." Henry seemed put out by the question.

Dee held her hand out for Claire to pass her the picture back. As Claire passed her the photo back they exchanged glances.

"Henry, who's this young girl? She looks too young to be staff," Dee asked.

Henry took a quick glance. "That's Elizabeth, Margaret's sister. She worked with the horses." He moved away towards the patio doors that led to the snug. "Now then, I fear I have taken up too much of your time. Let's return to the party."

Dee replaced the photograph she was holding on the window sill and they all followed Henry back out into the garden.

"On you go, ladies. It's been a pleasure meeting you," he declared, leaving them to make his way over towards the owner of the old book shop.

Dee and Claire could not believe what they had found. "Is it her?" Claire asked.

Dee nodded, "We've got to find Peter and Jake."

"Is one of you going to tell me what's going on?" Alison was getting frustrated at the cloak-and-dagger conversation."

"Sorry, police business," Claire said.

"Dee, come on, you can tell me. I understand why Claire can't, but what is it?"

Claire nodded and began humming to herself as Dee said, "The young girl in the photograph - Henry said it was Margo's sister."

Alison interrupted. "And?"

Dee grabbed Alison's arm and whispered in her ear. " She's the girl in the missing photo from Margo's house; the one holding a baby."

Chapter Ten

"Jake's going to be here any minute. Did Alison say anything further?"

"Afraid not," Dee replied trying to tidy the office so it looked a little more inviting.

"What are you doing" Peter asked her.

"Just trying to make the office look a little nicer."

Peter rolled his eyes and left her to it. He entered his flat, grabbed a plant he had on the side near his dining table, returned to the office and placed it on the corner of Dee's desk.

"That's nice, ta, The pot's lovely," She was really pleased to finally have some green amongst all the boring brown.

Alison was setting up for the day. She had seen Jake walk past the coffee shop window on his way to see Dee and Peter. She was desperate to know what was going to happen next, and whether they'd need her help. She had already decided, after overhearing them arranging to meet at Peter's office for some sort of brainstorming session, that she would give them ten minutes to get started and then take them morning coffee and pastries before she opened *Coffee Creams*.

Jake took a deep breath. After meeting Peter he wanted to have a tough talk with Ruth although the thought of having to meet her filled him with dread. At least his orders to Claire and Tom gave them a more straightforward task – going to see Lord and Lady Gaitley.

As Jake entered Peter's office, he immediately focussed on Dee sitting behind her desk, her hair shining as the winter sun came through the window. He couldn't help but notice how lovely she looked. Peter was at the whiteboard writing Elizabeth's name on it.

"Hi; grab a pew," Peter said pointing to the chair near his desk.

"What's all this? Very thorough. I like a good evidence board." Jake nodded his head in approval.

Dee sat quietly, giving Jake the once over. She didn't see how Claire could think he was so dishy, or hot, or whatever the term was that Claire had used when they first met. However, he did have something. She liked the neatness of his hair and clothes. He looked very much put together compared to Peter in his scruffy jeans and t-shirt. She turned her attention to the conversation the two men were having and commented, "Evidence board? Is that what you call it? The only thing about that…is that it's taken over the flipping office!"

Both men turned to look at her, shaking their heads. Jake carried on explaining that he was fuming with Ruth about the article and that he was paying her a visit once they'd finished up. "She's no idea what danger she's putting herself and Dee in."

"That's what I said to her yesterday. For a clever woman, she can be so stupid."

Dee said, "I'm here you know. What danger? What are you talking about?"

Jake took a step back, so Peter could get past him and Peter planted both his hands on Dee's desk and looked at her. "She said you were helping Jake and the police with their enquiries. Who's to say the killer doesn't think you saw something or know something? Get my drift?"

Jake noticed that Dee was getting paler and her eyes wider by the second. "It's nothing to worry about," he said loudly.

Dee turned to look at him. Angrily she shouted back. "Nothing to worry about? Course it is! I might be next. It could be anyone out there that killed Muttering Margo. You don't know who killed her do you, Peter? What am I going to do?"

From the corridor that led to Peter's office, Alison could hear the raised voices, mostly Dee's, and thought twice about delivering the goodies she was carrying, until nosiness got the better of her. Opening the door, she announced herself loudly; "Hello!"

The office fell silent. Peter was bending over Dee's desk; Jake was in the corner and Dee was sitting with her head in her hands, shaking.

Alison broke the silence. "Coffee and pastries. Thought this might help with the brainstorming."

"I might be next, Alison," Dee said.

"Next? No idea what you're talking about. You do look pale. Here eat one of these and drink that." Alison handed her a latte from the tray that Peter had taken from her, together with a cinnamon swirl from the brown paper bag she was still holding.

"Good timing," Jake said taking a pastry for himself. "We were just saying how annoyed we are with the article about Margo's death and how it might be misconstrued by our murderer, but I promise I won't let anything happen to you, Dee. I really won't."

Alison could see the colour returning to Dee's face but felt compelled to add to Jake's assurance. "They will look after you, Dee. Anyway you don't know anything about the murder or the murderer, so why would they come after you?"

"They don't know that she doesn't know anything." Peter's serious intent was marred by speaking through a bite of his pastry.

Jake shot Peter a glare and Alison could feel the tension in the air. She tried to break it. "Has anything new come to light from the garden party?"

Peter went over to the board and said, "Well, we know the girl in the picture is definitely Margaret's sister Elizabeth and that she worked with horses at the Manor House." Alison thought he looked like a teacher in the classroom, as he pointed at the photo on the board.

"Still need to know who the baby is?" Dee managed to say.

"Who would know?" Alison asked. "Could the baby have belonged to someone in the family or to a neighbour?"

They all looked to Peter who put the current impasse into words. "There's no record we can find of any baby born within the family."

Dee had an idea. "Alison you are a genius."

Alison looked puzzled. "I am?"

"Yeah, the neighbour. We need to talk to Albert. His wife worked at the Manor House and Margaret his next-door neighbour. He might know something."

"Already interviewed him. Not very helpful," Jake said with his head down, writing in his notebook.

Dee tilted her head to one side. "Old people don't like being interviewed. I imagine he would be much more talkative over a cup of tea and a piece of cake. My gran loves a good chat.."

Jake put his notebook and pencil away. "Looks like that's your next port of call; see if you can do any better than the professionals."

"I'll give it a go," Dee said standing up.

"You're not going anywhere without me," Peter insisted.

Claire and Tom were greeted at the door of Gaitley Manor by the housekeeper. Claire had remembered her name and the housekeeper looked taken back when Claire had addressed her as Ms Bay.

Tom explained that they would like to have a word with Lord and Lady Gaitley.

Ms Bay had politely but firmly told them, "Lady Gaitley is out and Lord Gaitley is recovering in bed from the garden party and has asked not to be disturbed. Perhaps you might call ahead next time so you do not have a wasted journey." With that she closed the door leaving Tom and Claire on the doorstep not quite believing what had occurred.

"Shall we take a look around the gardens while we're here?" Tom asked.

"Better not. Ms Bay might chase after us with her sweeping brush!"

The pair giggled and made their way back to the police car.

Lord Gaitley had managed to get himself out of bed and was hanging on to the back of a chair looking out of his bedroom window to see who had knocked at the door. He was shocked to see it was the police and headed back towards the bed. Just as his bedroom door opened, a stabbing pain in his abdomen doubled him over. He let out a loud groan.

"Lord Gaitley, Henry, what are you doing?" Ms Bay came running over to his side, and as soon as Henry could stand up straight, she helped him back into bed.

"Why were the police here?"

Ms Bay explained that they wanted to speak to him and Lady Gaitley. "They didn't say what they wanted. Someone has probably lost their wallet or purse at the party yesterday. I told them Lady Gaitley was out and that you did not wish to be disturbed." Ms Bay plumped the pillows behind Henry. "Is that better?"

The pain had gone and Henry felt a wave of tiredness come over him. He nodded and closed his eyes and Ms Bay left, closing the door quietly behind her so as not to wake him.

Jake and Alison left Peter's office together. Alison rushed back to the safety of Coffee Creams having learnt nothing that she didn't already know about the murder of Muttering Margo and a little worried that the murderer might be thinking she was helping with the case or knew something she didn't. She texted Jim to see what his thoughts were.

The little bell over the door chimed, and it was Albert. "You're late opening today," he said heading towards his usual table,

"Dentist!" Alison shouted after him.

As Albert sat down a black figure silhouetted by the sun was peering in through the shop window. Alison walked out of the back kitchen with Albert's usual order and let out a squeal.

"What's got in to you girl." Albert said.

"Did you see that; someone's watching us," Alison managed to get out.

"Just looking in to see how busy you are if you ask me. Why would anyone be watching us? It's something and nothing. Don't spill my tea Alison - you're all of a dither." With that Albert returned to reading his newspaper.

Alison's breathing was erratic; she needed to sit down. She couldn't think straight. She was a complete bag of nerves.

She was scared.

Chapter Eleven

Peter and Dee had gone over the questions Albert should be asked. He had also tried his best to give Dee a crash course on interview techniques. Although Dee had listened intently, she really wanted it to appear as if she was just calling round to have a normal chat with Albert. She felt sure she would be able to slide in a couple of questions if he was comfortable and not thinking he was being interrogated in any way.

"I'll head off. Take me a bit of time to walk there." She was popping her coat on as she said it.

"Not on your nelly."

"What?"

"I'm coming with you, Dee. I've already told you; you're not going out there walking across that park on your own."

Dee tutted and sat back down while she waited for Peter. He finally reappeared from his flat waving his car keys in his hand. "Can't ever seem to find these. They're never where I thought I'd put them."

"Hmm, funny that," Dee said with a hint of sarcasm. "Ever thought of getting a key hook or just putting them in the same pot all the time, then you know where they are. My gran puts her keys in the chicken."

Peter was now locking the office door. "Did you say chicken? Feel sorry for the chicken."

"It's a ceramic chicken, honestly!" Dee replied shaking her head as they made their way towards Peter's car. The pair were unaware they were being watched.

Arriving at Albert's, Dee looked towards Margaret's cottage. The garden was starting to look untended, Police tape fluttered in the wind, and she had an overwhelming feeling of sadness. Putting on a brave face she announced, "Right, won't be long," as she got out of Peter's car.

"I'm coming with."

"I don't think so," Dee retorted. "I can handle this on my own. It's just a chat, nothing more."

For once Peter knew he was beaten. "Off you pop then. Remember what we discussed."

Dee knocked on Alberts's door.

Fortunately, he hadn't stayed long at *Coffee Creams* that morning. He knew that Taylors the butchers had a special price on fillet steak and chicken breasts and as he was always one to watch the pennies, he hadn't wanted to miss out. "Oh hello, what's this then?" Albert was a little taken back at finding Dee on his doorstep.

"Just thought I'd pop in for a chat if that's okay?" Dee deployed her best smile. "I was hoping you could tell me a little about Gaitley Manor."

Albert gestured for her to come in. "Well I was just about to start getting my meal ready for tonight but there's not much I don't know about them up there at the Manor."

Dee found herself in the living room with Albert gesturing for her to sit down. She was quite surprised at how different it was inside to Margo's. Albert had removed the wall between the kitchen and the living room so it was all open although, like Margo's, he had patio doors going out into the garden. With the exception of a few newspapers and books scattered here and there, it was very neat and tidy.

"You have a lovely home," Dee shouted.

"Nothing wrong with my hearing, lassie," Albert shouted back. "Tea or coffee?"

"Tea please," Dee replied with a little laugh.

"So, you want to know about the Manor. Already had the police round asking questions. Has Peter sent you here?" Dee nodded. "What is it you want to know; fire away?" and Albert handed Dee her cup of tea.

"Well, you mentioned your wife worked there. What was it she did again?" She was hoping that Albert would just open up, grateful for a visitor; for someone to talk to.

"My Annie was the housekeeper till that new lot arrived. Annie loved Lady Caroline and Sir Henry. There wasn't anything she wouldn't do for them. Very generous lady Caroline was, always bought the kids gifts, never forget their birthdays or ours." Albert took a sip of his tea.

"When did Annie pass away?" Dee asked.

"A few years ago, now." Albert looked down into his cup. "Blame that lot up there, I do. They killed her you know; well them and bloody Muttering Margo with her gossiping."

"What?" Dee's eyes were out on stalks. "I don't understand."

Albert stood and went over to the kitchen. He stood behind the kitchen island that separated the two areas as if it was protecting him in some way.

"My Annie was let go by that Petra. Accused her of stealing a broach. A broach? Really! My Annie had loads of broaches; most certainly didn't need one of hers. Then again it wasn't probably that cow's broach in the first place. Bet it was one of Lady Caroline's." Albert turned to get something out of the fridge behind him. Turning round he placed a chicken breast upon the wooden cutting block sitting next to the sink.

"That's awful. Why would Petra think Annie would have stolen it?"

"Load of rubbish it was; just an excuse. She wanted to get rid of my Annie she did. Wanted to bring in her own staff. Sir Henry was really annoyed about what had happened especially when the so-called missing broach was found days later in another jewellery box. Fuming and upset Sir Henry was." Albert took a breath as he opened one of the kitchen drawers.

"Well, couldn't your wife explain to Sir Henry that it was nothing to do with her, especially if she'd worked there all those years. Surely someone else must have put it there by mistake."

Albert carried, on ignoring Dee. "We went to see Sir Henry. He was the one that told us the broach had turned up. He apologised to us both but said that what was done was done. The shame killed my Annie, it did."

"Shame?" Dee was shaking her head becoming more confused by the minute.

"Yeah, all those years she had worked for them. The shame of being accused of stealing. It didn't help matters with flipping Muttering Margo going around telling all and sundry that she'd been let go for stealing either."

"I'm sure no one listened to Muttering Margo. Sounds like a big misunderstanding if you ask me."

"Well lass, it wasn't long after that my Annie became ill, and I've no time for any of them. As far as I'm concerned, they killed her with their lies."

Albert had taken a mallet-like object out of the drawer and was now bashing hell out of the piece of chicken. It was obviously fated to be as thin as possible

Dee knew she had to ask questions about Elizabeth but Albert looked so angry that she needed to tiptoe gently into asking about Margo's sister. "Did Annie work there when Margo and her sister were there then?"

Albert looked up and stopped what he was doing. "Yes," he said simply.

Dee hoped he would carry on so she said nothing more and Albert finally put the mallet down and said, "Margo was the head gardener and got her little sister a job with the horses. Margo left several months after getting married but her sister didn't work there very long at all. Got another job in the countryside at some rival stables. Sir Henry wasn't happy about it at all. My Annie said after Elizabeth had left, Margo and Sir Henry could be heard having several arguments; not the done thing according to my Annie." Albert lifted the mallet from its resting place and started bashing the chicken piece again.

"Don't suppose you know which stables Margo's sister went to, do you?"

Albert shrugged his shoulders. "Somewhere in Yorkshire, I think. All such a long time ago now."

Dee sensing their chat was coming to an end asked what he was making.

"Chicken escalope," Albert replied, in a cheery voice.

"Ooh I could never make anything like that," Dee said, approaching the kitchen island to see what Albert was doing.

"Well first you bash it flat with this here meat tenderiser. Then you coat it with breadcrumbs."

"That's a right bit of kit, Albert. Are you a good cook then?"

"Annie taught me well. Found this in the garden." Albert waved the meat tenderiser at Dee. "It belongs to Ms Fancy-Pants next door. Her kids are always throwing or kicking things into my garden. Sometimes I throw them back and sometimes I don't." Albert took a deep breath "Useful this is; better than using a rolling pin, so I kept it."

Dee had a sinking feeling "When did you find that in your garden, Albert?"

"Other day. Same day as when you were here when Margo got her comeuppance."

Dee could feel a flush of red creeping up her neck. "I don't think Margo asked to be murdered Albert."

"Didn't she? Well she upset someone, going around muttering her lies. Got what she deserved if you ask me. Don't care if she's barking mad or not."

Dee made her excuses It was time to leave, and watching Albert bashing the chicken had made her feel sick to her stomach.

Peter, sitting patiently in the car, knew they had been followed. Years of training had taught him well. He'd picked the car up in his mirror a mile or so back. He got out slowly, watching as Shane brought out his camera to snap pictures of Dee entering Albert's house and then banged on the passenger side window causing Shane to jump, hitting himself with the camera as he did so.

"Is this how low Ruth has gone now? Following us eh? Best you can do? What are you hoping to take a picture of?" Peter shouted.

Shane put the window down. "Piss off. I'm entitled to do my job," he hissed back.

"Taking pictures of a young lady. Why, what for?"

"She's just gone into another old biddy's house. Might bump him off too!"

"Watch your tongue. Best you leave now!"

Shane didn't want to cause a scene. He was already on thin ice at the newspaper as it was. He turned on the ignition and sped away leaving Peter standing on the kerb alone.

Dee came out to find Peter pacing up and down at the side of the car. "All, okay?" she asked.

Peter had decided not to mention his run-in with Shane. It wouldn't achieve anything other than upset Dee for her to know she had been followed and photographed again.

"Yeah, all good, you haven't been long. Any news?"

"I need a glass of wine. Think Jake might need to be with us to hear this. I'd better call Edward. Best to let him know I'll be home late."

"Pub it is then," Peter said "I'd best call Jake to meet us there."

Dee nodded as she left a message on Edward's mobile. 'Why does he never pick up?'

Jake was pleased to hear from Peter. He felt like he'd wasted a whole day behind his desk. He hadn't learned anything new from their meeting in the morning and, since Tom and Claires visit to Gaitley Manor had proved unsuccessful too, he still needed that one break; He wasn't pinning much hope on Dee's visit to Albert either. When Tom had originally spoken to Albert although he had seemed shaken by the murder, he'd had nothing to contribute to the case and just seemed to want to be left alone.

Jake picked up his notes again, the photograph of the young girl with the horse was laid on his desk staring at him. He picked it up and ran a finger over the image. Looking into the eyes of Elizabeth, thinking out loud he said, "I'll find who killed your sister; I promise you I will."

Peter and Dee arrived at the pub in Amberleigh before Jake and the landlord made a joke about Peter becoming a regular and how much prettier the young lady with him was than the chap he normally sat with.

"What's that about?" Dee asked.

"I meet Jake here sometimes; he says you're better-looking company than Jake." Peter was laughing as he handed Dee her white wine.

Dee smiled in the landlord's direction and raised her glass to thank him. "That I am," she smiled.

Peter had been pushing Dee during their journey to Amberleigh to tell him what she'd learned from Albert that was so important it warranted a meeting with Jake. He'd eventually given up as Dee had made it very clear she wanted to tell them together. Instead, they had talked about what they were going to eat later. Peter's choice was between beans on toast or a pot noodle while Dee had stated she and Edward would manage with either a take out or a bowl of cereal.

Dee said, "I didn't realise you and D.I. Jones were friends like that."

"We've known each other a long time," but Peter's explanation was interrupted by the arrival of the subject, himself.

"Drinks?" Jake asked, one hand resting on Peter's shoulder.

"We're all good," Peter responded.

Dee raised an eyebrow. 'Maybe there's another reason the DI's single,' she thought as Jake took the seat next to Peter.

"Hope you've both got more news than I have," Jake continued. "Before you ask Tom and Claire came up with nothing. They couldn't get past the rottweiler of a housekeeper to see Sir Henry and Petra was out." He took a sip of his beer. "There's no more news forensically either and any other follow-ups we've done have hit a dead end. I'm getting frustrated to be honest with you. Why steal a photo of Elizabeth holding a baby and kill the sister? None of it makes sense."

"Actually, you know, "Peter said popping his pint back on the beer mat, "What if it's a burglary gone wrong. I mean, maybe it's nothing to do with the photo. I take it the frame surrounding the photo was worth a bit and what if Margo had just come home or she'd been in the garden and found them in her house and a scuffle breaks out - Dee said Margo was pretty agile for her age – and she ends up in the garden coshed over the head and they fled with the one thing they'd already bagged."

Peter lifted his pint to his lips for another sip and Jake gave it the briefest consideration before responding. "I don't think so, Peter. I've just got the itch about this one. It's personal. I'm sure of it."

Peter knew exactly how that sort of itch felt. He'd had it many times during his career and it wasn't to be ignored.

"So, when you've both quite finished, anyone interested in what I have to say?" Dee interrupted.

"Go on then." urged Peter, raising an eyebrow at Jake.

Dee began talking rapidly about Albert's house and its kitchen island and something about books and the garden.

"Whoa there!" Jake said. "We need to start at the beginning. Would you prefer to write it all down? Turn it into a concise report."

"No, I don't want to write it down!" Dee snapped back. "You need to listen."

Peter put a hand on Jake's arm. "Go on, Dee. Jake's got no patience. So, Albert's at the island cooking chicken - think that's where we'd got to."

Dee didn't get to continue for very long.

"Hang on, "Jake interrupted again. "Albert found a meat tenderiser in his garden on the day of the murder and didn't think to mention it to the police when questioned?"

Dee nodded and explained he was always finding things in his garden that Vicky's kids had thrown over.

"We need to pay Albert a visit in the morning."

"I haven't finished yet. He hated Margo and the Gaitleys. Said they killed Annie, his wife."

"What? This is quite a turn-up." Peter was holding his hands out as if hoping for some form of divine intervention. "What on earth could the Gaitleys and Margo have to do with her death? I thought Annie died of some type of cancer."

Dee shrugged. "Well he says it was the shame that made her ill. Petra accused Annie of stealing a broach. They sacked her you know. Turned out she hadn't; it had just been put back in the wrong place. Margo apparently went around Gamblewood gossiping to all and sundry that Annie had been sacked for a theft it turned out she hadn't committed."

Jake leaned forward. "Well, there's a motive for you."

Peter said, "Albert? Not a chance. No Jake, I don't think so."

"I do!" Dee blurted out a little too loudly.

Both men looked over their shoulders in case anyone else in the pub was earwigging. The landlord looked over and smiled, turning away to put a glass back under the bar, He knew better than to look as if he was trying to listen in.

"Look, you didn't see him bashing hell out of that piece of chicken. He's a lot stronger than you think. All I could do was visualise him smacking Margo over the head with that kitchen thingy. That's why I left. It scared me to be honest."

"So, we have a potential murder weapon and a person of interest." Jake crossed his arms.

Peter disagreed. "No Jake. We have two persons of interest."

"Two?" Dee asked.

"Yes. Vicky, Ms Fancy-Pants!"

Chapter Twelve

Dee poured hot water into her morning cup of coffee recalling how Edward wasn't too pleased that it was only the start of the week and as he put it, she'd *been out on the lash*. Dee had reminded him that it was work and Edward had reminded her that if that was the case Dee should get paid overtime.

Edward had also mentioned yet another meeting with an overseas client to take place on Thursday. He'd stated that he should be back Saturday morning as long as they secured the contract. Apparently, Edward and his colleagues would be out in London celebrating all their hard work on Friday night if all went to plan.

Dee had offered to join him and Edward had turned her offer down, a little too quickly for her liking. It would be nice if he asked her just once to accompany him. However, a couple of quiet nights to herself was no bad thing.

She had hardly read any of the romance novel for Alison's book group. If she was honest, she hadn't really wanted to go to London anyway. The thought of listening to Edward and his cronies spouting off about their achievements wasn't her idea of fun. 'Best leave them to it. I bet he doesn't get paid overtime either,' had been her final thought.

She decided to dress a little warmer as the weather was definitely becoming chillier. Jeans and a navy knitted jumper felt too plain so she added the scarf she had worn to the garden party, locked up the house and headed off to see Alison.

It had now become a thing before starting work to have a latte with Alison at Coffee Creams They had both fallen into the pattern easily and they enjoyed each other's company. Alison found herself looking out of the shop window hoping Dee would arrive early. She was nervous and anxious to tell Dee about the figure watching her the day before.

"Pleased to see you this morning," Alison said, practically dragging Dee inside and carefully locking the door behind her.

"I'm been watched!" Alison blurted out as Dee sat down in her usual window seat.

"Hang on. Watched? what are you talking about? Who's watching you?"

"Well, I don't know. There was a dark figure peering through the window staring at me. They just watched me and when I stared back, they left." Alison was struggling to breathe.

"Gosh, I'd have gone outside and asked them what they were doing," Dee said unthinkingly.

"Oh, you would, would you? It was scary. It was after I'd left your office and all that talk about you being in danger." Alison looked visibly upset "What if I'm in danger too?"

"You're fine. You've got nothing to do with this, honestly, Alison. I really think it was probably just someone deciding whether to come in or not."

Alison made a disbelieving sound and started to make two lattes, the noise of the machine frothing the milk precluding conversation.

As Alison popped the hot mugs down on the table and sat opposite her, Dee repeated herself just in case Alison hadn't heard her.

"I hope you're right," Alison said quietly hugging the mug with both hands. "Albert said that too; something and nothing he said."

"Albert was here too? Did he see them?"

Alison nodded, taking a sip of coffee. "I'm overthinking things as usual," she said.

"This isn't going to help you feel any better," Dee was shaking her head and twisting the scarf with her fingers.

"Oh no, what now? "Alison looked alarmed.

"I've something to tell you about Albert," Dee said taking a sip of her latte.

Peter was up early. He'd had a rummage through his wardrobe, thinking he'd better make more of an effort this morning in case he ended up at the police station. Jake had asked Peter to accompany him to interview Albert, hopefully in Alberts home but if things took a turn for the worse, he might find himself and Albert in a police interview room for the rest of the day.

Jake, Tom and Claire were digesting the news about Albert and Dee's suspicions over a morning cuppa.

"So, when are we going?" Tom asked impatiently.

"Let's finish these. Then we'll head off. Need to make sure they're both in. See if we can catch Albert first before he heads off to *Coffee Creams*. Once done there hopefully Vicky the neighbour will be back from the school run so you two can pop round for a chat."

Nods all round.

"I won't be seeing Albert today, then?" Alison asked.

"I'd be surprised," Dee replied. She realised time was ticking and she wanted to be in the office to see Peter before he left. Although Dee had protested strongly she had finally agreed to man the office and stay well away from Albert's. The outer door was to be locked and she must have her mobile on her at all times.

She gave Alison a big hug and told her once again not to worry. Alison watched her leave and once the door was shut spoke to the empty café. "Don't worry. There's only a flipping murderer out there!"

The door tinkled and Alison moved sharply behind the counter hoping the man standing there smiling and asking for a pot of tea and a bacon roll hadn't heard her.

Jake knocked on Albert's door at just after half past eight. They waited until an out of breath Albert opened it.

"Oh God! What's all this? I was just putting my shoes on."

Jake said, "May we come in please, Albert? we need a chat."

"No!" Albert would have slammed the door in their faces had Tom not already wedged his foot in the gap. "Go away."

"Albert it's me, Peter. Can I come in?"

Albert turned on his heel and was making his way down the hallway as he responded. "Do what you want but I'm not making any tea, so don't ask."

Peter and Jake sat on the sofa opposite Albert who had nestled himself in what could only be described as his comfy chair. Tom and Claire stood behind and waited.

"What's going on? I had that girl from your office here yesterday."

"There's a piece of kitchen equipment that might be important. A meat tenderiser you found tossed over the fence."

"I'll get it." Albert made a move to stand up.

"Just tell us where it is," Jake said and nodded at Claire who retrieved the tenderiser from the kitchen drawer.

She held it aloft for them all to see and Albert confirmed he'd found it in his garden. I'm sorry if I've caused any trouble," he said.

Peter said, "Albert, do you have a dishwasher?"

"Oh yes, Annie had one put in when we did the kitchen. Never use it though." Albert perked up a bit.

Jake looked at Peter knowing exactly why he was asking. "I'm sorry, Albert, but we'll need you to make a full statement down at the station and have your fingerprints taken - just to eliminate you, of course."

Albert nodded. "Do you think her next door used it to kill Margo then?"

"What makes you say that?" Jake asked.

"Well, she hated her as well as me. Those bloody dogs barking all the time. Who knows she might have flipped and gone and done her in."

Claire took a photo with her phone, sent it to Tom and Jake, and bagged the meat tenderiser. It had some weight to it.

"Just to go over things again, Albert," Jake asked carefully. "Do you remember seeing that?" Jake pointed at the bagged item Claire was holding, "…when you first saw Dee and Margo in the garden chatting together."

"No, it wasn't there then. I'm sure it wasn't."

Peter interrupted. "So, you saw Dee go into Margos and then you went out into your garden to spy on them?"

"No; well maybe a little. I'd only seen your girl at Alison's; knew she was new round these parts so I wondered how she knew Margo. Wasn't sure if she was family like; if the winds blowing in the right direction sometimes you can hear what people are saying." Albert looked down at his hands.

It was Jake's turn. "Did you hear anything?"

"No, Margo let out those flipping dogs. I couldn't have heard them anyway with all that yapping."

"Yes, yes," Peter said becoming a little frustrated. "So, when exactly did you find it in your garden Albert? Do you know the time, even roughly?"

"No; don't wear a watch see." Albert held his wrist up to show them. "But like I've already said I Heard Miss Fancy-Pants shouting at Margo so I came out to take a look at what was happening. I saw her run inside; then next thing I looked down and there it was. Just there." Albert pointed out towards the garden. "I went back in when her kids came out to play. Get on my nerves they do."

"Can you show me where in the garden you found it, please, Albert?" Jake asked and they all followed Albert outside so he could point out the spot where the tenderiser had landed. Albert shivered and Jake motioned to Claire and Tom to take him back inside.

"Bit heavy to throw from Margo's Garden to Albert's don't you think?" Peter asked Jake.

Jake looked perplexed. "I was having the same thought. Wonder if they jumped into Vicky's garden from Margo's then tossed it over into Albert's."

"Possible, but I noticed a padlock on the gate; probably to keep the kids in. Not an easy escape route that."

"Good point," Jake said hugging his arms around himself to keep warm. "Would you mind driving Albert to the police station so we can take his statement. Claire can go back with you. We need that piece of equipment down to the lab as soon as possible. I'll take Tom with me: see if Vicky recognises our potential murder weapon, maybe she's not been as truthful as we thought."

Dee's day was boring, there was no other word for it. She was so desperate to hear what was happening at Albert's. She constantly checked her phone but to no avail. Not one single message from anyone.

The office phone rang, making her jump. She sprang to her feet to answer it but it was just a wrong number. The boredom was getting to her. She kept staring at the door that led to Peter's apartment. "Shall I try it?" she thought and couldn't help herself. 'It's only a peek,' she told herself but it was locked. Tutting she went back to her desk.

Sitting back down, she opened her drawer, the one which contained the voice recorder and a camera. Wondering if either actually worked she set them on her desk and started playing with the camera. It was a compact, one of those that showed the image on a digital screen. It looked like it also had a video function built into it too. 'Pretty flashy, must have cost a bob or two,' she thought.

In her hands the camera sprang to life. Unsure on how to use it she spent a while googling the instructions. To her surprise, it turned out to be quite straightforward in the end.

She took a couple of photos of the office for practice; she was only used to using her phone these days. Thumbing through the photos she had taken she was pleased with the images but something odd caught her eye, the number forty-eight in the left corner of the screen. She knew she'd only taken four shots so without hesitation she went back over the other images in the camera. There were photos of dogs, pictures of a blonde lady and a young girl in different settings. 'Her granddaughter?' Dee thought. Then caught off guard, she blinked twice. There right in front of her were pictures of Margo, then some of Margo and Sir Henry together followed by ones of Gaitley Manor itself.

She put the camera down quickly on to her office desk. The images had spooked her. Putting her hands behind her head, she pushed her chair back. She looked at the evidence board and then back to the camera. Her thoughts were swirling rapidly; she was thinking twenty million things at once. She put her head in her hands hoping this would help to sort her thoughts into some form of chronological order. Nothing made sense.

The one thing she knew for certain was that Mary was now involved in some way but how and why? Those answers eluded her.

Chapter Thirteen

Peter had stayed with Albert while he gave his statement after which Albert had been driven home by a police officer. Complaining he was tired and hungry; he had wanted to be dropped off at *Coffee Creams* but Peter had finally persuaded him to go straight home but had suggested that maybe the police officer could go via the local fish and chip shop.

Claire was restless, waiting for Tom to return. She was hoping that Vicky might confess all and then this case would be over. Peter watched her pacing up and down in Jake's office. "Shall we get a cuppa?" he asked her.

"Yes, good idea. Do you think Vicky could have done this to her neighbour?"

"No, not if I'm being honest. My gut feeling is there's more to this than someone just losing the plot," Peter replied.

"Yeah, maybe. I'll get the teas," Claire said. As she left the room she turned to Peter. "It just doesn't make sense. There's just no motive for killing that old lady."

"No, but someone, somewhere had one."

Jake was relieved to be away from Vicky's clutches. She might just as well have sat on his knee for all her lack of subtlety and even Tom had noticed how uncomfortable Vicky made the DI. "Wasn't sure you were going to get out of there alive," he joked.

Rolling his eyes Jake said, "Me neither. Let's get back to the station; see if there's any news on our murder weapon."

In the staff canteen, Peter and Claire had finished their cups of tea when Jake and Tom entered. Claire jumped to attention but Jake gestured for her to sit back down and Tom went to fetch a mug of tea for himself and Jake. The others had declined his offer of refills.

"How did it go at Vicky's?" Claire asked impatiently.

"Not much to be honest," Jake said, looking straight ahead. "Sticking to her story, word for word. The only good thing is the meat tenderiser isn't hers. Or so she says."

"So, you have your murder weapon?" Peter said.

"I hope so. We seriously need a break with this case, but I don't think they'll find anything on it; forensically I mean."

"At least it's not been through the dishwasher, so you never know." Claire said, trying to be positive.

There was nothing else to say. They all looked into space in a silence disturbed only by the vibration of Peter's phone. "It's Dee." He realised he'd several missed calls from her. "I'll leave you all to it and head back."

"Can we go to the café?" Dee asked as she unlocked the office door to let Peter in. It wasn't really a question, more a statement and Peter realised he didn't have a choice. Dee was already pushing past him with her coat on.

"Okay, what's the rush?"

"I really need a coffee and some cake and I've something to show you. Come on."

Peter locked up and followed her. His quiet life of playing Candy Crush and looking for the odd lost dog now and again had really changed since Dee had entered his life. He smiled. He wouldn't have it any other way.

Alison although still a little jumpy felt much calmer. She had spent most of the day wondering if Albert was the murderer and how lucky she had been that they got on so well. She had given Albert no reason to smack her over the head and kill her and when she had phoned Jim to tell him all about it, he was under the bonnet of a car and had burst out laughing, saying that he'd never heard such rubbish in his entire life. Now she was pleased to see Peter and Dee entering her café.

"Usual?" Alison asked already placing two cups ready on saucers.

"Had quite a lot of tea today," Peter said. "I think I'll try one of those lattes that Dee has."

Alison nodded "Anything to eat?"

"I'm starved," Dee said "Can I have a sandwich please; ham salad."

"Make that two please, Alison."

Alison went into the back to start making the sandwiches while they settled themselves at the table in the window that had become Dee's favourite place to sit.

"How did it go? Is Albert our killer?" Dee asked, smiling.

"Of course not, but I do think we've found the murder weapon, or at least there's a fair chance it might be." Peter lowered his voice as a couple of ladies who'd been seated and chatting at the table behind them passed by on their way out and a customer with a newspaper moved over to sit at the now-empty table.

"How long does it usually take for forensics to see if there's any evidence on a murder weapon?" Dee asked a little too loudly for Peter's comfort and he brought his finger to his lips to tell Dee to be quiet.

"Just off to the loo," he stated, rising from his chair.

Dee watched Peter make his way between the tables and enter the loo, nodding to Alison en route. She was walking over with their drinks in her hands when Peter made his exit from the loo. To her surprise, he pushed past her and grabbed the newspaper from the customer at the table behind Dee's, eliciting a high-pitched shriek.

"What the hell!"

"Ruth, really, you've got to be kidding me!"

"Get stuffed, Peter. Got to get my info somehow." Ruth slammed a manicured hand down on the table causing her drink to wobble. "Jake won't take my calls and you and little Missy here seem to be pretty useless."

"No, I'm not! "Dee too was now facing Ruth.

Alison put Dee and Peter's lattes down on their table and said to Ruth, "Think you've finished your tea."

"I know when I'm not wanted," Ruth said haughtily, rising to her feet. Her departure was a dramatic performance in itself. She made her way towards the door flicking her hair and smiling at Peter, and as she grabbed the doorknob, she laughed. "Found the murder weapon have you? Thanks, Peter."

Jake was in his office mulling over the day's events. He needed the phone to ring. He needed the lab to call. Tom and Claire were typing up reports in the office opposite his. Both had their doors open and he could hear jovial banter. He missed that now he was a DI. He recalled back in his early days as a DC how he, Cami and Peter had had the same light-hearted relationship. 'Nothing stays the same.'

"Phone - line four." Tom was at the door. "Sir, line four."

Jake was brought back to reality to see the phone line flashing as Claire pushed past Tom and took the chair in the corner forcing Tom to stand.

"Shut the door then, Tom," Jake ordered as he pressed the flashing light and speaker button.

"Sorry Jake, it's clean," declared the voice on the other end. "However, it's a match for the impact wound; same shape and size. I'll send the report through."

"That's good enough for me. Thanks a lot for rushing it through." He ended the call. They all stared at the phone. It wasn't going to give them any further information.

Claire broke the silence. "How lucky was that? We'd never have found the murder weapon if Dee hadn't gone round to Albert's."

"No, probably not." Jake sat back in his chair folding his arms. "Probably not."

"What a witch." Dee meant Ruth.

Alison had asked the few customers she had left if they could finish up and leave as she was going to close early. All had agreed and as Alison had made Peter aware, his little spat with Ruth would be all round the village by teatime. "She's not nice, Peter. Never seen her in here before," said Alison.

"It's Ruth from the paper. She gets flipping everywhere."

"Is that who wrote about me?" Dee asked.

Peter nodded. "We might be in the shit with Jake if she prints that."

"Prints what? She doesn't know anything about the murder weapon."

"What Ruth doesn't know Ruth makes up!" Peter said, rolling his eyes.

"Let's change the topic. Are you allowed to tell me about Albert?" Alison asked Peter. He nodded and went on to explain what had happened at Albert's and how Tom and Jake had gone on to interview Vicky the next-door neighbour.

"Well, I have something to show you both," Dee said "Need to know what you make of this." She pulled the camera out from her bag and placed it on the table next to their plates.

"That's Mary's," Peter said. "I bought it for her birthday last year. Wonder why she didn't take it with her when she left?"

"Never mind that, look at this." Dee showed them the picture of Margo and Sir Henry chatting. "What do you think that's all about?"

"What else is on there?" Peter enquired.

"Just some dogs and pictures of Mary's Daughter and Granddaughter and of Gaitley Manor."

"Let's have a look," said Peter grabbing the camera. He went through the photographs one at a time.

"So?" Dee asked. "What do you think?"

"I think we need to get back to the office and phone Mary." Peter grabbed his coat and took a last slurp of tea..

"Why?"

"You see this?" Peter showed Dee and Alison the picture of the blonde lady and the young girl. "That's not Mary's Daughter or her Granddaughter."

"How do you know that?" Alison asked.

Peter was already at the door.

"Mary has two Grandsons!"

Chapter Fourteen

Back at the office Peter came up with a better idea. "Rather than phoning Mary, I think we should go see her."

"How exciting; a trip away. Where's she moved to?" Dee asked hoping it was Cornwall or Devon

"Just down to the coast, about three hours from here. A place called Shell Bay."

"Never heard of it," Dee said trying not to sound too disappointed. "Shall we phone first to see if she's free."

"Yep," Peter said rapidly writing down names and addresses from the rolodex on his desk. "I'll give her a call later on tonight. Shall we call it a day?"

"Can do. Edward's away from tomorrow till Saturday."

"Hm Yes," Peter acknowledged her but he never looked up.

"Heading off then."

"Be careful. Keep your mobile in your hand, Dee. Promise?"

"Promise," Dee said as she closed the door behind her.

Peter waited to be sure she was gone before he punched Mary's number in his phone. No response.

He'd keep trying. 'She's probably out walking Jasper.'

Jake, too, had decided to call it an early night. They had a specialist on paintings arriving in the morning to look at the ones that hung in Margo's house. He overheard Tom and Claire arranging to meet at the cinema and tried desperately to remember the last film he'd watched but couldn't.

"See you tomorrow, Sir," Tom said as he and Claire left arguing about how much a box of popcorn was going to cost them.

"Bye" Jake shouted after them.

They reminded him of himself and Cami at their age. Then the sudden feeling of helplessness came over him. Pulling himself together he decided to treat himself to a Chinese and a glass of red. After all they had found the murder weapon … or Dee had.

Peter was not getting any response from Mary's phone. Maybe she had changed her number. He tried to see if he had Mary's daughter's details anywhere but for the life of him, he could not remember her married name.

Edward was chatting away to Mr Wang in the Chinese loudly enough for anyone else in the restaurant who could be bothered to listen to how important the next couple of days were for the him and his company. Mr Wang nodded and smiled in all the right places but was fidgeting from one foot to the other.

'Jake looked up from his phone surprised to see that the man taking up Mr Wang's time and boring everyone else was none other than Dee's boyfriend. He made his way over. "Edward, isn't it?"

Mr Wang thanked Jake and made his escape.

"Yes, and you are?"

"DI Jake Jones," and he held his hand out to shake Edward's.

"Yes, yes. You're helping Dee and that chap she works for." Edward clicked his fingers, hoping the name would come to him.

"Peter," Jake said.

"Yes, that's it, Peter. What a mess Dee's got herself into. It's all so embarrassing, I must say." He took Jake's hand. 'Weak handshake,' was Jake's immediate thought.

"Well, I'd say more a case of wrong place, wrong time," Jake said calmly but his hackles were up. Just then Mrs Wang arrived with Edward's order and Jake watched him get into the sportscar parked next to his own VW Golf. 'Hit my car and I'll knock your head off.' He checked himself. He couldn't believe how much he had let Edward's words wind him up.

Mrs Wang tapped Jake on his arm. "Here you are; extra prawn toast for you from Mr Wang," she said. Jake acknowledged the kindness with a nod of his head to Mr Wang who was standing at the back of the restaurant. He felt they had a mutual understanding that Dee's boyfriend was nothing more than a jumped-up waste of space.

The next morning, Dee was looking forward to the little planned adventure. She felt a little nervous about meeting Mary who she desperately hoped would like her. She had decided to tie her hair up and make an effort with some makeup when her mobile rang.

It was Peter. "Pop some overnight things in a bag. Might not need them but you never know."

"Oh okay. Edward's away till Saturday so it's no problem if we need to stay over," her growing excitement spilling over into her voice.

"It's only a just in case. Not planning on it. On my way to your's in ten."

Dee thought about texting Edward to tell him, but then thought better of it. 'It's not a definite after all; only a maybe.'

Peter had an uneasy feeling, Mary hadn't answered her phone or retuned any of his calls. He didn't know why but, like Jake, he could feel the itch. With Mary's postcode in his satnav, he headed off to pick up Dee. The sooner they were in Shell Bay the better.

Alison had opened up as usual. A packet of crisps lay in the middle of the floor behind the counter. "Good morning to you too," she said happily. Finding a packet on the floor in the same place most mornings gave her comfort that someone, whether a former owner or regular customer was still there watching over her and the café. She went over to the picture of her and her mum that she kept by the side of the till.

She kissed the tips of her fingers and touched her mum's face. She did miss her. She made a mental note to call her in Spain for a catch up.

Suddenly the door slammed open and Albert barged in bumping into Alison.

"Hey!" she shouted out.

Albert caught her by her arm before she fell. "Sorry, sorry." He was clearly out of breath.

"You, okay?".

"Oh Alison, I need my usual. I was at the police station most of the day yesterday."

Alison didn't want to let on that she knew all about that but thought she might do a bit of digging herself. What if she could find out something from Albert that Peter and Dee hadn't.

"I wondered where you'd got to yesterday; thought you might be ill," Alison paused. "Police station? Whatever for? Let me get your tea and you can tell me all about it."

"Aye lass," Albert said, taking his coat and scarf off.

Jake hadn't slept well. The extra prawn toast had laid heavy on his stomach and he'd had one glass of wine more than he should have. He'd spent most of the night looking through the case file. With the file neatly settled on the passenger seat of his car, he decided to go into Margo's early before the others arrived.

Despite the garden needing attention now that Margo was gone the cottage was in good order. Jake had never owned his own house, only rented which his parents thought was a big waste of money. As far as they were concerned Jake should be spending his rent money on a mortgage.

As he looked around the cosy lounge he felt no sadness, just a feeling of warmth. It needed a clean now that forensics had finished and looking out of the patio into the garden the rain had washed away the blood stains. He felt like an intruder and was just about to shout out that if Margo was listening was it alright for him to be there. He was relieved he hadn't as just at that moment Tom and Claire arrived.

"You know I like this cottage," Claire said "It's just so homely."

"Yep," Jake agreed. "It does have something"

"I prefer Albert's. I like open plan," Tom offered.

"Uh no." Claire pulled a face. "This is how it's meant to be; warm, welcoming and cosy."

Jake agreed with Claire and he was about to enquire how good the film was when a man brightly dressed in a pea-green coat knocked on the door and walked in without being invited.

"Hello all; Charles Pond," the man declared, beaming at them and Jake couldn't help but smirk.

Claire was the first to speak "Welcome, Mr Pond. This is D.I. Jones. Thank you for coming."

Mr Pond shook Jake's extended hand and began to gush about the painting over the fireplace. The three of them swapped glances as Mr Pond asked if the painting could be taken down from the wall for a closer look. Jake even began to wonder if Peter was right and this had been an attempted robbery gone wrong.

Alison had decided to put the *Back in an hour* sign up on the door. Albert seemed ruffled and wanted to talk. As she sat down next to him with a latte she felt for her phone. 'You never know and better to be safe than sorry.'

"You had the murder weapon all the time?" she asked trying her best to look surprised.

"Well, I don't know if it actually is, but they took it away, they did. Anyway I had to give a statement at the police station. I think they think I done it."

"Killed Margo? Oh, Albert, that's silly. Why would you do that?"

Albert went on to explain about Annie, it was nearly word for word as Dee had told her.

"Look, Albert, if Annie and Margo were friends why would Margo go around saying things about her?"

"Always a gossiper that one; muttering things under her breath." Albert took a sip of his tea. "She said that if my Annie had stolen from them, she'd stolen from her."

"Stolen from her? From Margo? What's that all about?" Alison looked confused.

"Don't ask me. My Annie was really upset after Margo had said that to her. My Annie told her she wasn't making sense. What did anything at Gaitley Manor have to do with her? She'd left years ago and Annie most certainly hadn't stolen anything from Margo, I can assure you of that!" Albert's voice was strong and his tone adamant. "Telling you, lassie, Margo was bonkers. Didn't know what she was saying half the time."

They sat in silence for a little as Albert ate his toast until Alison decided it was the right time to ask if Albert knew of any connection between Margo and Sir Henry.

Patting his mouth with his napkin Albert said, "Margo and her sister both worked there, but everyone knows that. If anything, I don't think Margo and Sir Henry liked each other. My Annie said they argued a lot after her sister left. She'd gone to work at some other stables and Sir Henry didn't like it." Albert put his napkin back on his lap. "I saw Sir Henry call at Margo's a while ago though."

"Really," Alison was genuinely surprised "Wonder why?"

"Your guess is as good as mine," Albert said.

Peter was tired and frustrated from the drive. He'd had to listen to Dee telling him all the details of her mum going to live in Spain and how she had then moved in with her gran. As interesting as Dee could be, he actually wanted some peace and quiet to think. That itch just wouldn't go away. "Got to be close now. Must be around here somewhere," The satnav was showing the flag on the screen telling them they had arrived at their destination. Peter parked up. "Don't understand. It says we're here but we aren't." Peter was tapping the satnav hoping it would spring into action. It didn't.

"Shall we get out and have a walk round. Need to stretch my legs anyway: long drive that," Dee said

Peter agreed and they left the car and crossed over to the houses on the other side. It was a tidy street; seagulls could be heard above and the air did smell of the sea.

"Feels like Scarborough. Right then straight ahead according to this." Dee held her phone up. "Two minutes walking."

Peter followed Dee calling out that he'd never been to Scarborough.

Dee turned left at the top of the street into a little cul-de-sac of seven houses.

Peter's heart sank. All that way and she was out. "Her cars not here," he said.

"Might be parked in the garage."

Peter nodded as Dee stormed ahead to stop dead at a garden gate. "Defo this one?"

"Sure is."

Dee was already through the wrought iron gate and knocking at the door. There was no reply. She glanced behind her to find Peter had taken his notepad out and was looking for Mary's daughter's address that he'd written down once he remembered her married name.

"Think we'll try Angela," Peter said walking away.

"Is that her daughter?"

She got no reply. Peter was practically running back to his car.

"Are you sure you're not mistaken?" Jake asked Mr Pond.

"Absolutely not, dear man. These are definitely not fakes or even good copies. I believe this is the real thing and these two - small but beautiful - as well." Mr Pond was pointing at the two little pictures of the horses.

"Dare I ask for a value?"

"Can't give you an exact value, but in my opinion, we're looking at several hundred thousand pounds at auction." Mr Pond looked very pleased with himself.

Claire let out a gasp and Tom took a step back from the paintings.

Jake collected himself. His pulse was racing, "Can you have a look around the rest of the house please, Mr Pond. We're looking for anything of real value."

"It would be my pleasure."

Jake nodded to Tom to follow Mr Pond.

"Are you thinking attempted robbery, Sir?" Claire asked.

"Looks that way." Jake shook his head.

"What's wrong, Sir?" Claire asked.

"Didn't think Margo would have that sort of money tied up in paintings." Jake was still knocked for six by Mr Pond's valuation.

"Inherited maybe?"

"Think we need to do a little more digging into Margo's past." Jake declared.

Mr Pond returned with Tom and said that although there were some nice pieces of pottery, trinkets and photo frames there was nothing as valuable as the paintings. "However, I would be happy to take any of the items including the paintings to auction if the family would like to sell them."

Jake thanked him and showed him out while Tom rehung the paintings under Claire's direction.

"Better double-check these doors are locked. Think I'm going to put a constable outside here for the next few days just in case it was a robbery and they come back." Jake said.

"Not sure we can trust that Mr Pond either," Claire said. "He might have connections."

Tom and Jake agreed and Tom radioed through for assistance.

Albert had left *Coffee Creams*. He felt better after talking to Alison. As he crossed the park, he recognised Jake's car with a police vehicle parked behind it and he could see them coming out of Margo's house chatting and locking the door. It was an instantaneous decision to hide behind the nearest tree. The last thing he wanted to do was to speak to the police again.

Peter knocked on the blue door of Angela's house. They hadn't needed to drive as it turned out Angela lived literally around the corner in the next cul-de-sac. As they waited; they could hear movement and a moment later the door was opened by a surprised-looking woman.

"Peter? How? Why? Come in. Oh hello," Angela greeted Dee as she followed Peter over the threshold.

Pleasantries were exchanged and Angela asked them to sit down and said she would fetch some tea. Looking around, Peter spotted a picture of Mary and her grandsons which brought a smile to his face.

Dee followed Peter's eyes and went over to the picture. "Mary?" she asked.

Peter nodded and was just about to say something more when Angela returned. They sat back down as Angela handed out steaming mugs of tea.

"Thought we'd pay Mary a little visit. I haven't spoken to her in a while. Is she out?" Peter took a sip of tea trying to explain. "I tried ringing last night. Hope you don't mind us knocking. We thought she might be here."

"No not at all. I'm sorry Peter this is all my fault." Tears began to fall. I should have rung you but the last few weeks have been a bit of a blur.

"Take your time," Peter said softly.

Dee saw a box of tissues on top of the sideboard. She passed them to Angela who took a wad out and wiped away her tears. The room had fallen silent, and Angela looked directly into Peter's eyes to announce, "Mum's dead."

Chapter Fifteen

"Dead!" Peter exclaimed it so loudly that it made Dee jump.

Angela nodded and grabbed another tissue from the box nestled in her lap. Dee could see Peter starting to well up. She decided she would go and make a fresh pot of tea and give them both some space. She watched as Peter moved over to Angela and hugged her. They were both crying now, Angela trying to say something but so engulfed by her grief that the words wouldn't come out. Dee could feel her own tears starting to form but managed to fight them back.

Dee collected their used mugs. Angela managed a *thank you*, but Peter sat with his head in his hands not making any eye contact at all. She retreated to the kitchen and poured fresh hot tea into the rinsed-out mugs. She decided a sugar in each mug would no harm. Back in the living room she found Peter by the fireplace holding the picture of Mary they'd been looking at earlier. He replaced it as Dee passed him his cup of tea and thanking her with a half-smile, he looked away.

"I'll go get a breath of fresh air," Dee announced popping the two remaining mugs on the side table.

"No love, you're alright. Please stay," Angela said, patting the sofa where Peter had sat.

Dee picked up her tea and sat down holding her mug to her chest. Angela was visibly shaking so Dee asked her gently, "Would you like me to pass you your tea?"

"I'm alright. I'll get it in a minute. Sorry, it's all been a shock to be honest."

"Boys at school? "Peter enquired.

"Yes, they're just dealing with all this, coping very well if I'm honest or they seem to be on the outside. We're all devasted, Peter; we really are." Angela was now reaching for her tea. The mug shook a little in her hand as she lifted it. "It was just so out of the blue."

Dee wanted to ask a million questions but for once thought it was better to keep quiet.

Peter paced up and down but made no eye contact with herself or Angela. Keeping his head down he asked, "When did this happen?"

"Nearly three weeks ago now I think. Who knows? All the days have rolled into one. Yes; just coming up for three weeks."

"At home?"

"No, wish it had of been. It was an accident you see. That's why it's been such a shock."

Dee couldn't contain herself. "Accident?"

Peter glared at her.

Angela popped her tea back on the side table. "Yes, but they didn't believe me. The police, Peter, they just wouldn't listen to me. Jasper's gone too you know."

Angela was starting to shake again. Dee went to hold her hand.

"What do you mean; they won't listen? Won't listen to what?" Peter seemed angry.

"I need to start at the beginning. You need to help me, Peter. I feel awful for not ringing you. They haven't released mum's body yet. They're waiting for the coroner's report. Can't even book a funeral. It's just wrong, all wrong." Angela started to cry again.

"Tell you what," Dee said. "Are you free later on. We could come back when your husband's home. Then you can tell us all about it together."

"Yes, that's a good idea. The boys are out at football practice tonight, and another mum is bringing them home. That should give us a good couple of hours. Mick will be back about half four. Is that okay?"

"Of course. I'm so sorry to hear about your mum."

Peter was pleased that Dee had taken charge of the situation. The news of Mary's death had shocked and upset him to the core. They both hugged Angela at the door and walked back in silence to the car.

"You drive." Peter threw her the keys.

"I'm not insured," Dee protested.

"You are as of four days ago. Didn't I tell you?"

Dee decided not to answer but quietly got in the car. As they had made their way back to the car Dee had seen a sign for the beach. Sea air and a walk on the beach would do him good. She started the car.

A few minutes later, Dee kicked Peter out of the car and told him to have some time to himself. She watched him from the seafront as he walked along the water's edge. He cut a lonely figure. Not a word had passed between them on the way to the beach. Dee had not dared to even look at him. Her tummy rumbled and she looked around to see if there was a café nearby. Her eyes fell on a fish and chip shop in the distance so, leaving Peter on the beach with his thoughts, she headed off to buy them lunch.

Peter felt sick, sick to his stomach. He'd loved Mary. Mary had worked for him from the beginning. He remembered how she had walked into his office bold as brass asking if he needed any help. Without any hesitation she had looked around and noticed paperwork and bills scattered on the desk opposite his. He laughed to himself as he heard her voice saying, "This will be my desk then." Despite him saying he had no cases as yet, nor a single client and couldn't pay her, Mary had shrugged her shoulders and said she wasn't doing it for the money. She'd sat down behind the desk and got straight to work. She had believed in him when so many others didn't.

Dee had returned to find Peter had almost walked to the other end of the beach. Grabbing her phone she called him. The figure stopped and pulled his mobile out of a pocket to answer it.

"Lunch," Dee shouted into her phone and held the bag containing the two portions of fish and chips in the air for him to see. "Hurry or they'll get cold."

Peter hadn't realised how far he had walked and by the time he reached Dee she was nearly halfway though hers.

"Ta," he said quietly as he opened his portion. "Ta."

"It's okay. Do you good. They're 'bloody lovely' as my gran would say."

Peter nodded as he ate a plastic forkful of chips. "That they are. Fish and chips are always better eaten out of the wrapper outside."

Dee smiled in agreement. That was enough talking for now. They ate the rest of their lunch in peace watching the waves roll in.

Eventually, it was Peter who broke the silence. "Cold?" he asked Dee.

"Yep, definitely getting chilly."

"Let's go find somewhere for a hot cuppa."

Dee didn't need asking twice. She had noticed a little café two doors down from the fish and chip shop. It looked like a plastic tablecloth sort of place but she felt sure it would do a good strong brew which was what they both needed. "Just down there," she pointed.

Peter let her take the lead and followed her. He still couldn't believe Mary was gone.

The café was much nicer on the inside if nowhere near as welcoming as *Coffee Creams*. Peter went to sit down and Dee ordered for them both. There were a couple of cakes and brownies on offer but she felt full from the fish and chips and decided that they could have a cake with the second round of drinks if Peter felt up to it.

"What's the time?" he asked her.

"Just after two thirty."

Peter nodded; he couldn't muster up enough enthusiasm to check his own watch.

Dee poured and asked Peter if he felt he could tell her about Mary.

He looked out of the window. The sky was turning grey and he fought back a tear. "Going to rain," he said.

Dee nodded, moving a mug of tea closer to Peter.

They both looked out for a while in silence. Then Peter said, "Mary was a good person, Dee. She saw the best in everybody." he paused and took a deep breath. "She was with me from the start. The very same week I opened the office, she waltzed in sat at your desk and started sorting out all the paperwork. She wanted to do something interesting and I could pay her after my first big case."

"Did you get a big case then?"

"We had to find a missing girl who had run away."

"Did you find her?"

"Yes, we did. The young thing was on her way home anyway. It turned out living at her boyfriend's squat wasn't all it was cracked up to be." Peter paused and took a sip of his tea. "Then we had thefts, missing dogs and cats but nothing to write home about like a murder."

Dee interrupted him. "Sorry about this. I've been thinking, Peter. We're not getting paid for this case and I can't pay you for helping me."

Peter placed his mug on the sticky tablecloth and let out a belly laugh. It was so loud a couple of people turned to stare.

"It's not funny. I really can't pay you!" She felt he was laughing at her.

"Of course you can't. It's not about that. It's a long time since I've had a proper murder case to deal with. Besides I want to clear your name. We all know you didn't do it although I'm sure there's still a few in the village who think you did."

"Are there? Peter, that's not funny." Dee's bottom lip started to tremble.

"No there aren't" He reached across to tap her hand "Don't be silly. I'm only winding you up."

Dee hit his hand away and told him to sod off under her breath. Peter thought she looked great when she was angry with her cheeks a beautiful shade of pink.

"So, I haven't asked before but why did you set up as a private detective?"

"Bit of a story there."

"Well, I'm all ears, so go on. I get the feeling something happened," Dee urged.

"That it did. Easier to work on my own. Things happen when you're in the force, bad things, Dee. Saw too much, so now I prefer to work on my own."

"Well, you're not on your own. You've got me and you had Mary."

"True but Mary didn't get involved in cases or anything. Don't get me wrong, she had the nose for it and she was great at reporting but you're quite different to her. For one thing Mary would never get herself in the trouble you do."

"I didn't ask for it!" Dee could feel herself getting angry. "Not my fault Margo got herself murdered."

Peter used his hands to gesture for her to be quiet. Dee looked around and noticed other customers were now staring at her. Dee flicked her ponytail at them and turned to look out of the window. "So, what did happen then? Nice try on avoiding the subject."

"I suppose you'll find out eventually. Myself, Jake and another DC called Cami were called to a shop break-in, Jake and Cami were both DCs back then. I was the DI. I wouldn't normally get involved in a break-in but we were on our way back to the station when the call came in. We were the closest so I ordered Jake to turn the car round and head back to Amberleigh and it wasn't a shop break-in at all. It was a bank robbery. Heaven only knows who rang it in, but as we arrived it was still in progress. I ordered Jake to stay at the front blocking the door and call for back-up. I had Cami go round the back." Peter paused, looking down at his hands.

"I caught and arrested one of the men but the other one ran out through the back of the bank. He had a baseball bat. We found Cami unconscious with a serious head injury." Peter shook his head from side to side "Honestly that was the day I decided that I would only ever work alone and I'd never again put a colleague in danger like that…never again.."

"But it wasn't your fault. How were you supposed to know that was going to happen?"

"No, I didn't but in hindsight, I should have sent Jake round the back. He was stronger and bigger than Cami. She wouldn't have been able to stop or fight off the bastard but Jake might have stood more of a chance."

"Where's Cami now?"

"She died. They had to turn her life support off." Peter struggled to get the words out.

"That's awful. I'm so sorry. Were she and Jake good friends?"

"Yes they were. Tom and Claire remind me a little of Jake and Cami; he was the one that found her."

Peter rose and said he was off to the loo. He asked Dee if she wanted anything else on his way back.

"Another coffee, maybe." She was still full from the fish and chips . She was sitting motionless, taking in the enormity of what Peter had just told her.

With two coffees in hand, Peter made her jump as he returned to the table. "Miles away there," he said.

"Just a bit, I was thinking how hard it must have been for you both."

"Well to finish, I left. Caused a bit of a stir but it was the right thing for me to do and Jake asked for a transfer - went to North Yorkshire, Pickering way I think; don't quote me on that. I always kept an eye out for him. Knew he was going to make a good detective someday."

"You knew he was coming back to Gamblewood then?"

"I still have one or two friends at the police station, those who don't blame me for Cami's death - most did." Peter looked into the depths of his coffee. "I was pleased to hear Jake was coming back. The station needs someone of his calibre."

Dee caught her watch on the table edge as she put her coffee down forcing her to check the time. "Peter it's gone four!"

"Really? Come on let's go. I don't want to be late for Angela." Peter was already up out of his seat.

Angela opened the door; she looked better now than when they had left her. They both felt awful about the distress they had caused her and were apologising as she ushered them into the living room. Winter was definitely upon them. It was dark now at four-thirty and much to Dee's delight Angela had lit the open fire and its warmth and glow pleased her.

Angela asked them to sit down and Mick came to join them; a large man, quite burly with brown hair and a beard but he had kind eyes. "Beer, wine or a cuppa?" he asked.

"Sod it I'm having a wine; it's been a long day," Angela declared.

"Too right, love. Dee isn't it? Are you joining Angela?"

Dee didn't want to but it would feel awful if she didn't. "Just a small one. We've quite a long drive back tonight."

"Oh, are you not staying?" Angela asked.

"No," Peter . "I'll just have a beer, please."

"Right, you are," Mick said and disappeared into the kitchen. Angela said she wanted to wait for him before she told them what had happened.

Peter had his notebook out. "Here you are," he said to Dee, passing it to her. "Can you make notes, please."

Dee felt like a proper detective. She knew she wasn't and never would be but felt a sense of reassurance that Peter trusted her. "Of course I can."

Mick came back carrying the drinks. He had been over-generous with the pouring and his idea of a small one was not Dee's. She made a mental note to sip it slowly.

Peter said, "Please start at the very beginning. No detail too small. Tell me as much as you remember."

Angela began. "It was the twenty-ninth of September. Like I said three weeks ago."

Peter nodded to Dee. She took this to mean she should write it down.

"We got a knock at the door and can you imagine how shocked we were to find two police officers on the doorstep? They apologised for disturbing us and asked if it was alright for them to come in." Angela took a momentary breath. "Mick was here. We were just about to have tea."

"One police officer asked if it was alright if she sat with the boys in the kitchen while we talked to the other one," Mick interrupted.

"Did they give you their names?"

"Hmm…we've a card somewhere,. I can fetch it. Shall I get it?" Angela asked.

"I'll go," Mick said. "You carry on."

"I'll just wait for you."

"Theres no rush. We've plenty of time," Dee soothed.

Mick returned and gave the card to Peter who passed it to Dee. "Take a photo of that, please."

Dee did as she was told and handed the card back to Mick. He placed it on the side table and sat back down next to Angela. As he patted Angela's knee she began again. "It turns out they think that mum just missed taking the bend. They aren't sure if it was the low sun that dazzled her. They even said that Jasper might have jumped up onto her lap causing her to go off."

"Off what?" Dee asked without thinking.

"Off the road. It's a steep drop. They had no chance according to the police."

"Did the car catch fire?" Peter asked.

Dee was horrified. 'What sort of a question's that?'

"No," Mick replied.

Angela had started to well up. "Horrible isn't it. We were so shocked but that's nothing compared to then what happened."

"Have a sip of wine, love," Mick said, calmly.

"I don't know how long - a few days - the police are at the door again asking if they can speak to me about mum. They said they had done a post-mortem. You see I asked for that. Mum was a good driver, and Jasper never jumped up. He always sat in the footwell of the passenger seat."

Peter nodded and Mick put his hand on her shoulder.

"I know it's awful but I had to know if she'd had a seizure of some kind, maybe a stroke or even a heart attack. She really was a good driver so I just needed to know for sure, you know for my own peace of mind."

Angela took a gulp of wine which gave Dee time to write the last bit down.

"I understand. To be honest I think they'd have done a post-mortem anyway as standard procedure under the circumstances," Peter said.

"This is why we need your help, Peter. I've said to Mick, I can't believe you're here; you must have had a sixth sense or something."

"Go on. What did they want to talk to you about?" Peter needed to speed things along.

"The toxicology report had come back saying mum had a large amount of something with a fancy name but they explained it meant sleeping tablets in her system." Angela looked horrified at what she was saying.

"Did Mary take sleeping tablets?"

"Yes sometimes, but only the herbal ones. I offered to take them to mum's to show them the box, but they said they didn't need to do that."

"Odd," Peter said.

"They just don't believe me. They said mum must have got her medication mixed up and taken too many, I told them that was a load of rubbish. My mum would never do that, I even explained that the blood pressure tablets she had been prescribed didn't resemble the brown herbal sleeping tablets in any shape or form - plus mum kept the sleeping tablets in her bedside cabinet and her blood pressure tablets in the kitchen drawer downstairs. There's no way mum got mixed up. I feel like they're trying to say she was confused, had dementia or something. Mum had nothing of the sort!" The frustration in Angela's voice was plain for everyone to hear.

"It's alright, love. Calm down. Take a sec." Mick said, encouraging her to have another sip of wine.

Peter looked anxious; Dee noticed him fidgeting. "Do you know what Mary did that day? Where she'd been in the car? Any plans she had?" He sounded very official all of a sudden.

"Yes, yes. I told the police everything. They just didn't seem interested."

"Are you okay to tell me?"

"Yes … Mum had walked along the beach to the far end with Jasper. Jasper loved playing on the beach. They went most days. It had sort of become part of mum's daily routine since moving here. You know she loved walking - swam three or four times a week too." Angela took a deep breath. "There's a café at the end called Dolly's. It's quaint. Mum loved it cos they let dogs in and she said they were ever so nice to Jasper; always gave him a bowl of water and they had dog treats on the side that you could help yourself to." Angela was speaking much more clearly now.

"We met Mary there once or twice on a weekend with the kids and sometimes you'd meet your mum there too for a natter, didn't you?" Mick said, patting Angela's knee again.

"That's the worst of it, I was supposed to meet mum for elevenses that day but I didn't. I got a phone call from the school that Finn wasn't feeling well and I had to go and collect him."

"Was he ill?" Peter asked.

Dee looked at Peter. 'What's he asking that for?' She rolled her eyes and Peter ignored her.

"He really was. Turned out Finn had tonsilitis, but if I'd met mum, I have a feeling it wouldn't have happened. I might have realised she wasn't herself. Oh I don't know it's just not right. Somethings not right." The tears were falling again.

"Can you do anything, Peter?" Mick asked.

"I'll make some enquiries tomorrow. See if I can find out a little more. Did Mary have any plans to meet anyone at all?"

"No, just me. I was going to drive there and then afterwards mum would have walked back along the beach with Jasper and then driven back home for the afternoon. She loves that *Doctors* programme so I know she would have wanted to be home for that."

"Has Mary made any friends since coming to live here?" Peter dug a little further.

"A couple at the walking group but she didn't mention that she was meeting any of them. Not that day anyway."

There was a polite knock at the door and two shivering boys covered in mud bounced in. Angela went to the door and could be heard thanking the mum who'd brought them back.

"I'm starving," both boys said at pretty much the same time.

"Okay boys, in the kitchen. We'll leave mum to it." Mick shook Peter's hand and then Dee's. "You'll have to excuse me. Duty calls," he said.

"We'd better get off anyway," Peter said. "I'll be in touch soon, I promise." He swapped mobile numbers with Angela as a prelude to a protracted farewell.

Eventually, Peter and Dee were sat back in the car with the heated seats on. "Ready for the long drive back?" Dee asked.

"We're not going anywhere tonight other than to a hotel, can you see if you can find one and book us in," Peter said handing Dee his credit card.

"Really, why what are you thinking?"

"Think about it, Dee. Mary's as fit as a fiddle, member of a walking group, swims several times a week suddenly gets confused takes too many sleeping tablets and ends up at the bottom of some ravine."

"I know … I don't think a ravine got mentioned."

Peter scowled at her.

"Yeah, I get it, it does sound strange when you put it like that but could it be that Mary went to bed late and the tablets hadn't fully worn off, then driving and the low sun, like the police said. There's probably a very simple explanation for what happened, awful as it is."

"You're forgetting why we came down here in the first place; the photograph, the pictures of Sir Henry and Margo chatting." Peter sounded as if he was at the end of his tether.

"Oh God! Yeah you're right I had. So, what are you saying?"

"I'm saying get that hotel booked; we're staying down here for another day. We have investigating to do."

"Okay, I'm starting to think you don't reckon it was an accident," Dee said starting to google hotels in Shell Bay.

Peter tapped the steering wheel. "Not sure, but two deaths six days apart, one a murder the other in suspicious circumstances. One hell of a coincidence if you ask me!"

Chapter 16

Jake had woken up tired and frustrated. He'd had another bad night's sleep and if that continued, he'd have to seek medical help. He poured himself a strong coffee and looked around his flat. It was okay for a single guy but his parents didn't like visiting. They said it felt cold and uninviting. Compared to Margo's cottage, they had a point.

It was early but he felt the need to get to the station sharpish. He wanted to get his head straight. He felt all over the place which for him was unusual. He was blaming the lack of sleep but deep down he knew it was the case. It was constantly on his mind.

He needed some answers today. He was starting to hear rumblings that the top brass wanted Margo's murder sorted and quick. Making a mental note in his head of what he wanted to achieve, he needed Claire to do some behind-the-scenes work on Margo quietly and discreetly and he'd decided he and Tom should head to Gaitley Manor. If he had to produce his badge or get a warrant he would if that's what it took to interview Sir Henry and Petra. He was in a foul mood. 'God help anyone who gets in my way today.'

"Did we sleep well?" The landlady of the B&B asked as she served them a full English breakfast.

"Yes, fine thank you," Dee answered, a little too brightly for Peter's liking.

"Liar," he whispered at her over the table.

"Ok, I didn't sleep well at all; flipping Edward." Dee poured brown sauce all over her plate which made Peter wince.

"Want some breakfast with that sauce?"

Dee pulled a face back at him.

"Go on then, what's the boyfriend done now?" Peter didn't want to ask but felt he had to show some form of interest.

"When we got here last night and I'd got myself tucked in, I phoned him to tell him where I was, and what we were doing. Not all the details obviously. He said I'd disturbed him at work but I'm sure I could hear noises in the background like he was in a bar and other people chatting."

"Maybe it was work. It wasn't that late by the time we'd eaten, and got settled in here. Sure he was just out having something to eat."

"I know, yeah but he just hung up on me," Dee said, scooping baked beans on to her fork.

"Dick!" Peter said under his breath.

"What was that?"

"Nothing. So, you've spent the night worrying about him?"

"Not exactly. At about two this morning my mobile goes and its Edward wanting to talk to me all about the presentation. He was tipsy and I had to listen to him go on and on about some amazing contract he's going to win for the company and what a wonderful job everyone thought he'd done. They find out today if they get it."

"Two in the morning. Why would he call you then? Did he apologise about hanging up on you?" Peter tried to look interested.

"No, he didn't even acknowledge that, thinking about it. To be fair I was too tired to ask why he'd done that."

"Dick!" Peter repeated, a little louder.

"What?"

"Sausages are really good, aren't they?" Peter said waving his laden fork at her. "Let's make a plan for today so we don't waste time."

Claire was finishing her morning run which took her past the local newsagents. The picture on the front on the papers still bundled up outside caught her eye and she stopped to go back for a closer look.

"Shit!" She tried the door of the newsagents but it was closed. Claire peered through the window to see if anyone was there but couldn't see anyone. She made the decision to take one of the papers from the bundle and leave the money on top. Luckily, she always carried a couple of pounds with her. She tucked the newspaper under her arm and started running again. Claire had no idea where she had mustered the energy from but found herself running flat out. She needed to get home, change and get to the police station as quickly as possible.

Jake was on his second cup of coffee. He'd checked his e-mails and found himself staring at the clock. He stood to look out of the window, and watched Tom's car pull into the car park followed by Claire's. She got out and went to sit in Tom's. 'Maybe there's more going on with them two than I thought.' He smiled, turned away from the window and went back to sit at his desk.

"Oh no," Tom sighed. He couldn't believe what he was reading. "Have you read this?"

"Yep," Claire nodded. "Not good is it? Jake's going to hit the wall when he sees that." They were staring at the picture on the front on the newspaper showing Dee going into Albert's house, below which was a smaller photograph of all three houses and Margos still had police incident tape visible around it.

"I think you should show him," Tom said

"No chance. You're senior to me. You never know; he might have seen it already."

Claire was biting her bottom lip. Tom had noticed this was something she did when she was nervous. "Okay, c'mon, we'd better get this over with. Something tells me the shit is going to hit the fan," he said. As they approached the police station walking quietly side by side he added in a low voice. "I hope he's in a good mood!"

Peter and Dee left the B&B and drove back to the beach. There was only one car park at the top end where they had parked yesterday. It offered free parking and he felt sure this was where Mary would have left her car.

"Look around, on the floor and in the bins," he ordered.

"What for? I've no idea what I'm supposed to be looking for."

"Anything odd, I don't really know myself" The wind had picked up and Peter had to shout to be heard.

"It's not going to be here weeks later is it? And I'm not going through any bins."

Peter rolled his eyes. It was a freezing October morning, and no one was around; no shops or cafes open as yet. He pulled out the blue protective gloves he had in his pocket and picked up a stick that a dog had probably dropped and started searching through the first bin. He'd given Dee similar gloves and reluctantly she pulled them on.

It was Dee who first found something. An earring. It was a little flower with a pink stone in the middle. She thought it looked like a child's earring. She showed it to Peter who a clear plastic bag from his pocket and gave it to her. Se popped the earring in and the search continued.

"Morning" Jake shouted at Tom and Claire as they passed his door heading for the locker room. The two subordinates exchanged a look as they returned the greeting. He didn't like it; he knew them well enough to know when something was wrong. He hoped they hadn't had a lover's tiff which was going to affect them working together. He popped his head out of his office and into the corridor. He could see them through the glass door at the end of the long corridor talking animatedly. It didn't look like they were arguing but something was amiss and he knew it.

Claire was the first back she jumped a little when she saw Jake's head popping out from behind his office door. "Cuppa, Sir?" she asked regaining her composure.

"Yes please. When you're both ready, can you come in here? Bring your teas with you."

Alison had said goodbye to Jim and was opening up the café. She was expecting an early delivery and wanted to give the fridges a good wipe down before it arrived. Paula waved to her and Alison felt she had time for a two-minute chat so she popped over the road. "How are you doing? You'll be getting ready for Christmas soon."

"Sure am. You too I bet. Hope you're going to make your famous mince pies?"

"Absolutely, might do something with a little twist this year. I found an old cookbook of my grandma's. It had a recipe for a mince pie muffin. Thought I'd give it a go."

"Ooh that sounds gorgeous. Alison, have you a minute to come into the shop. I want to show you something."

Alison followed her inside. The shop was pretty and smelt wonderful, and she noticed one of the arrangements and asked if she could buy it for the café.

Paula nodded, putting the local newspaper on the counter. "Yes, have a look at that while I get it down for you. You can pop back during the day to pay if it's easier."

Alison instantly recognised the girl in the photo on the cover. "Is this todays? "she asked.

"Yes, picked it up from the petrol station this morning, you know her don't you? She works for Peter I believe."

"Yes, she does. Her name's Dee. Paula, can I borrow this please. I want to read it properly. I'll bring it back later when I come in to pay for the flowers"

"Sure; let me know your thoughts on that and will you bring me one of your brownies too? Fancy a treat tonight. It's all that talk of mince pies." Paula giggled.

Alison left as Paula's phone began to ring and she began taking an order for a dozen red roses. With the newspaper in one hand and the flower arrangement in the other, Alison made her way across the road to *Coffee Creams*. The fridges could wait. She needed to sit down and read the article from start to finish before her delivery arrived. Her phone beeped with a text message from Jim. It read *Have you seen the Amberleigh Gazette?*

Jake's fist hit his desk with force startling Claire. Tom thought she was going to fall and grabbed her arm but Claire yanked it away from him.

"This just beggar's belief. She's gone way too far!" Jake shouted.

A PC walking past the open office door was stopped in his tracks by the anger in Jake's raised voice. He stood to listen, but Claire saw him and promptly closed the door in his face.

"Do you see what she's implying or is it just me?"

Claire answered. "Yes, Sir."

"The photo doesn't help much either," Tom added.

"That's it! I'm going to commit a bloody murder myself!" Jake came round his desk, grabbing the coat lying across the office chair. In his hurry he almost sent Tom flying.

"I'll come with you, Sir." Tom offered with Jake already halfway out the door.

"You'd better!!"

Tom practically had to run to keep up with Jake and out in the corridor Claire overheard the nosy PC say to a colleague, "No idea who he's going to see but I wouldn't want to be in their shoes."

Passing them, Claire thought 'Neither would I.'

Peter placed the bag with the earring on the back seat of his car. "What's the time?" He asked Dee.

"Just after nine."

"Right, come on. Mary was a keen walker. If we walk at a medium pace, let's see how long it takes to reach the far end of the beach."

Dee didn't say anything. She followed Peter as he headed down the steps and onto the beach. She was shivering and wished she'd brought a warmer coat with her. "Better be a cuppa at the end of this," she shouted at the back of Peter's head.

He turned and gave her the thumbs up. "Keep your eyes peeled."

"For what?" Dee was trying to catch him up.

"Like I said, I don't know. Anything odd I guess."

Dee shrugged and walked a little closer to the sea's edge. It wasn't worth trying to converse; the wind and the crashing of the waves were so loud. Continually scanning the beach looking for anything that was unusual. Dee found a pretty pebble and a delicate little shell that she had picked up and popped in her pocket as souvenirs of the trip. Peter was way ahead of her in the distance. She sped up in the hope that she could catch up.

Alison was having quite the morning. There seemed to be a lot of chatter going on and more people in the café than usual. Alison knew a few of the customers but others were new. She had welcomed them all the same and decided they were from out of town and just passing through. She was keeping her eyes on the door for Dee, Peter or Albert to arrive but she wasn't expecting the next arrival to be D.I. Jones followed by a red-faced Tom.

"Gentleman, how lovely to see you both. Please take a seat." Alison gestured to the most recently cleared table as the café chatter faltered and stilled. She noticed people shifting uncomfortably in their chairs.

"Any sign of Peter?" Jake asked.

"Uh-huh. Sit down and I'll bob over with some tea."

Tom did as she suggested but Jake stood surveying the room for a moment before shrugging and joining his sergeant.

"Albert's not here. Is that who you're looking for?" Tom asked.

"No. Jake leant forward. "If he knows what's best for him, he'll be at home locked in with the curtains closed."

"There's a lot of people in here today."

"I know; too many if you ask me," Jake replied.

Alison brought them a pot of tea and two cinnamon swirls. "Here you are. Take it you've seen the Gazette?"

"Busy?" Tom said, trying to change the topic.

"I know." Alison was waiting for Jake to mention the article but all he said was, "Any chance you know where Peter is?"

"I had a text to say they've gone to see Mary in Shell Bay and decided to stay overnight."

Tom had managed to calm Jake down during their short car journey but now he seemed more riled than ever. "What?"

"Are you alright?" Alison asked as heads turned to look at them.

Jake didn't answer her. He wiped his mouth with the serviette and stood up to leave but suddenly they were surrounded by customers firing questions about Margo's murder. Tom tried to move some of them out of the way so they could make their exit knowing that Jake was at boiling point; he didn't know if he was angrier about the article or the fact that Dee and Peter had gone away for the night.

Somehow they made it to the door, and Alison saw Tom mouthing, "Sorry" at her as Jake shouted from the door way, "No comment!!."

"Right fifteen, maybe twenty minutes." Peter wrote the timing down in his notebook.

Dee had finally caught him up. Although she was out of breath she managed to say, "You, were walking faster than Mary probably did and she might have played a bit with Jasper, throwing a ball for him."

"Yes, we'll take that into account, but for now I'm working on the principle that if Mary had taken those sleeping tablets late at night or even in the early hours of the morning - would they have had enough time to wear off or not?"

"Depends how much she took, doesn't it?"

Peter didn't bother to answer. He knew Dee had a valid point but didn't like to think that Mary could have made a mistake like that. Like Angela, Peter couldn't imagine Mary getting confused and although he hadn't said it - and fortunately Angela hadn't even seemed to think of it – it had crossed his mind that it was possible Mary had taken her own life but if so why?

Jake was still fuming and Tom was worried that this wasn't going to end well as he marched into the offices of the Amberleigh Gazette looking for blood with Tom trailing after him.

"We've come to speak to Ruth," Jake snapped at the girl behind the reception desk.

"Please," Tom said politely, showing his badge.

The receptionist looked flustered and picked up the phone. They both watched her as she spoke and then put her hand over the mouthpiece and said sheepishly, " She's on her way down."

Tom watched the young girl trying to look busy but she was failing miserably as Jake paced up and down the reception area. "Sir?"

"What?"

"Sir, take it easy won't you. We don't want trouble, do we?"

Jake ignored Tom. He was going to do exactly what he wanted to do.

Alison thought about texting Dee to tell her about the morning's events but decided against it. After mulling it over, she decided she didn't want to be the one to tell Dee about the article if they didn't already know. She sent a message to Jim instead. He texted back. *Least one good thing out of all this mess very good for business.* Although Alison agreed that her day's takings were going to be substantially higher than normal it was coming at a price for someone.

Ruth had taken a moment to prepare and was beaming at her visitors, newly applied lipstick in evidence. "Well, who'd have thought? Come in here."

They followed Ruth into a side room although Tom turned round to thank the receptionist and caught her with a finger in her mouth making a sick gesture. He followed Jake but decided to stand by the door and watch the fireworks from a safe distance.

"To what do I owe this pleasure, or shall I guess?"

"What the hell are you doing?" Jake moved to lean forward over the desk that stood between them.

"Me? Moi? What have I done?" Ruth said, placing one hand across her chest.

"Why didn't you call me before you went to print?"

"You've been avoiding me, D.I. Jones," Ruth said haughtily.

"With good reason! I'm on a murder case and your stupidity isn't helping."

Tom watched Ruth flinch. Any minute she was going to come out fighting.

"There's nothing stupid about my article. If you have a problem take it up with my editor."

"I have a problem with what it insinuates. Do you think claiming that the murder weapon was found at Albert's house helps him?"

"Not my problem. Factually it was."

Jake imagined himself wringing her neck but somehow kept it professional. "What are your thoughts about insinuating that Miss Firth went to Albert's house to hide the murder weapon or furthermore to kill him with it?"

Ruth tapped a long fingernail on the desk in front of her. Smirking, she said, "Who's to say she didn't. She was photographed going into his house. Can't prove it either way."

"You also inferred that Albert could have murdered his neighbour."

Ruth tilted her head back and put her hands on her hips. "Well, seriously, I feel like I'm doing your job for you. Who's to say he didn't? I think you're the stupid one." Ruth paused. "Especially when the murder weapon was found at his house!"

Jake pulled himself to his full height. "You need to be careful, with no evidence you're putting the lives of innocent people at risk and hindering my investigation."

"Are you threating me?" Ruth's eyes were slits of fury.

"Me? Moi? Of course, not. Wouldn't dream of it."

Tom had to look away. He was trying not to laugh out loud.

"I think we're done" Ruth couldn't stand being ridiculed.

"That we are."

Ruth barged past Tom to open the door and leave. The girl behind the reception desk was pretending to be busy, shifting sheets of paper about.

Jake and Tom were almost at the exit when Ruth called after them. "Next time I can be of assistance don't hesitate to call."

Jake stopped and turned to meet her gaze. "With the kind of assistance you're offering and the damage you've caused to innocent lives, I wouldn't wait by the phone."

Ruth stood with her hands on her hips looking as if she was about to start spitting feathers but Jake marched straight outside before she could come up with a suitably cutting retort.

Behind them, Tom could hear the receptionist sniggering and Ruth telling her to shut up. As they walked back to the car he could hold it in no longer. "She's a right piece of work that one. Bit of a tough nut to crack."

"Hm, that she is but I've a few choice names for her myself!"

Tom's mobile beeped.

"There's a disturbance at Albert's house, Sir. He's outside threating journalists with a sweeping brush."

Jake rolled his eyes. "And so it begins."

Dee was struggling to keep up with Peter. He was ascending the steps from the beach to what looked like a cliff top. "Flipping Eck; this is a bit of a climb," she shouted, using the rail to help pull herself up.

Peter didn't turn round but carried on. "Nearly there. Just think how fit Mary was if you're struggling at your age." The truth was he too was out of breath but wasn't going to admit it. He was going to take himself seriously in hand when they got back. He wouldn't pass any police fitness test right now. that was for sure.

"Very funny."

They climbed the rest of the steps in silence. At the top there was a small car park with Dolly's café to the left and another little shop to the right already closed for the winter which probably sold all the usual beach necessities like buckets and spades.

They entered Dolly's, Dee's cheeks a cheery pink from the wind. A lady welcomed them and showed them to a table while a young girl didn't look up from folding serviettes in the corner.

"You've braved the cold and the wind. Walked here, have you?"

"Yes, nothing better than a good brisk walk," Peter replied.

Dee picked up the menu from the table. She wasn't hungry as she'd had a good breakfast but felt she needed a hot chocolate.

"Make that two. Haven't had a hot chocolate in years," Peter said smiling.

"All the trimmings?"

They both nodded. Dee was rubbing her hands together "It's nice here," and then excused herself to go and use the toilet. No sooner had Dee left the table than Peter's mobile rang and she smiled to herself as she heard him say, "Hi Jake; how's it all going."

"What? You're not joking?" Peter sounded worried and the girl folding the napkins pricked up her ears. "I'll wring her neck."

The young girl hoped he wasn't referring to the woman who'd just gone into the toilet. She seemed nice although, 'A bit young for him,' She thought.

"Of course; yes. I'll do my best. I'll see if we can stay away another night. Is Albert okay?"

The girl wondered if she should warn the woman in the toilet. The phone call sounded sinister to her.

"Good; pleased he's okay. Yes, yes; leave it with me, Jake. Do you think I should tell her?"

The girl had finished with the napkins but the one-sided conversation had taken her interest, and she went over to the table next to Peter's to toy with the salt and pepper pots so she could still hear what was being said.

"No, I agree. Best of luck Jake. Keep me posted and I'll phone you later."

Dee returned to the table and the young girl moved away. "How's Jake?"

A look of something akin to panic came over Peter's face. "Yep, he's good. I swear you have bionic hearing. Get much of that did you?"

"No. Any news on the case?"

"Not really. He's going to Gaitley Manor this afternoon. Hopefully he'll find out a bit more there."

The lady brought over two tall mugs covered in squirty cream and marshmallows. "I'll have to eat that, never mind drink it," Dee giggled.

"You're not from round here?"

"No. Probably obvious. Northern girl, me. Lovely here though. I really like Shell Bay"

"Well, I'm Shell Bay born and bred," the lady announced proudly folding her arms under her ample bosom.

"You might be able to help us," Peter said.

"Me? What with?" The lady looked puzzled.

"We came to see Mary who used to work for me. Angela, her daughter, said she came here with Jasper, her dog. Do you remember her?"

"Of course I do. I'm very good at remembering a face. Mary - if I've got the right one - I think she moved here to be near her daughter. Is that the one?"

"Yes, we've just found out she died in a car accident."

The lady picked up on the hurt in Peter's voice and pulled a chair over to join them. "Such a lovely lady - tragic accident. It was only a few weeks ago you know? Don't think they've had the funeral yet. Do you know when it is? I'd like to go."

"No, but I'll make sure to tell Angela to let you know."

"Yes, thank you. That would be kind of you."

Dee had been considering whether she should ask but in the end felt she had to. "Did anything unusual happen that day? Angela said that the accident occurred after leaving here - Dolly's."

"No, love. I said as much to the police. Just a normal day. Mary ordered tea and a cherry scone, with jam and butter no cream. She didn't like cream." The lady paused. "I think Jasper liked my cherry scones as much as Mary did. She always shared it with him. It's so sad he died too in the accident, poor thing."

Peter was impressed and sat back in his chair letting Dee take the lead.

"So nothing out of the ordinary then?"

"No, sorry. Nothing at all. Just another day at Dolly's." The lady put her hand on Peter's shoulder as she rose from her seat. "I'm sorry for your loss. I can tell she meant a great deal to you," and she left them to finish their hot chocolate.

"Not much there then," Dee said.

"No, but you were great. I think we have a new private detective in our midst."

"Really, do you think so?"

They finished their drinks and asked the young girl if they could have the bill. They watched her go into the kitchen to fetch the lady who returned to take their money, once again passed her condolences on to Peter and then cheerily returned to her baking.

As they made their way to the door, the young girl tapped Dee on the shoulder. "Can I speak with you both?" She was almost whispering and kept looking in the direction of the kitchen. "It's not true."

Dee said, "Sorry, what's not true?"

"That nothing happened."

The girl was playing with her apron strings and Peter thought she looked scared. "Talk to Dee," he said. "I'll wait outside."

"Are you okay to tell me?" The girl kept looking over her shoulder.

"I can but Brenda said it was nothing and not to mention it again. She said I was being silly. Brenda says I have a great imagination." The girl looked sheepish as she spoke.

"Well let me be the judge of that. Go on."

The girl took a deep breath and spoke quickly. "A woman banged into Mary's table, sent her tea flying everywhere. Mary was so gracious about it. She didn't complain or anything. The woman offered to replace the tea and she did."

"Okay. Why did you think that was strange?"

"It didn't look like a genuine accident. It was like she banged into the table on purpose and this is the bit I thought was really odd. Your friend had gone to the ladies to sort herself out - some of her tea had gone on her trousers you see, but the woman didn't wait for her to come back she just put the cup of tea on Mary's table and left." The girl paused, waiting for Dee to say something.

"Yes, yes. That is odd. Can you remember what she looked like?"

"No not really. I'd just started my shift when it happened, like I said. The woman had a big coat on, sunglasses and a head scarf. I think she was in the day before though, but I'm not sure."

"Sunglasses?"

"Yeah sunglasses."

"Thank you. Did you tell the police this?"

"Yes, they didn't seem interested. That's why Brenda said it was best not to mention it again; made me look silly."

"I don't think you're been silly at all and I'm sure Peter will agree. Thank you. You've been really helpful, truly you have," and Dee gave the girl a hug.

The girl watched her leave, but just as Dee reached the door to catch up to Peter, the girl caught her by her arm. "I want you to be careful," she whispered. "That phone call he took; I heard him say he was going to wring someone's neck."

Chapter Seventeen

Alison had run across the road to ask Paula for help. The café was so busy, she couldn't cope on her own and Paula had been happy to close early as all her orders were done and out for delivery.

"I can't cook," Paula had told her as she locked the door of Flowering Fancies.

"As long as you can clear tables and wash up, I'll be forever grateful," Alison had said.

Paula was shocked to see how busy Coffee Creams was. Every table was taken and three were waiting to be served. "Where have all these people come from?" she asked, tying an apron around her waist.

"No idea, but be careful what you say. Some might be paparazzi."

"Really? Do you think they're only here because of Margo's murder?" Paula whispered.

"They were all over D.I. Jones this morning. I think that article in the Gazette has created more than just local interest."

"Gosh, Gamblewood's never going to be the same again."

"I know. I'd better go serve. Are you ok to clear some tables for me please?"

Paula nodded and grabbed an empty tray.

"So how did it go?" Claire asked Tom.

"She stood her ground; gave him as good as she got, but he put her in her place at the end."

"Thought he'd tear her to shreds. Never seen him like that." Claire said.

"No, me neither, but I managed to calm him down a bit in the car before we got there. He seemed more annoyed that Peter and Dee had gone away together." Tom was smirking.

"Give over. Peter and Dee? I don't think so. Where've they gone?"

"To see Mary; she used to work for Peter."

"Oh, I see. Wonder why?"

"No idea, might be her birthday or something."

"Why would Dee go? You wouldn't go with your boss to see the person who's job you're now doing on their birthday."

"Well. how should I know. I'm only guessing." Tom was getting irritated at Claire firing questions at him.

"Sounds like there's more going on than we know."

"You're not wrong."

"Stop that," Claire said "You really are talking complete rubbish."

Jake was listening outside Tom and Claire's office door. He hoped Claire was right. He couldn't picture Dee and Peter together at all. Nor did he want to. Dee was nearer his age than Peters. It had rattled him though; Tom was right about that. Jake put the thought of the two of them together to the back of his mind and opened the door. "Claire, find anything out this morning?"

Claire stood up. "Yes, Sir. Something you might find of interest."

"I'm going to get myself a coffee. Anyone want one? Meeting my office in ten."

Neither Tom or Claire wanted coffee. "I wonder how long he'd been stood out there," he said.

"For your sake, I hope it wasn't long."

Albert was flustered. He'd had to take a tablet that Dr Glen had prescribed to calm his nerves despite the policeman on his doorstep keeping guard. D.I. Jones had assured him it was all a storm in a teacup and, "When they realise that's exactly what it is, they'll all get bored and go back to wherever they came from looking for a bigger story to report." Albert hoped the inspector was right. He went to the window and peeped around the curtain. He could see Miss Fancy-Pants from next door all dolled up, speaking to two of the journalists while someone took her picture. He was intending to make himself a cup of tea but, feeling drowsy, he sat down in his favourite chair and promptly fell asleep.

Claire was opening her notebook. Jake sat opposite her behind his desk drinking his coffee. Tom stood by the door.

"So, I've spoken to Mr Pond. Wait for this; he believes the large painting belongs to Sir Henry Gaitley." Claire paused. Jake looked gratifyingly astonished. "He couldn't say who owned the smaller paintings as they seem to be part of a collection, so the question is, why is a painting owned by Sir Henry hanging on Margo's wall?"

"Well, let's go to Gaitley Manor and ask him." Jake said.

"Are we going back to Angela's?" Dee asked Peter.

"Yes. I've just phoned her; she's going to give us the spare key so we can have a look around Mary's house."

"Really? Is she coming with us?"

"No, she has the boys to pick up from school. Probably best she doesn't; too upsetting at the moment for her if you ask me."

They had walked back along the beach at a gentler pace, Peter still looking like he was scanning the beach as they walked hoping to find something, whatever it was, so Dee had done the same. She was desperate to find out if he was thinking the same as her but it didn't feel like the right time to ask. They had reached the car just as the rain began to pour.

"The weather really has taken a turn for the worse," Dee had said, shivering as she got in the car"

"That it has."

Paula helped Alison close the café at three o'clock.

Alison normally stayed open till four but she'd had a busy day and couldn't thank Paula enough for all her help. "Think we deserve a latte and that brownie you wanted."

Paula agreed as she dried up the last coffee cup.

"Go sit down and I'll bring them over," Alison said "That was one busy day."

"Wonder if it's going to be that busy tomorrow?"

"Well, it's good for takings. Just unusual isn't it? This murder hasn't half caused a stir."

"It's that article. Like you said, it obviously stirred up some interest," Paula said, removing her apron.

"Hasn't it just. I really feel for Albert and Dee. Heard Albert had some trouble this morning too; he hit one of the journalists with a sweeping brush, he did."

"I was going to mention this later, when you came back to pay for the flowers. This Dee that you know; did you hear someone placing an order for a dozen red roses?"

"Yes, I did."

"Well, they were for her. They went out to be delivered to her house this morning."

"Oh no, that's a shame. She's not there; but I'm sure she'll be back tonight. Wonder what that twerp of a boyfriend's done now?."

Paula looked confused. "Don't think he's done anything bad. The card was to say that he'd won some major contract and he'd be back next week."

"Next week? Gosh she'll be upset. He's always in flipping London. Dee moved here to live with him you know, and I think she spends more time on her own than she does with him. Still nice of him to say it with flowers, as they say."

"He did seem full of himself on the phone to be honest. He tried to tell me about this contract but I can't have my phone clogged up with people going on about their business. Once he'd paid, I cut the conversation short. Honestly, I can't afford to miss any other orders coming in."

"Don't blame you. Talking of paying, let me pay you for mine," Alison said as she went over to the petty cash box she kept under her counter.

Jake knocked on Gaitley Manor's door, and no one answered so Claire reached forward and rang the bell. "Sure they'll hear that, Sir."

Sure, enough after a moment Ms Bay opened the door. "How can we help you?" she asked.

"We'd like to talk to Sir Henry. We'll only take a few minutes of his time.

"Have you an appointment?"

"We're the police; we don't need an appointment," Jake responded.

Petra arrived in the hall at that point. She had seen a car, followed by a marked police vehicle, pull up on the drive. Recognising Jake from the garden party, she had quickly changed out of her tennis gear into tight-fitting jeans and a white blouse and ran down to intercept them. "Ms Bay, please let them in. D.I. Jones if I'm not wrong." She held out a thin hand.

Jake shook it and asked if it was possible to have ten minutes with Sir Henry.

Petra smiled. "No problem at all. Follow me. Tea in the drawing room, Ms Bay."

"Right you are Lady Gaitley," and the servant disappeared down the corridor - towards the kitchen Jake presumed.

In the drawing room which Claire remembered from the garden party, Jake and Tom were trying not to be over- awed by its splendour.

"Can I help in anyway?" Petra asked, only looking at Jake.

"It's Sir Henry we've come to see. Have you been married long?"

"Fifteen years." There was pride in the reply.

Claire rose from her seat. "Is it okay if I have a look around?"

"Of course; just don't touch anything."

"I've heard Sir Henry's not been well of late?" Jake mentioned it as casually as he could manage.

"Yes, he does have an underlying heart issue but he seems to be having a lot of tummy trouble. Really knocked him for six to be honest. Dr Glen is looking after him."

The door opened to admit Ms Bay with a huge tray bearing tea and little cakes.

"That's lovely, thank you, Ms Bay," Petra gushed.

"Sir Henry's in the orangery. He's says if they wish to talk to him they can talk to him in there."

"Alright Ms Bay, you can go now." To Jake's interest Petra's accent seemed to slip a little as she said it.

Tea was poured and they were offered a dainty plate apiece.

Claire noticed a school photograph of a young boy on the window sill. "Who's that?"

"That's our son, Oscar."

"How old is he?" Jake asked.

"Fifteen. I fell pregnant straight away after we were married."

"Which school is he at?" Claire again.

"Boarding school." Petra failed to answer the question with any specifics and Tom noticed the smirk as she said it. "Now that's enough about Oscar; tell me did you enjoy the garden party?"

Inside Mary's house, Jasper's dog basket sat in the corner of the kitchen as did his empty food bowl, but the water bowl was full. It brought a tear to Dee's eyes.

Peter wandered around the downstairs rooms, through a small dining room into a nice lounge. Dee stayed in the kitchen. She wasn't sure why they were there and it was getting late. If Edward was coming home tomorrow, she really wanted to tidy around before he got back. "Finding anything?" she shouted through to Peter.

"Not yet. Have you?"

Dee hadn't realised she was supposed to be looking for anything so she quickly started opening kitchen drawers to make it look like she was doing something.

"Going upstairs," Peter announced.

Dee didn't answer him. She had found a diary in one of the drawers and was flicking through it.

Looking under Mary's bed, Peter could hear Jake's voice in his head telling him to keep Dee away for another night. 'Ruth has a lot to answer for,' Peter thought. He was trying to work out how he was going to tell Dee about the article and the media frenzy it had caused when Dee appeared in the doorway of Mary's bedroom, making him jump and bang his head on the underside of the bedframe.

"Bet that hurt." She couldn't help but laugh.

Peter got to his feet rubbing his scalp. "What you got there?"

"It's a diary. Found it in the kitchen. Look at this."

"Well, I say, that's a turn up."

"I know. Look at the date," Dee urged.

Peter had already clocked it. The fifth of October and a one-word entry. *Malton*. If Mary had been planning to go to Malton, then she wouldn't have been planning on killing herself on the twenty-ninth of September. As comfort, though, it was short lived. Either Mary's death had been a genuine accident … or something much worse.

"Look in the back, Peter. There's train times to Leeds and then on to Malton. And there's the name of a hotel too, so she must have been planning a little holiday or something."

"Maybe."

Dee could see the cogs turning in his head. "What are you thinking?"

Peter didn't answer her. He was already on his mobile. "Angela, hi. Just a quick question. Did your mum have a holiday planned in Malton?"

Dee could hear Angela asking where Malton was and then saying, "Mum never mentioned anything about a holiday – except that she was going away with the walking group for a night in October sometime."

Peter thanked her, saying they would pop the door key back through her letterbox on their way home. Dee was relieved to hear that they were heading home soon. She hadn't got round to telling Edward that she was away as he'd put the phone down on her and when he'd called her back, she couldn't be bothered explaining it to him at two in the morning; not that he seemed interested in her whereabouts anyway.

"Pleased we're getting off," she said.

"Yep. Let's take this with us. We can let Angela know we've got it once we're on our way."

"Okay, can we go now?"

"Yeah, come on," Peter said leading the way down the stairs.

Jake had listened to enough of Petra's rambling about herself and the garden party. "It's been lovely talking to you, but we'll go and speak to Sir Henry now." It was getting late, he was feeling hungry, and he'd noticed even Claire and Tom were becoming restless.

Petra stood. "I'll take you." As they made their way into the grand hallway, Petra linked her arm through Jake's. He didn't like it but thought it would be rude to pull away. Behind his back, Tom and Claire swapped glances.

Entering the orangery, Petra's voice became almost condescending. "Darling," she crooned, "D.I. Jones for you."

The room smelt beautiful, it was adorned with plants and at the far end at a circular table sat Sir Henry. "Jake come in, come in." Sir Henry beckoned as he rose up to greet them.

"No need to get up, Sir," Jake said.

"Join me, join me," Sir Henry urged. "None of that *Sir* stuff please, Henry will do very well."

The three of them joined him and Jake noticed Claire drawing Tom's attention to the old photograph placed on a low window sill.

"What's this all about then? We'll have to be quick; Dr Glen's coming shortly."

"I'll get straight to the point. We understand that one of your paintings has been found in Mrs Darnley's house. We wondered if you could explain that."

"Margaret's house, yes. It was a leaving gift. Lady Caroline insisted upon it. Margo as we called her always liked it when she worked here."

"That's a very generous gift," Tom observed.

"Lady Caroline was a generous lady," Sir Henry said abruptly.

"Is it all right for me to show D.I. Jones this photograph please?" Claire asked.

"Of course. Please pass it here." Sir Henry held out his hand for Claire to pass it to him.

"That's Margaret and Elizabeth in that photo, Sir?"

Sir Henry pointed them out to Jake.

"Pretty little thing," Jake said, "Elizabeth, I mean."

Sir Henry didn't answer.

"Elizabeth didn't work here long, I understand."

"No, she rather left in a hurry. Went to another stable. Better pay I was led to believe." Sir Henry didn't take his gaze from the photograph.

"Do you know which one?"

"Long time ago now. I know it was in North Yorkshire." Sir Henry placed a finger on the woman at the centre of the photograph.

"Is that Lady Caroline?" Jake asked.

"Yes." Sir Henry continued to trace the outline of the woman with his finger. "Beautiful isn't she? Such a lady. I still miss her every day."

"We understand that you argued with Margaret after Eliabeth left. Can you remember why?" Jake was treading carefully.

"No idea. Margo left here years ago and Margo and I arguing? Very unlikely" Sir Henry offered the photograph back to Claire who replaced it on the window sill.

"Have you seen Margaret recently at all?"

"I don't believe so. I'd have no reason to," Sir Henry claimed. "Terrible business. Poor Margo." With that he pulled himself to his feet. "It's been a pleasure. Please come and visit us again but Dr Glen will be here any minute."

That was obviously their cue to leave. They would have to come back another day. Jake had many more questions to ask.

Outside the house, Tom said to Jake, "I didn't know that Sir Henry and Margo had argued after Elizabeth left."

"Me neither. It's just a hunch."

"Imagine being given a painting worth hundreds of thousands of pounds as a leaving present," Claire said, dreamily.

"Yeah. Imagine!" was Tom's reply.

Dee and Peter were making good time on their way back home. Angela had still been at the house when they dropped Mary's door key back and had seemed more than happy for them to take Mary's diary with them.

"Edward's not picking up again," Dee announced.

"Did they get the contract?"

"Oh, this is annoying. I think I'll message him instead. I'll ask him. He seemed very confident they would."

Peter didn't answer her. He was wondering when the best time would be to drop his bombshell.

"Can I ask you something? It's a bit tricky," Dee said rubbing her hands together.

"As long as it's not about you and Edward I don't mind."

"No, it's about Mary. I can't help thinking that if it wasn't an accident - you know the sun and all that - do you think that lady spilling her tea had anything to do with it?"

"I do. What's your thought on what happened then?"

"You're going to think I watch too much telly, but let's just say it was done on purpose. The woman in a headscarf and sunglasses bangs into the table, spilling the tea everywhere." Dee paused for a brief moment" Do you think she might have put something in Mary's tea? You know the one she bought her to replace the spilt one. She could have put something in Mary's drink while she was in the ladies. You think that's far-fetched?"

"If it wasn't an accident, that's exactly what I think might have happened."

"So, what do we do now?"

Peter saw this as his chance. "We go to Malton."

"Really, when?" Dee asked, checking to see if Edward had replied to her text.

"Tonight."

"I can't go there tonight, I've no clothes and Edward's back tomorrow!" Dee sounded taken back "You'll have to go without me."

"Not happening. We're in this together. We can call in briefly for you to pick up fresh clothes if you want, but I mean brief."

"Where are we going to stay tonight? Malton's not that big and it's going to be really late when we get there."

"See if you can find somewhere just off the motorway, half way up for us to stay in tonight."

"My gran's not too far from Malton. Any chance we could call in to see her?"

"Absolutely; of course we can, but only on the way back after we've been to Malton." Peter sensed this might make the decision easier for her to explain to Edward.

"There's just one thing bothering me?" Dee said "Why are we going to Malton? What's the point? Mary was going there with her walking group; I can't see that it would have anything to do with the case."

"You see that's just it, Dee; was Mary going with the walking group? Or was it a cover for heading up to do some investigating."

"Investigating? Thought you said she never got involved in your cases. I don't get it."

"Maybe she was doing an investigation of her own. After all she had those pictures on her camera of Margo and Sir Henry together and the only connection they have is that Margo and her sister worked for Sir Henry." Peter was trying to help her out.

The penny dropped. "Oh, now I'm with you. Her sister left and went to work at some rival stables up North and you think it could be in Malton?"

"Who knows? It's a long shot. I could be wrong but if we don't go, we'll never know."

Jake was finally home, his tea in the microwave, He wanted to phone Peter to see if Dee was alright, but knew Peter would phone him when it was safe for him to do so.

Jake had driven around Gamblewood to see if any press were still hanging around. It looked as if they had all left or gone back to their hotels for the night. He had also driven past Albert's and Margo's cottages to check that the police officers on duty were all stationed and settled in for the night.

Ruth was having a long soak in a hot bath. She sipped on the glass of white wine smiling to herself. She'd enjoyed the confrontation with Jake. He'd really got under her skin and she liked it and she was hatching a plan in her head to see him again. The long and short of it was she fancied him.

Peter made good time back to Gamblewood but he drove straight past Dee and Edward's house.

"You missed it," Dee pointed out. "You need to go back."

Peter had missed it on purpose. He wanted to check that no media were camped outside for the night and was relieved to find no one loitering about. "Sorry; thinking about the case," he said, using it as an excuse. He turned the car around and as they headed up the drive his headlights picked out a large bouquet of flowers standing on the door step.

"Oh, look at that!" Dee sounded excited.

Peter parked and they both got out of the car and Dee rushed over to the floral display while Peter went to retrieve Dee's overnight bag out of the boot for her. Dee struggled to open the door while holding the flowers so Peter rushed over to take them from her so giving her two free hands. He watched Dee read the card that had come with the flowers; she made no comment, although when she took the bag from him there were tears in her eyes.

When she went upstairs to pack, Peter's curiosity got the better of him and he picked the card up to read it only to throw it back down on the kitchen work top where it landed next to the huge bouquet. He could feel the anger rising in him. 'Edward really is a total shit.' He'd not answered any of Dee's messages nor returned her calls, but instead he sent her flowers telling her he's away all week. 'What sort of a person does that?'

Dee sat upstairs on the edge of her bed, checking her phone again. Still nothing from Edward other than the grand gesture. 'All those roses must have cost a fortune.' In reality, she just wanted to talk to him. She wiped away a tear and sent him a text.

Thank you for the flowers. Congratulations on the contract. Am so looking forward to seeing you next weekend. Understand you're really busy at work but if you could call me, would love to hear your voice.

Dee grabbed some clean clothes and her winter jacket. If it felt cold down here it was going to be very cold up in Yorkshire. She popped a woolly hat and scarf into her bag for good measure. She was in the bathroom wiping away the mascara that had run down her face when she heard a beep on her phone. She ran to the bed where she had left it. Finally it was Edward.

The text was merely a thumbs up emoji.

She threw the phone down on the bed in temper. 'No word from him all day and that's how he replies.' "Screw you and your flowers!" She screamed at the phone.

Peter's voice drifted up. "Times a ticking."

She grabbed her bag and made her way downstairs.

"All okay?"

"All good." The lie was obvious

"Are you putting them in fresh water before we go?" Peter pointed at the bouquet.

"No, they can stay there!"

Peter knew not to say another word. 'They must have had a tiff; he hoped it wasn't about her going away for another night, but he had no choice. At Jake's forceful suggestion, he had to keep her away.

All locked up, Dee was huffing and puffing as they drove out of Gamblewood.

"I know it's none of my business," Peter felt he had to ask. "Is Edward upset about you coming up to Malton with me? I can always call him and explain if you like."

Dee was looking straight ahead. "He wouldn't pick up the phone if you did. He never does. How many times have I called him today?" Peter knew not to answer her rhetorical question. "How many messages have I sent him and when he does finally reply it's with an emoji! He doesn't care where I am or who I'm with. He never asks. He only cares about himself."

Peter was about to tell a big fat lie and say that wasn't true at all and he was sure Edward cared about her very much while deep down he hoped Dee was starting to see Edward for the self-centred person he really was. Fortunately, Peter was saved from having to say anything at all as a number flashed up on the dashboard screen.

"It's Angela," said Dee.

"Yeah. Let's see what she wants. Hope she's alright." Peter pressed the accept button on his steering wheel.

"Peter, it's me." She sounded out of breath.

"Are you okay? Has something happened?"

"Sort of. I've just had two ladies from the walking group here. They came to see if there was any news about mum's funeral." They could hear Angela taking a deep breath. "I thought I'd better let you know that the walking group went away last week to Whitby."

"Whitby? Not Malton then?" Dee asked.

"No, definitely Whitby. They're going to the peak district after bonfire night for a two-day walking trip. Is that in mum's diary?"

"We can check when we get to the hotel. We're driving at the moment and the diary's safely tucked up in my rucksack in the boot."

"Okay, so I don't know why mum was going to Malton. I thought I'd better let you know that she definitely wasn't going with the walking group, I don't understand why mum wouldn't have told me she had plans to go there, but she definitely didn't, Peter. I honestly have no idea why she'd be going there."

Dee had a sudden thought. "Angela, did your mum have an old school friend who lived there or an old family member that you can recall?"

Peter looked at Dee. He liked her thinking.

"No, we don't know anyone. All our family's based down here. That's why mum retired down this way to be near us all. Does any of this help?"

"It most certainly does."

They thanked Angela for calling and sat in silence as Peter drove, digesting the new bit of information.

Dee spoke first. "It's connected to the case, isn't it?"

"Think so. Looks like it."

"Peter, the woman in the head scarf and sunglasses - do you think she killed Mary and Margo?"

"It's a possibility. If I'm being honest, yes, I do." Peter didn't flinch as he said it. He just kept staring at the road ahead.

"But why?" Dee asked

"That's what we're going to find out."

Chapter Eighteen

Ruth had put on extra make-up, hairspray and perfume. The Gazette office had been busy with out-of-town journalists wanting to speak to her. Not one to miss an opportunity she wanted to dress to impress; not just for the journalists hanging about but for the inspector. D.I. Jones would see her again today whether he wanted to or not. She looked in the mirror, pleased with her reflection. Smiling to herself, she'd sit there all day if she had to, mulling over the tip-off she'd received last night.

Jake had spent most of the night awake again. He'd made the decision at some point he was going to make an appointment to see Dr Glen. He was worn out, the case really getting to him. There was still something niggling at him but he couldn't quite put his finger on it. He was also out of coffee. He'd pick some up on his way home after work. Coffee Creams came to mind. He needed to thank Alison and pay her as they'd left in a hurry yesterday. He'd call in on his way to the station, and then check in on Albert too.

Peter and Dee were finishing their breakfast.

"Straight to Malton then," Peter said.

"No."

"No?"

"No. I spoke to gran last night. She says the racing stable she knows is in Masham." Dee drained the last bit of tea from her cup.

"Malton; Masham? I suppose you could get them mixed up," Peter said placing his knife and fork neatly on his plate.

"There's a good hour and half between them. What do you think?"

"Shall we see how we're doing time-wise. We could try and find the stables at Masham first. If we get going, we might be there in a couple of hours, then Malton for lunch." Peter was already on his feet.

Dee agreed. They fetched their bags from their rooms and checked out.

Claire and Tom were already at the station. They were chatting over strong canteen coffee. "Wonder what time he'll be in?" Claire asked.

"Haven't heard from him this morning. Unusual; he's normally given me my orders by now."

"Fancy having a quick drive around Gamblewood? See if Albert is alright this morning?"

"Why not. I'll message Jake; tell him what we're doing," Tom said retrieving his mobile from his pocket.

Alison was in early. She wanted to get a head start in case she was as busy as the day before and she jumped at the loud knock at the door. She was surprised to see D.I. Jones standing there. "Come in, we're not open yet, but not a problem. Coffee?"

Jake spent the next few minutes apologising for turning up early and then a few more trying to persuade Alison to let him pay what he owed her from the previous day.

"I'm not having any of it. I had a good day's takings while you didn't look like you were having a good day yesterday at all. That article's caused quite the stir." Alison had to shout to be heard over the noise of the coffee machine.

"Quite." he shouted back and then as the machine finished, "Heard from Dee or Peter at all?"

Alison brought him over a steaming mug of coffee and a toasted current teacake. "They're on their way to Malton. Don't think they came back last night." She knew full well they hadn't as Dee had phoned her to complain about Edward from her hotel room.

"Malton. I used to be based up that way. Why Malton? Did Peter say?"

"Didn't speak to him. I spoke to Dee. She and Edward had a spat. He's away in London again all next week." Alison thought it might be good to mention that.

"Oh, I see. He's not my cup of tea," Jake said without thinking.

"Nor mine."

Alison stuck a poster advertising fireworks for bonfire night on the village green in the window. "Don't know where this year's gone. It'll be Christmas before we know it."

Jake agreed, finished his breakfast and went to the counter to pay.

"On the house D.I. Jones." Alison said.

"Please call me Jake. I hate all that formal rubbish."

"Where are you off to now, Jake?" Alison asked, struggling to use his given name.

"Going to see if Albert's alright. He had a tough day yesterday."

"Oh. I know, I heard about the sweeping brush incident."

Then they were both laughing. "Can you imagine the scene."

"Jake, I was going to mention this to Peter when he next came in, but he might not be back for a few days." She moved one of the chairs to straighten it.

"Go on, what is it?"

"When Albert was last in, he mentioned you finding the murder weapon in his house. You don't think he could do such a thing, do you?"

"No, I don't believe he could, but someone did."

"Well, he said that his late wife had a falling out with Margo over a broach." Alison could feel herself getting flustered. "I might have the story wrong but she was accused of stealing it from Gaitley Manor and Petra sacked her."

"Did she steal it?"

"No, I got the impression it was a misunderstanding, but Margo said something along the lines of, *if you've stolen from them, you've stolen from me*. Odd thing to say, isn't it?"

"It is rather," Jake said getting his notebook out to write it down.

"Do you think it's important?"

"Not sure, but you never know. Is there anything else?"

"Yes. He also said that Sir Henry and Margo didn't like each other very much. Especially after her sister left, they used to argue apparently, but - listen to this - he saw Sir Henry going into Margo's house."

"Really, recently?" Jake was writing at speed.

"Don't know; you'll have to ask Albert." As she said it, a couple came through the door asking if she was open.

"I definitely will," Jake said holding the door for the newcomers.

Peter had pulled in for petrol. Dee felt better after a night's sleep. She had phoned Alison to tell her about Edward and Alison had set her mind at rest. "He was probably out celebrating and wasn't thinking straight." Dee could see Peter paying at the kiosk and quickly sent a text message to her gran saying they were nearly at Masham after taking her advice and that she was looking forward to seeing her later on that day.

"Right Masham, here we come," Peter said as he got back in the car, throwing a packet of pastilles into Dee's lap. "Thought they'd keep us going."

Dee opened the packet and offered one to Peter. "I keep thinking about the connection between Margo and Mary. There isn't one is there?"

"That's been playing on my mind too. I don't think they were friends either. I know Mary definitely spoke to Albert's wife Annie. Think they used to meet up for a cup of tea sometimes, but I never heard her mention Margo at all."

"If there's no connection between them then why would someone kill them both? Maybe the deaths aren't connected at all. When all's said and done the only thing we have linking Mary and Margo is that Mary had photographs on her camera of Margo and Sir Henry."

"Yes, think we need to have a look in Mary's diary again - see if anything jumps out."

Dee suddenly had a lightbulb moment. "Peter, you know who the connection is?"

"Do I?"

Dee couldn't contain herself. "It makes perfect sense - it's Sir Henry."

"Sir Henry!" Peter didn't want to belittle her, so he tried not to burst out laughing "What possible connection could there be between Sir Henry and Mary?"

"I don't know, but I'm sure there is one."

Peter shook his head and carried on driving.

Jake had arrived at Albert's. Before leaving he'd spoken to the constable who had assured him that no journalists had turned up as yet.

"Morning," Albert said as he opened the door.

"Just come to check you're okay after yesterday."

"Tea?"

"I'm okay thanks. I've just been to *Coffee Creams*."

"Wish I could. Feel like a prisoner in my own home, with that lot out there."

"No, it's not nice; unpleasant business," Jake said, checking his phone. He'd had a message from Tom which could probably wait but just then he heard someone enter knocking on the door Albert had left ajar.

"Hello, Albert." It was Claire Brown. "We understand D.I. Jones is here. Okay if we come in?"

"You're like flipping buses, all coming at once, suppose you'll want a cup of tea?"

"That would be lovely. Tom's talking to the man outside. He'll be in in a minute."

Albert looked put out, but put the kettle on, muttering under his breath. Before it even boiled Tom joined them in Albert's lounge. "Morning all."

"What have I done now?" Albert asked sarcastically. He finished making the tea and handed Tom and Claire their cups, fetched his own and settled himself in his favourite chair.

"Just wanted to make sure you're alright, you had a bit of a day yesterday," Claire said softly.

"You're not wrong, lassie. Anyway those pills Dr Glen gave me sorted me out. Right good nap I had; I did."

"Hopefully they've all gone home now," Tom said referring to the journalists that had been camped on the doorstep.

"Or crawled back under their stones," Albert said.

They all laughed, which seemed to put Albert at ease.

"Can I ask you a couple of things, Albert?" Jake asked.

Tom and Claire looked at each other. They had no idea what Jake could possibly want to ask.

"I understand that Margo and your wife had a falling out over a broach. Is that true?"

Albert looked down into his cup of tea, his hands starting to shake. "News travels fast round here. doesn't it or should I say gossip does."

"It's okay, Albert," Claire said. "Any information we can gather might help. That's all."

Tom took his notebook out and wrote down the key points about the theft accusation, Annie's sacking and Margo going round the village telling all and sundry that Annie was a thief.

"They killed her; they really did. She fell ill after all that. I'll always blame them. My Annie would be here today, she would, if it wasn't for them and Margo."

Although Jake already knew about all about the incident with the broach from his conversation with Peter and Dee in the pub it surprised him how venomous Albert seemed and Tom and Claire were equally taken aback by what was, to them at least, new information. They swapped a look that Jake knew only too well and Tom wrote *motive* in large letters in his notebook.

"I understand Margo and Sir Henry didn't always see eye to eye after her sister left. Do you know anything about that Albert?" Jake asked.

"No, I don't think they liked each other very much. My Annie told me that they argued sometimes. No idea why though. Might be to do with her sister going to work at another stables - not sure. Look we've been through this all before!" Albert was shaking visibly and had gone quite red in the face.

Jake said, "A little bird tells me that you might have seen Sir Henry visit Margo."

Now Tom and Claire were thoroughly confused.

"Yes, I did. Came a few times actually," Albert answered, keeping his eyes firmly set on the cup in his hand.

"Recently?"

"Aye, he was here the day she got herself done in."

Claire interrupted Jake as he was about to ask his next question. "Albert, are you saying that Sir Henry visited Margo on the day she was murdered?"

"What part of that don't you understand," Albert snapped back.

Claire felt the hair on the back of her neck stand up. Albert might be annoyed but there was no need to take that tone of voice with her.

"Albert, may I remind you, you're talking to a Detective Constable." Jake said.

"Sorry." The apology was mumbled.

"Have you any idea what the time was when Sir Henry visited Margo - even roughly. Was it after Dee visited Margo or before?"

"I'd have to think about that."

They all sat quietly, giving Albert time to think.

"After. Yes it was after." Albert shuffled his body towards the edge of his chair.

"Are you sure? Absolutely sure?"

Albert nodded. "I'd forgotten about that. Am I in trouble?" he asked.

Peter and Dee found themselves outside the most beautiful wrought iron gates adorned with horses. There was an intercom built into the wall on the right-hand wall.

"I'll go," Peter announced much to Dee's relief as she had no idea what she would have said.

Peter returned as the gates began to open.

"How did you pull that off?" Dee asked.

"Where there's a will there's a way," he answered smugly.

They drove up the drive towards the buildings at the top, passing two fields to their left which contained several horses grazing or minding their own business and as they approached the buildings an older woman dressed in riding gear came out to greet them.

Peter got out and, with an outstretched hand, was already introducing himself when Dee reached his side. Following Peter's lead Dee shook the woman's hand too.

"How can I help? You've travelled quite some way." She was well-spoken but not overly posh.

"We're trying to trace an Elizabeth Darnley. It's some time ago now, but we wondered if you'd heard the name at all?"

"No, unfortunately not. Can I ask why?"

Peter had prepared an answer. "We believe she died in a horse-riding accident, but her sister has recently passed and we understand there might have been a child that the estate can be passed down to. We're trying to trace them."

Dee was shocked at how convincing Peter was but had the presence of mind to flick through the photographs on her phone. "Hmm, just a minute, got it. Does the name *Elizabeth Blunt* mean anything to you?"

"No I'm sorry. No Blunts or Darnleys here and I don't think anyone with those names has worked at any of the stables around here. We all tend to know each other pretty well. I wish I could be of more help."

"There's quite a few stables around here then?" Dee asked.

"Plenty, but mostly much smaller than us."

"Any in Malton you might know of?" Peter had his fingers crossed.

"There's one, on your way into Malton - small but very good - if you think this Elizabeth might have worked there."

"Well we can call that way and ask."

They said their goodbyes and thanked the woman for her time. As they approached the gates to leave, they automatically opened.

"Blunt. Good call that, Dee. Pretty impressed."

"It was Margo's maiden name. I knew I'd taken a photo of Margo's wedding certificate; just had to find it." Dee was feeling quite proud of herself.

"Any pastilles left?" Peter asked her.

"Nope; you've eaten them all."

"That Ruth might have a point. Maybe it was Albert after all. He's got a motive and a temper, and the murder weapon was found in his house," Tom said as the threesome stood beside their cars.

"No. I know where you're coming from and it looks like it could point to Albert but now there's Sir Henry in the mix." Jake said.

"Well, it lets Dee off the hook, well and truly," Claire pointed out. "After all, Margo must have been alive when Henry went to see her."

"Not necessarily. Maybe Sir Henry found Margo dead in the garden and didn't report it."

"Why wouldn't he report it and surely you'd knock on the door before entering someone's house."

"Not if they knew each other better than we think they do, Tom," Jake replied.

"Me and my best friend just knock and walk into each other's houses all the time," Claire said.

"Exactly. I'll meet you up at Gaitley Manor. We need to pay Sir Henry another visit since he lied to us yesterday."

"Sir?" Tom looked puzzled.

"He clearly told us he'd not visited Margo or argued with her didn't he? Remember?" Jake was halfway into his car. Now he straightened up momentarily. "Well they did argue, even if it was a while ago and he visited Margo very recently according to Albert. So, he lied."

"Ah, yes, Sir."

Both Tom and Claire found themselves wishing they had Jake's memory for detail.

Petra had finished another Tennis lesson. Not that she needed lessons. She was a highly competent player. She'd arrived home to find Dr Glen's car on the drive yet again. Entering Gaitley Manor she rolled her eyes at Ms Bay as she passed the kitchen door, put on her best fake smile and headed into the drawing room.

"Dr Glen, how are you? How's my Henry doing?"

The doctor rose as Lady Petra entered the room. He didn't like her much but fortunately he wasn't her GP. "I'm fine but Sir Henry's not."

Sir Henry was on the sofa. He looked tired and in pain.

"Oh dear. I'll get Ms Bay to bring us some tea."

"Not for me thank you. I need to get back to the surgery." Dr Glen returned his stethoscope to his bag and addressed Sir Henry. "I'd like you to try and get a little more fresh air."

Sir Henry was about to answer but Petra interjected. "We can do that, can't we dearest. We can have a little walkie round the garden this afternoon."

The doctor was tempted to remind her that she wasn't talking to a child, but thought better of it. "I'll come back later. I'm going to run more blood tests," he announced as he made his way to the door of the drawing room and Petra offered to walk him out.

After shutting it behind Dr Glen, Petra leant against the door and Ms Bay came to join her in the hallway.

"He's to have more blood tests," Petra said, "…and more fresh air."

Ms Bay didn't answer. She tutted and looked up at the ceiling.

It seemed to be taking Peter and Dee longer than expected to reach Malton and Peter had wanted to be there for lunch. He still had the long drive back to do and found himself yawning.

"Do you want me to drive?" Dee offered

"No, I'm good. Maybe you can drive a bit of the way home tonight."

"I thought we were coming to see what Mary was up to not to look for Elizabeth?"

"We are, but I'm more convinced than ever that Mary was on to something, or knew something that someone didn't like."

"So, what are we going to do when we get to Malton?"

"Phone Jake; have something to eat."

"Phone Jake?"

"Yeah, I want to know how he's getting on with the case. I'll give him a call, see if he's free for a catch-up next week." To Dee, the remark seemed somehow flippant. She didn't realise he needed to check if the journalists had left Gamblewood and, depending on Jake's answer, he might feel it best to keep Dee away from home another night.

"Look!" Finally a sign for Malton.

"Thank heavens." Peter was more than relieved. He needed the loo.

Unhappiness was becoming Jake's normal mood. Making their way to Gaitley Manor, they had been instructed to turn around and get back to the station as soon as possible. Jake had forgotten he would be needed at the press conference about Margo's murder that had been called at Gamblewood Village Hall.

Ruth was the first to arrive. She was so grateful for the late night opening at the hairdressers where she had overheard a woman by the name of Mrs Powell moaning to another woman waiting to have the foils taken out of her hair, that she was having to get up early because, "Mr Butt's away on holiday and I'm the second key holder for the village hall so it's up to me to go and open up, put all the chairs out and make some drinks for a police press conference." The two ladies had then gone on to discuss the murder but said nothing else of any significance or interest to Ruth so she interrupted to ask what time Mrs Powell might be there to open up and sympathised with her at how awful it was that she had to put all them chairs out on her own. Making a firm mental note of the time was important as she wanted to be sitting on the front row, right in the middle.

There was no way Jake was not going to see her. She settled herself exactly where she wanted to be. Only a few other journalists and photographers were starting to arrive, and under no circumstances was she budging.

Claire watched Jake disappear into the superintendent's office for a briefing. They knew he was going to hate every minute of it but it was the only way to stop any further media attention. She was inputting the details they had gathered from Albert while Tom was trying to see if there was any CCTV of Sir Henry's car in the area on the day of the murder.

When Jake finally emerged he just said, "Time to go."

Claire and Tom followed him out of the station to the cars parked side by side in the car park. "Are you okay, Sir?" Claire asked him.

"Will be when this press conference is all over and done with and we can get back to what we should be doing."

"What should we be doing?" Tom asked him with mock innocence.

"Investigating Tom, bloody investigating," Jake shouted as he slammed his car door.

Malton turned out to be a pretty market town. They managed to park easily in the market square and found themselves amidst a maze of shops, estate agents and places to eat so, they decided to have a wander round and stretch their legs.

The one and only stables they had passed on the outskirts of the village had proved to be another blank. No one had heard of either Elizabeth Blunt or Elizabeth Darnley. They also didn't know of anyone who had died in a horse-riding accident from their stables or any other. Once again it was reinforced that they were a tight-knit community and most of them knew anything and everything about each other.

"Fancy here?" Peter said, now really desperate for the loo.

"Yeah, can do." Dee was not really bothered where they ate and the coffee shop looked as good as any. It had a shop selling cakes and bread on the right-hand side and, on the left, dropped down a couple of steps into the café area. Peter had already rushed to the toilet leaving Dee to ask for a table for two and a menu to look at.

"I'll be back shortly," the waitress said, beaming.

Dee checked the menu and singled out either mushrooms on toast or rarebit. She felt spoilt for choice.

"Any good?" Peter asked as he sat down to join her.

"Too good, I could order everything."

Peter agreed with Dee once he'd seen the menu and he decided to order the rarebit which he'd never tried before. Dee settled on a prawn sandwich. The waitress was chatty but not overfamiliar and said she would pop their order in.

They didn't discuss the case. Instead, they chatted about the weather and Dee's gran until the waitress came back with their drinks and said their food would not be long.

Ruth was getting excited; she liked a good press conference. She was ready with her own questions to fire at the Inspector although she was irritated by a journalist from out of town who was too big for his chair. Sitting down next to her he caused her to have to move over a little. "If that skirt gets any higher, they'll see your crown jewels," he joked and Ruth ignored him. As far as she was concerned her long legs were her best assets and she wanted Jake to see them.

"Mutton dressed as lamb," the other journalist muttered under his breath.

Camera flashlights lit up the room as the five police officers entered the hall and sat down behind the long trestle table covered in a white tablecloth.

The Superintendent opened proceedings and then passed the microphone over to Jake for him to give an update and answer any questions. As he got to his feet, he noticed Ruth sitting slap-bang in front of him. On seeing her, he paused just for a brief moment. She was pleased with herself; not only had he seen her but her appearance seemed to be having the desired effect and she kept crossing and uncrossing her legs to the annoyance of her neighbour in the audience.

He whispered, "Go to the bloody toilet."

She hissed back. "Piss off!"

Jake stared at the back of the room, as he had been trained to do, while he gave the update. Tom and Claire stood behind him. They too had noticed the performance Ruth was giving and were finding it hard not to laugh.

"Looks like Jake has an admirer," Claire whispered to Tom.

"He wouldn't go anywhere near that for love nor money. What does she think she's doing?" Tom whispered back.

At the end of the update, Jake asked if there were any further questions. A couple came from the back of the room that Jake could answer easily before Ruth rose to her feet, wriggling her skirt down as she did so.

"When will you be making an arrest, D.I. Jones? Any time soon?" Ruth was putting on her sexiest voice.

Before Jake could answer, the Superintendent grabbed the microphone out of Jake's hand. "Thank you for coming. That will be all," he announced.

As the room emptied, the Superintendent turned to Jake and said, "You should arrest whoever that was sat on the front row. I've never seen anything like it. So unprofessional."

Jake couldn't agree more. He thought Ruth a total fool.

Dee and Peter finished their meals and were settling the bill when Peter asked the waitress if she had heard of anyone going by the surname of Darnley or Blunt in the village.

"No, I'm sorry, but I haven't lived here long. I can fetch the owner for you. She was born here."

"That would be great, thanks but not to worry if they're busy."

The waitress said she would check if the owner was free and returned with a stout lady asking how she could help. When Peter repeated his query, she said, "I'm sorry no. You don't have any other names or anything else to go on?"

Peter looked fed up. "Afraid not."

"Our friend Mary and her dog Jasper were coming here for a holiday; don't suppose you know if they've been here before or if you've ever met them?" Dee knew it was a long shot but she thought she'd give it a try. "I have a photograph of her on my phone. I'll just find it."

The owner looked at the photograph. "No, don't think I've seen her round these parts. There's plenty of Marys that live here but not one with a dog called Jasper, that I know of. Sorry love."

They thanked her and made their way to leave but as they did so, a woman dressed in jeans and a woolly camel-coloured jumper stood to intercept them. Dee noticed her lovely skin and how neat her blonde ponytail was. It was hard to put an age to her.

"I heard you mention the name Blunt. Can I ask why you're asking?"

Peter decided to describe Mary as an old family member he was trying to trace, and that they'd been tipped off that she liked to holiday in the area at this time of year.

"I think I might be able to help you but I only have an hour. My name's Helen. I think I might know your Mary." Somehow she looked nervous.

"Why do you think you know Mary?" Peter asked quietly.

"I heard you mention a dog called Jasper?"

Dee and Peter nodded.

"I was meant to meet her, if it's the same Mary. She asked me if I knew any dog-friendly hotels nearby as she wanted to bring her Jasper with her but she never showed up."

"Can you remember the date you were meant to meet Mary?" Dee jumped in before Peter could ask her anything else.

"We'd arranged to meet on the fifth of October," Helen replied.

Jake was finally back in his car. It was late afternoon as he pulled up outside the manor house and Dr Glen's car was on the drive. Tom and Claire were just behind him in a marked official vehicle so Jake waited for them before he rang the bell.

"See the doctor's here again," said Tom.

"Good; I'm pleased. I want a word with him," Jake said as Ms Bay opened the door.

"He's with the doctor," she announced.

"That's fine, we'll wait." Jake already had one foot in the door and Ms Bay moved back to let them in.

Petra had heard the DI" s voice and rushed into the hallway from the kitchen, tears rolling down her face.

"Are you okay Lady Gaitley?" Claire asked.

"Ooh this," Petra answered wiping her tears away with her hand, "It's my eye drops. I've just popped them in."

Claire said, "I suffer with dry eyes too from time to time," but Petra ignored her.

"Dr Glen." Jake shook the man's hand as he emerged from the drawing room into the hallway.

"Everything alright, D.I. Jones? I hope you're not here to upset my patient?"

"Absolutely not. Is it alright if I walk out with you?" Jake asked.

"Of course."

That left Tom, Claire, Petra and Ms Bay in the hallway staring after them.

A shout from Sir Henry broke the silence. "When are we eating Ms Bay. Is that you standing out there?."

"Yes, Sir," and she pivoted and went into the drawing room. The others followed her in. "What time would you like to eat?"

"Back again I see," Sir Henry gestured for Tom and Claire to sit down but Petra went to stand by the window where she could watch Dr Glen and D.I. Jones deep in conversation. "Six thirty would be good," he answered Ms Bay.

As Ms Bay left the room, Tom asked, "How are you feeling?"

"Just had more blood tests taken, but having a good day today."

Petra came back to sit with them and moments later Jake walked in apologising. "Sorry about that. Just had to speak to Dr Glen."

"Not about me, I hope? What can I do for you, this time?"

"Is it okay, Lady Gaitley, if you show my D.C. around? "Jake asked.

"I'd rather not," Petra said.

"Petra, show our friend here the music room and the library," Sir Henry said and Petra did as she was told.

Jake noticed that Sir Henry looked a bit clammy. Waiting for the door to close, he turned to face him. "I'm going to get straight to the point. I believe you lied to us yesterday. You said you had not visited Margo recently, but we have a witness who saw you enter Margo's on the day she was murdered."

Sir Henry opened his mouth to say something but all that came out was a groan. He suddenly fell to one side of the sofa clutching his chest and rolled off the sofa and onto the floor. Jake ran to him and opened his shirt collar. "Get an ambulance, and quick" he shouted.

Ms Bay entering with tea and biscuits panicked and dropped the tray causing such a clatter that Claire and Petra raced back to see what had happened. As they entered the drawing room, Jake was shouting at Tom. "He's having a heart attack!."

Chapter Nineteen

Helen had to leave quicker than they had hoped. An emergency at work. "All part of the job, so sorry. Here's my mobile number. Will you call me later?" She scribbled it down on a napkin.

Peter took the napkin from her "Go, go. I'll pay your bill. Sort it tomorrow when we see you." He made a shooing motion with his hand.

"Really are you sure? You're such a gentleman; not many of you left around; thank you. See you tomorrow." She was already halfway out the door.

"That one's always running around. Another medical emergency, I take it." It was the same waitress who had served them.

Peter didn't acknowledge the waitress. His mind was in overdrive and Dee had to nudge him with her elbow. "Peter - bill."

"Sorry yes, yes. You were saying?"

"Must be another emergency, to run off like that."

"Yes, it must be," Peter replied getting his credit card out of his wallet. "Has Helen lived here long?"

"All her life I think. She was the only one who made me feel really welcome when we moved here. It's not easy being newcomers in a place like this."

"How did you meet her?" Dee asked.

"Primary school. Our girls were in the same class; still are."

"Oh, Helen has a daughter. Is she married? I don't think I noticed a ring."

"No, very much a single mum. Always has been. Think Clara's dad was in the forces. Didn't come back, unfortunately. Don't know if he even knew about Clara if I'm honest."

Peter and Dee exchanged a look, and thanked the waitress once again for their lovely meal and her time.

The cold air hit them as they left the café. Dee wrapped her scarf tightly round her neck and popped her woolly hat on.

"Wish I'd got one of them," Peter said.

"You need one of those," Dee said pointing at a flat cap in a shop window selling outdoor wear.

"That I do," he said, making his way inside with Dee only too glad to follow him in and get out of the wind.

When they emerged from the shop, Dee was laughing. "You look like a local now." Not only had he bought the cap but also a matching scarf.

"Much warmer now. Think I look quite dapper in fact," he said doffing his cap at her and they laughed like a couple of school kids.

As they walked around the market square, Dee said "Think we need a plan. I said I'd see my gran on the way home."

"I've been thinking about that. Looks like there's not much we can do for the rest of the day. It's going to be dark soon. The nights are really drawing in. I'll message Helen tonight to arrange where and what time to meet her tomorrow. Why don't you take the car and spend the night at your gran's. I'll stay here and get a hotel."

"The car? I can take the car, are you sure?"

"Sure, I am. I'm not going anywhere tonight. How long will it take for you to get to your gran's from here?"

Dee tapped away on her phone. "Just over an hour if I'm lucky with the traffic. Where are you going to stay?"

"Well, there's plenty of hotels, but I'll try there." Peter pointed over at a large white building just off the square and they walked into the reception to be warmly welcomed from behind an old desk by a neatly-dressed woman.

Peter asked, "Have you got a room available for one night." He was lucky; he had a choice of a twin or a double and he opted for the double and asked about the car park.

"It's free car parking and you're more than welcome to leave your car there."

Peter took the room key which was attached to a large silver horse.

"Makes the keys harder to lose and if you did leave it anywhere in the village they usually get returned very quickly."

"Let's get the car then, drive it round here, and you can get off," Peter told Dee.

Once again, the cold air hit them as they walked to retrieve the car.

"How lucky was that; to meet Helen I mean," Dee casually said. Since meeting her, Peter had not said one word about it.

"Very. Sometimes a bit of luck is all you need."

"Do you think she was earwigging on our conversation?"

"Good job she was. Otherwise we might have been going home tonight, none the wiser."

They reached Peter's car and he threw the keys at her. "Here you are. I'll jump out in the car park and grab my things from the boot."

Dee settled herself in the driver's seat. She was looking forward to seeing her gran. Since they were meeting Helen tomorrow it meant she could stay overnight and spend a meaningful amount of time with her.

"Did you text Jake?" Dee asked as they pulled into the hotel car park.

"No, I'll do it once I'm settled, with a pint in my hand. Are you messaging Edward, to tell him you are at your gran's?"

"Like you, once I'm settled with a glass of wine in my hand."

Peter laughed as he retrieved his overnight bag from the boot. As he bobbed his head down to say goodbye, Dee asked him, "Peter, I know we didn't have long with Helen, but do you think she was really meeting Mary?"

"We don't have any reason not to believe her. The date matches and Helen can't have known that. See what she knows about the Blunt name and why she was meeting Mary - if indeed she was. I'm looking forward to meeting her tomorrow."

"Bet you are!" Dee said with a wink.

"Drive safely. I'll text you the time once I've heard from her," Peter shook his head as he closed the car door.

The ambulance had arrived at Gaitley Manor and Sir Henry was in the back of it hooked up to machines and drips.

"Would you like to come with us Lady Gaitley?" the paramedic asked.

"No, D.I. Jones can follow you. I'll go with him."

The paramedic closed the doors and the ambulance sped away to Amberleigh General Hospital.

Petra threw her arms theatrically around Jake. "Oh my poor Henry, poor Henry," she wailed. Claire thought she had looked more like she was crying when she'd put her eye drops in than she did now.

Jake extracted himself. "It looks serious. We need to go."

"Shall we follow, Sir?" Claire asked.

"I think under the circumstances, you should."

Petra climbed into the car beside Jake and immediately asked, "What on earth did you say to him? He's so fragile at the moment."

"Nothing to cause a heart attack, Lady Gaitley, if that's what you're implying?"

"No, no. Please call me Petra. I wasn't meaning that at all." With that she put a hand on his knee.

Jake had to almost shake it off. He started the car and put his blue lights on. He wanted to catch the ambulance up and he didn't want to be confined in a car with Petra any longer than he had to be.

Ruth had returned to the office to type up her story after the press conference. She noticed that the girl on reception giggled as she teetered on her high heels past her. Ruth gave her a filthy look but as she entered the office some looked away while others laughed or sniggered.

"Alright, what's going on?" Ruth shouted.

"That's what I want to know! Get yourself in here now!" the editor bellowed at her from his office door.

"What the fuck." She had no clue what was going on.

The woman who worked at the next desk to hers took great delight in showing her a short clip Shane had taken of her.

"You're fucking kidding me! How dare he?"

Shane had taken the necessary photos required at the press conference, but he couldn't help but take a video of the performance that Ruth was putting on for all to see on his phone. By the time Ruth got back to the office it had done the rounds.

"The bunny boiler from *Fatal Attraction's* back," one of them shouted as he sat on the edge of his desk crossing and uncrossing his legs. There were howls of laughter.

"That's enough! Ruth now!" the editor shouted even louder.

Ruth went into his office and closed the door.

Peter sat with his pint and a newspaper in the hotel bar. He had a message from Jake who was at the hospital with Sir Henry and would call him as soon as possible. He liked the hotel and town very much. He looked around at the people near him chatting away. Some had dogs with them and that suddenly sparked his interest. He grabbed Mary's diary. He'd brought it down with him to go through it once he'd eaten, but a thought had popped into his head and he was right; he was staying at the same hotel Mary had noted in the back of her diary. He left his pint and paper on the table, asking the barman to keep an eye on them, while he popped to the reception.

The same woman was on duty although it looked as though she was getting her things together to leave for the day.

"Sorry, to ask. Are you okay to check if a Mary Cutler was staying here, please, on the fifth of October?"

"I can if you give me a minute. I'll just log back in."

"I really appreciate it. Thank you."

"Fifth of October? Yes we had a Mrs Cutler staying here." She then corrected herself. "Sorry that's not true. Mrs Cutler was meant to be staying here. She'd paid in full and extra to bring her dog too, but she was a no-show. Anything else I can help you with?."

"Would you be able to see if Mrs Cutler stayed with you before?"

"Yes, she did. Back in early September. That seems to have been her first stay with us according to the file. Is that all? I really need to be off."

"Yes, thank you, you've been really helpful. Sorry to keep you."

Peter had suspected as much but had wanted to be sure and now he was. He'd just sat back down in the bar to finish his pint when his mobile vibrated in his pocket. It was Jake. "Now then D.I. Jones, what are you doing at the hospital with Sir Henry? Don't tell me someone's tried to kill him too."

The barman's ears pricked up.

"Heart attack? What's the situation now?" Peter said, aware that heads were turning to listen to what he was saying. He lowered his voice, thanked Jake for the update and said he would call him on his way back tomorrow.

At the bar he ordered another drink. "Same again please?"

"Sounds like you need it." the barman said.

Dee had finally finished her phone conversation with Edward. He was pleased that she had gone to see her gran and had something to do while he was away. Dee tried to tell him about coming to Malton with Peter but he'd cut her off to talk about the contract and told her he could be earning a massive promotion. Dee told him she was pleased for him but he seemed to have completely forgotten that she was trying to clear her name in a murder case.

Once inside the warmth of her gran's house engulfed her like a hug. Her gran was fussing over a roast dinner announcing that Dee looked like she'd lost weight and she was worried about her. "Tell me from the beginning, when did it happen? How are you and Edward doing?"

"Gran, one thing at a time. It all started with me falling over a dog at Muttering Margo's house," Dee explained while pouring out two glasses of wine.

"Muttering Margo; unfortunate name," her Gran said.

"Very," Dee replied as they clinked glasses.

Peter had finished his second pint and needed to order some food; he was definitely feeling peckish. He was at the bar asking for a menu when, to his surprise, Helen walked in.

"Helen! Are you meeting someone? Can I get you a drink?"

"No, and yes. I've come to find you. Hope that's okay?" Helen's cheeks reddened a little.

"Please sit down. What would you like?" Peter was feeling uncomfortably awkward, he hadn't expected company let alone female company and wished he had taken a shower.

"A white wine would be lovely." She turned to the hovering barman. "House white is fine, Fred. Shall I sit here?" She pointed to the table with the newspaper strewn all over it.

"How did you know I was here?" Peter asked as he set their drinks down on the table which Helen had already cleared, neatly folding the newspaper and moving it to the side.

"This is the only one that takes dogs and since you were asking about Mary, I thought you might be here. Just a hunch," she said, taking a sip of her wine.

"Who's looking after your daughter; a boyfriend?" Peter hoped there wasn't one.

"Absolutely not; no - no boyfriend. Clara's having tea and doing her homework round at Debbie's, the waitress you met today. Our girls are in the same class."

"Yes, she mentioned you had a daughter."

"Oh, she did, did she? I'll thank her later. What else did she tell you?"

"Only how lovely you are."

Helen's blush made her prettier still.

Sir Henry lay in a private ward surrounded by machines but in a stable condition. They were going to run more tests in the morning. Dr Glen had arrived and was speaking to the consultant and Jake decided there was nothing more they would gain from being there and told Petra they would be leaving.

"Can you take me home D.I. Jones? It's been such a long day." The requested favour was accompanied by fluttering eyelashes.

"I thought you would be staying."

"No, nothing to do here. I feel they'd like me out of the way."

Jake beckoned to Tom. "Can you take Lady Gaitley home please?"

"Our pleasure." Tom knew full well it would be no pleasure at all.

Petra seemed about to say something but changed her mind. She looked like she'd sucked on a lemon.

Dr Glen had finished talking to the consultant and waved at Jake to come and talk to him. "For you," he said. "Only take one to start with. See how you get on. Must go."

As they reached the double doors, Jake looked down at the box in his hands. Sleeping tablets.

Dee and her Gran had finished eating and were sharing another glass of wine.

"So, I'm up to date on the murder, and they know you definitely didn't do it, so you're no longer a suspect?" It was the umpteenth time some such question had been asked.

"Gran, of course they know I didn't do it. I'm helping Peter find out who did. Talking of Peter, he's not messaged me yet to tell me when we're meeting Helen tomorrow."

"He'll be enjoying a pint or two, if he has any sense," her gran replied. "Now, let's talk about you and Edward."

Ruth's cheeks were as red as her lipstick when she left the editor's office. He had pretty much wiped the floor with her, telling her how unprofessional she had been and how she had done nothing for the reputation of his newspaper except make it a laughing stock. Ruth had had nothing to say; the video evidence was damning. She had left agreeing to take three days off while things calmed down at the paper. The editor didn't want to lose a good journalist and he had already decided that Shane, on the other hand, would not be there on her return. He didn't like his underhand ways and taking a video of a colleague without her consent was the final straw. For now, he'd keep that to himself. Ruth needed to stew on how she'd behaved and he needed to show the rest of his staff what happened if they turned on each other. As far as he was concerned, they should always have each other's backs.

Jake was enjoying a glass of red wine at home. He laughed as he remembered Ruth's antics at the press conference and then grimaced at the thought of Petra's hand on his knee. 'What's wrong with these women,' he asked himself. He had thrown himself into his job, even more so after Cami died. He wasn't going to let her down. She would have made a brilliant detective. He'd had girlfriends before, a few if he was honest but no one serious. He'd just never met that one. Dee's face popped into his head. He could see her red hair and green eyes smiling at him. 'Yeah right,' he told himself. 'She's too good for that prick of a boyfriend, but if she's too stupid not to see what everyone else can then more fool her. Maybe love is blind after all.'

Peter ordered food from the bar. Nothing fancy. A burger for himself and, for Helen, a chicken wrap. They were both in stitches trying to eat them without food going all over the table or themselves.

"Shall I get you another glass of wine?" Peter asked.

"No, I'm all good. I have to be in early for a surgery in the morning, but after that I'm free till three o'clock. Then I have to pick Clara up from school." A piece of chicken fell from the bottom of her wrap onto the plate. "Lucky!" she giggled.

Peter nodded. "What kind of surgery?"

"Mrs Anvil's cat. She's pregnant but there's a complication so we're delivering them by caesarean first thing as she might go into labour anytime and we don't want that to happen."

"No, sounds awful, poor thing." How long did you have to train to be a vet?"

"Not long at all. I'm not one. I'm a veterinary nurse." Helen smiled. "What do you do?" Noticing him shift a little in his chair at the question, she added, "It's ok I won't judge."

Peter leaned closer and said quietly, "I'm a private detective."

He got back a look of complete surprise. "No way. How exciting. Are you here on a case?"

"Sort of."

"Mary? Is she your case?" Helen moved in closer still so no one could overhear.

"That's why Dee and I need to talk to you tomorrow. We're hoping you can help."

"Ah yes, the pretty girl you were with. Actually, where is she?"

He realised Helen had to be wondering if anything was going on between him and Dee and he needed to dispel the notion. "Dee's gone to visit her gran. She doesn't live far from here. Dee's lovely. Gets herself into right scrapes through and yes, she is pretty, not that she knows it. Has a dick of a boyfriend - treats her rotten. It's a good job I'm not her father. I'd have sent him packing ages ago."

She liked his answer. "Is Dee part of the case? Can I ask? Are you allowed to tell me any details about it at all?."

"Dee's my new assistant." He paused and looked at her "I'm having such a lovely time. Is it okay if we talk shop tomorrow. Say twelve thirty - same cafe? I'll treat us all to lunch before we head back to Gamblewood."

"Alright." She was sure he would tell her all in good time, so, she smiled at him and said, "Twelve thirty's good by me. Now tell me all about Gamblewood before I have to go. I've never heard of it."

"He works away a lot, doesn't he, your chap? Do you miss him?" Dee's gran was treading carefully.

"Yeah, I guess so."

Concerned at how unenthusiastic Dee seemed, her gran said, "Young love should be full of laughter and lots of fun."

"Oh, it is. It's just that when you live together, it's also full of washing, ironing and cooking and we all know how bad I am at that."

"Bless him. What's he said about your cooking?"

"Not a lot. Probably a good job he's not there half the time. I might have poisoned him by now!"

They both laughed but then a serious look came over her gran's face. "Love, if it doesn't work out, you can always come home," and Dee's hand was grabbed and squeezed.

"Thanks, gran," She kissed the old woman's cheek.

Petra was tucked up in bed, enjoying having it all to herself when Ms Bay brought her up the cup of herbal tea which was supposed to aid sleep.

"How's Sir Henry? I thought you might have come and told me when you came in." Ms Bay sounded put out.

"Not dead, if that's what you're asking," Petra replied.

Ms Bay could not help noticing the disappointment in her voice.

Chapter Twenty

Dee had finally received a message from Peter saying not to rush. They were meeting for lunch at twelve thirty. There was also something about Sir Henry and a heart attack. She packed up her things and headed downstairs as she could smell the bacon and eggs her gran was cooking.

"Looks like Sir Henry's in hospital. Heart attack, poor man," Dee said as she entered the kitchen.

"That's terrible, from what you were saying last night, I wouldn't be surprised if that Lady, whatever her name is, put him there. Sit yourself down. Just buttering the toast and then breakfast is ready."

Peter had finished a magnificent full English in the hotel breakfast room and was unsure how he was going to eat any lunch at all. However, he'd noticed some maps showing a local walk in the foyer. He'd grab one on his way back to his room to pack.

Already in his office, Jake was hoping Sir Henry might be feeling well enough to answer some questions. He was awaiting Claire and Tom when his office phone rang. The call required only simple responses. "Yes, Sir. I understand. I'll wait till he comes home."

"Morning, Sir." Claire shouted followed by, "Morning" from Tom.

"Morning you two. Just pop in for a minute. We've had it from above that we're not allowed to go anywhere near Sir Henry till he comes out of hospital."

"Oh, we were just saying that's where we thought we'd be going today, Sir."

"Me too, but the hospital is definitely out of bounds. Tom, can you carry on looking at the CCTV footage before and after the day of Margo's murder. We need to make doubly sure we've not missed anything, Claire, see if you can find anything on anyone from Margo's family, the sister especially, I'm going to speak to Peter this afternoon, he's in Malton."

"Malton? What's he doing up there?" Tom asked.

"No idea, but I guess we'll find out soon enough."

"Sir, can I change the subject? Are you going to the firework display on the village green on Friday?" Claire asked.

"Haven't thought about it. Are we in November already?".

"Yes, Sir, Tom and I are going."

"Don't see why not. Yes I will. Thanks guys. Now let's get on," and Jake dismissed them with a wave of his hand.

"Do you want me to get you a cuppa?" Tom asked halfway out the door.

"No thanks. I'm going to pay another visit to Margo's house; make sure we've not missed anything there either."

Petra was packing a large leather bag when Ms Bay came in to make the bed. "Are we going somewhere?" she asked Petra.

"We aren't, I am - or I would be if I could find that yellow bikini."

"Bottom drawer," Ms Bay told her, drawing back the first pair of curtains to let the light flood in. "Where are you heading?"

"Going to stay at the spa hotel; you know where I play tennis. Looking forward to a few days of pampering. You're okay to be left in charge here aren't you?"

"Of course. I thought you might be going to the hospital to see how Sir Henry's doing."

"Nah, they don't need me there. They made it quite clear he'll be in for a few days," Petra said stuffing the yellow bikini into her bag.

"Don't you think it might be an idea just to pop in, show some interest, see if he's had any blood test results? You could call in on your way."

"I could, but I'm not. I've got a four-ball starting shortly."

"I'm sure he'd like to see you." Ms Bay plainly didn't feel it would be in Petra's best interests not to show up at all.

"He'll be happy being fussed over by all those nurses. He's in the best place. He'll be fine. Right, that's me off. I'll be back at the end of the week."

"Are you going to the firework display on Friday?"

"That poxy thing? Definitely not. Lady Gaitley will be having one of her headaches," she said smiling. "Ta, Ta."

Petra left and Ms Bay started to make the bed.

Dee was back in Malton, she'd been to the hotel bar and checked out the café, but Peter was nowhere to be seen so she decided to grab a coffee and sit back in the car. So much for getting there early.

In the lounge of Margo's home, Jake was uncomfortable about leaving those pictures unguarded.

"There has to be something. Come on, Margo, give me helping hand." Jake spoke out his thought aloud and his brow furrowed. Something was urging him upstairs to the spare room.

Ruth had ordered her first drink of the day. She sat on a padded sunbed in a white towelling robe by the side of a huge pool that had a bubbling hot tub at the far end. She had booked to stay at the luxury spa hotel on a whim. She felt so humiliated at her own behaviour at the press conference and its aftermath. She really had made a fool of herself. A few days away pampering herself was just what she needed.

A guy wearing tennis gear walked past her and went to speak to two ladies lying on sunbeds near hers. They were discussing the lesson they were going to have after lunch and she heard him asking if he could push it back half an hour. Both ladies agreed there was no issue and as he walked away, they burst into childish giggles.

"Excuse me," Ruth called as he walked past her sunbed. "I overheard you talking to those ladies. Do you have room for one more. I'd really like to learn how to play tennis?"

"Yes, see you on the court, one thirty," he said smiling so Ruth could notice his perfect teeth.

She checked her watch. She had plenty of time to go and buy tennis gear from the shop inside the hotel. In typical fashion for her, she wanted the shortest tennis skirt they had. It wouldn't do any harm for the tennis pro to see her amazingly long legs.

Peter had seen Dee climbing back into the car with a coffee and he tapped on the window making her jump.

"Where you've been?" Dee asked him.

He showed her where he had walked on the map and asked if he could have a sip of her coffee.

"Shall we go and get a table at the café. You can get yourself a drink and we can ask if they have one in a quiet corner."

Peter agreed.

"Hello again," the waitress greeted them.

"Hi Debbie," Peter said. "Do you have a table out of the way. We're meeting Helen here."

"Yes, follow me."

Dee whispered, "How do you know her name's Debbie? She never said yesterday."

Peter patted the side of his nose with his finger. "Never you mind," he told her.

"Do you think Helen will turn up?" Dee asked him as they sat down.

"Yes, I'm sure she will."

The waitress returned with menus and took their drinks order. Peter said they would wait to order food till Helen arrived and as it happened they didn't have long to chat about Sir Henry and then about the roast dinner that Dee had shared with her gran.

"Hello there," Helen said with a smile. "Hope I'm not interrupting."

"Absolutely not. Here, have this chair."

As Peter pulled the chair out for Helen, she was removing her coat to reveal a jumper with a sheep on it. She had a white shirt on underneath it and tight dark jeans. Dee, always obsessed with what people wore, thought that there weren't many people who could pull off wearing a jumper with a sheep on the front, but then she remembered those iconic pictures of Princess Diana in her famous jumper.

"Love it," she complimented her.

"Thank you. It's one of my favourites."

The three of them ordered their lunches and chatted about Malton the weather and Helen's job before Peter said, "We need to get down to business."

"Quite," Helen said firmly, flashing Peter a cheeky smile.

"So, when did Mary first get in touch with you?" He passed Dee his notebook and pen.

"Sometime in September. She said she'd been here on a holiday and it turned out we might have family in common."

Debbie brought their meals over, so, they thanked her and waited for her to leave before Dee asked, "How did Mary get in touch with you?"

"Facebook. I ignored the messages to begin with, but then she mentioned the name Blunt and like I said to you both yesterday, I'd heard that name mentioned in my family before, so then I was curious; nothing more than that." Helen took a bite of her sandwich. "We arranged to meet here on the fifth of last month, but she never came."

"Is that your surname?" Dee asked.

"No. Mine's Randall"

"Can you fill us in on what you know about the Blunts, Helen? Anything you can tell us would be really helpful," Peter said.

"I'm going to have to start at the beginning, it's a bit of a long story." Helen said.

"We're all ears," Peter replied and Dee nodded in agreement.

Claire felt she was banging her head against a brick wall looking into the Darnley family. She hadn't discovered anything that they didn't already know.

"They really led quite boring lives. Margo out lived them all; quite sad isn't it and no children in the family either. Wonder who inherits Margo's estate now? I suppose it'll go to the government," Claire said looking across at Tom.

"Probably." Tom was distracted. "Come and look at this. Who's car do you think that is?"

Staring at the grainy picture on the screen, Claire was suddenly excited. "No way! Gosh I hope the D.I.'s back soon."

Jake had found a pretty box with flowers on it under the bed in the spare room. It was almost hidden but should still have been found in the original searches. It was covered in dust and had obviously been there for years. He sat down on the bed and gently removed the lid to find it crammed with photos. Many were of Margo. In some of them she was young, in others a little older and then with a man he knew must be Margo's husband. There were a few of Margo's family too. He put them to one side in a different pile. At the bottom of the box was an envelope. It looked fragile so he gently opened it, pulling a piece of paper from the envelope which looked like a letter, but as he started to read, he realised it was Margaret Darnley's last will and testament.

"Can I check I've got this down right?" Dee asked Helen.

Helen nodded, exhausted from talking so much and Peter had ordered them fresh cups of coffee.

"Your mum wasn't your mum; she took you in when your mum died," Dee said, tapping the words she had written down with her pen.

"Not exactly taken in," Helen corrected her. "My real mum already lived with my mum, so I was more kept than taken in, if that makes sense."

"And you only found out about all this recently when your mum passed?"

"Yes, the solicitor had been keeping a letter for her. I was given it when she died." Helen looked down at her hands. "I've brought it with me. Would you like to see it?"

"May I?" Peter said softly. "We know its deeply personal from what you've told us. Are you sure you don't mind us reading it?."

"No please do. Was Mary part of the Blunt family?"

Peter was taken aback by the question, He looked at Dee who didn't know what to say. "Okay, you've been honest with us, so we need to be honest with you. We're looking into the murder of a woman called Margaret Darnley and Mary's suspicious death."

Helen looked at each of them. "I've got nothing to do with it. I don't know a Margaret Darnley or this Mary. I've never met either of them. You know Mary never showed up. Peter I have a daughter; I can't be involved in anything like this." Helen was shaking.

Dee grabbed her hand. "It's fine. You've nothing to worry about, honestly nothing at all."

"Helen," Peter said "Can we take a copy of this to show it to the D.I. back in Gamblewood?"

Helen couldn't speak. She was so flabbergasted she only managed to nod her consent.

Peter handed Dee the letter. She took photos of it with her phone and handed it back to Helen.

"Dee, can you give us a minute?" Peter asked her.

She rose and headed to the ladies, taking her phone with her. Once she was safely inside the cubicle, she opened her phone to read the letter.

"Helen," said Peter, taking her hand. She didn't pull away. "I think you're connected to the Darnley family. Margaret's maiden name was Blunt. There was a photograph of her sister holding a baby which has since gone missing, Margaret's sister died in a horse riding accident when she was very young."

"Do you know the sister's name?" Helen asked.

"Elizabeth."

"It can't be a coincidence can it?"

"I don't think so. In the letter your mum clearly states that your birth mother was called Elizabeth Blunt."

"That would make Margaret my aunt?" Helen was asking as Dee returned to the table.

"Yes," he said.

"So why was Margaret murdered? And what's Mary got to do with it? How is she involved?"

"We don't know why Margaret was murdered but Mary was my secretary, before Dee. I think she was definitely looking into something to do with the Darnley family, but we've no idea why."

"At least we found you," Dee chipped in. "You must be the baby in the photograph that I saw."

"What photograph?"

Dee started at the beginning. Missing out only the gory details about the murder, she explained all the events that led to her seeing the missing photograph.

"But if you've found me and my aunt's been murdered…Am I in danger, Peter?" Helen was wide-eyed and shaking.

Jake carried the little flowery box and its contents to his car. He wanted to get back to the station to show Tom and Claire what he had found but first he thanked the police constable on duty for doing a good job.

Ruth's tennis lesson was over. The other two women had made it very plain they were not happy sharing the tennis coach with her so she went to reception to book a private lesson for the next day. It had not gone unnoticed by any of the women how much attention he had shown her. She was leaving reception, turning to go and grab a smoothie from the cafe, when she caught a glimpse of someone in the lift as the doors closed. She was almost certain it was Lady Gaitley.

Peter had managed to convince Helen that she was not in any danger. They had offered to give her a lift home, but Helen felt she needed the time it took to walk home to take everything in before picking Clara up from school. Dee had then left Peter to say goodbye on his own. She had the impression Helen wanted to say something privately to Peter.

Dee tried to pass Peter the car keys but he wouldn't take them. "You can do the first half of the journey; I'll do the rest." He wasn't looking at her but watching Helen disappear out of sight.

"Do you think she is safe?" Dee asked, opening the car door.

"I hope so, Dee. Come on, let's get going. I need to call Jake."

Back at the station, Jake put the flowery box in the centre of his desk with a flourish as if he was going to perform a magic trick.

"Can I open it?" Claire asked.

"Yes. Don't forget your gloves."

Claire quickly went to fetch some.

"You know what's in there, don't you?" Tom asked.

Jake smiled. It was enough of a confirmation for Tom. They waited patiently having seen how excited Claire was to look through the contents herself.

"Right then, here we go," she announced. She removed the lid carefully as if she thought something was going to jump out at her. "Oh. look, photos. And what's this?" She was holding the envelope.

"Open it," Jake encouraged her.

Claire removed the letter from the envelope and began to read it. Then in a surprised voice, she said, "I thought this was a letter - but's it a will!"

Tom took his own gloves out of his pocket and Claire waited till he was sorted and then passed him the will.

Claire picked the box up and examined it carefully, turning it around in her hands.

"What are you doing?" Jake asked.

"My grandma had something similar to this and she would let me play with it when I was little. Her's had a secret…" She stopped talking mid-sentence. She could feel a catch on the inside and pushed it with her finger. The bottom of the box sprung free and a tiny bracelet fell onto Jake's desk.

"What's that?" Tom asked.

Claire picked it up. "I had one of these when I was born, although I think mine was a christening gift. It had my name engraved on the inside."

"Does it have a name?" Jake asked.

"Yes," Claire replied. "Helen Blunt."

Chapter Twenty-One

Alison was fed up. She was missing Dee coming in on a morning even though it had only been a few days. Albert hadn't been in either and all the newspaper journalists had gone too. It seemed extremely quiet. Too quiet. Maybe she would clean those fridges out today.

She jumped out of her skin as her phone beeped to let her know she had a text from Dee. She couldn't open the message quickly enough. It said she and Peter were on the last leg of the journey back and she was asking if Alison fancied coming round for a glass of wine or two and a good catch up.

Alison didn't need asking twice. *I'll bring some food* she replied.

Peter had phoned Jake from the car while Dee had been driving. He hadn't wanted to say too much, so he mooted a discussion over a pint in the Star and Crown. Jake said he had major news for him too but it could wait. They had left it that Peter would text after dropping Dee off.

Ruth ordered Steak and Chips. She was feeling a little tipsy. A salad for lunch and running around on a tennis court had made the wine go to her head quicker than usual. Her attention was caught by a shrill voice from the other side of the restaurant.

"Petra, darling; Petra!"

A turn of the head and she saw Lady Gaitley walking in, dressed expensively from head to toe in camel and Ruth being Ruth, she clocked the gold chain hanging around Petra's neck as Chanel. Ruth watched the woman make her way over to a heavily bejewelled woman across the restaurant.

"Bethany, how gorgeous you look. Loving this," Petra gushed, touching the silk scarf at the woman's neck.

"A little something I picked up in Milan, darling." It was said loudly. Everyone in the restaurant now knew where it had come from.

A waiter rushed over to them with two glasses of champagne. They didn't bother to thank him.

Ruth's food arrived, brought to her by the same waiter who had served Petra and her friend their champagne. She looked at her meal in dismay. It wasn't a generous portion and she was hungry. Politely she asked if she could have an extra portion of fries with her steak.

"That makes a refreshing change," the waiter said under his breath, glancing in the direction of Petra's table.

"Pardon?"

"Nothing, ma'am," the waiter said.

Dee and Peter made it back to Gamblewood in plenty of time. The time had passed quickly on their return journey. They had talked nonstop about Helen and recapped everything they knew so far about Margo's death and Mary's potential murder, trying to piece it all together.

"See you in the office tomorrow," Peter said and Dee hurried in for a quick shower before Alison arrived.

Jake was already in the Star and Crown. He'd bought two pints, exchanged pleasantries with the barman and taken a seat in their usual spot. He was looking through his phone checking that he had everything that he needed to show Peter, when his former boss arrived.

"Evening," Peter said and raised a hand towards the barman who simply nodded to acknowledge he had seen Peter come in.

Acclimatising comments about the weather, how it was November all of a sudden and that Christmas would soon be upon them were all too brief before Peter pushed Jake into their real business. "Sir Henry? Tell me all what happened and how he's doing."

In a few brisk sentences, Jake told Peter every detail - about the paintings, their worth and who they were once belonged to, how Sir Henry had lied about visiting Margo and then when questioned his inconvenient heart attack.

"Dee was right." Peter rubbed his chin.

"What does she know about Margo and Sir Henry?"

"No more than we do, but she's convinced that the connection between Margo and Mary is Sir Henry."

"Mary who used to work for you?" Jake was becoming confused. "In what way is Mary involved in all this?"

"I think she's been murdered too." Peter rose from his stool. "We need another pint."

Ruth watched the tennis coach like a hawk. He'd walked into the restaurant, straight over to Petra and her friend. Ruth grimaced as she watched him chat with them, his hand moving slowly up and down Petra's back. She grabbed her phone from her handbag and took a couple of photos of the three of them.

Finishing her meal, she was having her coffee as the threesome rose to leave and the tennis coach spotted her and came over to speak to her, Petra and friend in tow.

"Hear you've booked a one-to-one tomorrow," he said, showing his perfectly white teeth.

"Yes, looking forward it."

Ruth heard Petra's friend say to her, "I bet the old crow is," as the three of them made their way towards the lift.

Petra looked back over her shoulder. She was sure she'd seen that woman somewhere before.

Alison and Dee, deep in conversation, were on their second glass of wine.

"Your gran sounds like one in a million. Hope I get to meet her one day," Alison said.

"Yes, I'll have to invite her down. After all Christmas is coming. Wonder where everyone will want to spend Christmas?" Dee said to Alison but she was really asking herself.

"We're at Jim's mum's this year. My mum isn't coming over from Spain this Christmas. What about your mum?"

"Oh gosh. She'll be busy with the bar as usual I imagine," Dee said looking a little sad.

"Well, Christmas is still a few weeks away. Things can change. Anyway, I didn't come here to talk about Christmas. Tell me all about this Helen you found."

Dee went on to explain about Mary looking for Helen, how they'd found her by chance in a café and that it looked like Helen was probably related to Muttering Margo.

"Oh, lordy me. You just wouldn't believe it. Do you think this Helen is the baby in the missing photograph?"

"We do, but for the life of us, we don't understand why Mary would have pictures on her camera of Margo and Sir Henry talking. We can't put it together. There's no explanation why."

"Well, I don't want to be the one to point out the obvious, but why didn't you ask Mary when you went to see her?"

"We can't. She's dead."

"Dead? Mary?" Alison's eyes were huge.

"Murdered. Peter thinks Mary was drugged. So do I."

Alison seemed on the cusp of bursting into tears. "You'd better pour me another wine and start at the beginning. What on earth's going on?"

Dee hadn't realised how brutal she had been in her delivery and had forgotten how long Alison had known Mary. "I'm sorry. I just blurted that out without thinking. We still have no proof."

Alison was looking into her now empty glass. "Poor Mary. I really liked Mary; we all did."

Yeah, I'll give them a call, Peter. I don't know anyone down at the Shell Bay police Station but I'll get on to it. I'll find out as much as I can about Mary."

"Ta. So, the other big news is, we think we've found a relative of Margo's."

"Really? Who?" Jake asked, shifting in his chair.

"She's so lovely. She's called Helen."

"Helen, you say? I've something to show you." Jake brought up a photo of the bracelet and the enhanced photo of the name engraved on it.

"Where's this from?"

Jake told Peter about the box under the bed and its secret compartment.

"What are the chances of that?" Peter said staring at the photo on Jake's mobile.

"It's the same maiden name as Margo's too. Claire checked that out. Do you think the Helen you've found is this Helen?"

"I do. Helen has a letter that was left to her. Here read this." Peter passed his phone over to Jake and watched Jake's expression change as he read the copy of Helen's letter.

"Oh my. So, we know Mary was trying to find Helen but do you know why?"

"No; we were hoping Mary could help us with that," Peter said finishing the last of his pint.

"Sir Henry comes home tomorrow from hospital. We'll give him the morning to get settled but we're going in the afternoon whether he likes it or not. We need to question him." Jake placed his empty pint glass beside Peter's. "Do you and Dee want to come? he might talk more freely having you both there"

"If you don't mind. I have some questions of my own," Peter said. "I'd better get going; it's been a long day"

"Peter, just before you go there's one more thing I need to show you." Jake was flicking through photos on his phone again. "Here." He passed his phone to Peter. "Tom found it going through the CCTV footage on the day of Margo's murder. Must have missed it the first time, it's a bit blurred but we've had it enhanced."

"Whose car is that?" Peter looked stunned.

"Petra's," came the reply.

Chapter Twenty-Two

Dee woke with a sore head and dry mouth. She and Alison had gone through two bottles of wine and she was feeling very hungover. Dee wondered if Alison was feeling as rough as she did.

She picked up her mobile to check for messages and to text Alison. The only message she had was from Edward. *Be home early. Mr Wang's for dinner and watch fireworks on the Green.* She was so happy at the thought of a romantic meal followed by fireworks that she practically jumped out of bed. However, her head got the better of her and she found herself falling back onto the bed. "I'm too old for this," she moaned.

Jake was up early and on his way to the police station he passed Claire on her morning run. He made a mental note to take a leaf out of her book and start running to keep his fitness levels up. In the meanwhile he decided to grab a smoothie from Alison if she was there to set himself up for the day. Then he remembered about the firework display and turned around to go back to the garage he had just passed. It would be nice to take some sparklers along.

Peter was already in the office. He'd been on the phone checking that Helen was alright although she had teased him about phoning her so early, "And yes Clara and I are fine and I'm looking forward to seeing you tonight." He had so much to tell Dee he thought he might get the coffees in for once. He put his coat on and headed out into the cold November morning to *Coffee Creams*.

Alison, too, was in a mess. Her head hurt. Before dropping her at work, Jim had brought her up some paracetamol and a large glass of water followed by a black coffee and a couple of slices of toast. Alison thanked him, but Jim just took the mickey out of her. It had been a while since Alison had come home tipsy and he'd found it hilarious.

Alison was trying her best to set up the coffee machine when Jake appeared at the door.

"D.I. Jones."

She sounded to him as green around the gills as she felt. "Are you okay?"

"Self-inflicted I'm afraid. A bottle of wine too many at Dee's last night. Coffee?"

"Could I have one of your smoothies, please. Going to the firework display tonight?"

"Yes, Jim loves fireworks. Feels like I've got fireworks going off in my head right now." Alison laughed as she put fruit and ice into the blender.

The bell tinkled over the door as Peter walked in and Alison rushed round from behind the counter to fling her arms around him. "Oh, I'm so sorry to hear about Mary."

"Me too, Alison."

Alison asked what he wanted and went to finish Jake's smoothie and make two coffees in take-away cups but the bell tinkled again and Dee walked in, looking and feeling sorry for herself.

"Well, a full house," said Alison. Do you want to have these coffees here instead?"

Peter looked at Dee. "I think we'd better."

Jake was already reaching inside his pocket to get paracetamol tablets for Dee who was so thankful she could have hugged him.

"I'm glad we're all here. Alison, can you close just for a few minutes? Is that okay?" he asked.

"Do you lot ever look at the time, it's ten past eight, I'm not actually open.".

The four of them settled at the table, Alison having locked the café door so they couldn't be disturbed and they thanked her for her generosity as she had brought them chocolate croissants over to have with their drinks.

Jake started. "Alison, Dee; I don't want you mentioning Mary's death to anyone. Have you told anyone else at all about it?"

"No, I wasn't in a good state last night, so I said I'd tell Jim all about that and Helen tonight," Alison said.

"I've told my gran everything, but that's it," Dee said.

"Have you told Edward, Dee?"

"No, haven't seen him all week I might have mentioned it tonight though."

"Well don't. The less people know the better. If Mary's death was murder and not an accident then we don't want the killer to know that we know. We need to keep it between us, do you all understand?"

Dee and Alison nodded.

"Do you think the same person killed Margo and Mary?" Alison asked.

Peter answered her. "We don't know Alison. The only thing we know for sure is we all need to keep quiet about Mary's death and finding Helen. We know Mary was looking for Helen and now she's dead. We don't want to put Helen in any danger too. Keep everything you know about this case to yourself."

"I'm a bit scared now," Alison said.

"Just be vigilant and keep your eyes and ears open," he reassured her.

Dee had been sitting quietly listening and the truth suddenly dawned on her. "If they've killed twice, they might kill again."

Ruth had finished a lazy breakfast in her room and was making her way to the pool area. She just had enough time for a coffee, thumbing through one of the many magazines dotted around before her manicure, but she could hear the woman who'd been with Petra the night before. She stood and popped her head round the corner. Both women were there, Petra in designer flipflops and a kaftan that Ruth knew would match the swimwear underneath. The tennis coach had his arm round Petra's waist as they waved their friend good bye.

Ruth quickly scuttled her way back to the café area by the side of the pool. A moment later Petra entered waving at the poolside attendant, who went to grab two white towels to hand her. The tennis coach was nowhere to be seen and Ruth watched as Petra put on a performance for everyone as she undid her kaftan to reveal her figure.

"Like what you see?" The voice behind Ruth made her jump.

Ruth spun round like a cat, finding herself facing the beaming tennis coach. "A little too thin for me," she retorted.

"I'm looking forward to this afternoon. I need a good workout. Hope you're up to it?" and he winked.

"Let's hope you can keep up."

Neither noticed Petra watching her tennis coach chatting to *the old crow* from last night.

Claire and Tom were waiting for Jake to come in. It was unusual for him not to be in by eight if not before. "He passed me this morning, while I was out on my morning run. Must have been going somewhere else. Maybe he's called in to see Peter," Claire suggested.

"Think he met up with Peter last night," Tom said.

"Looking forward to tonight?"

"Sure am. Love bonfire night."

Jake's head bobbed into view around the door. "Major meeting. Be in my office in five please. Lots to catch up on before this afternoon."

"This afternoon?" Tom asked.

"Sir Henry's out of hospital," Claire chipped in.

"Exactly and we're interviewing him this afternoon."

Peter and Dee were looking at their evidence board. It was quite full now and things were jumbled.

"It's all mixed up," Dee said

"It is. Let's get it all sorted in a timeline order."

"Timeline?" Dee didn't understand.

"We just need to put what we know has occurred in date and time order, that's all," Peter said, moving a picture of Mary next to Margo.

It took them a while to reorganise the board and once finished they stepped back to admire their morning's work as the office phone rang but it turned out to be a wrong number.

"Just this to go on," Peter said taping a fuzzy picture onto the board.

"What's that? I've seen that car before. It's not a good photo."

"Take a closer look. It's an image taken from CCTV footage. Jake forwarded it to me this morning."

"It's on the day of the murder. Have you seen the date?" Dee announced squinting at the image."

"It's Petra's car."

"Is that Petra driving it?"

"Can't tell who's driving it, you can only just make out the number plate," Peter said going to sit back at his desk and Dee followed suit.

"Jake told me that Sir Henry lied about seeing Margo. He also told me last night that painting's worth several hundred thousand pounds. Maybe it's him driving?" Peter didn't sound convinced by what he was suggesting.

"Or Petra, herself. Remember the woman in the scarf and sunglasses down in Shell Bay bumping into Mary's table."

"Could be Dee, could be," Peter said, checking for messages on his mobile phone.

Alison finished tidying away after the lunch time rush. Albert had come in but much later than usual or he might have seen Peter, Dee and D.I. Jones leaving. She didn't want Albert asking her any more questions about the murder or what they were all up to. She was worrying about Albert. He looked quite pale and very far from his normal, cheery self. He'd made it very clear that he wanted to sit quietly, read his paper and be ignored.

As Albert was leaving to go home for lunch Alison asked him if he was going to the firework display to be told that Albert could see them from his bedroom window if he wanted to watch them.

He'd left without so much as a goodbye.

Claire and Tom were astounded at the news that Dee and Peter had found Helen.

"Are we going then?" Tom said, chomping at the bit to get to Gaitley Manor.

"You're like a giddy puppy," Claire chastised him. "Calm yourself down."

"Yes, indeed," Jake agreed with Claire. "There's no hurry."

Jake's office telephone rang and he dismissed Claire and Tom while he took the call. It was the Superintendent demanding an update.

On the tennis court Ruth was bouncing around waiting for the pro to appear. He was late and she wasn't happy. She had paid for ninety minutes coaching and ninety minutes coaching is what she would have.

"Sorry, sorry," the coach shouted as he ran down the steps. "Something always comes up."

"Bet it does, where you're concerned."

He grinned back. "Let's play."

Peter and Dee sat in a layby close enough to see the gates to Gaitley Manor.

"Why aren't we going up to the house?" Dee asked.

"We need to wait for Jake, we agreed to meet here and go in together." He was checking his watch.

"Are you in a rush?"

"No," Peter lied.

Petra had finally made it home. She had not noticed Peter's car parked in the layby as she passed.

Ms Bay was not impressed and scowled at her as she entered through the back kitchen door and made her way to the grand staircase. "Sir Henry arrived back just after eleven," she told Petra.

"I'm here now. I just got tied up."

"He's in the drawing room. He's got hot tea and I've put a thick blanket over his legs. Do you want me to light the fire?" Ms Bay asked.

"Maybe around four as it's getting dark," Petra said mounting the stairs with her bags. "I'll go see him in a tick."

Jake came up behind Peter's car and flashed his headlights. Peter put his window down and signalled with a thumbs up and Jake pulled out again, followed by Tom and Claire in their marked car.

"How exciting is this?" Dee said as Peter pulled out to join the convoy but he didn't answer her. His head was in investigating mode.

Ms Bay answered the door to find a gaggle of people on her doorstep. "What do you want now, and why are you here?" Ms Bay asked pointing at Peter. "You're not police."

"We're here to talk to Sir Henry as are Mr Gill and Ms Firth," Jake said matter-of-factly, giving nothing away.

As they entered, Ms Bay said, "You'd better wait there. I'll check to see if Sir Henry is comfortable. He only came out of hospital today and Dr Glen is due any minute."

"That doctor is never away," Dee said under her breath, but they all heard it.

Ms Bay returned from the drawing room to confirm with a gesture that they could go in.

"Peter," Sir Henry said. He looked pleased to see him. "Please sit down. Dee isn't it if I remember rightly. Now then what can we do for you?" He had virtually ignored the police officers.

Jake spoke before Peter could answer. "We've come to ask you some questions, Sir Henry."

"Like last time, and looked what happened then."

Peter could see the hostility in Sir Henry growing. "Jake - D.I. Jones - maybe you could speak with Lady Gaitley or Ms Bay first. Give me a couple of minutes with Sir Henry on my own, if that's okay?"

Jake nodded. He knew Peter's softly, softly approach.

The drawing room opened and in stalked Petra. "I hope you are taking it easy with my Henry?" and she rushed across to sit next to him and take his hand.

"Where have you been?" Sir Henry asked, pulling his hand away from hers.

She flushed a little. "Those meds must have knocked you for six, sweetheart. I've not been anywhere. I've been here all morning."

Henry threw her a dirty look, but he didn't want to make a scene in front of other people. Instead, he said, "Of course, darling. Do you know all this medication is sending me bonkers." He looked over at Peter. "It's been a horrid time."

Peter didn't believe a word of it.

Neither did Jake. "Lady Gaitley is there somewhere we can go to have a little chat, please."

"Of course. We can go to the library." Petra smoothed down the blue dress she was wearing with a wiggle. Dee knew that was for Jake's benefit, but he didn't seem to notice.

"Lovely scarf," Claire commented as Petra passed her to go out into the hallway.

"It's from Milan."

"Dee, come with us please," Jake asked.

Dee looked at Peter. She wasn't sure why she should go rather than stay with him but all he said was, "Yes, that's fine. Maybe you could see if Ms Bay could make us some fresh tea."

"Bit rude that. Why can't I stay and see what Sir Henry has to say?" Dee asked Jake her cheeks flushed.

"Dee, sometimes we just have to try another technique. Peter thinks it's best if he talks to Sir Henry one to one. He might open up a bit more. He definitely didn't want to speak to me, but he'll have to eventually,"

Dee felt better for there being a clear reason but on the library threshold, she felt a tickle in her throat which rapidly worsened into a coughing fit with tears streaming down her face.

"Come on. We'll get you a glass of water," Claire said. "The kitchens down here."

Ms Bay was fussing over making a tray for Petra. As they entered, they heard her talking to herself about herbal tea and checking there was enough sugar in the sugar bowl.

"Could we have a glass of water please? Dee has one of those tickly coughs."

Ms Bay stopped what she was doing, went over to one of many cupboards, opened it and reached for a glass which she handed to Claire. "There's good old tap water or iced water in the fridge."

Claire chose the fridge as Ms Bay went back to setting a tray.

"There's a lot of medication in here, Ms Bay."

"All Sir Henry's." The answer came without Ms Bay even looking up.

Claire noticed something that wasn't Sir Henry's. "Even the eye drops?" Claire asked.

Ms Bay looked up, obviously annoyed. "No, they're Petra's; Lady Gaitley's."

Claire poured Dee her glass of water. The ice-cold water was soothing but Dee noticed Claire looking over her shoulder. "Everything alright?"

"Yeah; something and nothing I'm sure."

"Follow me," Ms Bay ordered. She was not leaving them in her kitchen. They had snooped enough as far as she was concerned.

Petra thanked Ms Bay for the tea and Dee remembered Peter had asked her to ask Ms Bay for fresh tea. When she did, Ms Bay did not directly answer. She just put her nose in the air and, with a huff, retreated from the library leaving Claire and Dee standing there, feeling like spare parts with Jake and Tom already comfortably settled in conversation on the sofa opposite Petra so, Claire excused herself to go to the bathroom and Dee followed her.

"What are you doing?" Dee asked. "Do you really need the loo?"

"No, just an excuse. Gives us a chance to have a wander. Just need to avoid Ms Bay."

Claire opened the door into the orangery first. "I love it in here, don't you?" she turned to ask Dee but Dee was gone. She poked her head out into the hallway but Dee was nowhere to be seen. Claire shrugged. Perhaps she really had needed the toilet.

Dee was having no luck finding a bathroom downstairs and decided to try her luck on the first floor. She opened a few doors that led to other sitting rooms, a room that displayed crockery and a couple of bedrooms until finally she stumbled across her goal. She was just finishing and about to flush the toilet when she heard footsteps which continued past the loo, and then stopped again. It had to be Ms Bay. She stayed quiet and the footsteps resumed and faded away.

Dee left the bathroom and made her way to the top of the steps but she could hear a door creaking down the hallway, so, she quickly opened the door behind her and found herself in Sir Henry's office.

"Sir Henry, we've known each other a long time. Will you answer me honestly?"

"It's Henry and yes I'll do my best. I just don't understand what Margo's death has to do with me."

"It's not just Margo's death. I think someone's killed Mary too." Peter watched Sir Henry's face closely but all he saw was baffled indignation.

"Mary, no! Peter, why would anyone kill Mary? This is all totally ridiculous. What is going on here? You have to find out." Sir Henry's words came out in short bursts.

Peter gave him a minute to digest the news of Mary's passing. He thought the man looked genuinely shocked and the shortness of breath supported that view. He knew he had to tread carefully. Sir Henry was an unwell man and he didn't want to see him back in hospital.

"Henry, why did you go to see Margo on the day she was murdered?" Take your time but you have to be honest with me."

Sir Henry took a deep breath. "I'm not well Peter. You know that. Margo and I had unfinished business, shall we say."

"Is this to do with the painting over her fireplace?"

Sir Henry looked surprised. "Lady Caroline gave that painting to Margo when she left. She said it was a sort of leaving gift. However, when Lady Caroline passed away - she was only forty-seven you know - in her will, she left Margo two more paintings from one of our collections. I always felt there was more to it than mere generosity."

"And was there more to it?" Peter asked, hoping he wasn't pushing his luck.

"Not according to Margo. She shooed me out of the house and told me not to come back."

"That was on the twenty-third of September. You'd not been to see Margo before then?"

"I saw her in summer." Sir Henry lapsed into silence.

"You're not telling me everything. Please, I can't help you if you don't." Peter was running out of time.

Sir Henry looked worried. "There is something." He pulled the blanket around his knees tighter. "On my first ever visit to Margo's, I saw a photograph of Elizabeth with a baby and that's when I knew. I went to visit Margo several times afterwards. I wanted to know what had become of the child - I was aware Elizabeth had passed away in a riding accident. Margo said she didn't know but I didn't believe her." Sir Henry paused, gathering his breath. "Peter, I asked Mary if she could speak to Margo on my behalf to find out where the child is now."

"Mary was looking for the child in the photograph for you. Why?" Peter was trying to stay as calm as possible.

"Lady Caroline had lost yet another baby. You have to understand Lady Caroline was very upset and locked herself away for a while. I was young - twenty-nine - and Elizabeth was pretty and well I think you can guess the rest. I'm dying and I want all this to go to where it rightfully belongs. I have a lot of making up to do."

"You believe the baby in the picture is yours?" Peter's heart was beating rapidly.

"That I do. I'd asked Mary to speak to Margo to see if she would tell her anything about Elizabeth and the baby that she wouldn't tell me."

"I take it Mary did speak to Margo?"

"Yes, and it turns out that as dotty as Margo was, she too wanted to find out what had happened to the child. According to Mary, Margo wanted to put things right. It was Margo who sent Elizabeth away when she realised she was pregnant. She didn't want to cause Lady Caroline any more distress, but she hated me from that day on and now I know why." Sir Henry was breathing heavily. "On the day - the twenty third - Mary had asked me to meet her at Margo's. Said she had news that would please both of us, but when I got there Margo slammed the door in my face and told me to go away. She said I'd caused enough upset and if Mary had found out anything important about the child, she should be the first to know."

"Did you just leave, or try to speak to Margo again?"

"No, I felt Margo was right. She did deserve to know first. It was her sister after all. I left, Peter. She was alive when I left."

Peter could hear the door to the drawing room opening "Did you ever meet with Mary to talk about what she'd found out?"

"No, I tried phoning a few times, but Mary didn't pick up. Then when I heard about Margo's murder, I called her again and left her a message." Sir Henry looked pale. "Peter, Mary never returned any of my calls."

Ms Bay entered with a tray of tea and fairy cakes. Her face looked like thunder. "Dr Glen is on his way," she said. "Looking at Sir Henry I think he's had enough."

Jake learned nothing much from Petra. When questioned about the car she said only, "I could have been coming back from playing tennis, or the shops. Who knows? Just because my car was in the area doesn't mean I was going to see a woman who was clearly unhinged." Petra had spoken clearly and precisely but seemed a little too rehearsed for Jake's liking although she had a point. They had no proof that her car being near the scene of the crime was of any more significance than any of the other cars in the vicinity on that day.

Jake checked his watch as he headed to the library door. Claire and Dee had been gone a while. "Thank you for your time, Lady Gaitley. We'll just have two minutes with Sir Henry and be on our way."

Petra nodded. "Tell Henry I will be in to check on him shortly; need to powder one's nose." The fake posh accent was clearly evident. When the door had closed behind them, she grabbed the arm of the chair to steady herself. Her nerves were shot.

Claire was loitering in the hallway when Jake and Tom came out of the library and she came with them back into the drawing room but there was still no sign of Dee.

Before Jake could ask his one burning question of Sir Henry, there was a loud knock on the door, and, without being invited, Dr Glen entered. He did not look amused. "What's all this then? All you people? " Sir Henry's just out of hospital. This won't be doing him any good - no good at all."

Peter stood up. "Alright, we'll be off."

"Just a minute," Jake said. "One question, Sir Henry if I may? How did you get to Margo's on the twenty-third of September - taxi or car?"

Sir Henry didn't flinch. "Dr Glen drove me."

Dr Glen merely nodded in agreement as he rummaged through his capacious bag. He removed a small package and, as Ms Bay walked in to remove the tea tray, he handed it to her. "Here. Now please tell Lady Gaitley this is the last time. I'm not her G.P. and if she needs more eyedrops she must go and see her own doctor"

Ms Bay thanked him, even apologising for any inconvenience that Lady Gaitley had caused and left carrying the tray of used china.

Peter and Jake thanked Sir Henry for his time and Jake said they'd make their own way out.

Dee was by the front door waiting for them. Claire wanted to ask her where she'd been, but thought better of it.

Outside Jake told Tom and Claire to return to the station and before getting into his car, asked Peter and Dee, "Going to the firework display tonight?"

"Yes, looking forward to it," Dee said.

"No, not me" Peter answered.

They parted company agreeing that Peter would call Jake later to fill him in on his conversation with Sir Henry.

Making their way back to the office, Peter said, "Sir Henry believes he's Helen's father."

"I told you, there was a connection between them and Sir Henry. That does make sense, but why kill Margo and Mary?" Dee went on to answer her own question. "Inheritance, that's why."

"Um, yes." Peter checked his watch again. "Rather than going back to the office, I'll drop you straight home so you can get ready for tonight."

"That's great, thank you. Don't you fancy the fireworks then?"

"No, not tonight."

Before Dee could get out of the car at Edward's house, Peter asked, "By the way, where did you get to at Gaitley Manor?"

"Sir Henry's office."

"What were you doing in there?"

"It was quite by accident but look…" Dee took out her mobile phone. "I saw these on the wall behind his desk. They're similar to the ones Margo had."

The pictures did indeed look like the ones Lady Gaitley had left to Margo in her will.

"And this…" Dee showed him a photo of a car parking ticket. She enlarged it to show Peter more clearly. "Look at the date - the twenty-eighth of September – at Shell Bay."

"And you found this in Sir Henry's office? Just lying there?"

"No, it was in the bin."

"Dee, don't tell anyone about this. Enjoy your weekend. We'll talk more about it on Monday. Can you forward those pictures to me, please."

"Sure," Dee said as she closed the car door.

"Bloody hell!" Peter grabbed the steering wheel. He needed to hurry. He had a train to catch.

Chapter Twenty-Three

Moving into December was frustrating with no significant breakthrough in solving the murder of Muttering Margo.

Bonfire night had gone without a hitch apart from Dee finding an old newspaper in Mr Wang's Chinese that was left out for people to read while they waited for their takeout. It featured a photo of her going into Albert's house and implied that she was a potential suspect as was Albert. Dee had exploded in the restaurant like one of the rockets in the firework display and Edward was forced to call Alison to come and calm her down. Alison had made Dee see sense, and a pleasant evening was restored even if Edward had got on Dee's nerves and everyone else's by comparing the event unfavourably with the sort of displays happening in London.

Dee was now struggling as she felt she should be doing something more to find the murderer. Despite Peter telling her she had to be patient, she was getting bored. She felt like she was manning the office on her own. The phone had hardly rung at all and when it did it was usually a wrong number. It irritated her that Peter had been able to get away to Shell Bay to spend a few days there with the police. She suspected he was enjoying spending time down with Mary's family and on the phone he had even mentioned going fishing.

Her boredom was exacerbated by Edward's absences in London while Alison had spent the last week in Spain visiting her mum. Then she received a text from Alison asking if she was free to help put the Christmas tree up in the café. Jim normally helped but he was away with the rugby club lads on a stag do. Dee couldn't get out of the office quick enough.

Claire and Tom were moping around too, without any new information coming in. They had checked and re-checked data, and CCTV footage and interviewed all the car owners in the vicinity of Margo's house on the day of her murder, all to no avail.

"Doctor Glen's car is there – look!" Tom shouted over his desk.

"I know. Sir Henry was telling the truth about Dr Glen dropping him off." Claire had seen the footage many times.

"You don't see him get out though, do you?"

"Well, you can't. It's the angle of the camera but he said he did, and we've no reason not to believe him." Claire tapped the end of her pencil against her lower lip "Did Jake ask him how he got back to Gaitley Manor once Margo had closed the door in his face?"

"No idea, we'll have to check back through our records."

Claire was already working away on her computer.

Jake was in Amberleigh at the only solicitors it had. He had wanted to know if Margo's will would stand up in court if anyone came out of the woodwork to contest it. The solicitor said it was valid and one of the witnesses had been Dr Glen so there was no need to look into it any further. Everything was left to her niece Helen Blunt.

"Why do you think Margaret would have the local doctor witness it?" Jake asked.

"Many do. Nothing unusual in that. Shows they're of sound mind too at the time of making their will. Please don't think I'm being rude but…" The solicitor stood up.

"Yes, time is money," Jake said, thanking him on his way out.

Peter was back in Malton. He'd arrived the night before to watch Clara perform in her school's Nativity play. He was as much taken with the young girl as he was with her mother. He didn't know how much longer he could carry on keeping his visits a secret and he didn't want to.

"It's the tree-lighting tomorrow," Helen said. "Clara and I love Christmas."

Peter agreed wholeheartedly and he put his arm around her as they walked through the park. "Helen, we need to talk; fancy a coffee?"

"Am I in trouble?" She nudged him playfully.

"No," he laughed.

They came across a log cabin selling mulled wine in the park and decided that was a much better idea than coffee. They sat next to each other on the nearest park bench to drink them and Peter came to the point he'd wanted to discuss. "Helen, I think it's time you met Sir Henry."

"What if he doesn't want to? I thought you hadn't told him about me yet."

"I will. I needed to be sure, that was all. It really is the right time for you both to meet. He will love you as much as I do."

Peter did not realise exactly what he had just said.

"Love me as much as you do?" Helen was smiling from ear to ear.

Peter had never felt so sure about anything in his life. He turned to face her, "I do love you Helen - and Clara too."

Alison and Dee were happily chatting away as they decorated the café with Christmas decorations. Alison had decided to close early. She, like everyone, would be staying open late tomorrow for the Christmas light switch on.

"Is Peter okay with you being here?" Alison asked.

"I messaged him but he's not answered," Dee replied, untangling tinsel that had seen better days. "He won't mind. if I'm helping you and I've put the office phone on divert to my mobile so if anyone rings, I'll know"

"Look at you - all tech savvy. Where is he anyway?"

"It was fishing the other weekend, then he went to see Angela another, then fishing again and do you know I don't think I bothered asking him about this weekend."

"Any news about Margo at all?"

"No, but there seems to be a lot going on behind the scenes that I don't know about. It's really frustrating if you want me to be honest." Dee suddenly sounded down in the dumps.

Alison said, "After this do you fancy going to Amberleigh for a look round the shops. I fancy going to that shop again - I can't remember its name. I'd like something nice to wear for Christmas. You never know someone somewhere might be throwing a party we can go to."

"I'd love that."

"Shopping? or going to a Christmas party?"

"Both," Dee replied laughing.

Jake had called Claire and Tom to meet him at Dr Glen's practice. He'd called ahead to make sure the doctor was there.

"Sir, what's happening?" Tom asked.

"Dr Glen witnessed the will for Margo and he said he was the one who took Sir Henry to Margo's on the day of the murder. We could justify a chat."

The surgery was quite modern inside despite its dated exterior. The receptionist said she had been informed they were coming and they were to go straight through to the office at the end where Dr Glen welcomed them. "This is a surprise, D.I. Jones. How can I help you?"

Jake shook the doctor's hand and sat down on the available chair. Claire and Tom had to stand.

"We understand you witnessed Margo's will. Is that correct?" Jake asked not wanting to waste any time.

"Yes, I did. Can't remember who the other witness was. Might have been a neighbour. It was a long time ago. I've done many more since. Is there a problem?"

"Did you read the will?"

"No, I never read them. None of my business, D.I. Jones. It's more that it means I can attest they were compos mentis at the time they made their will. Some don't want family reading them before their death. You never know what goes on behind closed doors."

"No indeed. Can I ask you about the day of Margo's murder. You said you took Sir Henry to Margo's house. Can you tell me about that, please."

"Yes, I'd been to check in on Sir Henry. It feels like I'm there most days at the moment. Do you know he had a good couple of days back in September – the nearest I'd seen him back to his normal self - no pain, no nothing. Then sadly it came back again. Mind you, Sir Henry was much better when he was in hospital. The consultant said he had no stomach pain at all - it was just his heart. Might all be in his head you know."

"Yes," Jake interrupted him. "Can we get back to you taking Sir Henry to Margo's?"

"Yes, I did. I was up at the Manor house and he whispered to me that he needed help and that it was really important. I've known Sir Henry a long time. We're more like friends so naturally I offered to take him and I said I'd stay outside till I saw him go in. As it happens, I went to turn the car around and no sooner had I dropped Sir Henry outside Mrs Darnley's house than he was back on the pavement flagging me down. I pulled over and Sir Henry got in. He was very flustered. I remember because I wondered if he needed a tonic to settle his nerves. He said that Margo was a mad woman and she'd closed the door in his face."

"Do you know why he was going to see her?"

"No, none of my business," the doctor said, looking Jake straight in the eye.

"Did you ever hear Sir Henry mention Mary Cutler at all?"

The Doctor looked taken aback. "Peter's Mary? No, why would he do that?"

"Thank you for your time, you've been most helpful," Jake said without answering the doctor's question.

On the way back to the car, Claire said, "So, he did pick Sir Henry back up and take him home. Clears that one up."

"Yes, it does, but is he telling the truth. Time will tell," Jake said under his breath.

Ruth was back at work; she was pleased Shane had been sacked. Her colleagues were being overly nice to her, presumably fearing for their jobs too. It wouldn't last long but she would enjoy it while it did.

"Do you have that info on Sir Henry's son," Ruth shouted across at Gina whose head was buried in her computer.

"Yes, I'm just printing it."

Ruth went to wait by the printer which whirred into action.

"That should be what you wanted!" Gina shouted.

Ruth looked at the piece of paper in her hand and gave Gina a thumbs-up. It was definitely what she wanted.

Dee and Alison were having a cheeky glass of wine in Amberleigh to celebrate finishing decorating the café for Christmas before visiting the dress shop that Alison wanted to go to.

They had agreed that they would go to the light switch-on together.

"It won't be as good as the one in London," Dee said, mocking Edward's previously stated opinion.

"Course it won't. How could it be? If he loves London so much why doesn't he live there?" Alison saw the look in Dee's eyes. "Sorry, have I overstepped the mark?"

Dee started to cry. "I think I'm going home," she managed to get out in between sobs.

"What are you talking about?" Alison was shocked at Dee's outburst. She found a tissue in her bag and passed it over.

"Edward's got a huge promotion, but he has to move to London, and I don't know if I want to go with him." Dee blew her nose.

"Is it that you don't want to go to London to live or that you don't want to go live in London with Edward?" Alison asked, not having a clue what the answer would be.

"I don't know. Both maybe. I like it here; I want to stay, I like my job, but I think I have to go. Edward starts his new role in the new year and it turns out the house isn't his; he only rents it and he's given them notice."

"Without discussing it with you first?"

"Yes, he just thought I'd go with him. So did I until recently. I'm not sure what to do." Dee had tears streaming down her face.

Alison put her arm around Dee's shoulders to comfort her. "You'll be fine. It'll all work out for the best, you'll see. How long do you have to decide?"

"Not long, I suppose."

"Come now. Let's finish these and go do a little shopping to take your mind off things."

"Hey look at that."

When Alison looked out she saw what Dee had seen. Ms Bay coming out of the fancy clothes shop. "She's got expensive tastes for a house keeper."

"Hasn't she just," Dee said, noticing the scarf Ms Bay was wearing.

The new week was upon them, and Jake went to see Peter hoping Dee would be there too. He found them deep in conversation and surprised to see him.

"Shall I go and fetch coffees? Unless you like that powdered milk stuff." Dee pulled a face at the tin that sat beside the kettle.

"No. I'm all good ta. I've come for a chat about things. I think we're just missing one piece of the puzzle. Maybe on your evidence board."

"Puzzle, what piece?" Dee asked.

"And there it is," Jake announced. "Just knew it. Neither of you thought to mention this? Where did you find that?"

"Dee found it in the bin in Sir Henry's office," Peter said. "Jake, as a friend, can you give me a couple of days, please?"

"Yes, you can have a couple of days, I've still some loose ends to tidy up. I'll call you."

Dee went over to the board to see what Jake had been looking at. "Why was he looking at the car parking ticket? And what's that about a couple of days?"

"Dee, we need to get to the Manor house and tell Sir Henry all about Helen and we need to be quick." Peter was already halfway out the door.

Dee grabbed her coat, knocking the old hat stand over. She didn't bother picking it up, but locked the door and ran after Peter.

Jake was back at the police station "I'm going back to Shell Bay and you two are coming with me."

"Do we need overnight bags, Sir?" Claire asked.

"We could be there a couple of days, so yes," he replied.

Peter had made sure that Sir Henry was alone. Petra was at the tennis club and Ms Bay was in Amberleigh collecting dry cleaning, so, they had a good hour of uninterrupted time.

"You look brighter," Peter said.

"Yes, I've had a lot of blood tests recently. Then, as soon as I came out of hospital I started having the stomach pains again, but today's a good day."

"Sir Henry, I've found Helen. I think you'll put yourself in danger if you tell anyone about her. Can you keep this to yourself?"

"Helen, really?" Sir Henry stammered. "Can I meet her, Peter. Will you talk to her? Do you think she'll meet me?"

Watching Henry, Dee could see tears of joy starting to well up in his eyes.

"Yes, Henry. Helen wants to meet you too, but we need to do it soon."

"I'll meet her today…or tomorrow. How soon can we do this? Peter, can you take me to her?"

"Yes, we can. Dee, can you call Dr Glen? I need to speak to him. I need to know you're well enough to travel and if you are we'll go first thing tomorrow."

"How can I ever thank you? You too, Dee. Helen - is she okay? What's she like?" Sir Henry was bursting with questions.

"Dee, sorry to ask but I need to speak to Sir Henry privately for a moment."

"I'll go outside and call Dr Glen," Dee said. "Don't worry I'll make sure no one's listening." She closed the door behind her and walked towards the kitchen, phoning Dr Glen's practice as she went. Suddenly, she heard a noise coming from the kitchen. Her heart jumped. No one was supposed to be there. She pressed the end button on her mobile and opened the door.

"Ms Bay, how lovely to see you." Her brain was racing knowing she needed to buy Peter more time with Sir Henry.

"Is it? What are you doing here again? Thought I recognised the car on the drive."

"Peter has known Sir Henry a long time. He wanted see how he was doing after the heart attack. Can I help myself to a glass of water?"

"Do as you like. Do they want tea or coffee in there?"

"No, they're fine. Just me. Still got a bit of a sore throat."

Dee started to open the cupboard the glass had come from last time but Ms Bay pushed her out of the way. "I'll get that for you." She wasn't quite quick enough to prevent Dee catching a glimpse of something unusual.

"Shouldn't that be in the fridge?"

"What are you talking about? Here get your water and get out of my kitchen." Ms Bay was glaring at her as she handed over the glass.

Dee did as she was told. With glass in hand, she headed to the orangery. From there she could see if Ms Bay came out of the kitchen.

She phoned Dr Glen. "This is Dee, Peter's assistant. He's asked me to call you. Is it okay for Sir Henry to travel? She got her answer and said, "Thank you for that, Dr Glen. I need to ask you one more question." Dee asked it with her fingers crossed, finished her call and ran back to the drawing room to signal Peter with a thumbs-up.

Peter said, "See you tomorrow. Don't forget the reason you're having to go away for a few days. Stick to that story, no matter how much Lady Gaitley questions you."

Sir Henry nodded as Ms Bay came in. "Think you two should be going now. Would you like some tea or coffee, Sir?"

"Coffee, Ms Bay. I would like a coffee."

"Right, you are. I'll just see these two out." Ms Bay said it with her arms folded, brooking no debate.

"Am I coming with you?" Dee asked once they were back in the car.

"Not to Malton, but if you want to see your gran you most certainly could come in the car. Probably best in case anything happens to Sir Henry. We don't want him to have a turn given all the excitement."

"Is that okay? I need to talk to my gran and you'll pick me up on the way back?"

"Of course. I'm not going to leave you up there." Peter laughed. "I'll drive you home."

Jake, Tom and Claire were enjoying first class on the train to Shell Bay.

"This is a first," Claire said.

"And the last." Tom laughed, shovelling a cream cake in his mouth.

"They're meeting us at the station?" Claire asked Jake.

"Yes, they're sending a police car. And if I'm right, this is it."

Dee came home to find Edward enthusiastically packing boxes and her heart sank. "I'm going up to see my gran for a couple of days. She's not been well."

"Oh. I was hoping you could get some packing done. Never mind, we still have a few weeks. Isn't it exciting. London here we come."

Dee went upstairs to pack her overnight bag. She noticed that he didn't ask how her gran was. 'What if she was really ill?' It made her mad.

Peter was walking from his car to the office when he noticed Alison locking up. She was beckoning him.

"Everything alright? Love the Christmas Decorations."

To his surprise, Alison unlocked the café door again. "Can you come in. I need to talk to you. It's really important."

"Of course," and he followed her into *Coffee Creams*.

Ruth was sat at the bar of the luxury hotel and spa. She was waiting patiently; her next big scoop in the palm of her hand. Hearing voices, she looked up.

She loved being right.

Chapter Twenty Four

Peter dropped Dee at Leeds railway station. She had said she was happy to get a taxi from there and it would make it easier for Peter and Sir Henry to reach Malton by lunch.

Having dropped Dee, Peter asked, "You stuck to the story?"

"That I did."

"Any trouble?"

"No, the only one who looked concerned was Ms Bay, but then she does like to fuss around me," he replied.

"Any issues with Petra?" Peter asked, changing gear.

"No, she had a massage booked today at the spa. I do believe she was almost pleased I was going into a private clinic for more tests, but not for the good of my health you understand. More that I'm out of her hair for a couple of days."

Peter nodded; he knew exactly what Sir Henry was inferring. "Feeling well?"

"Top form, top form."

In her luxurious office at the Shell Bay Lodge Hotel on the cliff top looking out over the bay, the manager said, "Sorry to keep you waiting." She was neatly dressed with a scarf tied to one side like a flight attendant. "How can I help? I understand you're looking into a potential murder here in Shell Bay."

"Yes, Miss," Jake said.

"Mrs Turnbull, but please call me Fiona."

Jake nodded. "Fiona did you have anyone staying here in or around the twenty-eighth of September with the name Gaitley?"

"I can check for you. Give me one moment." Fiona tapped away at her computer with the most perfect set of nails Claire had ever seen. "No, I'm sorry."

"Can you print a list of guests who were staying here?"

"Yes, that's no problem. I'll do that from the twenty-seventh to the twenty ninth. Does that help?"

"Very much so." Jake was impressed with her efficiency. "Do you have CCTV at all?"

"Yes, but only in the lobby and outer perimeters of the hotel. Would you like to see it. We keep everything for at least six months."

Jake turned to look at Claire and Peter. He could tell they were equally impressed with Fiona.

"There." She handed Jake three pieces of paper, which he promptly passed to Tom. "If you come with me, I can find you a room to sit in. I'll call Jeff from security to set you up with a computer and get you going. Is that okay? Do you want to follow me?" Fiona was already up and moving out from behind her desk. They moved after her like children following their teacher.

"Here you go." Fiona opened the door into what looked like a temporary office. Jeff will be here in a minute to get you set up and Flo will bring you some tea and coffee. Are you hungry?"

They all declined and thanked Fiona as she left. No sooner had she gone then she was replaced by Jeff, who introduced himself, set up the computer and then showed them how to access all the files from the last six months. He then left them his number saying they only had to call and he would be there immediately if they needed any help. The three of them were astounded by the courtesy. It wasn't the norm at all in their experience.

They weren't alone for long. "Here we are, get your chops round that. I'm Flo if you need me. I know you told Fiona you weren't hungry but you need good food when you're working." She put a well-laden tray down in front of them. It held tea and coffee, a platter of cheeses, meats and crackers as well as a generous plate of scones covered in jam and cream.

"I think I've fallen in love," Tom told Flo.

Flo let out a laugh so contagious they all began to laugh.

"Time to get to work," Jake ordered." Claire, you know what to do, Tom we need your eagle eyes to do their magic."

Dee felt she was home; a proper home. Her gran's perfume and the smell of her baking warmed her heart.

"My love; gosh you look frozen. Get in here. I'm making you a hot chocolate."

Dee sat in front of the roaring fire her gran had already lit.

"Take that coat off. Here we go," her gran ordered returning with a steaming mug. She didn't pry but somehow she knew something was wrong. "Now before we get talking, I've made a shepherd's pie for tonight and a Victoria sponge for later. I know it's your favourite."

Dee put her head in her hands and burst into floods of tears.

Helen was nervous. Clara was at school but would be home by four, and Peter had phoned to say they were nearly there.

She had set the table for a light lunch and hoped Sir Henry would not judge her on her mis-matched plates. She needed a wee but heard the car pulling up on the drive. She wanted to peep out to take a look but thought that would be rude so she took up a position near the door waiting for Peter to ring the bell.

As Peter helped Sir Henry out of the car, Sir Henry wobbled a little. "Okay?" Peter asked him.

"Right as I can be."

Peter rang the bell and Helen quickly answered it. She looked nervous, so, Peter gave her a big hug and a kiss on the cheek.

"May I do the same?" Sir Henry asked.

Helen didn't hesitate. "Yes you can."

Peter could feel a tear coming to his eye and wiped it away before anyone could see. Helen and Sir Henry were in a tight embrace, neither letting the other go.

"And there we have it," Jake said as they all looked at the grainy image in front of them.

"You were right," Tom said. "Well done sir."

"What now?" Claire asked.

"We'll stay tonight and head back tomorrow. Just going to see if there's any more information regarding Mary's car. I just want to double check it wasn't tampered with." Jake picked up a scone. "How gorgeous are these?"

Alison had finished up and closed for the day. Albert had not been in for two days running and she was concerned. She had told Jim she was going to call on him with some of her special mince pies. He approved, saying it was a lovely thing to do.

She rang Albert's doorbell. There was no answer. She tried again. Still no answer. She tried the side gate. It opened easily and she went into Albert's back garden. A lonely football stood out like a sore thumb in the centre of his lawn. She peered through the patio doors. Albert was either dead in the chair or sound asleep.

"Now cake always makes you feel better," Dee's gran said handing her a plate with a large piece of Victoria sponge on it." Now you stop this crying. We've some serious talking to do."

Dee grabbed the cake and started to eat. She hadn't realised how hungry she was and smiled at her gran lovingly while she took bite after bite.

"Now you listen to me. I have a few pennies put away and if you need that now, you can have it. It will help you pay the rent till you get on your feet or you can come home, Dee. No one will judge you. You have to do what's right for you, but this will always be your home." Dee's gran put her hand on her shoulder. "Now, no more tears and if you go to London, I will support you in your decision but the decision has to be yours, no one else's."

Dee nodded and handed her gran back an empty plate.

"Now that's my girl. Fancy a glass of wine. Its five o'clock somewhere in the world."

Dee burst out laughing and followed her Gran into the kitchen. She felt so much better already.

Peter, Helen and Sir Henry had enjoyed a wonderful afternoon. Conversation had flowed easily between them and Peter noticed how alike father and daughter were.

The door burst open and in ran Clara. "Peter, mum didn't say you were coming." She gave him a big hug. She then stopped in her tracks and stared at the old man staring back at her. "Who are you?" she asked, edging to her mother's side.

Helen began stroking the child's hair. "Clara, please sit down. We have a story to tell you and this is your grandfather. He lives in a place called Gamblewood."

"It's okay," Peter said soothingly and Clara sat down at the table.

"I'm Henry," Sir Henry said, "…and you are beautiful - like your grandmother. Would you like to see?" Clara nodded and Sir Henry pulled out a folded-up photo that he had removed from its frame in the orangery. "That's your great aunt and that's your grandmother."

Clara said, "She's not very old, is she?"

"No," Sir Henry said. "But very pretty, just like you."

"Do you like horses?" Clara asked out of the blue.

"Yes, I do, I love horses."

"So do I. I prefer horses to people, but I like to dance too."

"You're more like your grandmother than you could ever know," Sir Henry laughed.

Alison banged loudly on the patio doors, as she reached into her pocket for her mobile so she could call the emergency services.

Albert woke up with a start, grabbing his chest. All he could see was a black figure at his patio doors trying to get in. He got up as quickly as he could, grabbed his walking stick and started waving it at whoever was there.

Alison was so taken back at Albert rushing towards the patio doors waving his walking stick at her, she stumbled backwards and let out a scream.

Albert saw the figure fall. He rushed out of the kitchen door and stood over her with his walking stick in the air.

"What's going on there?" The shout was from Vicky in the next garden who had heard the scream as she was putting her bins out. "Shall I call the police?"

"It's me Vicky, Alison from *Coffee Creams*. No, no police needed."

"What in the hell are you playing at, lassie?" Albert was still holding his stick over her.

"I came to check on you, you stupid old bugger. You've not been in for a couple of days. Put that stick down."

Albert helped her up and inside. "Tea or something stronger?" he asked.

"Do you know, I'm going to get off. Jim's expecting me. I just wanted to make sure you were alright." She said it with an overwhelming feeling of dread.

"That's nice of you. Hope you're, okay?" Albert was addressing thin air for Alison was already out of the kitchen door. She ran to her car and once inside locked the doors and tried to catch her breath, banging her fists on the steering wheel.

"How stupid, stupid," she was telling herself out loud.

It had suddenly dawned on her that they still didn't know who had killed Margo. To see how quickly Albert could move and to find him standing over her with his walking stick about to strike had made her realise he was more than capable of killing someone, and, after all, the murder weapon had been found in his house.

Chapter Twenty-Five

Dee waited outside Leeds Station to be collected by Peter holding a plastic container filled with her gran's homemade mince pies and chocolate mini-Yule logs. She had enjoyed the time she'd spent with her gran. They'd done some Christmas shopping, been out for a meal and sung Christmas carols together as they put up her gran's Christmas tree. Dee was now feeling festive and started waving as soon as she spotted Peter's car.

Peter put the passenger door window down and said, "Pop your stuff in the boot Dee. Bit of a full car going back. Okay next to Clara?"

Dee looked into the back and smiled, "No problem."

"What are those?" Sir Henry asked.

"These are my gran's seasonal treats," Dee replied.

"Well don't put them in the boot!" Sir Henry laughed.

Jake, Claire and Tom had returned from Shell Bay with all the information they needed. The D.I. had raced off somewhere leaving Claire and Tom watching two police officers put up the Christmas tree in the station's reception area.

"Do you have a tree?" Claire asked.

"We have two. Mum loves Christmas. We all do. You?"

"A little one. We only have a tiny lounge. How spectacular was that tree in the hotel?"

"Very," Tom replied.

"You know I'm going to save up and take my mum to Shell Bay next year for Christmas even if it's only for one night. She's had a tough time with dad running off like that." Claire was pleased at the thought.

"You know, you could see if there's any last-minute deals for this year. Nice Christmas present that," Tom suggested.

"Not just a pretty face, are you?" Claire shouted back at him as she rushed to their office to google it.

Tom stood there smiling. All his Christmases had come at once. Many a true word said in jest indeed and he hoped Claire did think he wasn't too bad looking.

Alison had Christmas carols blasting out at the café when the bell over the door tinkled and Albert walked in. "Morning, no bruises from last night?" he asked.

"No, I'm all good, thank you. Tea and a currant teacake?"

He answered her with a nod as he took his usual seat.

She could feel her mobile vibrating in her apron pocket. It was Dee so she replied straight away. "Albert, we've been invited to the Manor house tomorrow afternoon. Do you fancy it?" she asked him innocently, as she'd been instructed.

"Can do. What for?" he asked her.

She had to think on her feet. "Mince pies and whisky I think."

"I'll definitely go. Can't stand that Petra woman but at least Sir Henry will have the good stuff out."

Peter had told Dee as much as he could in front of Clara to bring her up to date on the case. Jake had sent him the CCTV footage from the hotel so he passed Dee his phone to look at it. He then asked her to text Alison and said he needed Sir Henry to contact Dr Glen once he was home.

"Alison's replied. We're all good with Albert," Dee told Peter.

He nodded, pleased.

"Just a thought, where are you and Clara staying tonight?" Dee asked Helen.

"A B&B in Amberleigh. Peter's booked it. Exciting isn't it, Clara?"

Clara nodded and carried on looking at her book on different breeds of horses.

Dee nudged Clara "Bet you're happy not to be at school too?"

"I like school, but mummy says it's alright. I'm not missing much and we break up next week. Can I ask you a question?"

"Yes, what is it, Clara?"

"If you had a horse, what would you call it?"

"I did have a toy horse once. I called it Flame because it had a long red mane, a bit like me." Dee touched her own long red ponytail.

"What would you call yours, Clara?" Sir Henry asked.

"I think I like the name Sapphire" Clara said, returning to her book "Do you think that's a good name for a horse, mummy?"

"It's a beautiful name," Helen said, kissing the top of her daughter's head.

"Dee?" Clara said.

"Yes, Clara?" Dee looked at her wondering what was coming next. As did everyone else in the car.

"Can I have a chocolate mini-Yule log please?"

Everyone laughed.

Ruth was back at her desk, typing away. She was pleased with the result of the article she had written as was her editor. All she had to do now was wait. The timing had to be right when it went to press.

"We're all ready for tomorrow. Think we should call it a day," Jake said.

"It's early, Sir, are you sure?" Claire queried.

"I've some personal stuff to sort out," Jake said without thinking and then realised his two colleagues were staring at him, their mouths agog.

"Not what you're thinking; Christmas shopping. Don't you have some presents to buy too?"

"I have. I've no idea what to get my dad," Tom said.

"Shall I come with you, Tom?" Claire asked.

"Brilliant. We could pop into that new gin bar. Fancy it?"

"That I do," Claire said and made her way to get her coat that was on the back of the door.

"Don't overdo it. Busy day tomorrow," Jake shouted after them.

Peter dropped Sir Henry home first. It was agreed that it was best if Petra didn't see Peter dropping him off, so, Sir Henry said he would walk from the bottom gate. There was lots of hugging when saying goodbye and Helen had tears in her eyes when she got back in the car.

"Are you alright?" Dee asked her.

Helen nodded.

Dee noticed that Peter had a little chat with Sir Henry once Helen was back in the car.

"He looks amazing, so much better than he has been, doesn't he, Dee?" Peter said climbing back into the driving seat.

"He does," Dee agreed.

Dee said her goodbyes and watched them drive away. She was surprised to find the house in darkness. Inside she was horrified at what she saw. There were packing boxes everywhere. 'How on earth did Edward have so much stuff?' There was a note on the kitchen counter top from Edward. It said he was sorry he'd missed her call last night and for the mess. He had left her two large boxes upstairs that he felt was more than enough as she didn't seem to have much to pack. He had not started on the garage but if she had time before he was back, could she make a start on it. Apparently, he thought that would be really helpful.

Dee threw the note in the bin. She went to the fridge. There wasn't much in it but enough for a sandwich and, luckily, a full bottle of wine. Dee opened the wine and poured herself a large glass. "Here's to you Edward Holloway! You can pack your own flipping garage," Dee said raising her wine glass in the air.

Peter dropped Helen and Clara at the B&B after a quick meal stop on their way to Amberleigh. Clara was tired from the journey and it was agreed it was best for them both to get an early night. Peter kissed them good night and said he would see them in the morning. Then he checked his mobile and, as he'd hoped, Jake had messaged to say he was in the Star and Crown.

Dee woke up excited for the day. She wanted to wear her green trouser suit. The colour matched her eyes and she'd not worn it as yet because it had been a little tight. After her shower, she dressed and much to her delight the green suit was, if anything, a little loose. She tied her hair up in a high ponytail and was applying a little makeup when she heard the front door being tried. She grabbed her phone and ran down the stairs. It was Edward.

"Hope I didn't startle you. Managed to get back early. How did you do with your packing?" he asked as he came over to kiss her on her cheek.

"No, you didn't startle me at all. Everything good at work?"

"Yes, it's just so busy, let me tell you." Edward stopped talking for a second. "You look nice."

"Thank you. Got to go." She smiled back at him, leaving him open-mouthed and surrounded by all the packing boxes.

Jake, Claire and Tom were having a final meeting before heading over to Gaitley Manor.

"Get much shopping done?" Jake asked.

"I did very well, and Claire's very good at pressie shopping if you ever get stuck," Tom said.

Claire beamed. "Did you get everything done that you wanted to?"

"I had a very good afternoon thank you. Now are we all up to speed?"

"Yes, Sir," they replied simultaneously.

Petra was having a lazy morning; she didn't fancy playing tennis or going to the spa.

"Morning," Ms Bay said as she brought her breakfast in bed. "Where's Sir Henry?"

"He's tending to his plants. He was worried about them; you know with having been away." Petra rolled her eyes.

"Did you ask him about the tests he's had done? What have they said about his results?" Ms Bay sounded concerned.

"No idea. I didn't ask him. Why would I?"

"Why wouldn't you?" Ms Bay shot back at her and made her way out of the bedroom, closing the bedroom door behind her with a bang. Petra looked up with a mouthful of scrambled egg and shrugged.

Helen and Clara finished a lovely breakfast. Peter joined them at the end and the landlady brought them an extra cup and a fresh pot of tea.

"You both look lovely," Peter said, taking Helen's hand across the table.

Clara made a vomiting sound, and they all cracked up, laughing.

The morning passed quickly and Alison was able to turn the sign to closed. She ran her finger over her mum's young face in the photograph by the door and set off.

Peter was in his apartment. Dee wondered what on earth he was doing in there. He was making a lot of noise. She could hear him opening drawers and closing them. He'd left the door ajar and she couldn't resist a look.

"Peter, are you alright? Do you need some help?"

"No. I'm all good," came the reply from what she presumed was the bedroom.

She was staggered at Peter's apartment. It had a white kitchen and a black dining room table with matching chairs for four people which was placed perfectly to the left of the kitchen. He had a huge L-shaped sofa facing the fireplace and a TV on the wall above it. It was really lovely. She'd expected it to be scruffy and for much of it to have seen better days a bit like the clothes Peter wore although Dee had noticed he had smartened himself up of late.

"Let's go," Peter and noticing Dee's apparent surprise, he added, "I don't like to live in a mess."

"It's lovely, and no brown."

Ms Bay was busy folding the last of the towels when she heard the front door bell. Tutting, she wondered who it could be, and opened the door to find the doctor on the doorstep.

"Come in, Dr Glen, I didn't think we were expecting you till next week?"

"No, Sir Henry called. Asked me to pop in. Is he in the drawing room?"

"I believe he's in the library. Shall I fetch him?"

"It's fine, I should know where it is by now."

Ms Bay had just put her foot on the first step of the stairs when the bell rang again. "What now?" She found D.I. Jones and his colleagues at the front door.

"Dr Glen has just arrived. You'll have to wait till he leaves."

Jake showed his badge. "It's fine. Sir Henry is expecting us."

Ms Bay looked confused. "He's in the library."

"Thank you."

They were heading down the hallway when Petra came down the stairs, in a tight, black, knitted dress and long, high-heeled boots. "Ms Bay, what's going on? Who's in there?"

"Dr Glen and the police. I've no idea what's going on. You'd better find out," Ms Bay said and made her way up the stairs with the towels.

Petra was about to enter the library when the doorbell rang for the third time and she went to answer it.

"Sir Henry's asked to see us," Peter said. Dee was beside him.

"You'd better come in," Petra said. "I do believe we're all meeting in the library." She took then in and if she was surprised by the gathering she put a good face on it. "Gentlemen, lovely to see you all. Ms Bay will be here to sort some drinks and nibbles shortly."

Sir Henry was on his feet, chatting happily with everyone. Petra didn't like it. She left and went straight to the kitchen where Ms Bay was already putting cups and saucers on a tray. "You really should have told me about this," she said to Petra.

"I didn't know about it," Petra said. "I really didn't."

The doorbell rang again. "Who's he invited now," Petra said, looking perplexed. "I'll get it; you carry on." At the door was an elderly man. "Who are you?" she said in a haughty voice.

"Albert. Sir Henry's invited me."

Petra was taken aback. "He's invited you?"

"It's his house. He can invite who he likes."

"How dare you talk to me like that. I am Lady Gaitley."

"You're about as much a Lady as I'm a Gentlemen," Albert hissed at her "I take it they're in there; I know my way around."

Petra watched him scuttle off towards the library. She could hear them all chatting happily about their Christmas plans and saying how well Sir

Henry was looking. She then heard Sir Henry greet the horrid man who had just arrived like a long-lost friend.

She reapplied her lipstick in the hallway mirror - she always kept a spare lipstick in the cabinet below it for emergency top-ups – and hurried into the library.

"Petra, darling," Sir Henry said as she entered. "Come and join us. Where did you get to?"

"Just organising things. This is all a bit of a surprise. Henry, you are such a devil. You must have forgotten to mention it. You've got Ms Bay in such a spin."

"Yes, I must have," Sir Henry said, looking directly at Peter.

Ms Bay came in carrying a tray laden with hot tea, cakes and biscuits. "I'll just pop some sausage rolls in. I'll be back shortly."

"No need for that. Please stay; take a seat." Jake pointed her to one of the empty chairs.

"Thank you. "she said. As she took her seat, she noticed Claire check her phone and leave the room.

Jake began. "I hope you don't mind Sir Henry and myself inviting you all here today. We have the little matter of Margaret Darnley's death to discuss."

Albert interrupted him. "Do you mean Margo, Muttering Margo?"

"Yes, I do, Albert. As we all know Margo was murdered on the twenty-third of September, and we believed Dee was the last one to see her alive, making her our prime suspect." Jake smiled looking over at Dee, the light catching her red hair. He couldn't help noticing how green her eyes were and that the suit she was wearing complemented them perfectly.

She smiled back and Jake had to turn away. He felt as if he'd been caught out staring and he needed to concentrate.

Jake turned to look at Sir Henry. "Now as it turns out that's not true. You…" Jake pointed at Sir Henry. "You visited Margo on the day of the murder after Dee had already left. We've a witness to that, don't we, Albert?"

"Yes, I saw Sir Henry go into Margo's," Albert declared.

"That's rubbish. I never went in. I've told you this."

"Yes, Sir Henry and that is the truth. You didn't actually go in. Dr Glen can vouch for that. So, the question is who did and why did they kill Margo?"

Dee noticed that Tom had positioned himself in front of the library door.

"I believe it's best to start at the beginning. Margo had three very expensive paintings in her house, worth hundreds of thousands of pounds. Did someone know that? Was it a robbery gone wrong?" Jake turned to Albert. "Did you know about the paintings?"

"What would I know about paintings?" Albert said.

"Annie never mentioned to you that Lady Caroline had given a painting to Margo as a gift and that the other two were left to Margo in Lady Caroline's will?" Jake stared hard at Albert.

"Yes, she did," Albert replied. "It's not fair is it. My Annie got nothing. All those years she worked here and my Annie got nothing."

Sir Henry patted Albert on the hand. "I'll make it right, I promise," he said to him.

"So, Albert, was it you who went round to steal the paintings. Maybe you didn't think Margo was there. Was there a scuffle of some sort and you hit her on the head with the meat tenderiser you'd taken with you?"

"I found that in my garden. It was hers next door. I've told you that too. I'm an old man. Don't be so ridiculous."

"Not too old to threaten Alison with your walking stick, eh Albert?"

Peter and Dee exchanged looks, shocked by what they'd just heard.

"I said I was sorry. I thought she was trying to break in?" Albert looked upset.

"So, if you didn't want to steal the paintings, that brings us to Dr Glen." Jake turned to face him.

"Me?" Dr Glen fiddled with the stethoscope around his neck.

"Yes, you." Jake paused for a moment. "Who's to say you didn't go back to Margo's after you dropped Sir Henry back home. You knew about the paintings and their worth. You'd seen it in Margo's will when you witnessed it."

"I don't go around killing my patients D.I. Jones. I'm a doctor. I make people better." Dr Glen was as red as a beetroot. "I witness lots of wills. I told you that also."

"Margo had no family, so who did she leave them to?" Albert asked.

"Don't ask me. I didn't read her will," Dr Glen answered.

Jake looked at them all one at a time. Then he told them. "A lady named Helen Blunt." Dee noticed Jake nod at Tom who opened the door to admit Helen and Claire.

Helen looked immediately to Peter for reassurance and said, "I'm Helen, I'm Margo's niece."

"Well, I never," Albert declared. "Annie never told me Margo had a niece."

"No," Jake said. "Annie wouldn't have known. Margo and Elizabeth kept it to themselves and Helen is Elizabeths daughter."

"Elizabeth? She died ages ago. Went to work in some stables up north. Nasty accident, I think," Albert blurted out.

"Thank you, Albert, that's enough."

"Sorry, love." Albert looked across at Helen. "I wasn't thinking."

Helen smiled and mouthed silently to him that it was okay.

"If Margo wasn't murdered because one of you wanted to steal the paintings, then why was she murdered at all? Could it be for inheritance reasons?" Jake asked staring at them.

Albert couldn't hold his tongue "Other than the paintings I don't believe Margo had much to leave to anyone. Why would someone murder her for any inheritance?"

Jake once again surveyed the room. "Helen's father is Sir Henry."

There were gratifying gasps around the room.

Petra finally spoke. "That's rubbish. Oscar is Sir Henry's only child. I've never heard Sir Henry mention her once. She could be a fraud for all we know."

Peter didn't like Petra's tone at all. "Helen is not a fraud." He spoke with authority.

"And how would you know?" Petra said, in a condescending manner.

Peter reached into his pocket and took out an envelope. "I have the DNA results to prove it."

Dee looked really surprised as did most of the others and Petra was taking deep breaths, trying her hardest to keep her wits about her.

"Petra, your car was seen near Margo's house on the day she was murdered," Jake said.

"So, what? There were plenty of other cars there too. Doesn't mean anything." She was glaring at Jake. "I told you I could have been coming back from anywhere."

"Yes, you could - from murdering Margo."

"Why D.I. Jones? Why would I murder her? You're not making any sense."

"Like I said inheritance. Maybe you had found out that Sir Henry had a rightful heir." Jake watched her intently.

"Oscar is his rightful heir; I'll be having those DNA results re-done," she spat out.

"That's not true Petra, but I will always ensure Oscar is taken care of," Sir Henry said.

"What are you saying? That you're not Oscar's father? Is that what you're implying?" Petra was beside herself.

"That's exactly what I'm saying," Sir Henry stood up and walked over to Helen. "Oscar could never have been mine; I had a vasectomy a long time ago. Didn't I, Dr Glen?"

The doctor nodded. "Yes, you did, Sir Henry."

Sir Henry looked back at Petra. "Lady Caroline lost so many babies and a piece of her died with every one. In the end I could not see her hurt anymore. I asked Dr Glen to make arrangements for me at a private clinic."

Sir Henry took Helen by the hand. "It was by chance that I found out about Helen. I had an affair with Elizabeth, Margo's sister. Not for long but long enough. I'd been to Margo's to ask her why Lady Caroline had left her the paintings in her will on top of giving her the other originally. I always felt there was more to it. Margo wouldn't tell me but then I saw a photograph of your mother…" He smiled at Helen. "…holding a baby. I knew immediately that the baby in the picture was mine."

"Hang on," Albert said. "So why did Lady Caroline give Margo those paintings?"

"To be passed on to Helen one day. I believe Lady Caroline knew all about Helen. I understand she wanted to raise you as her own, Helen, but Elizabeth wouldn't let that happen, so Lady Caroline did the next best thing and found Elizabeth a job at a good stable and arranged for her to live with a lovely family called the Randalls. Lady Caroline never told me she knew about Helen; she took that to the grave with her."

"This is all ridiculous. Why didn't you tell me you'd had a vasectomy before we got married?" Petra was walking up and down. "You lied to me."

"You lied to him," Albert shouted at her.

"Where's this story come from?" Petra shouted back.

"It's not a story. It's all in a letter my mum left me when she died. Not my birth mother but Mrs Randall, my mum." Helen spoke quietly.

"So, who does your sprog belong to?" Albert shouted at Petra.

Laughter was close to the surface among the observers and Claire and Tom were having to look down at their shoes to control themselves.

"No need to talk like that Albert," Sir Henry scolded him. "But I believe he'll turn out to be the son of Petra's long-time tennis coach."

Petra turned away to stare out of the window.

Jake finally got a word in. "If I'm correct, Sir Henry, you used someone to help you find Helen."

"Yes, I did, but it wasn't only me. Margo was also trying to find Helen. After Elizabeth died, Helen disappeared - vanished into thin air. Helen was only weeks old when it happened. Mrs Randall raised Helen as her own registering the birth as hers. They moved several times, making it hard to trace. We both wanted to find you, and we asked Mary for help."

"Mary; I miss Mary," Albert piped up.

Jake gave him a look. "Mary was also murdered."

"Bloody Hell!" Albert couldn't believe what he was hearing.

"We believe she was drugged in a café. A woman bumped into her table spilling her tea and then bought her a fresh one out of kindness or so Mary thought. However, that was laced with sleeping tablets. We have the toxicology report that confirms this. Totally unaware that she'd been drugged, Mary got behind the wheel of her car and didn't make it home. Her car left the road and went off the edge of a cliff. Mary and her dog never stood a chance." Jake finished speaking and stood looking at them all for a moment.

"Mary was killed for helping Margo and I look for Helen," Sir Henry said solemnly.

"Petra Gaitley, we're arresting you for the murder of Margaret Darnley and Mary Cutler," Jake announced, nodding at Tom.

"What, I've done no such thing."

"Your car was in Shell Bay where Mary lived the day before and on the day of the murder. We also have a car parking ticket with your fingerprints on it proving your car was parked at the Shell Bay Lodge

Hotel and we have CCTV footage of you in the hotel and outside the café at the time Mary was drugged."

"I haven't done anything. I really haven't. I didn't know anything about this Mary or her." Petra pointed at Helen, her body shaking.

"No, you didn't," Dee took a step forward. "…but you did, didn't you Ms Bay?"

They all looked at the housekeeper.

Peter said, "What are you doing Dee?"

Dee carried on, ignoring him. "Ms Bay knew that Margo was looking for Helen. Margo told me that the girl in the photo holding a baby was an heiress and I bet at some point you bumped into Margo and she told you too." Dee looked straight at Ms Bay. "Most of the village had probably heard her say it come to think of it. After all Margo wasn't called Muttering Margo for nothing. She went round this village saying all sorts about anyone and everyone. Most people ignored what she said, but you didn't. You listened and you didn't like what you heard."

"How on earth would I know about this Margo woman looking for anyone. I've never heard such rubbish," Ms Bay shouted.

"You found out that Sir Henry had been visiting Margo and talking to Mary. You ask how I know? I'll tell you." Dee looked straight at Ms Bay." I know you like to listen at doors. I've seen you. I was upstairs. I had been in Sir Henry's office. I saw you as I came out of the office listening outside the drawing room door, earwigging when Sir Henry was speaking to Peter. I also think you listened in on any phone calls that Sir Henry had with Mary. If Sir Henry had listened carefully, he would have heard the click of you picking up a phone in one of the other rooms." Dee caught her breath. "Once you knew that Margo was telling the truth and it wasn't just an old lady going around muttering under her breath but there was a potential blood relative who could inherit Gaitley Manor and all that comes with it, you knew what you had to do. You had to get rid of Margo and any evidence that Helen ever existed."

Dee stopped to took a quick sip of her tea, and carried on. "Once again you were eavesdropping and overheard Sir Henry asking Dr Glen to drive him to Margo's. It was you driving Petra's car that day, not Petra. You took Petra's car and followed Sir Henry and Dr Glen to Margo's. That's how you found out where she lived. You watched Sir Henry leave Margo's - or should I say being sent away with a flea in his ear - and then you knocked on her door moments later. I'm not sure exactly what happened between you and Margo. Detective Inspector Jones can sort out the details but it was you who killed Margo." Dee looked at Jake for confirmation and he nodded back, allowing her to carry on.

"Now we need to talk about the murder weapon. The meat tenderiser you used to kill her with belonged to this house. It was from your kitchen. It was an expensive piece of kitchen equipment and I noticed when Claire and I were in your kitchen the day I had a tickly cough, you had all your kitchen utensils hung up. There was one missing but the gap wasn't big enough for the tenderiser. Then it dawned on me while I was visiting my gran that like her you like everything to match and I'm sure if you check the handles of the other utensils in Ms Bay's kitchen, they'll be a match for the murder weapon. I'm not quite sure how you managed to get it into Albert's Garden but then I had the thought that Petra's car would have a few tennis racquets in the boot, why not use one of them to hurl it over the gardens. I was surprised you didn't bring it back here with you to be honest. Then we'd never have found it."

No one spoke, they were all just staring at her.

"Let's move on to Mary. I found photos of Sir Henry and Margo talking together and pictures of Gaitley Manor on Mary's camera that she had left behind in the office when she retired. That is when Peter and I realised Mary was involved somehow. I think the photos were taken to show you, Helen. Nothing more than that."

Dee turned to stare at Ms Bay. "I believe you listened in to the phone call that Mary made to Sir Henry, you know the one where she arranged to meet them at Margo's house to tell them some important news. That was to tell them both that she had found you, Helen."

Turning back to Ms Bay, Dee continued. "Well you couldn't have that could you, so you took Petra's car to Shell Bay. I think you either found out where Mary lived from Margo before killing her or, lots of people knew where Mary had retired to, so, maybe you found out by just asking around the village. Once again, we can let D.I. Jones tie that one up.

"Like I said you used Petra's car to go to Shell Bay. Unfortunately for Petra you wore one of her scarfs. Maybe it was conveniently left on one of the car seats. You tied it round your head and put on Petra's sunglasses that she probably keeps in her glovebox to disguise yourself."

She turned to Petra. "You see, that's why she looks like you on the hotel CCTV footage, but it's not you; it's Ms Bay."

Jake was about to say something but Dee shut him up with a stare and continued. "You orchestrated the whole bumping into Mary's table fiasco, and replaced her cup of tea with the one you had laced with sleeping tablets."

"What are you talking about now? "Ms Bay raised her voice.

"You went to Shell Bay the day before you killed Mary. I think you watched Mary's movements. You probably followed her to the café. I think you asked about her, how often she went, and when you found out Mary went to the cafe every day, you hatched the plan to drug her. You knew it wouldn't take long for the sleeping tablets to take effect - just long enough for Mary to walk Jasper back along the beach and get behind the wheel of her car to drive home. Mary and Jasper didn't make it home thanks to you, Ms Bay."

"This is the most stupid thing I've ever heard." Ms Bay stood up. "Why would I be interested in murdering them? Tell me why?"

"Okay, if I have to," Dee sighed. "Ms Bay isn't who you think she is, is she Petra?"

Petra looked away.

"Albert, you were right all along about Annie. Petra moved the broach and hid it. She then accused your Annie of stealing it so she could sack her."

"Told you. You're a witch," he shouted across at Petra.

Petra didn't flinch.

"Why did you do that, Petra?" Sir Henry asked.

"Do you want to tell him?" Dee asked.

Petra shook her head.

"So she could give Ms Bay a job here. Ms Bay is Petra's mother."

"What?"

"I've had enough of this," Ms Bay shouted.

"I haven't finished yet," Dee said.

"There's more?" Jake asked.

"Yes. Ms Bay needed to get rid of Sir Henry. You were to be her third victim."

Sir Henry looked horrified.

"With Mary and Margo gone, that only left you who knew about Helen. Ms Bay didn't want her daughter and grandson to miss out on all this…" Dee spun round with her hands in the air. "So, you had to go too."

"How was she planning on doing that?" Sir Henry asked.

"She was already killing you. That's why you've been ill. She was putting eyedrops in your food and it also explains why when you weren't here you got better. I spoke to Dr Glen and he confirmed that it was Ms Bay who ordered the eyedrops saying it was on Petra's behalf. Petra didn't need them; she has her own eyedrops from her own G.P. Petra's are kept in the fridge but if you look in the cupboard where the glasses are kept you'll find two if not three bottles of eyedrops hidden in there.

"Dr Glen also confirmed how poisonous eyedrops are when swallowed. Who knew, but you did, didn't you Ms Bay? Sir Henry, she was slowly poisoning you."

Sir Henry looked as if a feather could knock him over.

"But Dee we have Petra's finger prints on the car parking ticket from Shell Bay," Jake said.

"Yes, that's unfortunate. I bet Ms Bay didn't bank on Petra going into Sir Henry's office. I bet that threw you a little, Ms Bay, when you heard that. It did me. My guess is Petra found it on his desk or maybe the floor, picked it up and threw it in the bin. D.I. Jones, how did you get the ticket from Sir Henry's office for analysis?"

Peter said, "He didn't. It was me. I made an excuse to come back. I sneaked up to Sir Henry's office and retrieved it from the waste bin. When you showed me the photo, Dee, I knew it was an important piece of evidence. Then to be honest I forgot about it. I had a train to catch. I remembered when Jake showed up looking at it on our evidence board. It was still in my pocket. I should have handed it in to the station straight away on the day but I didn't. Sorry about that, Jake. I gave it to Claire as soon as I remembered."

Claire nodded. "That's true, but Dee, how did you know that Ms Bay is Petra's mother?"

"That's easy. Alison and I were shopping for dresses in Amberleigh for your garden party, Sir Henry. Petra had bought a dress that Alison liked that was in the dress shop window. Turned out to be a very expensive dress and the lady who worked there said it wouldn't fit Alison anyway. Like you do, we both took it that the dress would have been too small for Alison, especially when you look at how tiny Petra is. However, that wasn't the case at all. The dress would have been too big for Alison as Ms Bay was wearing it to the Garden Party. You would not spend that amount of money on a dress for your housekeeper, but you might on a dress for your mother. Secondly, there's the scarf."

Jake looked bewildered. "What scarf?"

"Yes, I think if you check Ms Bay's room you will find the scarf she used as a head scarf to disguise herself in Shell Bay, the one she's wearing on the hotel CCTV footage, when she drugged Mary,"

Jake nodded at Claire who left the room.

Dee turned her attention back to Ms Bay. "I saw you wearing it the other day in Amberleigh. This time I was Christmas dress shopping with Alison. I'm sure it will be the same one. I'd recognise a Chanel scarf anywhere.

"That got me thinking Perhaps Ms Bay took a liking to the scarf after wearing it in Shell Bay and kept it. If you think about it, Annie got sacked for a stolen broach that wasn't actually stolen, so, why wouldn't

Petra sack Ms Bay for taking one of her scarves?" Dee paused for dramatic effect.

"Because she's your mother, Petra."

Claire returned holding a clear plastic evidence bag containing the scarf for all to see.

"Yep, that's the one," Dee said, feeling pleased with herself.

"Ms Bay, I am arresting you for the murders of Mary Cutler and Margo Darnley and for the attempted murder of Sir Henry Gaitley. Read her her rights, Tom."

"Mum, did you, do it? You didn't have to do any of this. I don't understand. Why?" Petra was crying and grabbing her mother's arm.

"I did it for you. This is all yours, my darling. You deserve everything. It belongs to you." Ms Bay turned to Sir Henry. "You make me sick, trying to take it all away from her and my grandson."

She then turned on Dee. "Think you're clever don't you? That muttering idiot was going all over the village telling people that she knew who the real heir to Gaitley Manor was and then that Mary had to go and stick her nose in, hanging around and taking photos. Nothing but interfering old bats the pair of them." Her malevolent gaze switched to Sir Henry. "And I wish I'd finished you off quicker."

Tom escorted Ms Bay out to the police car her hands in cuffs, behind her back.

"You're coming too, Missy," Jake said to Petra.

Claire didn't handcuff her, but escorted her by the elbow to another waiting police car.

Alison and Clara came out of the drawing room. "Mummy," Clara shouted, letting go of Alison's hand and running to Helen.

"I never did get that mince pie or my whisky," Albert moaned.

Two weeks had passed since the arrest and Christmas day was just around the corner.

It was late and Ruth was sharing a whisky with her editor in his office. Not only had she had the scoop of her life, reporting on the murders and the potential murder of Sir Henry, she had shocked readers with her revelations about Petra's hotel rendezvous with friends and her tennis coach. Her editor had promised her a nice Christmas bonus and she'd decided to treat herself. Her suitcase was packed and ready to go. She was flying off to celebrate Christmas and New Year in the Bahamas.

Sir Henry was relaxing on his sofa in the drawing room. He had thrown the most fabulous Christmas party. Helen, Dee and Alison had helped to organise it. "Ladies that was wonderful," he said to the three of them. "Alison, the food was exceptional."

"Thank you, Sir Henry…Henry," Alison corrected herself.

All the other guests had gone and Jake Jones stood near the piano, admiring the Christmas tree. He looked around. Claire and Tom were standing chatting about their New Year plans, Helen and Peter were together on the sofa opposite Alison, Dee and Sir Henry. Jim was playing a game with Clara on the floor. Then Alison nudged Dee who stood up by the fireplace.

"I have something I want to say, I've decided not to go to London with Edward. I'd like to stay here. Not sure how it's going to work but I really want to."

Claire asked, "Are you just going to see each other on a weekend?"

"I won't be seeing him at all," Dee said smiling. "I had a lucky escape; he definitely was not the one for me."

"Thank heavens!" Peter shouted, relieved Dee had finally seen sense.

"I'll drink to that!" Alison said laughing.

Helen tapped Peter on his knee and taking the hint he went to join Dee by the fireplace. "Dee, you said you'd like to stay?"

"Yes, I would."

"Well, I'd like to give you an early Christmas present." He handed her a blue box, wrapped in pretty ribbon.

Jim came to join Alison on the sofa and Clara jumped on Helen's knee as Dee opened the package. Inside were two keys. "What's this, Peter. I don't understand." Dee held the keys up to show everyone looking completely confused.

"That one is the key to my car. I transferred it into your name this afternoon."

"Really?" was all Dee could manage to say.

"And that one is the key to my apartment," Peter said.

"What? I can't live there. I don't understand, Peter. I like you a lot but I'm sure you don't want me living with you."

"No, I won't be living there. You can live in the apartment rent-free, as long as you cover the bills; that's all I ask."

"So, hang on, where are you going to live?"

"With Helen and Clara."

Clara had been sitting on Helen's knee. Now Helen popped her off onto the sofa and came to stand at Peter's side. Slipping her hand into his, she gave him a kiss on the cheek.

"Really, I can live in your apartment and you've given me your car?" It was all starting to sink in.

Jake watched Dee embrace Peter as she thanked him. "I can't believe I missed picking up on you two getting together," Dee was wagging her finger at Peter and Helen. "Some flipping detective I'd make."

"You would be a good detective, Dee," Jake said.

"Absolutely," Alison agreed. "Look at how you solved Margo and Mary's murders."

"Glad we all agree," Peter said. "In the new year Dee will be doing lots of studying. I've already put you in for your P.I. exams." Peter sounded so excited for her.

"No way! Me a P.I." Dee could hardly contain herself and once again flung herself at Peter to hug him. "And are you both going to live in Margo's house?"

Helen answered. "No Dee, I've sold it."

"Really, who to?"

Jake stepped forward. "Me," he said.

Dee looked at Jake, her eyes wide with surprise. "I love that cottage," she said to him.

"Me too," Claire butted in.

Jim went over to Jake and shook his hand. Claire nudged Tom. "That's the personal business he was sorting out when we went Christmas shopping."

Dee interrupted the general chatter about Margo's house and its wonderful garden. "If I'm living in your apartment and Jake's bought your house, Helen, where are you three going to live?"

Sir Henry rose to his feet. "Here, with me," he said proudly.

"I've one more thing to say," Peter announced and the room went quiet. He didn't need to say anything more because Helen raised her left hand to display her new engagement ring.

Clara and all the women ran over to congratulate Helen and to have a closer look.

The men were patting Peter on his back as Sir Henry made a polite but loud cough.

They all stopped and turned to look. Sir Henry was holding a bottle of champagne and, as the cork flew across the drawing room, he laughed loudly.

"Merry Christmas everyone!"

Milton Keynes UK
Ingram Content Group UK Ltd.
UKHW022058260924
448786UK00012B/598